IN THE GARDEN OF MONSTERS

CRYSTAL KING

IN THE GARDEN OF MONSTERS

Crystal King

//MIRA

/IIMIRA™

ISBN-13: 978-0-7783-1057-0

In the Garden of Monsters

Copyright © 2024 by Crystal King

For questions and comments about the quality of this book, please contact us at
CustomerService@Harlequin.com.

TM is a trademark of Harlequin Enterprises ULC.

Mira
22 Adelaide St. West, 41st Floor
Toronto, Ontario M5H 4E3, Canada

Printed in U.S.A.

To Joe, for whom I would willingly go to hell and back.

Midway upon the journey of our life

I found myself within a forest dark,

For the straightforward pathway had been lost.

Ah me! how hard a thing it is to say

What was this forest savage, rough, and stern,

Which in the very thought renews the fear.

So bitter is it, death is little more;

But of the good to treat, which there I found,

Speak will I of the other things I saw there.

I cannot well repeat how there I entered,

So full was I of slumber at the moment

In which I had abandoned the true way.

Dante, *Inferno*, Canto I

PROLOGUE

Bomarzo, Italy, 1547–1560

It took me years to find Giulia Farnese, but no time at all to win her confidence. I did so with an unassuming cherry rose tart. It had been nearly a hundred years since I last looked upon her face, but from the moment she pulled the golden tines of her fork away from her lips and she looked to me, not her husband, I knew my influence had taken hold.

"You truly are a maestro, Aidoneus," she said, closing her eyes to savor the sweet, floral flavors. "And a welcome addition to our kitchen."

"Madonna Farnese, you flatter me." I gave the couple a polite bow, my gesture more fluid than human custom, and turned back to my earthly duties.

"It seems you will eat well when I am gone," Vicino joked behind my back. "But don't eat too well, my beauty, or you won't fit into those lovely dresses."

Giulia laughed, and my heart warmed. Oh, she would eat well, I vowed.

Very well.

★ ★ ★

The next day, as Vicino Orsini gave his wife a peck on the cheek and vaulted onto his horse, I watched from the rooftop terrace, my gaze lingering on the horizon where earth met sky—a threshold I knew all too well. Then, with a flick of the reins, he led his men down the road into the valley. They were headed to Venezia to escort the Holy Roman Cardinal, Pietro Bembo, to Rome. Afterward, Vicino would depart for Napoli and Sicilia on business for Papa Pio IV.

Jupiter had blessed the region of Lazio with a warm spring, and a week after Vicino left, Giulia asked me if I wanted to take a walk. I suggested we explore the wood in the valley below the palazzo. She readily agreed, which did not surprise me. It was impossible for her to ignore the aphrodisiac qualities of my food, let alone the timbre of my voice, and the brush of my hand against hers. The first time she startled at my warmth— no human runs as hot as I—but she did not ask me to explain. In all the centuries past, she never has. This alone stoked the fire of hope within me.

She led me on a thin path through the verdant tapestry of the forest, where sunlight, diffusing through the emerald canopy, dappled the woodland floor with patches of gold. Beneath our feet, a carpet of fallen leaves, still rich with the scent of earth, crunched softly. We moved through clusters of ancient evergreen oaks, their gnarled limbs reaching out like weathered hands, and past groves of squat pomegranate trees with their ruby-hued fruits catching the sunlight and casting a warm, inviting glow.

Upon reaching a clearing surrounded by several large tufa stones jutting up through the grass and weeds, I was immediately drawn to one of the stones embedded in the hillside. The exposed side was round and flat, and it hummed, a song of the earth, a low vibration that warmed the deepest depths of me.

Giulia could not hear the humming, but she was surely aware of it in some hidden part of her, for she turned to me then.

"I love this wood," she said, her arms outstretched toward the stone. The early morning light brightened her features, making her blue eyes shine.

"I can see why."

She twined her hand in mine. "I come here often to bask in the feeling. The moment I arrived in Bomarzo, I felt like I had been called home, to my true home. And this wood, this is why. It reminds me of a fairy tale, or a place from the ancient, heroic myths."

It was then that I had the idea. The stone—it hummed because the veil to the Underworld was thin there. Perhaps...yes... if the wood was enhanced, and energy from the darkness was better able to pierce the surface into this realm I would no longer have to spend years attuning to Giulia when she reappeared in the world. Instead, she would be drawn closer, and I would find her faster. It would work. I was sure of it.

"Vicino doesn't like me walking here alone. Too many wolves and bears, he says."

I could sense a wild boar in the far distance, but no wolves or bears. "I think we're safe here." I gestured toward one of the big misshapen rocks. "Sometimes I like to imagine rocks as mythical creatures. Like that one. It could be a dragon poised to fight off danger."

"*Ooo*, I can see it. The big open mouth, ready to take on any wolf, or even a lion." Her enthusiasm was exactly what I had hoped for.

I waved my arm toward the large, round, smooth rock behind it. "And that should be a great big *orco*, with a mouth wide open. And it eats up and spits out secrets."

"An ogre that spits out secrets?" Giulia laughed.

"Oh yes. This *orco* would tell all. *Ogni pensiero vola.*" I made my hands look like a fluttering bird.

She wore a wide grin. "All thoughts fly! How perfect. But if he eats up secrets, there should be a table inside this *orco*. It could be his tongue."

As we wandered through the wood, dreaming up new lives for the monstrous rocks left eons ago by a force of nature, I was delighted to see how invested she was in the game.

"There are so many stones," she said, clapping her hands together. "We could make a whole park of statues. I will write Vicino tonight."

I did not expect it would be quite so easy. Usually it took a long while to convince Giulia of the merit of my ideas. But the pull of the Underworld was strong here and my influence was far greater than it would have been in Paris, or some backwater hill town in the wilds of Bavaria or Transylvania.

On the walk back, she paused by another enormous stone that jutted out of the ground, the size of a giant. She leaned against it. "Can you keep a secret?" she asked coyly.

"Of course."

"This secret is only for you." She leaned forward and grasped the edge of my cloak, pulling me toward her. Our lips met and she melted into me.

In the years following, as Vicino began work on the garden, a change was palpable in the air. Each evening, as the twilight deepened, a subtle energy began to emanate from the heart of the valley. I found contentment not just in the evolving grove, but also in my closeness to Giulia. Our time together, so abundant and intimate, felt different. I had never waited so long to make my attempt, but I nurtured this earthly bond, knowing it was essential for the garden's growth.

The day finally arrived when Vicino ushered Giulia into the heart of the Sacro Bosco—the Sacred Wood—the name he had fondly bestowed upon the garden. As she crossed the threshold, I sensed it—a strengthening of our connection, more profound than ever before. It was time.

That night, the chicken with pomegranate sauce I prepared was met with Giulia's usual lavish praise, although I knew she took in the single pomegranate seed garnishing the dish as a courtesy, not a desire for the fruit. As she savored each bite, I felt a loosening in the ethereal shackles binding her heart. A vivid, red-hued hope blossomed within me.

Postdinner, I retreated to the palazzo's highest balcony, my gaze drawn to a nascent light in the wood below. The light, though barely perceptible, was imbued with a power that seemed to bridge the realms of mortal and divine. A faint green luminescence that whispered of unwanted things to come. It pulsed like a languid heartbeat, beckoning to something—or someone.

I was immediately compelled to find Giulia. Amid the soft murmur of the salon where she played with her children, I enveloped her in my senses and the flower of hope within me withered. Her heartbeat, steady and unsuspecting, echoed the rhythm of the garden's glow.

1

Rome, 1948

"Julia, I still don't think you should go," Lillian said as we sat down at the base of the Spanish Steps near the entrance to the famous Babingtons Tea Room. It was late in the afternoon and the sunlight glowed against the boat-shaped fountain that Bernini's father had designed nearly three hundred years before.

I sighed. Lillian and I had been arguing ever since I had received the invitation to sit for Salvador Dalí. "You know this is an opportunity I can't pass up. And you also know how much I need the money."

Dalí had made waves in the city papers because he was in town creating sets for the Rome Opera. But he was also painting on the side, which was good for me. I had graduated from the Accademia di Belle Arti in the spring but continued to take classes to maintain my student visa, and I modeled to pay the bills. Dalí had inquired about me by name—I don't know how he'd heard of me, but it was often difficult to find a naturally blond model in Rome and I assumed that another person I had sat for referred me. He wanted to paint me in the guise of an ancient goddess—Proserpina, the

Roman counterpart to Persephone. Lillian was convinced it was a bad idea.

"Come on. He admires fascists, for god's sake. You have to be pretty bad to get kicked out of the Surrealists for having weird views."

"I know, I know. But he's been spending a lot of time in New York, so maybe he's changed. It's only for a week. He's one of the best painters in the world, Lil, and watching a maestro like him at work isn't something I can pass up. It's only a week." But I hated that she was right and felt guilty that I still planned to go.

Lillian tried a different angle. "Okay, then. But he's also a deviant. You'll be naked in front of him."

"His wife will be there," I protested. "There's nothing to worry about. He only has eyes for Gala."

Lillian, who worked as a shopgirl at a luxury clothing store, had never understood how I could be just as comfortable dressed as I was undressed. But the art scene had always been comfortable with nudity, sexuality—and promiscuity—while the rest of the populace was not.

My friend pulled a ribbon from her pocket and began tying up her long, dark hair. "You don't even like surrealism."

"That's not true," I insisted. "I just hate *most* surrealism."

In fact, I was somewhat obsessive about surrealism, but it was no longer in vogue to say so. Abstract expressionism had taken the art world by storm and I wanted to sell my work, so I followed the trends, inspired by the likes of Kline and Rothko. But, oh, the surrealists tugged at my heart and soul. It had been Dalí's *Dream Caused by the Flight of a Bee Around a Pomegranate a Second Before Waking* that had lured me in when I was in Madrid. The painting of a naked woman—Dalí's longtime muse, his wife, Gala—resting on rocks in the middle of the ocean, a pomegranate by her side, had a lot going on. In the sea, another monstrous pomegranate births a rockfish that spits out two tigers, their mouths wide open, their claws ready to rip the woman apart. There was also a floating gun and Dalí's first spindly-legged elephant. But it was the pomegranate that had really caught my eye—how it opened up, bursting with life, and yet the woman lay asleep, unable to react to all the emotion and life around her, lost in a dream.

There was something in that painting that resonated with me, that made me feel a little less fragmented. I couldn't explain that to Lillian. She would never understand. She knew the newest version of me, a fabricated tale: born in Italy, raised in Manhattan by an eccentric aunt after my parents' tragic deaths, and educated in Boston before returning to Italy postwar.

But the truth is, my earliest memory is emerging from the Pantheon years before into the streets of Rome and a stranger's kindness to help me reach the *accademia*. Beyond this, my past is a void; I have no recollection of family, childhood, or schooling. A doctor once dismissed my amnesia as temporary, but it never resolved.

To dispel any awkwardness, I concocted a fictitious past. This story satisfied the curious and accounted for my advanced intellect and erudite speech—traits I never fully understood in myself. I claimed an education at Radcliffe and feigned ties to high society, a narrative that seemed plausible enough to explain my idiosyncrasies.

But the way I felt when I looked at that painting by Dalí was one of the reasons I couldn't turn this job down. There was a connection there and I had an inexplicable need to discover what it was.

Lillian looked at her watch. "I really should go. I don't want to be late for my shift. But I hate you gallivanting off to some town no one has ever heard of with a couple of fascists to pretend to be some Properseena goddess in a wild garden of monsters."

"Proserpina. *Pro-ser-pin-ah*," I corrected. "I know, the name is confusing. You could just say Persephone. And don't worry. I'll be home before you know it, and much richer. I'll take you out for dinner on the Veneto."

"On the Veneto?" She whistled. "I never did ask how much he is paying you, but now I want to know."

I pulled out the invitation with the details and handed it to her.

"Holy mackerel, Jules," she gasped. "Seventy-five thousand lire a day for seven days? That's what, about a thousand bucks? Dear lord."

"I know. Pennies from heaven. It will be nice not to be a starving artist for once." And with that kind of cash I'd be far from starving. "But, Lil, this is less about the money. It's the chance of a lifetime. To learn from a master, to be depicted as one of my favorite mythical heroines, and to be…"

"Dalí's muse," she finished for me. "I know." She kissed me on the cheek and hugged me goodbye, giving me one last admonishment to be careful.

At four o'clock on the dot, a sleek black-and-red Alfa Romeo pulled up, with a wood-paneled Fiat station wagon following behind, laden with luggage and easels strapped to the roof. Salvador Dalí stepped out of the elegant car, walking cane in hand, and looked around. The artist wore a beautiful dark gray double-breasted suit, complete with a pink-and-gray tie, and I worried that he might find my outfit, a simple black sweater over a red dress, lacking. I approached slowly, working up my courage, but Dalí caught sight of me and waved me over.

"Are you my *modelo*?" he asked with a thick, clipped Catalan accent. His mustache curled upward just barely and his hair was slicked back, his eyes dark and piercing. His ears, which stuck out a bit too much from his head, were his least attractive feature. He had about twenty years on my twenty-four.

"Julia Lombardi," I said, extending my hand to the artist. Dalí clasped it with both of his and kissed it, his lips caressing my skin in a way that would make any woman swoon.

"You *are* a goddess," he said, rolling the *r* in a most dramatic way. He stared at me as though I were a landscape or a rare, precious object. "You are exquisite, your skin so pale, like you have just stepped forth from the darkness. I was right to ask for you."

I blushed.

He let go of my hand and looked around at the crowd. "Am I stealing you from a boyfriend? Has some dark Italian knight swept you off your feet before I got here, my Proserpina?"

I swallowed, thinking about Lillian's warning of him being a deviant. Unfortunately, it wasn't the first time some man asked me that within a minute or two of meeting. I thought of my last boyfriend, a Roman who was controlling and manipulative. "I sent him away. He was inadequate."

Dalí fell into a fit of deep laughter. "All are inadequate for the beauty that is Proserpina. Only the darkest knight will satisfy the light within you."

"A princess in need of a knight?" said a woman with a heavy Russian accent, as she stepped out of the car. "It's a good thing you aren't a knight, Salvador."

I breathed a sigh of relief. I had heard so much about Gala. The woman was not just Dalí's wife, but also his manager. She had inspired many a poet and artist: Éluard, de Chirico, Ernst, and Breton, to name just a few. It was said that many of the surrealists did their best work during the time they had been in love with Gala. I found that particularly interesting because she was rather plain of face, with a long nose and a disapproving stare. Yet she moved with a sexuality and an assurance I envied.

She walked up to me and took my chin in her hand, her grip harder than it needed to be. "Good. Your skin really is like porcelain."

"Imagine her as Proserpina, pomegranate seeds across her flesh, dotted like a thousand ants," said Dalí. He had long been known for adding lines of ants into his paintings. Together, they eyed me like I was a treasure in a museum.

I stood there awkwardly, until finally, Dalí tapped his cane on the ground twice. "Are you ready? I must warn you that where we are going is like nothing you have ever seen. I was in Bomarzo fourteen years ago with my friend Maurice Yves Sandoz, and I saw the wild wood there. A surreal place full of monstrous statues. Giants, a screaming ogre, sirens, a Pegasus, gods and goddesses, and of course, Proserpina."

I lifted my suitcase and gave him a nervous smile. "I am ready, Signor Dalí."

"No!" He tapped me on the shoulder with his silver-tipped walking cane. "I am Dalí."

I jumped, surprised at the strength of the gesture. "Very well, Dalí," I said, wondering if perhaps Lillian was right about not going. But no, I couldn't back down now. I drew a breath and gave him a nervous smile. "I look forward to vanquishing the monsters."

His driver retrieved my suitcase to put in the boot, then escorted me to the seat next to him. As we sped out of Rome, it felt like I was traveling through a tunnel, and every mile we drove, it was as though the light was growing a little brighter, that we were heading toward a beacon that might help me navigate the uncertain path of my future. Strangely, just as my past was blank, so, too, was my ability to envision a future, leaving me with a sense of emptiness and an unshakable feeling of being different. But for the first time, I felt a spark of something like hope.

The engine roar made it difficult to hear the Dalís' conversation, and the driver didn't seem interested in small talk, so I enjoyed the ride in silence, mesmerized by the beauty of the Lazio hills beyond Rome's walls. I hadn't traveled far outside the city and was glad for all the fall colors.

We could see Palazzo Orsini long before we arrived in Bomarzo, the boxy *castello* looming high above the trees, its ramparts gray against the blue of the November sky. A cluster of medieval houses crept up the hill and tumbled against one another until the line of buildings blurred into the edges of the palazzo itself. A lone bell tower stood out higher than all the rest of the edifices, jutting coarsely skyward. It looked like a place out of a dark fairy tale.

We couldn't take the cars up to the palazzo, as the medieval streets were far too narrow. Instead, we parked at the bottom of the hill and Dalí hopped out of the car and led us at a fast pace through a short tunnel and up a narrow road lined with centuries-old houses to the unassuming entrance, leaving the two young men in the Fiat with our luggage. I was surprised to see the face of the most important building in the city was so bland, a double door framed with stone, set into a simple medieval wall, chipped and cracked in spots.

"Something is wrong with this palazzo," Gala said as she raised her hand to the door knocker.

"What do you mean?" I asked her.

She rubbed her hand along the worn metal. "It's just a feeling. That something is out of place."

But it did not deter her. She lifted the knocker, its sound reverberating off the buildings around us. A man more arresting than any other I had ever seen opened the door for us. He was beyond a cliché, even more beautiful than stars in the movies. He was too perfect, too handsome, too…everything. His eyes were pale green, like shining sea glass. Thick, ridged eyebrows gave him a serious air. His dark hair was long and slicked back on the sides, his lips full. He seemed familiar, but I knew I hadn't met him before.

"*Benvenuto.* Welcome," he exclaimed, his voice deep and rich with the barest trace of an accent, one I couldn't discern.

Gala moved toward him like a moth to a bright flame, reaching out for a handshake. She didn't seem inclined to let go of his hand, but somehow, he extracted himself and fixed his eyes on me.

"Julia."

How did he know my name? I was just the model, a person of little importance. It was surprising that either Dalí or Gala would have mentioned me.

"You are welcome here, Julia." His eyes never moved from mine as he took my hands in his.

I almost gasped as the heat of his touch lit every fiber of my skin on fire. My mind whirled with the sensation of something terribly familiar. But then he let go and ushered us inside. I looked at my hands. *What just happened?*

"I'm Ignazio," he said as I stumbled across the threshold. "I am your steward. I will see to your every need."

"*Every* need?" Gala said, laying a hand upon his arm and winking at Dalí.

I couldn't help but raise an eyebrow at Gala's suggestion. The rumors about her open sexual inclinations were rampant in the art world, but to see her so willfully flirting with another man in front of her husband was something I hadn't expected. Dalí, however, did not appear upset at all. On the contrary, the conspiratorial smile he gave her seemed to signal his approval. The idea they were in it together, that they both found some measure of pleasure in her flirtatious proclivities, was fascinating.

For his part, Ignazio deftly removed her hand from his arm and carried on as though he had not heard her comment. He led us on a tour of the six-hundred-year-old property with numerous long corridors, rooms full of antiques, weary frescoes, and shabby tapestries. The floors were bare, save for some decorative black-and-red tile in the main halls. Our steps echoed as we walked. It was darker than I liked. The electricity wasn't bright, and the wall sconces cast queer shadows.

"The palazzo is not as grand as many other places you may visit, but it's full of history and forgotten memories," he said, his tone wistful. "So many memories."

The back of my neck tingled at his words. Someone had walked over my grave, Lillian would have said.

As we walked from room to room, Dalí peppered Ignazio with questions about the Orsini and particularly about Vicino's obsession with alchemy, which he had read about. Our host was

pleased to oblige the maestro and explained that Vicino was interested in the transmutation of the soul, in finding true enlight-
enment. "And if he turned metal into gold along the way, well,
that would be a happy circumstance, wouldn't it?" he mused as
he led us to the ramparts and ushered us outside.

"Below us is the *boschetto*, the little wood. Beware, there are
monsters there." He pointed to a spot far down in the valley,
but, in the fading light, it was difficult to see anything other
than the dome of a small white building, which I took to be the
tempietto. "Tomorrow you will meet them."

I thought that sounded rather ominous but didn't say so.

As we peered down at the garden, the sky began to transform,
moving from yellow to pink, to the deepest violet, to dark blue.

"This," Dalí breathed, "is the *only* painting I could never paint."

We stared, mesmerized as the colors flowed across the sky,
leaving the landscape awash with nature's brilliance.

"It's a gift," Ignazio whispered to me as he placed his fingers
on the small of my back. It was the barest of touches, but it gave
me a heady feeling of déjà vu and sent a distinct rush of warmth
up my spine. I wanted to pull away, to break free from whatever invisible bond this man had wrapped around me, but my
body was transfixed, as if tethered by an unseen force. "I think
Sol is sending us his good luck."

"Sol?" I whispered back, my heart pounding, confused. Why
would the sun god be sending "us" his luck?

Ignazio remained silent, a cryptic smile gracing his lips as he
pivoted away. He shifted his focus to the Dalís, narrating tales of
the abandoned Torre di Chia, a thirteenth-century lookout tower
in the distance, jutting up like a mysterious obelisk in the forest. This sight stirred something within Dalí, who launched into
a frenetic monologue about elephants and fantastical towers on
their backs. But his words floated past me, mere specters of sound.

I stared at the ever-changing sky, its hues shifting in response to the sinking sun. Yet it was Ignazio's strange words,

and more bafflingly, his touch, that captivated my restless mind. It wasn't just heat that emanated from that fleeting contact; it was something far more disquieting—an energy that crackled and jolted, like the dangerous dance of a live wire. It was heat; it was sparking, jolting. *It was like a brand*, I thought. A mere human shouldn't evoke such a visceral, almost primal, reaction in another. I didn't believe in magic or the divine, yet there was something that felt distinctly otherworldly—magnetic, or dangerous, even—about our host.

"Let's not go to the cellar today," Ignazio said as he led us back into the palazzo. "Another day, perhaps, I can show you the prison cells."

"Who would they have kept in the cells?" Gala asked the question before I could.

"People who didn't pay their taxes, town criminals, prisoners of war. The usual ruffians. A few murderers."

The way he said this last word made me shudder.

"You are cold, Julia?" asked Dalí.

"A little," I said, not knowing what else to say.

Ignazio winked at me, and my heart clenched. "A meal will warm you up. Let me show you to your rooms so you can rest a little first." He led us to the second floor. The red carpet on the stairs beneath my feet was frayed, with a few white, threadbare spots. I was struck by how quiet the *castello* was. At no point during our tour had I heard any sounds other than those we were making: the plodding of our footsteps on the hard floor, the swoosh of our clothes, the chattering among us. There was no door being closed somewhere off in the distance, no water running in the kitchen, no hired help murmuring or scurrying about.

We stopped at a set of interconnected rooms that were intended for Gala and Dalí. I stood awkwardly near the wide double doors as Ignazio showed the couple everything they would need to know about their stay. Gala's voice floated toward me, and although I couldn't see her, it was clear she was fawning over our host. Then Ignazio appeared and ushered me out of the room, shutting the Dalís in behind him.

"Here we are," Ignazio announced, stopping at the door to my room.

"Thank you," I stammered. "This is lovely." And it really was. The gold-edged frescoes of ancient myths adorning the walls, the baroque-era, red-velvet love seat, the luxurious four-poster bed, and even the dark wooden beams overhead were stunning. Modern stained-glass lamps graced the tables, the only sign I hadn't stepped back centuries in time. He pointed out all the amenities: extra blankets and pillows, a basin with water to wash my face, a plush bathrobe, and a pair of fuzzy slippers. I had not imagined I would be sleeping in such a luxurious fashion.

Ignazio motioned for me to enter, but I hesitated, unsure if I wanted to be in a bedroom with this man. After making his way to the window to close the curtains against the blackness, he eyed me intensely, as though he intended to say something but thought better of it. Then he neared me, moving close enough that I could smell him—a heady scent of smoke, leather, wood, and cinnamon. For a second, I thought he would reach out and touch me, and I didn't know what I would do if he did, but he just swept right past me, pausing only briefly at the door.

"You can freshen up," he said, pointing to the basin in the corner of the room. "Then join us in the dining hall. You must be hungry." And with that, he was gone.

He was the one who sounded hungry—for me.

Going to the window, I parted the velvet curtains, hoping for a glimpse of the *boschetto* below. But the landscape was dark, save for the few houses lit up far in the distance. It was in moments like these I often tried to remember some of the blankness that furled out behind me.

I reveled in the darkness and the starry tapestry above me. To my surprise, three shooting stars streaked across the sky in quick succession. First, the display of the sun, then the brilliance of the night.

I hoped Ignazio's mysterious proclamation about Sol might be true—that the gods were bestowing something good upon us. If not Sol, then perhaps I could call upon Astraeus, the Titan god of the planets and stars. I made a wish on those stellar gifts, that some of their light would help me find my way.

Just as I was about to close the curtains, a green glow flared down in the valley. Faint at first, it grew brighter, illuminating the obscure corners of the landscape in an eerie radiance. I couldn't pinpoint its origin, but I knew it wasn't anything mundane. It wasn't a fire, that much was clear, and its ethereal luminescence ruled out the possibility of it being a car's headlights or a flashlight. It was mesmerizing yet unsettling, almost as if it tapped into some deeply buried instinct. The light began to pulse faster and faster, intensifying in brilliance. Leaning against the window frame, I analyzed its rhythm with a sense of growing astonishment, my breath catching when I realized that the pulsing light was eerily synchronized with the beat of my heart.

I shut the curtains and stood there, the hairs on my arms standing on end as I tried to calm my breath. The sound of laughter from down the hall brought me back to my senses. I was being ridiculous. There couldn't have been anything there in the garden. With great hesitation, I opened the curtain again.

The glow was gone.

2

"I saw a weird green light in the valley," I told the elderly servant who escorted me to dinner. "Do you know what it might be?"

"Impossible," she said without looking at me. "No one goes into the Sacro Bosco at night." She strode ahead, cutting off my opportunity to ask anything more, and led me to a set of ornate doors, bowed her head, and departed.

For my first meal in Bomarzo, I had chosen to wear an elegant black dress with puffed sleeves that made my arms look sleek. The front draped seductively, and the skirt was nearly floor-length, not quite pencil thin but fitting. My black-heeled shoes had been a gift from Lillian, a Ferragamo pair with a tiny nick on the sole that couldn't be sold at the shop. The dress was my most flattering, and I wanted to inspire Dalí on the eve before he was to begin painting me. I took a deep breath and entered.

Green helical columns topped with gold capitals were painted onto the walls of the immense hall, giving the sense that they propped up the ceiling. The golden brocade curtains had been drawn to close out the night, but a fire in an intricately carved marble fireplace lit up one corner of the room. A long dining table dominated the middle of the chamber, surrounded by several dozen plush chairs. Gala and Dalí were already there and stood at one end of the table. Dalí wore a black double-breasted suit with a blue pocket square. Gala had donned a dress much in the same shape as mine, but her skirt was of shiny black silk that flowed sensually when she moved. They were talking with two men who looked to be near my age.

"Paolo," one said by way of introduction. He reminded me a little of Sinatra, but with an outsize nose and an Italian accent. "I'm the photographer."

"Pleased to meet you, Julia," the other chimed in, extending his hand. "I'm Jack." He was tall and blond, with striking blue eyes and the body of an American footballer. His smile immediately endeared him to me. I guessed he was the muscle who would haul Dalí's materials around.

"You're American," I said, surprised and pleased to have someone there who sounded like me.

"Born and raised in Idaho," he said proudly. "I served in the War. Infantryman, part of the Fifth Army under General Mark Clark."

"Under General Clark? You helped retake Rome."

He nodded. "And when it was over, I wanted to come back and see the city properly. I came with a girl, and when she went home, I decided to stay. I barely know an iota of Italian, but I get by."

"Ah. Italy is the better lover?"

He chuckled. "That she is."

"I went to school in Boston, but I'm from New York," I lied to him as I lifted a flute of prosecco from the tray a waiter held toward me.

"To New York," Dalí exclaimed, holding his glass aloft, eyes sparkling. "An enigma of its own creation, draped in shadows and light!"

"It is a place of poetry," Gala said, clinking her glass to mine.

"New York is indeed a poem, but not of steel towers reaching for the heavens. No, New York is a symphony of vibrancy and chaos, an orchestration of the primeval and the enigmatic. It's a pulsating, monstrous organ of crimson ivory echoing its rhythm into the ether." His hands moved as if conducting an invisible orchestra. "New York isn't a prism of light. It is not a sheet of cold white. It is a ballad sung in red, fiery red!"

I had no idea what he was talking about. Jack and Paolo only looked amused, as if this sort of poetic nonsense was common with Dalí.

"I think of New York as an inverted heart," Gala said. "The veins of its streets an organized snarl, pumping energy, pumping people in and about."

Dalí's eyes grew wide. "Yes, pumping! PUMPING," he shouted.

I wanted to laugh at this bizarre, campy behavior, but I didn't know if I would offend my eccentric employer. Jack, however, burst into a gale of hearty chuckles.

"You dirty fiend," Gala said, smacking him playfully. "Get your mind out of the gutter."

"Gala, you admonish me?" Jack laughed even harder. "You're always the first to tumble into the gutter."

Gala licked her upper lip seductively at Jack.

Glancing at Dalí, I saw his eyes alight with a different kind of intensity, the corners of his mouth hinting at a knowing smirk. His gaze lingered on the exchange, drinking in the moment, his fingers lightly tapping the stem of his glass in an erratic rhythm. It was not disapproval that radiated from him, but something much more akin to heightened interest. The air around him seemed to thrum with a fresh, palpable energy. In that moment, I found myself questioning Jack's role in Dalí's retinue, wondering if he had been brought to Bomarzo as anything other than a handsome plaything.

Ignazio entered the room just then, sporting a black tuxedo with a white bow tie and white gloves. "Dinner is served."

His voice rang across the room, and both Dalí and Gala released a little gasp similar to the one I stifled. Our host's beauty was impossible to describe. I looked away.

Fortunately, the arrival of the food provided a perfect distraction. The servers were also dressed in tuxes with white gloves. Some carried in platters covered in silver, and others wheeled carts with elaborate statues made from food—castles of painted sugar, a woman with a dress made of lettuce, a peacock with all its feathers on full display.

"Tonight you will dine like the gods," Ignazio declared in his smoky voice. "I have chosen your dishes carefully, and I trust you will be pleased with my selections."

Parsnip soup garnished with a pomegranate seed was placed before me. I wasn't fond of parsnips, and when it came to pomegranates, I generally disliked the seeds and avoided them whenever I could. While I loved the juice and the pop of the seed's skin against my teeth, I didn't like their pith and grit. I eyed Gala's seafood stew with jealousy as she lifted a spoonful of tomato broth and shrimp to her lips.

"You do not like parsnips?" Paolo asked me in halting English. I started to respond, but Dalí interrupted.

"You are in Bomarzo now, and I declare you Proserpina! You must eat the pomegranate seeds."

I was alarmed by his insistence but decided to play along. "If I do, I'll be trapped in the Underworld." I lifted a spoonful of soup to my mouth but avoided the jeweled seeds.

"Eat the seeds," Dalí instructed me, jabbing his finger toward my soup.

"Fine," I said hesitantly and took another spoonful, with one ruby-red seed. The combination of flavors was unexpected; it filled my mouth with a savory sweetness I had never experienced. I closed my eyes to immerse myself in the pleasure. The moment my eyelids dropped, I was plummeted into the middle of a spinning mélange of images and feelings—a palace with ephemeral Gothic spires, dark and beautiful; hands hot on my shoulders and a breath in my ear; and finally, the sensation of being dragged away from someone I deeply and dearly loved. Then it passed and I could taste the pomegranate juice on my tongue once more.

Startled, I opened my eyes again and found Ignazio staring intently at me from the doorway. For a second, I couldn't breathe under the weight of his gaze. The stare broke when the wind suddenly gusted around the corners of the *castello* with a loud whistle, causing the fireplace to flare up. Alarmed, I looked back to see if Ignazio would tend to the fire, but he was gone.

I was staring into my soup, trying to understand the odd daydream, when Dalí's arm brushed against mine.

"What are you doing?" I asked him.

He took up my soup bowl and placed his vichyssoise in front of me. "This soup was wasted on you—you ate a seed, and you weren't whisked off to the Underworld." He seemed disappointed. "And I prefer it to a bowl of cold leeks and potatoes."

He spooned the soup into his mouth.

"Delicious! Poetic! Now *I* am Proserpina!" He waved his spoon in the air as he spoke.

I was shocked and a bit irritated. The soup had been good after all, far more so than I could have anticipated, and I would have been happy to finish it.

Thankfully, the soup course was an anomaly, and we were all served the same dishes for the rest of the meal. Following a pasta course, which included tortellini in *brodo*, spaghetti with chiles, garlic and olive oil, and *garganelli* with mushrooms, the servants brought out platters of roasted pheasants with their heads and feathers made to look alive, foie gras tarts, a tower of sausages made from goose and duck, and a boar's head with an apple in its mouth.

I shook my head when a cheesy soufflé was placed in front of me. "I don't know how I can eat all this."

"Me either," Jack said.

"Just have a little of everything," Gala instructed. She was looking at Jack, not at me, and I wondered what might be going on under the table that I couldn't see.

Between courses, Ignazio returned with a little *digestivo* on a silver tray. "Ratafia," he said as he placed the glass in front of me. His arm brushed my shoulder as he set it down. I recoiled from the intense heat of his touch, which sent my heart racing again.

"Mi dispiace," he said. But when I looked up, his slight smile made it clear he wasn't sorry at all.

I smelled the glass of liqueur.

"Cherry, nutmeg, cinnamon, and clove," Paolo said, anticipating my question. He tilted his head back and downed his glass. "Every *nonna* has her own recipe."

I sipped it and was delighted. It also had the fortunate effect of making me feel like I had not yet indulged, when just ten minutes before I was sure I might burst.

Dalí declared it the most exciting meal he had ever eaten. "Someday, I will write a cookbook," he declared. "I will fill it with the magic of Dalí and the magic of the food that can satisfy Gala."

The wine had started to go to my head and emboldened me. "Do you always talk about yourself in the third person?" I asked the maestro.

"Darling, I am the only Dalí! How else am I to talk about myself?"

I chuckled along with everyone else, but I couldn't help but wonder if the performance ever stopped. Dalí was gesturing again, telling a vivid account of when he wrote a story at the age of seven about a child taking a walk with his mother during a rainstorm of falling stars. But mixed into his tale was a brief, unsettling remark about the child's encounter with a group of people, described with a choice of words that hinted at prejudice. It was a fleeting moment, but it was there, subtly coloring the whimsical imagery with something darker. Everything else he said was curious, outrageous, and endlessly fascinating. It was easy to be enthralled by him. But I wanted more—I wanted to know how he painted and created—not this endless show of artistic narcissism. I hoped that when he painted me, he would be different, and I would discover the real genius of Salvador Dalí, unmarred by those subtle undercurrents.

"I think these are the monsters in the garden," Jack said when he beheld the platter of cookies shaped like elephants, mermaids, sirens, unicorns, dragons, and a little sitting bear. "They are the same as the statues Ignazio described when he first told us of the *boschetto*."

"The symbol of the Orsini," Paolo pointed out, holding up the bear.

I chose a cookie shaped like Cerberus, dipped it into the silkiest, most decadent chocolate mousse I'd ever tasted, and bit off one of its three heads.

Dalí wagged a finger at me. "Why do you eat your protector with such gusto?"

"My protector?"

"That beast guards the Underworld, and thus you, little Proserpina. You need to let his strength fill you up with each bite, not let your teeth deflate his spirit."

I gave him a weak smile. He was really taking the idea that I was Proserpina too far. "I see." I examined the rest of my cookie and carefully broke off another head, wondering if the rest of the week would merely be an exercise in bending to Dalí's will.

When the plates were cleared, Ignazio brought out more prosecco and a bottle of whiskey. As he poured, Dalí suggested that Gala read her tarot cards for us.

"My Gala, Galachuka, Gravida, my Lionette! She who is never wrong," Dalí said, his voice full of awe. "My wife is prophetic, angelic, demonic, the very picture of desire." He leaned over and kissed Gala's cheek.

"It's true that Gala's never wrong," Jack said to me. "And she's clairvoyant."

Of course she is, I thought wryly.

Jack noticed my skepticism. "She really is. She can sense things that we can't. It's uncanny."

Gala beamed at Jack as she began to shuffle the cards.

"Let's start with you, Salvador," Gala said, and Dalí pulled a card and laid it on the table. It showed a man with his hand in the air, holding a wand, with a cup, sword, and pentacle on a table before him, and an infinity loop over his head like a halo.

"The Magician. You always draw that card." She laughed.

"That is because I am *el mago*! It's the card of infinite possibilities of creation through the force of one's will." Dalí smiled at me and took a sip of his whiskey. "*Sì*, this is a good omen for my painting."

"The Magician is a conduit between the spiritual and material realms," Gala told the rest of us. "This connection gives Salvador the energy he needs to transform his visions into reality. He's right about it being a good omen." She ran a hand along her husband's cheek. "You'll have the power to manifest what you desire while you are here."

Gala reshuffled the cards. "Now, one for our week here at Bomarzo." This time she had Jack pull a card. It was an ominous one, featuring a satyr with bird feet and goat horns, a man and a woman chained to the pedestal upon which he perched—the Devil.

Gala furrowed her brow. She was silent for so long that Dalí reached out a hand and put it on hers. "My Gravida, are you all right? Is it bad?"

"I don't know." She picked up the card and looked at it. "This card means entrapment, emptiness, lack of fulfillment. Obsessive or secretive behavior. Fear, domination. I fear there is a force at work here that will not be in our control."

"That sounds so dire," Ignazio commented. He had returned to refill our glasses. "There must be more to such a reading, no, Signora Dalí? What if it was a tale of two lovers?"

"Yes, the card could be interpreted as lust, temptation, or hedonism."

"The pursuit of life's earthly pleasures," Ignazio said, handing me a new goblet of prosecco. I was careful not to touch his fingers as I took the glass. He turned back to Gala. "Will you read a card for me?"

Gala brightened at the suggestion. She shuffled the cards and Ignazio plucked one depicting Adam and Eve with an angel looking down over them.

"Interesting. It appears I've drawn a card that reflects my theory—The Lovers," he said.

"But it is reversed," Gala said, noting that the card was upside down.

"What does it mean?" I asked.

"Imbalance. Something is opposing the lovers, keeping them from being together."

Dalí tapped a finger on the card, indicating the fruit tree behind Eve, around which a snake was entwined. "Some scholars believe Eve didn't eat an apple, and it was actually a pomegranate."

"I've heard that, too," Ignazio chimed in. "I believe it to be true."

Dalí clapped his hands together. "If only you had pulled that card, Julia. Proserpina you would truly be!"

Ignazio picked up the card, lifted it to his lips, and kissed it, then handed it back to Gala. "*Grazie*, Signora Dalí."

"You're welcome," she said, sliding the card back into the deck, clearly disarmed.

"Julia, it's your turn," Jack said. He nudged Gala, who tore her eyes from the door Ignazio had disappeared through and returned her attention to the deck.

"Fine," she said, her voice flat. "Your turn, Julia."

But I didn't want a card to tell me about my future. I wanted to know about my past.

"I would have preferred The Lovers," I muttered when I saw that I'd pulled the Death card. It featured a knight waving a flag emblazoned with a double rose somewhat similar to those I'd seen all over the *castello*, the emblem of the Orsini family. There were bodies strewn about the feet of the knight's skeleton mount, and a pope in front of the horse, pleading with Death.

Gala shook her head. "You know nothing. This is a very good card."

"I don't see how."

"Oh, but it is. You're undergoing a transformation. The old you will die, and the new you will be created. Don't be a ninny, Julia. Let go of your stupidity, of what you know, and accept what comes your way, no matter how much it frightens you. Let yourself be ripped apart and made anew."

Despite her cutting remarks, Gala was oddly jubilant, as though she had just given me her own great gift.

"I don't need a new me." I stammered, unable to tell her I was desperate to know about the old me.

"I have reinvented myself almost every day, and look where it has got me," Dalí interjected. "I am the greatest living *artiste*. I am the dream, the madman who is not mad. I am Dalí!"

Distraught about the notion of reinventing a me that I didn't know in the first place, and tired by the events of the day, I excused myself a little while later. I set my hair in rollers, put on my pajamas, and climbed into bed. I was tipsy, and I hoped my fuzziness would carry me into a deep sleep. But when I rolled over and put my hands under my pillow, I encountered something there. I pulled it out and turned on the lamp.

It was a tarot card. The Lovers.

My breath short, adrenaline rushing through my veins, I flung it from me as if it were on fire. How had that card ended up under my pillow? It was the card Ignazio had pulled. Was he the one to place it there? But how had he gotten it from Gala? Did he have a deck of his own?

When I had calmed, I went to retrieve the card but couldn't seem to find it. I turned on the rest of the lights and searched all over for it—under the bed, in the bedding, behind the night-stand, at the edges of the room. But to no avail. The card had disappeared.

3

A knock on the door roused me from my restless sleep. When I opened it, the servant from the night before swept past me and deposited a breakfast tray on the table near the window. She reminded me of someone, someone I could not place in my empty past, but whom I knew I deeply cared for. As she opened the curtains, letting in the November light, I asked for her name.

She stopped and turned to me as though just realizing I was in the room. "Signorina, I am Demetra," she said with a wide smile that warmed my heart. She must have been quite beautiful long ago.

I peered down at the landscape behind her, relieved to see it looked just like it should, a pretty valley full of fields and dotted with little groves of trees in the resplendent colors of fall.

"It's a beautiful day. I hope you enjoy it," Demetra said as she made to leave.

I stopped her with a hand on her shoulder and thanked her for bringing me breakfast.

"Oh, Julia," she said as she stared into my eyes and lifted a cold hand to my cheek. The smell of her skin reminded me of damp earth. "You should not have done me wrong."

"What do you mean?" I asked, pulling away from her.

Her eyes flared with alarming intensity. "Don't you get tired of doing this over and over?"

I was stunned. What on earth was she talking about? But just as I opened my mouth to question her, the light in her eyes dimmed, and she looked at me, confused, her face once more placid, her eyes blank, as though she were staring through me. "Is there anything else you may need?" she asked, as if nothing had just transpired between us.

Shaken, I said no, and she left without another word.

There was a note with my breakfast, telling me to meet Dalí outside the palazzo at ten o'clock. After a bite of bread and cheese, I decided on the perfect ankle-length, flowing dress the red-and-pink colors of the pomegranate.

When I stepped outside, I was glad to find it was unseasonably warm and I would probably be able to forgo my cape as the day progressed. November could be rainy, but I didn't see a single cloud in the sky. It was always much warmer in fall and winter in Rome than it was in many parts of Europe, and there were still many days when I wouldn't even need a jacket.

Dalí and Gala weren't waiting outside the door as the note had said, but Jack was leaning against the wall nearby. "They're in there." He pointed down the narrow street toward the duomo, a little white church with double, curved staircases leading from the road to the door. We walked toward the church.

"I must say, you look beautiful. The maestro is lucky to have you for a model."

I blushed. "Thank you. I do like this dress."

He chuckled. "And the dress likes you."

"I wish I were painting instead of modeling," I said wistfully. "But I do hope I can learn from Dalí while I'm here."

Jack raised an appraising eyebrow. "Ah, you are a painter?"

At my nod, he grinned. "I haven't met a woman painter yet. You are a rare breed."

I gave him a rueful laugh. "I wish it weren't so."

"Well, I'd temper your expectations. Dalí is a terrible teacher."

I laughed. "Maybe I can learn from observation, or perhaps by appealing to his ego."

A dove cooed from the top of a nearby building and Jack lifted his head to look at it. A blond lock fell into his eye, and he brushed it away. "You are a smart one, aren't you? That's exactly the way to manage our maestro."

I liked Jack. I liked his American-ness, his accent, his manner, his way of dress. He was handsome but wholesome. And while he was a little flirty, he was also polite. To me, he seemed like a bit of normalcy in a place that was very strange, with people who were very strange. There was also something about him that drew me in, made me feel instinctively safe.

"Why are you with the Dalís?" I asked.

He shrugged. "Well, when Gala heard they would be here for a week, she insisted. And if you haven't noticed, she's not someone you say no to. But, in theory, I'm to help haul around easels and scare off ghosts."

"Ghosts?" I asked, concerned. I pulled my wool cape close around me, suddenly cold.

"You are too serious." He laughed. "But have you seen this place? Surely a ghost or two must roam its halls. I even heard a woman died in the garden a few centuries ago."

"I hope not."

As I spoke, one of the church bells gave a loud clang, then fell still. Both Jack and I looked up at the bell tower, startled. And, as if on cue, Dalí emerged from the duomo, Gala and Ignazio in tow, and my heart began to beat wildly at the sight of our host. Had he really placed that tarot card under my pillow?

Spying me, Dalí cried out, "My Proserpina!" Rushing across

the piazzetta, he lifted my arms and twirled me around. "You are magnificent, my beautiful goddess—I cannot wait to paint you. Gala, look at this girl!"

"Charming," Gala said dryly, her lips pressed into a thin line as she looked me up and down with a critical eye. She'd latched on to Ignazio's arm, which he tolerated only until they reached the bottom of the stairs. Then he discreetly disentangled himself from her. "Though a goddess shouldn't need costume jewelry and gaudy fabric to make an impression," she added dismissively, toying with her own ostentatious necklace.

"A goddess can wear whatever she likes," Ignazio said. He eyed me intently.

"Can we see the garden now?" I asked, hoping to take the attention off me. After seeing the green light the night before, I was nervous about entering the garden, but having Ignazio's attention was even more nerve-racking.

"Certainly. Come." He strode forward and we followed dutifully behind, like the story of the Pied Piper leading along the rats.

Paolo joined us just as we were heading down the lane toward the parking lot. He carried a big camera bag on one shoulder and a tripod on the other.

A new Lancia Ardea pickup, with benches built on both sides of the open truck bed, waited to take us down the hill to the *boschetto*. Ignazio extended his hand to help Gala up into the truck, though she still managed to stumble—clearly on purpose so he'd have to catch her, which he did, righting her without ceremony or any sign of emotion. Then he motioned toward me. I wished I could climb into the truck myself—I didn't want him touching me again—but the dress I was wearing restricted my movement, and I, too, would stumble without assistance. Fortunately, he extended his arm rather than one of his peculiarly hot hands, and I held the white canvas of his jacket as I raised myself up. He was staring at me, adulation in his blue-green eyes, as though I really were a goddess. I turned my head hastily, just in time to see Gala stiffen. She must have seen how Ignazio had looked at me and didn't like it.

"Here we are. The Sacro Bosco—the Sacred Wood," Ignazio announced when we stopped in a little clearing mostly overgrown by vines and half covered by bushes. I looked at the high grass and noted that I shouldn't have worn one of my nicest pairs of heels.

This time, Jack helped me out of the truck. He nodded at my shoes. "If I have to carry you, I will."

"I hope it won't come to that," I said. But looking at the vines ahead, I thought it might. "Besides, you have all the equipment to bring." I indicated the French easel and stretched canvas that Paolo was unloading from the truck.

"For you, I would drop it all."

I smirked but was secretly pleased by his gallantry.

Ignazio started down the thin, overgrown trail. He stopped when we were a few dozen or so paces away from the dirt parking area. "Now we are officially in the garden of monsters," he warned us with a dark grin. "They're monsters made of stone, but sometimes the creatures may appear quite sinister. Worry not. For the most part, you have nothing to fear."

I couldn't tell if he was joking or not. Considering the green glow I had seen the night before, he might not be jesting after all.

"Have you had to rescue many of your guests?" Gala asked, her tone teasing.

"You are the first visitors we've had in years, though there are curious trespassers on occasion." Ignazio pointed down the path ahead. "This is a back passage into the Sacro Bosco or, as it is often called, the *boschetto*, the little wood. The original main entrance, now unused, is on the other side of the garden. There you'd have been greeted by two worn sphinxes, one of which bears an inscription that reads 'You who enter here put your mind to it part by part and tell me then if so many wonders were made as trickery or art.'"

"So, the statues are riddles to decipher?" Jack asked.

Ignazio gave him a brilliant smile. "Or are they just art? Come, let us find out."

I fell in step behind him, marveling that we were walking along paths that were centuries old. The air felt charged with magical energy, although I was sure it was only my excitement to be sitting for Dalí. Then I stumbled, nearly crashing into Gala, who grunted as I used her arm to steady myself. Regret washed over me for having worn my best pair of heels; it was an attempt to make an impression. And indeed, an impression was being made, but not in the way initially intended.

A bleat emanated from somewhere deep in the garden. "That didn't sound like a monster," Jack remarked.

"There are a few locals who let their sheep graze near here," Ignazio explained. "They think the monsters scare away the wolves."

Jack and I exchanged looks. He clearly thought the same as I—Italian superstitions truly made no sense.

"Wait," I called out to Ignazio as he started forward. "We were told that the locals are afraid of this place, because of a woman who died in the garden. Is that true?"

"Yes. A long time ago. Several women are rumored to have died in the garden. The details are lost to history, but superstition remains long in the mind." Ignazio's eyes did not leave mine as he spoke, and it was as though he was imploring me to discern some hidden meaning in his words.

My heart skipped a beat.

"It's a shame," he continued. "The *boschetto* was once a place of great wonder and beauty that was much talked about among the Italian nobility."

"Are there ghosts?" Jack asked, elbowing me playfully in the ribs.

"Perhaps." A fire seemed to light in Ignazio's eyes, but he said no more.

Jack elbowed me again. "I told you there were ghosts."

I gave him a little chuckle, but it was a nervous laugh.

We had come to a small stream banked by bushes colored with autumn's brush. A wide board had been placed across the shallow water. As we traversed the wobbly bridge, I felt that I had somehow pierced a veil of light, shadow, and *something* indescribable. This feeling was coupled with an intense sense of déjà vu. It was as though we were entering someplace that was not part of our real world, but despite that, it was as familiar to me as if I were walking into a home of my own. I had a distinct impression that I had trodden this path before, many times.

Arriving at a fork in the trail, Ignazio steered us down the short trail to the left, which brought us to an enormous monster with a wide-open mouth and several square, chipped teeth. Upon its head was a striped globe topped by a small castle.

"I think he wants to eat us," Gala said.

Dalí stood in the monster's open mouth, touching its chipped teeth. "Let him eat," he declared as Paolo began snapping photos.

"This is Proteus Glaucus," Ignazio explained. "He became a sea god after eating a magical herb."

"What is that on his head?" Jack asked.

"You've seen the Orsini bear and the double roses throughout the palazzo—the globe and the castle are also family symbols."

"But what does it mean?" Jack eyed the statue, clearly puzzled.

Ignazio shrugged. "It's set apart from the rest of the statues on this dead-end path. Perhaps it's meant as a sign that one has lost their way. Or perhaps it's a warning?"

"A warning?" Gala folded her arms across her chest and tapped her fingers against her arm as though she didn't believe anything Ignazio was saying.

"A final warning to turn back, away from this garden of monsters."

"Should we?" I asked without thinking. After I spoke, I had an odd feeling that perhaps we should. All my conversations with Lillian came flooding back to me. Was it really wise that

I was in a creepy garden with complete strangers? And one of them a known freak of a sort?

I stared at Proteus Glaucus. For all my lost memories, somewhere in my past I had absorbed the depths of the myths. Glaucus had loved the nymph Scylla, but she was repulsed by his scales and webbed hands. He asked the witch Circe for a love potion, but his charms had already enraptured Circe. When Glaucus rebuffed her, she took revenge, turning Scylla into an oceanic form of a hydra.

Ignazio shook his head, his eyes catching mine. "There is no reason to turn back. The *boschetto* welcomes you, Julia." Then, almost as an afterthought, he waved a hand at my companions. "All of you."

He moved back down the path and the others followed dutifully behind. But I paused to look back at Proteus Glaucus and his empty stone eyes and big square teeth. His mouth was wide open, as if in a shout. Scylla's twelve feet and six heads came to my mind, sharpening the warning he was casting into the garden.

To not fall in love.

I thought of Jack and his bright blue eyes and of the heat of Ignazio's touch. And almost on cue, they both paused and turned back to look at me. When Gala realized the reason for their halt, she screamed at me, her mouth open wide like the stone sea god.

"You stupid girl, keep up!"

I swallowed hard and picked up my pace.

Farther down the footpath, we came to another fork, three thin trails in the brush. One of the forks led down a perilous set of stairs. On that lower trail, an enormous head rose above the stone retaining wall. Dalí gave a cry of excitement before charging down the steps, and we followed after him. As we neared, we could see the giant held another man upside down by the legs. The giant's face was well wrought, etched with lines. His hair was curled, and his carved beard was lush and full. His body was thick with muscle. The man he held showed his agony, his mouth open in a scream, his eyes empty and wide. Gala knelt to pick the moss off his face.

"There is more going on here!" Dalí went close to the statue and pointed up between the two stone men.

Indeed, it did look as though the giant might be performing some intense sexual act upon the other man.

Ignazio pointed to a partially eroded plaque on the nearby wall. He put his finger on the word *Anglante.*

"If you know Ariosto's epic poem, *Orlando Furioso,* then you know that Orlando was the Lord of Anglante. The story is that Orlando was driven mad when the beautiful Princess Angelica did not return his love. In his fury, he raged through the land, destroying anything in his path. In this vengeful state, he met two woodsmen with a donkey pulling a cart of logs. Rather than waiting for them to move aside, he kicked the donkey so hard it landed over a mile away. Then he took one of the terrified woodsmen by the legs and tore him in half. And clearly, you can see here the giant is ready to tear this man in two."

Ignazio paused to watch Gala stroke the tortured man's face. When he continued, his voice took on an ominous tone. "This is one of my favorite statues in the garden. I think of it as a warning, that passion may render love into something evil. It can light the fire of desperation, anger, or even hate."

Ignazio looked off into the depths of the garden. I followed his gaze through the greenery but did not see anything. I wondered who among us this warning was for—it seemed more than just a story to me.

Dalí startled me with a shout. "Paolo, get your camera!" Dalí and Gala posed with the giants, then motioned for me to come forward so Paolo could take a couple of photos of me standing next to the statue before we went back up the crumbled stairs.

To my dismay, Ignazio walked with me. My body hummed with his nearness, a humming that filled me with conflict. It may sound like a terrible cliché, but he truly was the most attractive person I had ever laid eyes on. Still, there was something about him that seemed off, *wrong*, even, and I wasn't sure I wanted this man's attention. And yet he was all I could think about, especially since I had found that damned tarot card under my pillow. I wanted to ask him about it, but I hesitated, thinking that by doing so I might encourage him, which was certainly not what I wanted.

"How long have you lived in Bomarzo?" I asked to cut through the silence between us.

"A long time. It feels like centuries."

"You don't like it here?"

"This is where I need to be—now. With you."

Distracted by this proclamation, I stumbled on the stairs. I don't know how he caught me so quickly, but suddenly his arm was around me, preventing me from pitching forward and breaking my face or, at least, mucking up my dress. His warmth spread through me, quick and hot, pooling in all my limbs, making me think of lava bubbling inside a volcano. I made a strangled noise and he let go, and the sudden absence of such heat was even worse. I shivered despite my cape and the sun upon my face. My head swam with dizziness, and I began to wonder if perhaps I was coming down with something.

We continued up the stairs, and at the top was a massive, decrepit rectangular rock, covered in moss. "A toppled mausoleum with Etruscan images," Ignazio said as we neared. It didn't look like a mausoleum, but rather it seemed to be a broken block of stone with carvings that were difficult to make out. "A woman is buried beneath it."

"Really?" I couldn't see how the rock could be moved at all, much less to bury someone there. "Who?"

His eyes found mine. "Her name was also Julia." He smiled at me, a smile that would melt any woman's heart. But his words chilled me to the bone. He didn't explain further, instead leaving me there, staring at the massive block of stone, as he went up the path the others had taken.

I didn't know what to do. Was he threatening me? Something told me he didn't wish me harm and was merely imparting information. Compelled to touch the moss-covered sculpture, I laid my fingers against a spot where the tufa was bare of moss.

Julia... A woman's voice whispered in my ear. Dear god, was Jack right about the ghosts? Was she saying my name, or the name of the woman buried beneath the heavy rock?

"I'm here," I whispered back, hoping if I made light of the situation, I would dispel the ridiculousness of my imagination.

Attenti al mostro...

Beware the monster. I jolted back from the stone, short of breath, thinking my heart might never slow again.

Julia...

The whisper grew louder, seemingly coming from somewhere on the trail in front of me. I moved toward it.

"Julia," Gala said, louder, appearing at the top of a little hill. Her anger rang out across the *boschetto*. "Don't dawdle. There are pictures to take!"

Though I didn't appreciate being scolded like a child, I was relieved to know it was only Gala calling my name. I looked back at the destroyed mausoleum behind me.

But if Gala had been calling for me, why had she been warning me about a monster?

We were in a garden full of them.

4

My companions were at the *tempietto*, a small Doric-style octagonal temple with a cupola that rested on the edge of a vast field, encircled by a rock wall with a broken gate that hung half-off the hinges. Though a bit shabby, the tiny structure was still exquisite. A series of Tuscan columns made from *peperino* stone cut through the center of its square patio leading toward the entry to the dome. Paolo had his camera out and was filming Dalí entering the building. The artist had somehow come across a friendly white cat and had decided to carry it on his shoulder.

"This should have been the last building you come to as you emerge from the garden," Ignazio was explaining to Gala when I arrived. He motioned toward a set of stairs that led into the rest of the garden. "I had intended to take you down the main path so you would see the *boschetto* laid out in order, from earth to hell to heaven. There are the earthly creatures—those that are created by the gods, then comes the entrance to the Underworld, through the mouth of the ogre, or *orco*, which you'll see soon. From the *orco* you eventually come to the bench of Proserpina, up the stairs past the loyal Cerberus, and then, finally, you find yourself here." He gave Gala a pointed look. "But you took an alternate route, arriving here first."

Dalí raised his eyes to the little dome. "Vicino Orsini's wife, Giulia Farnese, is buried here, *sì*?"

Ignazio nodded. "Some say Vicino Orsini may have been laid at her side, but there are no records of this."

Giulia. What coincidence was it that there were three of us with the same name in the garden? The Julia under the heavy rock mausoleum, the lady Farnese, and me, breathing in the air they no longer could.

Ignazio pointed to the ceiling of the entryway, which was decorated with Farnese lilies and Orsini roses, and explained how they symbolized the union between them.

Gala asked him about the empty circles surrounding the temple's base.

"Stolen over the years. They were zodiacal and biblical scenes."

"This doesn't seem like a religious place," Jack said.

"Oh, it is, very much so, just not religious in a Christian sense," Ignazio explained. "At the time Vicino created the garden, he must have worried about being accused of blasphemy. Including some biblical imagery may have been an attempt to stave off such charges. But the truth of the matter is that the *tempietto* is the final resting place for those going to the Greek or Roman afterlife, the representation of Elysium, not that of heaven."

Paolo bade me enter and exit the temple so he could get me on film.

I was readying myself for the walk toward the back of the *tempietto* when the cat that Dalí had been holding came to me and twined itself around my legs, purring. It looked up at me and meowed.

"Pick him up, Proserpina," Dalí said. "He likes a shoulder."

I did, and the little beast immediately climbed to my shoulder and rubbed his face against mine, purring even more loudly. His almost melodic meows endeared him to me. I didn't remember ever having a pet, so I wasn't sure how I was supposed to behave, and the cat's affection took me by surprise.

"Wow, he really likes you," Jack marveled. He reached out a hand to pet the little beast, but the cat stiffened against me and swatted at him. "But I guess he doesn't like me."

"I've never seen that cat before." Ignazio frowned, and I wondered why he was concerned about its appearance. Surely there must be dozens of cats wandering around the wood. Italy was full of stray cats.

The animal started to trill a little song. "I name him Orpheus," I said. It instinctively felt like the perfect name. The cat seemed to approve as he rubbed his head against my ear.

"Why Orpheus?" Jack asked.

"When Orpheus came to the Underworld seeking the return of Eurydice, Persephone—Proserpina—was moved by his tears and agreed to let her return above."

"And you are Proserpina, no? And even now, he cries in your ear. The perfect name!" Dalí was exuberant. "Now, Paolo, we shall film our Proserpina."

Orpheus jumped down but stayed close. I let Gala fuss over my clothes and hair, but my mind was on the story of Orpheus and how he lost Eurydice because of the gods' condition that he would not look back until the couple had both returned to the world of the living. When Orpheus, in his anxiety, turned around too soon, Eurydice disappeared back into the Underworld forever. It was a story that had always resonated with me—of true, deep love lost. Just thinking about it made me want to tear up.

Gala slapped me. "Pay attention!"

I gasped and instinctively raised my hand to my cheek, shocked. It wasn't a slap hard enough to leave a mark, but it was a startling violation. Orpheus hissed at her, and Gala made to kick the cat, but he easily evaded her boot.

Gala didn't let me protest. "We don't pay you to daydream, Julia. Now start walking. And smile." She pointed at the *tempietto*.

Orpheus seemed to be waiting for me. I picked him up, glad that he had hissed at Gala in my defense. He went right to my shoulder. Furious about the slap, I plastered a smile on my face and walked the twenty feet through the catwalk of columns toward the inner sanctum, admiring the arched ceiling and its rosettes above. Light filtered in from circular windows around the dome's edges and from little openings in the tip of the cupola.

As I entered the little room, I thought I heard my name again.

But Orpheus only purred louder in my ear, which convinced me that I imagined the whispers, that perhaps I really was just tired or coming down with something.

Brushing the thoughts away, I scanned the room. How odd there was no plaque for Giulia, who may be resting beneath my feet—nothing to mention a date of death, no words of love or memory.

I turned toward the door, ready to strut out for Paolo's camera. *Julia…*

This time I heard my name loud and clear. There was no way I could have imagined it. Before I could react, two birds flew through the cupola windows and dive-bombed Orpheus, then fled just as quickly as they'd swooped in. Orpheus howled and bolted, his claws piercing my dress and skin as he pushed himself off my shoulder. I shrieked and attempted to run but only managed to pitch forward, landing in the dust and leaves covering the *tempietto* floor. As I fell, I thought I saw the faintest ghostly figure against the far wall, the figure of a woman. There was something familiar about her, but I didn't have a chance to understand why before the shape disappeared and Jack appeared by my side.

"Are you all right?" he asked, lifting me up. "That cat just streaked by us like it had seen a ghost."

"I think it did," I said, dusting myself off.

Jack pulled a leaf from my hair. His skin smelled earthy, fresh like a spring morning. "You're joking, right?"

I could only give him a nervous laugh before the rest of the Dalí entourage crowded around the temple entrance.

"I'm fine," I said, willing my body to stop shaking. "I just need some air." I pushed my way through them and out of the *tempietto*, wondering if the ghost had been communing with the dead Giulia buried there or if her words were intended for me.

"What did you see?" Ignazio asked, concerned.

What did I see? Not "are you all right" or "what happened," but what had I seen? For a moment, I considered telling him about the ghost, but something held me back.

"Two birds flew down from the windows and went after the cat. He launched himself off my shoulder." I looked at my hands; they were still trembling.

"What kind of birds?"

"Turtledoves," I said, not understanding what difference it made.

He sighed and nodded. "They must have a nest somewhere up high."

It would be unusual for birds to be protecting a nest in November, but I didn't bother to contradict him. "Heh," I said instead, "I thought doves were peaceful birds." I touched the spot on my shoulder where Orpheus had clawed me and felt blood. A nasty set of claw marks were bright against my skin. Ignazio reached a hand toward my wound, but I recoiled, afraid of the heat of his touch.

He frowned but didn't comment on my action. Instead, he pulled a handkerchief out of his pocket and dangled it toward me. Conflicted, I took it and winced as I pressed it against the wound. Despite all my internal warnings about this man, I wanted Ignazio to take care of me, to help, and a part of me wished I hadn't pulled away from him.

"We'll need to clean that up so it doesn't get infected. There is a first aid kit in the truck," he said. "I'll take you to the spot where I think Maestro Dalí will want to paint you, and then I'll go back and get it. It's not far."

"Grazie." Much as I wanted him to help, I didn't want him to touch me again. The jolt that rushed through my body and mind when he merely brushed against me was overwhelming enough, and I didn't think I could handle more.

After I reassured everyone I was fine, Ignazio led us down another set of stairs to the top of a wide hippodrome lined with huge statues of acorns and pine cones resting on pedestals and set between long benches. Partway down the stairs was a level spot with a small statue about four feet high that was half covered in moss and surrounded in weeds. Emerging from this wild nature were three heads, oddly added to the top of the stone body—Cerberus.

"He's guarding the dead in the Underworld," Gala said, jerking a thumb back toward the *tempietto.*

Thinking of the ghostly woman I had just seen, I shivered as Orpheus emerged from the brush and began to rub his face on one of Cerberus's legs, marking his territory. "Perhaps he's not so savage after all." I chuckled. Despite his three heads, the dog looked rather docile. I ran a hand over one of its snouts as if to test my theory.

But Gala didn't hear me. She was already down in the hippodrome, directing Jack on where to set up the easel. Instead, it was Dalí who appeared at my side. He, too, extended a hand and rubbed one of the beast's snouts. "You're right. He's not so savage, not like this. But I always picture him as he was in Dante's *Inferno.*"

"How so?" I asked.

"Canto six, on gluttony," Ignazio, who had just appeared seemingly out of nowhere, chimed in before Dalí could respond. Then he proceeded to recite the poem, his voice mesmerizing, the accent smooth, though not quite Italian, not quite like any I could identify:

> "'Cerberus, cruel monster, fierce and strange,
> Through his wide threefold throat barks as a dog
> Over the multitude immersed beneath.
> His eyes glare crimson, black his unctuous beard,
> His belly large, and clawed the hands, with which
> He tears the spirits, flays them, and their limbs
> Piecemeal disports.'"

"But this Cerberus could barely tear apart a rabbit," I said, pointing at the statue.

Ignazio raised an eyebrow at me. "You assume this is always his form."

"The Cerberus in my mind is wild, rearing back, towering over Dante, black and dangerous," Dalí said.

"You are right. He is dangerous," Ignazio said, then went down the stairs.

I stared after him, wondering what he meant.

"You have nothing to worry about, little Proserpina," Dalí said, his hand stroking each of the dog's heads in turn. "He's your protector, remember?" He winked at me and followed Ignazio.

I began to trail after them down the stairs, but the scrape of stone against stone pulled my attention back. Cerberus's heads seemed to have moved, to have turned upon its stone body pedestal so that one was squarely facing me when I could have sworn it wasn't before. Unnerved, but sure I had dreamed it, I hastened down the stairway.

When I caught up to the group, Paolo was setting up his camera in the new location, and Dalí was instructing Jack on his requirements for painting that day. We were before another giant statue, this one of a woman, her legs spread apart to form a bench, her body a backrest for any who would sit down. Her hands were missing, and her fine carved features had eroded, leaving a face lacking any detail, though from her dress, it was plain that she was once regal. Upon her head was a crown that looked like a basket, one I imagined once held carved fruit. I was inexplicably drawn to the bench, craving to be nestled in the figure's wide arms—the figure I instinctively knew represented Proserpina—to sit upon the ancient stones and look down the length of the hippodrome.

"The goddess Proserpina," Ignazio verified, waving his arm expansively toward the bench.

"*Sì*," Dalí exclaimed. "A purple paradox. Proserpina in the arms of Proserpina."

Gala had taken a rag from Dalí's box of equipment and started to dust off the bench. I helped her remove some of the leaves and other debris that had accumulated over the years. There was still a lot of moss on the seat, but I thought that would be good extra padding if I were to sit on the hard bench for the next few hours.

"I'll go get the first aid kit," Ignazio said, leaving us to our preparations.

"First aid kit?" Jack asked, concerned.

I moved the handkerchief and indicated the gash where Orpheus had pierced my skin. Pinpricks of blood dotted the cloth. As I pulled it away, the smoky scent of Ignazio lingered, and I resisted the urge to put it to my nose and breathe in deep.

"That cat gave you a mean scratch," Gala said. She seemed less concerned about me and more concerned that my skin had been marred. I didn't know why it mattered—I could hide the gash in photos, and Dalí didn't have to paint it.

"We were both startled," I explained, feeling like I had to excuse the episode somehow.

Orpheus seemed to realize we were talking about him and jumped up on the bench.

"No, no, no," Dalí said, coming toward us. "Proserpina first."

He picked up the cat and dropped him on the ground. Then he took me by the arm and bade me to sit upon the bench.

Together, Gala and Dalí began to arrange me, and soon I was lounging along the bench, one leg dangling off the side, the other outstretched, my arms above my head, my face turned away from Dalí. I felt oddly comfortable in the arms of the goddess, despite the bizarre pose.

"*Bellissima,*" Gala said, the Italian word sounding strange in her Russian tongue. "She is perfect."

Might this be one of the only times Gala would compliment me?

Paolo took several snapshots of me before Ignazio returned with the first aid kit. He set the kit on the edge of the bench next to me and dug out a piece of gauze, upon which he poured some iodine. Leaning forward, he pressed the gauze against my skin. It seemed he was being careful not to brush against me with his fingers as he wiped off the blood, and for that I was grateful. But his very nearness set my body tingling. It was a confusing combination of lust tinged with terror, and it set me on edge. How could I be attracted to someone I was also inexplicably afraid of? He had been nothing but kind to me, yet underneath his beautiful exterior I could only sense darkness—*wrongness.*

"Welcome home, little goddess," he said to me, his voice low enough that the rest of the entourage would not hear.

The hairs on the back of my neck stood up. Home? What was he suggesting? While I was desperate to figure out where my home really was, I didn't believe this bizarre garden was it. I thought of the other Julias buried in the ground not far from where I sat. No, he couldn't have meant that, could he? A lump rose to my throat. I was about to break my pose and pull away, but Ignazio waved a hand, indicating the stone where I reclined.

"The bench," he said.

"Ah." I was glad to look away from Ignazio and up at Proserpina's eroded face. I willed myself to be calm, to take slow breaths.

Ignazio fetched an Elastoplast from the kit, pulled off its paper and applied it to the wound with great care. In the few seconds before he backed away, I was overcome with a great urge to reach up for him, to bring him to me, to seal his lips against mine. I cleared my throat and turned my head away. His lips curled upward in a satisfied smile. Then he left, ascending the steps toward the *tempietto*. I shuddered, tamping down any remaining vestige of desire. I was not one to play with fire.

After his departure, Gala fussed over me, arranging my limbs again and fixing my clothing. "You stupid girl. I would have had him kiss it better," she said.

I couldn't respond, sure my cheeks were the same shade as my dress.

Just then, Dalí, who had wandered off while I was being tended to, gave a shout from the other end of the hippodrome. He stood near a statue of a siren, waving something in the air. "Pomegranates," he exclaimed as he rushed back to us, raving about finding the fruit-loaded trees. He had two ruby-round orbs in his hands, which he placed, one in front of me and the other to my left, upon one of Proserpina's stone legs.

"Tomorrow we will remove the dress," he said as he stepped back to look at me.

"Of course." I shrugged, just as Orpheus jumped up and curled himself into a ball in my lap, tucking his face into my belly. I expected Dalí to shoo the beast away, but he only said *"bueno"* and then returned to his easel.

A subtle shift in the air drew my attention. Ignazio was there, standing slightly apart from the rest, that damned smile at the edges of his lips. I had been wrong to assume he had departed. Crimson heat rose to my cheeks with the thought of his eyes upon my naked body. I looked away, wishing I hadn't agreed with Dalí so easily. Perhaps I could have bought at least another day of clothing.

"I'll return soon with the midday meal," Ignazio told the

group. This time I watched him make his way back to the truck. I was glad for his departure and relaxed the moment he vanished down the trail. Gala, Jack, and Paolo also left us, eager to explore more of the garden, while Dalí began to paint me—a preliminary sketch in oils. He planned to create many images of me, and I knew it wasn't feasible to develop entire paintings in the garden. It was the perfect time to ask him about his techniques.

"You are sketching me in oil—will you paint it in oil, too, or will you use a different medium?"

Dalí paused and regarded me. "Why do you wish to know this?"

"I am a painter as well. I didn't just model for the *accademia*. I graduated in the spring."

He snorted. "Women are not suited for art. You are a muse, you are a goddess, but you are not an artist. You will never be an artist."

"That's a terribly backward view," I ventured boldly. "There are many female artists."

Dalí laughed, loud and long. The sound was eerie against the silence of the hippodrome. *"C'est un spectacle,"* he said in French. "Nothing more. A brief shine before history obliterates all memory of them."

"I am not a spectacle," I told him.

"Neither are you a real painter. Now hush, Proserpina. I'm paying you to model, not comment on art."

I pressed my lips together, willing myself to be quiet, to not say the words I wished to say. And I closed my eyes, so I would not cry. I thought of Artemisia Gentileschi, Mary Cassatt, Dorothea Tanning, Helen Lundeberg, Frida Kahlo—women I admired for their talent and verve, women whom Dalí had just declared to be nothing more than inconsequential. I pictured Meret Oppenheim's *Object* in my mind. Her fur-lined tea set had captured the world's imagination a decade back, in a way that even Dalí's melting clocks could not.

I fumed as he painted. My whole reason for coming to this

damned place was dashed with just a line out of Dalí's mouth. I wanted to retort, to spit back all the things that the art world and tabloids said about him—that he was a sellout who cared more about commercial success than art, that he was a Nazi sympathizer and lover of dictators like Hitler and Franco. That he was a shallow self-promoter, a consummate narcissist, a political opportunist who had compromised his art for fame.

I wanted to scream all these things at him, but I remembered the number on the piece of paper that I had shown Lillian, a monetary sum I could not conceivably make in any other way, and I kept my mouth shut. But I decided then that the opinions of this man would not sway me. Besides, I reasoned, he was right about one thing. I hadn't paid him to teach me. He was the one who had hired me for an outrageous fee and I had gratefully accepted it.

I counted down from one hundred to calm myself. Maybe Lillian had been right in her worries about my visiting Bomarzo.

After a time, I did fall into a dream state, thinking of what the Sacro Bosco might have been like when Vicino Orsini first created it. In my mind, the tangled mess of weeds before me was instead filled with grassy paths between beds of flowers and herbs. I pictured the women in their beautiful dresses, the men in their jackets and ruffled shirts, and musicians playing in the rotunda that overlooked the hippodrome. I could hear their happy murmurings, the women's laughter, the grand stories of the men. It was almost like a memory, a good one, one that had made me content.

At some point, Jack roused me from my fugue. "Ready for lunch?"

I sat up and looked around. Dalí had already set aside his paints and was making his way up a crumbling moss-covered stairway behind Proserpina's bench. I made to stand but my leg had gone to sleep. Shaking it, I winced with the sensation, and Jack extended his arm to help me up.

"Those steps would be much faster, but clearly, we have to take the long way," he said, pointing to the staircase on Proserpina's right, which led deeper into the *boschetto* but was blocked by a massive tree that had fallen long ago.

"That would have been a great shortcut," I agreed as we headed up the stairs. "This leads around the edge of the garden, rather than through it." At the top stretched a vast field, half of which was sowed with wheat, the other half with corn. On the far edge of the field, I could make out the silhouettes of a man and a donkey. "I always associate cornfields with America," I said with wonder. The truth was that I wasn't sure I had ever seen a cornfield in person, but I couldn't tell Jack that. My "memories" of the United States were built upon images I had seen in newspapers and films.

Jack laughed. "It's wacky to see something so familiar here, isn't it? But don't worry, we don't have to find our way through the cornfield."

We walked along the edge of the field until we saw a monstrous vase rising out of the weeds of the garden, towering over us by four or five feet. "How strange," I said, marveling at the size. I pressed my hand against it.

The whisper came to me again, faint this time. *Julia, don't... Julia, Julia, don't...* I snatched my hand away.

Jack didn't seem to notice. "Gala saw Ignazio before he left for lunch and asked him about the vase. He said it represents Bacchus's entry into hell, with his goblet in hand."

"I think someone is buried here," I said, certain it was true. There were ashes within or under the vase. I could sense it. And this time, I somehow knew that the voice had been talking to me. It was a warning, but a warning I didn't understand.

"Now you are letting your imagination run wild," Jack said, giving me a light sock in the arm.

I laughed, but I was unnerved. How could I feel such conviction about something I had no knowledge of? And why had this ghost chosen to communicate with me? Why not Jack or any of the others? I changed the subject to quell my rising anxiety. "So, why do you think Vicino Orsini created so many monsters to represent death and the Underworld?"

Jack laughed. "We humans are all obsessed with money, sex, and death, aren't we? But wait, you ain't seen nothin' yet."

There weren't many trees in that part of the *boschetto*, and two statues were visible a few paces ahead of us—a monstrous elephant with a castle on its back, and a bizarre, doglike dragon fighting off lions. As we neared, I could see Dalí had mounted the elephant and stood in its castle, holding an arm out, pointing the beast forward. Paolo was at its base, filming.

"We're up here," I heard Gala say. It sounded like she was right next to me, but when I whirled about, I didn't see her anywhere.

Jack nudged my arm and pointed up a path toward a gigantic face, its mouth wide open in a scream. I gasped. This must be the screaming ogre that Dalí mentioned yesterday. Gala stood inside the mouth of the monster, below its two stone teeth, waving at us.

"But I could hear her perfectly," I said in awe.

"An acoustic trick that Ignazio showed us. Killer-diller, huh? Come on—there is a mountain of food up there."

We made our way up the dirt trail to the *orco*. Pomegranate bushes laden with fruit flanked the stone of the monster's cheeks, the surrounding ground littered with fallen fruit. As we approached, I saw it had a tongue—a table carved from *peperino*. Above the mouth was an inscription: *OGNI PENSIERO VOLA*. All thoughts fly. Or at least anything said in the mouth of this ogre.

Jack went right in, but I stopped to admire the incredible structure before me. The "tongue" table was laden with food, and around the interior of the monster was a long bench carved into the rock. What a feat of engineering this must have been to create.

Dalí waved me in, and I stepped forward, crossing below the enormous teeth, but as I did, the stone walls seemed to press closer to me. My world spun terribly out of control, and everything became a blur...the faces of my companions, the food on the table. As the *orco* became awash in shades of gray that grew darker by the second, a roaring sound filled my ears, and the smell of smoke overwhelmed my nostrils.

I came to my senses in the fiery hot arms of Ignazio, who must have caught me before I smashed my head on the table. *"Ogni pensiero vola,"* he whispered in my ear.

The world stopped spinning abruptly and all the puzzling sensations I was experiencing ceased just as quickly. There was no smoke, no roaring noise. I took a deep breath. Ignazio righted me and let go.

"Be careful, Julia," Jack admonished. "Those shoes really are terrible."

"Grazie," I said to Ignazio, but I wasn't sure I was thankful. What did he just do? Why had everything righted with his whisper? *All thoughts fly.* I moved away from him to the opposite side of the tiny room.

"Grab a plate, Julia. Eat up," Gala instructed. "You clearly need some sustenance to fulfill your duties this afternoon. It would not do to have you faint on the job."

I pursed my lips and said nothing, surveying the spread before us instead.

Lunch was set up buffet-style, and I looked on in awe as Ignazio described the dozens of little dishes sprawled out on the table: garlic rolls; canapé of chicken liver, truffles, and woodcock; little salads with *bresaola* and pomegranate seeds; *maccheroni* with bread crumbs; apple and pomegranate fritters; pastry puffs with cheese and mortadella; *coratella*, a much revered Roman dish made of lamb's liver and offal; roasted mushrooms; potato salad; *Romanesco* broccoli with pomegranate and pine nuts; roast chicken stuffed with prosciutto; and a ricotta tart for dessert. I wondered how much Dalí was paying for such catering.

"Please, partake," Ignazio said when he'd finished. He laid a hand on the artist's shoulder and held it there for a moment, which I thought odd—it seemed a gesture of power, and Dalí was not someone who let anyone other than Gala dominate him. I expected the artist to move away or say something, but Dalí didn't even seem to register it.

Nor did he seem to notice that Gala had her hand high on Jack's thigh, a sight I couldn't help but see when I took my seat on the bench.

"Mon Dieu," she said in French after biting into a golden croquette of some sort. She closed her eyes, savoring the flavor. "Potato."

"Try the broccoli," Dalí instructed me, pointing to the whorls of green on my plate. I lifted the *Romanesco* to my mouth but purposefully lost a pomegranate seed to the floor. A bird would find it later, I supposed. I took a bite. The broccoli, to my surprise, wasn't cold. We were a long way from the *castello*, and I did not smell or see any fire to warm the food.

Dalí looked unsatisfied. "Did you have the salad? The pomegranate seeds are the ultimate complement to the chicory and *bresaola*."

I gave him a sheepish smile. "I'm not partial to salad."

He pointed at a fritter on my plate. "Then you must have the fritters."

I couldn't understand his weird insistence that I eat certain foods, although I noticed they all had pomegranate seeds. Dalí being his freakish, surreal self, I assumed, wanting me to really fill Proserpina's shoes. Fine. Much as I hated pomegranate seeds, perhaps if I ate a fritter he would leave me alone. I lifted the pastry off the plate and thought I heard the faintest of whispers.

Julia...don't...

I was tired of my mind playing tricks on me. I took a bite. The crunch and sweetness of a pomegranate aril hit my tongue, and for a moment, I was transported. My senses were overwhelmed by a rush of indescribable love, so profound that it seemed to permeate my very being. I felt as though I was floating, ensconced in the warm embrace of someone deeply familiar yet distant. Passionate kisses, whispered promises—I experienced them all, vivid as if happening in the present.

I heard a whisper. *"Ogni pensiero vola."*

And then, as suddenly as it had come, the sensation was ripped from me, leaving an aching emptiness where that feeling of pure love had been. My world was spinning, my eyes refocusing on the stone room around me. I was struck by the heady aroma of smoke and leather, as if remnants of that ephemeral moment had followed me back.

Ignazio bent down to pick up my fork, which had clattered to the floor in my daze. "All thoughts fly," he said, smiling at me. "Don't worry, I'll get you a clean one."

"I'm not hungry anymore," I replied, standing up. I had to get out of the mouth of that monster. Leaving with as much decorum as I could muster, I rushed down the path, away from the *orco*.

I had never been faint of heart, having dizzy spells. And the whispers... What did they mean? What was wrong with me? One second dizzy, but then suddenly not. And I was left haunted by the intense love and passion that had been so cruelly snatched away.

I hurried past the elephant with the castle on its back and the dragon fighting off the lions and found myself at the foot of a giant statue of a seated woman, her mossy legs before her, a wide bowl upon her head, from which a wild abundance of autumn flowers grew—cyclamen, autumn iris, chrysanthemums, winter honeysuckle. It was an outlandish, impossible bouquet. Who had planted such a chaotic arrangement in that basin? Surely it didn't grow that way on its own. The statue looked in the direction of the *orco*'s mouth, where I could see my companions talking as though nothing had happened.

As I neared the statue, I began to feel nauseous, my stomach roiling with each step. I stopped, clutching at my belly, wondering if I might lose what little lunch I had managed to eat. I looked up at the statue. Her face was serene, beautiful, her hair tumbling down her back. A little cherub seemed to be whispering something in her ear.

Ceres.

It came to me in that moment, her name. How, I couldn't tell you. I only knew the woman was familiar, as though I had always known her. The comfort of her arms, the way her hips so generously curved, the swell of her breasts, her hands caressing me, the feel of her lips against mine. Before me was an image in mossy *peperino*, but there was more to this statue, just as I instinctively knew there was more to the myth of Ceres, of Pluto, of Proserpina. It wasn't the same as the tale written in the pages of the books on my shelves, the story passed through centuries of mortal telling. No, the truth was different, twisted up, and it had little to do with motherhood and everything to do with passion, betrayal, and deceit.

I didn't have time to ponder this stunning new understanding, for at that moment the ground began to vibrate beneath my feet. At first, it was a soft, barely perceptible feeling, but it grew until the earth was shaking violently. The stone of the statue in front of me seemed to be moving—no, rippling—as the earth shifted. I looked around at the few trees that stuck up between the statues, hoping that none would fall on me.

"An earthquake," Jack said, appearing behind me. "I was in one once in California."

Terror drove me to him. Between my nausea in the mouth of the *orco*, the whispers, the memory of stolen love, this sudden earthquake, and the strange recognition of the goddess before me, I could no longer pretend I was fine. I threw myself into

Jack's arms. He held me and stroked my hair until the ground stopped shaking.

"You are safe, Julia. You are safe," he said.

But even with Jack holding me, I didn't feel safe.

"Can we go back to the bench where I was modeling?" I asked him after I had calmed a bit.

Thankfully, he did not ask me to explain why—if I spoke too much I might start crying like a child. He might understand my need to escape the area of the earthquake, but he wouldn't understand why I thought sitting on the bench might give me comfort that he could not. He offered his arm and led me back to the bench. As soon as I sat upon it, a sense of calm flooded through me.

Jack sat down next to me and put his arm over my shoulders. "Are you okay?" he asked, concerned.

I nodded. I liked his arm around me. "Much better, thank you. I don't know what came over me."

"Have you been in an earthquake before?"

"No, we didn't get them where I grew up," I said, unsure if that was true.

Jack stood abruptly, distancing himself from me as the sound of Dalí and Gala's voices and footsteps came down the stairway behind the bench. When Gala reached us, she went to Jack and put her arm around his waist.

"There she is, my Proserpina." Dalí patted my shoulder, then went to his easel. "Are you ready?"

"At least the earthquake didn't topple your painting," I said, marveling that the easel was still standing upon its thin wooden legs.

"Earthquake?" Gala asked.

"You didn't feel it?" That made no sense. The *orco* was a mere hundred and twenty feet or so from the statue of Ceres, separated only by a few trees and some bushes. A shout from one to the other would easily be heard.

She looked at Dalí and Paolo, who shrugged and shook their heads. "We didn't feel anything."

"I felt it," Jack exclaimed, coming to the rescue of my sanity. "Maybe the stone in the monster's mouth was so thick it prevented you from feeling it, but it was a really big one."

"No earthquake will bother Dalí!" the artist shouted in the direction of the statues near the *orco*, as if offering a challenge. I shuddered at the thought that one might respond. He turned back to me. "Now, little Proserpina, you are ready to begin again?"

I wasn't, but I didn't know how to articulate how confused I was about everything that had happened so far that day. Save for the scratch on my shoulder, my body was fine. I looked at Dalí and reminded myself yet again about the massive sum of money waiting for me when I finished. Regardless of what he thought about women painting, I would observe him at work and ask questions all the same. I would learn, even if he didn't realize he was teaching me.

Besides, I was coming to realize he had little to do with why I was really here. In his art, I'd be the physical representation of Proserpina, the mythical Persephone. People around the world would recognize me as her when his painting fell into public purveyance. That and the pull of the garden, the ghost whispering in my ear, the heated connection with Ignazio, and now the inexplicable familiarity of Ceres, solidified my determination. They were somehow all connected. There was something here, in this wild place of Sacro Bosco, something that might help me understand myself. I was determined to figure it out, no matter how much it scared me.

"I'm ready." I settled back against the bench, hoping that the meditative state that sitting sometimes put me in would be a balm to my troubled spirit.

5

The afternoon passed in a haze. I dozed while Dalí painted. At some point, Ignazio brought out folding chairs for the others, who collapsed in them gratefully in between their forays into the garden. Orpheus returned and curled up in his spot, purring against my belly.

"Time to go." Gala shook my arm, rousing me. "This place is becoming creepy."

I looked around and saw that dusk had begun to fall. The sirens at the other end of the hippodrome glowed in the last rays of the day's light. Paolo was waiting, his camera bag and tripod on his shoulder. "Can I see?" I asked Jack, who held the canvas as Dalí packed up his easel.

He turned around to face me, bringing the painting into my view. My face had been sketched in great detail, and the outline of my body was there, and I was hardly surprised to see a pomegranate floating in space, a few inches from my figure. But rather than being held by Proserpina, as I had expected, my image was in what I could tell would become the mouth of a terrible *orco*, the beginnings of a vast ocean beneath and a wide pink-and-blue sky above.

"Why am I in the Mouth of Hell?" I asked Dalí.

His eyes bulged in a mix of surprise and incredulity. "Where else would Proserpina be?"

"Judge not," Gala warned me.

I nodded, unsure what I would have said, even if my opinion was wanted. But I was glad he hadn't decided to have me model in the mouth of the *orco*.

Ignazio was waiting for us at the truck to take us back up to the palazzo. On the way, the others filled me in on the parts of the garden I had yet to see.

"There is an old stone amphitheater, covered in moss," Paolo said. "They must have put on some magnificent performances there at one time."

"The tilted house is my favorite," Jack said.

"Tilted house?" I asked.

"It's like a house in one of Dalí's paintings," Gala said, patting her husband's knee.

"No, it is like how it *feels* in one of my paintings," he corrected her.

We hit a bump and Paolo slipped off his seat, knocking into the wet canvas, the top of the *orco* and part of the ocean transferring to the sleeve of his jacket.

"*Idiota! Stupido sciocco!*" Gala cried out, smacking him across the face with the back of her hand.

Paolo drew back and looked down at the blue-and-black smear of paint on his clothing, mortified. Rather than reclaim his seat next to Jack, he sat down next to me, and I could see a red mark just beginning to bloom on his cheek. I felt for Paolo. It was the second time that day that Gala had slapped someone—and I still recalled the feeling of her hand hitting my cheek. Was she always so awful?

"My Lionette." Dalí put his arm around Gala to calm her, speaking to her in a mixture of Catalan, French, and English.

I surveyed the damage. "Dalí can fix anything," I said, looking at the canvas. I hoped that the situation would diffuse if I appealed to the artist's ego. "Do not worry."

Gala harrumphed and turned her head to look out of the truck toward the palazzo looming on the hill above us, but my tactic worked on Dalí. "A trifle," he exclaimed after he'd lifted his head to survey the damage. "This is nothing. I can fix that with my eyes closed."

Beside me, Paolo released a sigh of relief.

"Grazie per la sua gentilezza," Paolo said, thanking me for my kindness when we got out of the truck and Dalí and Gala were out of earshot.

"Non era niente," I told him. For it was nothing.

"Questo è un brutto posto. Lo sento nelle ossa. E queste persone, non si prenderanno cura di te. Stai attento."

This is a bad place. I feel it in my bones. And these people, they won't take care of you. Be careful. I opened my mouth to respond, but Jack spoke before I could.

"Gala is prone to outbursts," he said calmly. "Don't take it personally."

Clearly, he hadn't understood the cameraman's words of warning. I wanted to ask Paolo what he meant, but he had already turned from me and was hoisting Dalí's easel over his shoulder.

"Julia, may I speak with you?" Ignazio asked as we trekked up the long stretch of road toward the Orsini palazzo.

"Sure," I said, although my heart had already begun to pound at his nearness.

He fell in step with me, waiting until Paolo and Jack were some distance ahead of us before he began to speak. "They told me you felt an earthquake when you were in the garden," he said, finally.

"*Sì*, I did. So did Jack, but the others said they did not feel it. I don't know how—it was quite strong."

"I felt it too."

I looked at him, shocked. "You did? But the others didn't."

He gave me a dark, sly smile. "I am more accustomed to the unusual nature of the garden than they are. Where were you when it happened?"

"In front of the statue of the woman with the mossy legs and the vase of flowers on her head." I didn't want to tell him I knew her name.

He nodded. It seemed to be the answer he expected.

"I regret that the *boschetto* wasn't kind to you today. I imagine fainting in the mouth of the *orco*, then feeling an earthquake so shortly after must have left you unnerved."

He sounded truly sympathetic, and despite my better judgment, I warmed to him a little.

"You haven't eaten much today. You must be famished," he said.

My belly rumbled then, and I hoped he couldn't hear it. "I am."

"There will be a big feast tonight. Partridge, pheasant, perhaps a little *pollo alla diavola*."

The devil's chicken. My breath caught, although I shouldn't have been as taken off guard as I was. It was a common Italian dish I had eaten many times before. It derived its name from its spicy nature and because it was traditionally cooked over coals, not because of any sinister association.

"Are you the devil?" The words were out of my mouth before I could stop them. I didn't know what provoked me to be so coy and I could only hope it came out as a joke. I dared a glance at him.

"Only if you want me to be, Julia," he replied with a wink.

My jaw dropped a little and I paused, unsure what to make of such a clear, brazen suggestion.

"Julia, are you all right?" Jack asked me as we entered the palazzo. "You look like you've seen another ghost."

I shut my mouth and strengthened my resolve. "I'm swell. Really."

Ignazio informed us that dinner would be served in two hours and that we were free to roam the premises if we desired.

"Perhaps you could give me another tour," Gala purred. "I was so tired when we first arrived."

"I would be delighted to answer any questions you have," Ignazio responded, quashing any hope of her getting a private tour from him. He ignored her pout and turned on a heel to head down the corridor.

"Jack can give you a special tour, Galachuka," Dalí offered in an attempt to appease his wife. "I will go with you—for inspiration," he added, giving me a little jab in the ribs with his elbow. "Perhaps you need inspiration, too, little goddess. Come back with us." His eyes roamed to my chest, then flitted over to Jack.

"I think I'm inspired enough," I said. There was something about Dalí and Gala, with their peculiar aura and unsettling demeanor, that made the idea of any closer encounter with them deeply unappealing. I could embrace the unconventional, but the thought of entangling with them churned my stomach in a way that no adventurous spirit could overcome.

I excused myself and went to my chamber, which I was relieved to see was just as I had left it. I half expected to find some new surprise under my pillow, but it was crisp and smooth. Throwing myself onto the bed, I stared at the frescoed ceiling, unable to believe the events of the day—the *boschetto*, the doves in the *tempietto*, fainting, the earthquake—it was all too unbelievable to be true. I thought about Ignazio's words—he regretted that the *boschetto* hadn't been kind to me, as if a garden had a choice in how much kindness it imparted on someone. As if *he* could control it. Who was this man?

Realizing it would do me no good to lie there letting my thoughts run rampant, that I was only ratcheting myself up, I decided to freshen up and to take the opportunity to explore the palazzo on my own. I started with the library we'd passed when Ignazio was showing us to our chambers. The shelves had beckoned me with the delicious odor of old books and the tantalizing thought of discovering something about this unnatural place.

It was just as you might imagine an old library in a castle would be. The walls were lined with thousands of books from floor to ceiling, with two ladders on wheels and a track to reach the highest shelves. A massive globe stood in an alcove near the window where a large desk and chair were positioned for easy viewing of the garden below. When I flipped the switch, the lights gave the room a cozy orange glow. Déjà vu ripped through me again, the sight of the library infusing a familiar sense of belonging within me, as though I had spent many an hour in this very room. I tried to tell myself that I had just been in a similar library in one of the many palazzi I had toured in Rome, but I knew that wasn't true. It was *this* library that was familiar, and it bothered me that I couldn't remember why.

Wandering along the shelves, I admired the dusty volumes, mostly written in Italian, though I did notice some Latin, Greek, and French titles too. I was astounded to see that many were hundreds of years old. Just as I was about to pull a volume of Dante's poetry off the shelf, the sound of a book falling to the floor on the other side of the room startled me. I whirled around, expecting to find Dalí or someone else touring the palazzo. But there was no one else in the room. My heart in my throat, I went over to investigate the fallen volume.

It was a simple, black, leather-bound book, a little bigger than those Pocket paperbacks that were so popular. I picked it up and was surprised to find it was a journal written in crisp, clear Italian. A woman's hand. Flipping to the inside front cover of the book, I found both a date and a name. *Giulia Farnese, 1560.*

I looked around the library, suddenly terrified. What spirit wanted me to find the journal of Vicino Orsini's wife? For there was no other explanation—someone or something had pulled this book off the shelf. It didn't fall on its own. There were thousands of volumes in the library. Why the one penned by a woman who shared my name and was buried in the *tempietto* in the garden of monsters below? What message was I being sent? From whom?

"Who are you?" I whispered to the empty room. When there was no response, I calmed myself with a few deep breaths, then took the book to the plush couch on the other side of the library, one of the few items in the room that wasn't a relic of the past but a modern addition. I sank down into the cushions and opened the journal. The writing was clean, but my Italian was intermediate at best, and many of the words were archaic, having been written so long ago.

I could understand the basic gist of the text but felt like there was more to it than I was grasping. Why else was I supposed to see it? The first few pages were full of anecdotes about Giulia's seven children—Corradino, Marzio, Alessandro, Scipione, Orazio, Ottavia, and Faustina—and spotting the word *incinta*, I gathered that she was pregnant again. I tried my best to scan through the journal, to see what could be so vital for me to know, but it was hard.

Just then, I heard Dalí call my name. Jumping off the couch, I rushed across the room to put the journal back before he found me with it. I don't know why I did it, other than I didn't want to share my discovery with the others. Jack appeared in the doorway as I slid the journal back onto the shelf.

"Ah, there you are," he said. He entered the library and looked around. "So many books. How could you read all of them in one lifetime?"

"It would be hard," I admitted.

"Did you find anything good?"

"There are a lot of interesting tomes on these shelves," I said, not wanting to admit I hadn't looked at any of them except the one that had fallen on the floor for me to see.

He approached the book display on a podium near the window. "What's this one?"

The cover had beautiful gold etching and contained only a single word: *Poliphilo*. A more extended Latin title was on the spine. Carefully, I opened the book and found the inside filled with beautiful woodcuts—wondrous images of people, animals, and what looked like a garden. The text seemed to be a mix of Greek, Latin, and even hieroglyphics, and the typography was unique, often creating shapes on the page with the words.

Jack leaned in to look at the images, putting his arm over my shoulder as though we had long been friends. "What is this book?"

I showed him the spine. "Hypnero...to...ma..."

"Hypnerotomachia!" Dalí exclaimed, coming up behind us, Gala in tow. *"Hypnerotomachia Poliphili,"* he said with ease. *"Que fantástico.* It was published in 1499. What a find this is. *The Strife of Love in a Dream."*

"You know this book?" I asked, stunned by his seemingly boundless intellect.

"It is the story of Polia and Poliphilo. Of course I know of it. It is a story of love, of dreams, of architecture, of ecstasy!"

I thumbed through it and came upon an illustration of an elephant with an obelisk on its back.

"Hey, I know that elephant," Jack said.

I did too. It was the same as the Bernini statue in front of the church of Santa Maria sopra Minerva, near the Pantheon in Rome, though noting the book's year of publication, this image probably inspired the sculpture. Dalí had always said he had taken his inspiration for his spindly elephant with an obelisk on its back in his *Dream Caused by the Flight of a Bee around a Pomegranate a Second before Waking* painting from the statue, so I should not have been so surprised that he knew of its original source.

"It's a famous book," Ignazio said from the doorway. "A story of love in a fantastical place. Vicino Orsini designed much of the garden based on the dreams within the *Hypnerotomachia.* It's interesting that you discovered this book tonight. Your dinner is based upon a meal that Poliphilo had during his dream."

"Who was Poliphilo?" I asked.

"He's the illustrious hero of the tale. The story is that Poliphilo can't sleep because his beloved, Polia, has shunned him." He paused and looked at me, as though there was some understanding between us, which was certainly not the case. "But," he continued, "he falls into a fitful dream, in which he is transported into a forest, where he encounters magnificent temples, dragons, wolves, nymphs, and other beasts as he searches for Polia despite the danger and distraction."

"Are they ever reunited?" Jack asked.

"Polia spurns him over and over, but eventually, when Poliphilo is on the brink of death, the goddess Venus convinces Polia to accept him. She kisses him, and he rouses from his fever, much like the prince and princess in *Sleeping Beauty*. But just as they are about to embrace, Polia disappears as Poliphilo wakes from his feverish dream."

"Love is cruel," Gala said. She sounded bored.

"Indeed," Ignazio agreed, turning his gaze to me once more.

"I don't blame Polia for running," I said, forcing myself not to look away. "Such infatuation is rarely wanted."

Ignazio was not deterred. "Sometimes people don't know what they truly want. Sometimes they are victims of the lies they tell themselves."

"I always know what I want," Gala said. "And, right now, I want dinner." She tried, once again, to take Ignazio by the arm and lead him away. This time he let her.

Seeing them together left me deflated. It was the oddest feeling, akin to watching an ex-lover go off with his new girlfriend. I was pondering the ridiculousness of such a sentiment when Jack put an arm around my shoulders and led me out of the library.

"Such magnificent backsides," Dalí commented from behind, thwapping me on the side of my leg with his cane.

"I'm not sure whose derriere he prefers more—yours or mine,"

I said to Jack as we descended the elegant staircase to the first floor.

"Likely mine," he said, laughing. "But I think he's mistaken." He stole a glance at my behind.

At this, I warmed. While I didn't think I wanted Ignazio's attention, having Jack's wasn't something I minded at all.

6

"Aside from a great camera, there is nothing more wonderful than a great library," Paolo exclaimed, his eyes lighting up when I told him about the thousands of volumes I'd discovered, including *Hypnerotomachia Poliphili*, which had so excited Dalí. "If you ever want help reading anything in Italian, I would be honored to translate for you."

I thought of Giulia Farnese's journal. Perhaps I would take him up on his offer. But I hardly knew him... Was he someone I could trust not to tell the others? I paused to listen to the quartet—two lutists, a flutist, and a drummer, playing medieval music—wondering if I might find a quiet moment alone with Paolo. Glancing around the room, I didn't think that would likely happen that evening. By the looks of it, we were in for another night of gluttony.

The tablescape was even more elaborate than it had been the night before, the long dining table covered in an extravagant green silk tablecloth with a pearl border and gold fringes that reached nearly to the floor.

The servers, who wore green and gold to match the tablecloth, scampered about, setting up for whatever wonders were in store for us. One invited us to wash our hands in a golden basin from which a fountain of perfumed water flowed. Then he escorted us to the table, oddly placing us all on one side, me in the middle, Dalí and Jack to my sides, Gala and Paolo to theirs.

It suddenly struck me as odd that, aside from Demetra and the servants who brought us our food, I hadn't seen a single one of the help within the palazzo. How could that be? Granted, I had been away much of the day, but there were no sounds of others talking in the palazzo, no footsteps, no glimpses of someone else in a hallway. Even queerer, none of the servers acknowledged us beyond a few short words to explain the food. They did their jobs with impeccable precision, so carefully that while we were busy oohing and aahing over the food, it was easy to disregard that they seemed utterly devoid of personality. The thought set me on edge.

Two servants brought out a massive buffet cart, the front shaped like a boat, the back like an ancient Roman triumphal chariot. It looked to be made of pure gold, decorated with little sea monsters, shells, and precious stones, and it was breathtaking. How had such a treasure not been plundered for a museum? Especially during the war, when metal resources were scarce, and every piece of art was coveted by Hitler.

Dalí squealed with glee. "We should include such a cart in the cookbook of Gala!"

"A marvelous idea," Gala agreed. "But, darling, I think you have other things to accomplish before we worry about making a cookbook."

The chariot contained all manner of items—napkins, glassware, wine, flowers, candles, and the basic condiments and spices that would rest upon the table. In unison, the servers set the table before us.

"Do you think these are real?" I asked Jack, picking up my

fork and waving it at him. The utensil was heavy and it, too, appeared to be made of gold.

"Of course," he said, as though gold forks were an everyday object. He seemed distracted, his head tilted to the side as though he were listening to someone other than me. But Paolo was looking away from him.

"Would they mind if I stole one?" I joked.

"Probably not," Jack said. Again, he answered as though this was a perfectly normal thing to ask.

I raised my eyebrow at him, puzzled at the response. "Are you serious?"

For a moment, Jack's gaze seemed to glaze over, as if he was momentarily lost in a separate reality. Then, with a slight start, he seemed to snap back to the present. "Look at all this gold—who would miss a fork or two? Go ahead, hide one away and see what happens. Besides, you are beyond reproach."

I couldn't tell if he was joking or not, but my shocked expression seemed to trigger a flicker of clarity in his eyes.

"I'm teasing," he said after a beat, but his voice was still unnaturally even.

Concerned, I put my hand on his forearm. "Jack, are you all right?"

He paused, his eyes briefly showing confusion, quickly masked with a forced smile. But his smile was too sudden, too bright. "Perfectly." He grinned, full of emotion once more. "And boy, oh boy, am I hungry. And you better be, too, because here it comes." He gestured toward an approaching server.

The meal began with five tiny fritters of saffron-colored dough, drizzled with a rosewater glaze and served on plates made of some sort of yellow, transparent stone. If I didn't think it impossible, I would have sworn it was topaz.

Ignazio came forward with a glass carafe. "From Elysium itself," he said, as he poured us each a glass of the golden wine.

"You jest," I said, catching his eye.

"Do I?" Again, that dazzling smile.

A jolt ran through me, and I looked away, heat rising to my cheeks. Picking up the glass, I buried my nose in it, wishing for him to depart. I let out a breath when he finally did.

The bouquet of the wine was truly divine. I thought it smelled of apricots and toffee, although Gala patently disagreed with me.

"Sandalwood and lemongrass," she declared.

"Candied walnuts. Fallen leaves," Dalí said, sipping the wine and closing his eyes. "Pure hedonism."

To sip it was heavenly, transporting even. If it had been the last thing I ever drank, I would have died happy.

After this welcome refreshment, the tablecloths were changed to a purple silk, the same color the servants now donned. How had they found the time to change? I marveled as one of them scattered white rose petals across the table while two others brought each of us five cuts of fat capons, roasted and shining with flecks of gold, accompanied by a snow-white bread and a sauce Ignazio informed us consisted of lemon, sugar, pine nuts, and cinnamon.

"This must have cost a fortune," I said, shocked at the display before me.

Gala chuckled. "My Dalí makes money every time he twists his mustache."

Dalí twisted the end of his tiny mustache and winked at me.

They were smiling and laughing, but something felt unnatural about his response. Gala was impressed by the display of luxury before us, but Dalí was not nearly as amazed at the meal. While I knew the Dalís were wealthy, this was beyond opulent. I wanted to understand how he could possibly take such excess for granted. "Why go to such lengths for so few of us?"

Dalí gawked at me in the same way that Jack had when I asked him about the gold forks. "This is what Dalí deserves! It is not extravagance," he finally answered. "This is how gods and goddesses dine. You should know that, little Proserpina."

Though Gala laughed, a wild laugh, I found Dalí's conviction unnerving. Did he actually think of us as gods?

Giving him a weak smile, I cut into the capon and took a bite. I wasn't ready for the explosion of flavor upon my tongue. This was no ordinary chicken. I was torn between savoring the dish and devouring it. It was tender, smoky, and juicy. And the rest of the meal promised to be just as sublime.

As we waited for the next course, the conversation turned to current events. Dalí made an offhand remark praising General Franco's leadership in Spain, which immediately soured my mood, knowing the dictator's brutal tactics during the civil war.

Sensing my discomfort, Dalí continued, "Of course, I do not agree with all his methods, but a firm hand is sometimes needed to bring order."

I chose my next words carefully. "Order through fear and oppression rarely leads to anything good. We all saw the costs of fascism during the War."

Dalí waved his hand dismissively. "Politics is boring. Controversy and shock—that is what really motivates the masses."

He leaned in with a gleam in his eye that I found unsettling. "Imagine a painting of Hitler. Now imagine Hitler engaged in a most personal and private act. What a delightfully outrageous idea!"

An uncomfortable silence followed. Dalí chuckled. "Now, drink up. We should enjoy this night. The only 'politics' an artist should care about are those of the unconscious mind. That is the only truth."

I murmured agreement, though his cavalier attitude toward oppression and his provocative hypothetical unsettled me. It was my first glimpse of the moral—and, to my mind, dangerous—flexibility behind Dalí's genius. Dalí did not actually stand for or against any political ideology. He was not interested in moral outcomes. His provocative art stemmed from a relentless desire to shock and court controversy by any means, not explore deeper truths. Dalí's primary motivation was garnering attention for himself, not any sincere political position. He leveraged the names of leaders and ideologies opportunistically to further his artistic career, apathetic to real-world consequences. His amoral approach troubled me but revealed the cunning pragmatism behind his success. We spoke no more of politics, but the conversation left a shadow over my impression of him.

Fortunately, we were distracted by the next part of the magnificent dinner show. The servers, now in yellow, dressed the table in a satin cloth of the same color, and brought out a roast partridge with another yeasty milk bread, and a sauce that smelled of almonds. The plates appeared to be made of peridot. The fourth course was brought by servers in crimson and the table was relaid in crimson cloth. The dish was succulent slices of roast pheasant on plates of emerald, dressed in a sauce of pine nuts, orange juice, and cinnamon.

"This is ridiculous," I said to Jack when Ignazio announced the fifth course, exactly nine mouthfuls of peacock in a pistachio sauce. "Kings don't even dine in this sort of luxury."

Jack smirked at me. "And you know that how?"

He had me there. "Really, Jack, who eats peacock anymore?" I asked, looking down at the sapphire plate before me.

"It's rather amazing, I have to admit," he said, placing his hand next to mine on the table, now laid out with a violet linen tablecloth. "But I've seen many unexpected things since I met the Dalís. I've learned to just enjoy." He smiled, gently stroking my fingers, and a thrill shot through me. A normal thrill—the bubbly, happy kind, not the hot, dark-edged, dangerous kind that infused Ignazio's touch.

Gala noticed immediately. "Jack, come here," she barked, and he dutifully got up and went to her, bending down to let her whisper in his ear.

"What did she say?" I whispered when he returned to his seat.

"To stay away from you," he said, covering his mouth with his hand.

But his foot found mine under the table, and my cheeks grew hot with the notion that I might be a rival for Jack's affection.

Despite enjoying the attention from Jack, I couldn't help but drink Ignazio in when he appeared before us to announce the dessert course. Dear god, he was beautiful. He wore a black suit with red embroidery—a stark contrast to the servers, now in white, who waited at the edges of the room, ready to take our plates. His dark hair was a little wild, but everything else about him was perfectly tailored and groomed. He gave us a graceful bow, and when he stood again, his eyes were fixed on me. Perhaps it was because I sat in the middle of the table, but it seemed as though I was the primary person he honored with that bow. He flashed a smile at me, and again, the urge to reach for him conflicted with the simultaneous urge to run from the room and never look back.

Jack's touch on my upper thigh broke the spell. I must have let out a little gasp, for he quickly withdrew his hand and looked toward Gala. She wasn't paying attention.

"Are you okay?" he asked me, but there was a mischievous look in his eye.

I was unable to answer. The air in the room felt heavy, and I had the distinct sensation that I was caught in a hopeless trap between these two men.

Ignazio moved toward us. "For you, my queen," he said, laying a semitransparent red plate before me.

"Jacinth!" Dalí waved a hand in the air in a gesture of approval.

The jacinth plate contained four bite-size confections, each topped with a single pomegranate seed and covered in powdered gold.

"I am not a queen," I managed, though the notion did give me the strangest thrill. I brushed the seed aside and bit into one of the sweets. "Oh, heavens." I determined they were made from dates, pistachios, rosewater, and perhaps a healthy dose of magic. I took another bite. If I thought I could have died happy from the sweet wine, I was even more convinced I could from this treat. I glanced up at our host to share my appreciation, but he was looking in Dalí's direction.

"Proserpina," Dalí admonished me. "You have not eaten the pomegranate seed." He pointed at my plate, the discarded aril glinting in the candlelight.

"Why do you care?" I asked him, unamused. "And you realize my name is Julia, don't you?" I said it teasingly, hoping not to offend, but then I wished I had put more force into those words, because he seemed to miss my point.

"Yes! Julia of the Julii," he cried out, raising his hands toward the heavens.

I didn't understand what he meant, but at least he seemed to acknowledge I had an actual name, though he wouldn't let up on my eating the pomegranate aril.

"Now, Proserpina, you must eat the seed," he begged me. "How else will you return to your Pluto?"

"I don't have a Pluto," I said, exasperated.

Ignazio cleared his throat. "While you may not believe in Pluto, you're missing out on the true delight of this confection, Julia. The chef prides himself on creating the best possible combinations of flavor, and without the pomegranate seed, you will not understand the true measure of his genius." He nodded at the remaining candies on my plate. "Please, try it as the chef intended."

At least he had the courtesy of getting my name right, I thought as I considered the dessert before me.

"Don't eat it if you don't want to," Jack said in an exaggerated whisper. "But you know you want to."

Don't... Another whisper echoed in my ear, the same whisper I had heard in the garden and the library.

All eyes were upon me. I *wanted* to eat the sweets—the first had been delicious—but not under such duress and not with the seed on top.

"I can't possibly eat them all," I finally said. I offered a compromise to our host. "I will have one if you will help me eat one."

Ignazio eyed me hesitantly.

"I will help you, Proserpina." Dalí reached for the candy.

"Perfect. I'll have one, you have one, and Ignazio can have the other." I looked back at our handsome host, daring him to defy this wish of mine.

"I have already eaten my fill tonight," Ignazio said with a slight shake of his head.

"Very well." I lifted the plate to pass the confections to Dalí.

"Fine, fine." Ignazio stopped me with a note of concern. "I'll eat one."

I smugly took one of the sweets, and after Dalí had taken up his morsel, I tipped the plate toward Ignazio. He gingerly accepted the remaining candy.

"Together," I said, lifting the morsel to my mouth.

A brief emotion akin to fear flashed in Ignazio's eyes, but then it was gone, and I wondered if I had been mistaken. In unison we ate the candy. When he closed his eyes to savor it, I shut mine.

As the sweetness melted on my tongue, an intense, warm darkness enveloped me. I found myself in a shadowy, labyrinthine garden where the scent of roses and night-blooming jasmine was intoxicating. I sensed rather than saw a presence, a formidable figure lurking just beyond my vision. Though the feeling of love and passion overwhelmed me, there was also an unsettling undercurrent, like the rumble of distant thunder. Whispers seemed to dance around me, seductive yet laced with something I couldn't quite place—danger, perhaps, or even betrayal. A voice called out, deep and resonant, uttering words I couldn't understand but felt I should. Just as I was about to turn, to glimpse who—or what—was behind me, the vision shattered.

A massive crash against one of the windows caused Gala to

scream. When I opened my eyes, Dalí had jumped to his feet and was staring wildly in its direction. Paolo and Jack ran to the window, yanking open the velvet drapes, but Ignazio didn't move or even open his eyes. He stood as if locked in a spell.

"Well, will you look at that," Jack said, pointing to the detailed dust marks of five birds that must have slammed up against the panes.

"My lord," Gala exclaimed, her hand upon her chest as if to protect it.

"They must have hit at the exact same time," Paolo observed.

Jack shook his head. "How could they do that?"

There was a brief silence as we stared at the impressions on the window. Ignazio stood next to me, his fists clenched, his normally calm demeanor replaced by a visible tension in his body and an angry fire in his eyes. "Poor doves," he said finally.

I wondered why he assumed they were doves.

"Should we go see if they are all right?" I asked, horrified.

"This side of the *castello* is on the edge of a cliff, remember?" Gala said.

"When a bird hits the window, it means death is nigh." Dalí waved his walking stick around wildly. "Someone is going to die," he squealed.

"That's just a superstition," I said, but as the words passed my lips I wondered if I believed it.

"But there are five bird marks," Jack pointed out. "Does that mean five deaths?" He was being facetious, but it was a chilling thought, and no one responded.

After a long moment, Ignazio stepped forward and closed the curtains. When he turned around, all concern had disappeared from his face, and he was smiling. "We must not let a freak accident mar our evening." He briefly touched Gala on the shoulder and led her away from the window.

"The musicians," I observed, suddenly noting that they'd never stopped playing. "The disturbance should have broken their song, but it's like they didn't even notice it."

Jack looked back at the quartet, who were not far from the window. "That is weird," he agreed, but he didn't offer a guess as to why they didn't react to the crash. Instead, he put his hand on my back. "Maybe we can dance later…" he said in a low voice.

I didn't picture the group of us doing much dancing, and besides, Gala had warned him to steer clear of me, but his touch gave me comfort.

Ignazio led us to a smaller salon decorated with accents of red and gold, but the mood had shifted, so much so that Paolo announced he was retiring for the evening.

I sat on one of the love seats, and to my surprise, Gala joined me—I assumed to keep Jack and me apart. It worked. Jack deposited himself across from us in a chair next to Dalí. Ignazio brought us goblets made from pink glass and poured us a much more significant portion of the golden drink than he had given us earlier. Then he said good-night, and the music in the other room stopped, replaced by only the crackling fire in the fireplace.

"Please, stay," Gala implored him. "Have a drink with us."

"I cannot. But thank you, Signora Dalí, for the offer."

"What if we want more wine?" Dalí asked.

Ignazio raised an eyebrow. "You won't."

Then he was gone, and I could have sworn the room temperature dropped a degree or two.

I didn't feel up to drinking much, but it was hard not to indulge in the wine, which I was beginning to believe may have actually come from the gods. It made us jovial, giddy even. And as the conversation jumped from art and surrealism to Jack growing up on his grandparents' farm on a ridge overlooking the Snake River in a forlorn place called Burley, Idaho, I found myself thinking that perhaps the peculiarity of the day wasn't all that peculiar, that it was just me, because this moment with these people felt good, and I was happy.

Eventually, though, I set my wine aside. I didn't want to destroy my good feelings by taking them a step too far.

Gala motioned at my glass. "I'll have that if you don't want it."

"By all means," I said, picking it up and pouring my wine into hers.

"This wine is outstanding, isn't it?" She leaned over to me, giggling.

I giggled with her. "It's the best I've ever had."

Her smile dissipated. "But something is wrong," she said, slurring her words slightly. "With the wine. With this place. With all of it." She waved her arm wide.

"I know what you mean," I said, feeling my world tilt back to the stranger side of the day.

She put her hand on my cheek, an intimate caress. "No, you don't. Because something is wrong with you too."

"What do you mean...?" I began to ask, but she leaned in and stopped my words with a kiss. Although I was a bit shocked, I was tipsy and feeling a new affection for Gala, who had been somewhat mean and cold to me until now. I let myself get lost in the sensation for a moment, but she pulled away abruptly.

"Eww," she said, wiping her mouth with the back of her hand as I sat there, horrified and embarrassed. "Now I remember why I don't like women." She stood and deposited herself into Jack's lap.

"Now, now, Gala, I'm sure Julia is a perfectly fine kisser," he said to her as she slid a hand into his hair. But he only had eyes for me. "You just don't have enough practice with the fairer sex. Let me try—I would like to find out the truth of the matter."

"I would observe this and declare judgment," Dalí said, his mustache twitching.

But I wasn't about to have my sexual prowess tested in such a way. "That won't be necessary," I said, getting up. "I'll leave you to your games."

Dalí and Jack protested, but Gala only muttered something in Russian that I thought was probably akin to *good riddance*.

I stumbled back toward my room, the effects of the wine hitting me even harder after I stood. The *castello* was creepy at night, silent, the fixtures in the hallways far enough apart that there were little dark spots between the splashes of light. If I hadn't drunk the wine, I probably would have been terrified. I wasn't *drunk*, not like I had been at some of the art school parties I had attended with Lillian. But everything around me was slightly fuzzy, and as I neared the library, I decided it would be a good idea to retrieve Giulia's diary and take it back to my room with me. The curtains were open and there was just enough moonlight for me to see the switch on the wall. I pressed it and went to the shelf, and although there was likely no one in the castle that might have taken it, I was still relieved to see it there. I had just shut off the light and was turning the corner when I ran smack into Demetra.

"Oh!" I exclaimed, angling my body so she couldn't see me slide the journal into the deep pocket of my wide-legged trousers. For some reason, I didn't want her to know I had borrowed it.

"It's rather late to be in the library, signorina," she said, her voice devoid of emotion.

"I thought to borrow a book to read in bed, but they're all in Italian." I wasn't about to tell her I could read a little of the language.

She pushed past me and shut the door to the library, staring at it intently for a moment. Then, without another word, she headed down the hallway.

Back in my room, I locked the door behind me. I considered looking out the window to see if the mysterious green glow was there again but decided I would rather not know. Instead, I pulled on my pajamas and settled into bed with the journal. If only I had an Italian dictionary with me. So many of the words were unfamiliar, though I understood enough to glean that Giulia's stories sounded an awful lot like they were about the monsters in the garden. I reread the pages a few times and determined that she was perhaps dreaming them, not describing the statues in the *boschetto*. One phrase in particular jumped out at me: *Abbiamo preso il passaggio segreto per il boschetto. We took the secret passage into the little wood.*

Secret passage? Many castles of the time period had subterranean passages to enable the nobles to escape if the keep was besieged.

A knock on the door startled me. I sat up in bed, my heart pounding.

"Julia?"

At Jack's voice, I breathed a sigh of relief, slid the journal into my nightstand drawer and opened the door to find him leaning inward on the frame, one arm above his head. He had a sweet drunken smile on his face. "Julia."

"What are you doing here, Jack?" I asked. "Where are Gala and Dalí?"

He waved a hand down the hallway toward their room. "I had them go ahead."

"But they're expecting you," I said. It wasn't a question so much as a request for confirmation.

"Gala is always expecting me. But I don't always give in to her." He looked down at me with a wide smile.

"I see," I said, backing up a step as I realized that he was at least a foot taller and could easily see down my top, which was rather revealing. He took that as an invitation to come in, but I put a hand on his chest to stop him.

"I can't stop thinking of you kissing Gala," he said. "There is nothing wrong with you. She's a fool."

"Humph. I think I might be the fool," I said, the humiliation of that moment coming back to sting me. Worse, I knew she was right, not about me being a bad kisser, but about there being something wrong with me. The blackness of my past covered me like a cloak.

Jack cupped my cheek with his hand. "Would I be a fool if...?" He leaned down to kiss me, and I decided to let him.

His kiss was different than Gala's—harder, more purposeful, but still tender. He wrapped his arm around me, pulling me close, then laced one of his big hands in my hair, heightening the moment's intensity.

When the kiss broke, he looked at me with a goofy grin. "Not the fool," he said.

I knew he was hoping to step farther into the room, shut the door, and take me to bed. And a large part of me wanted that too. Gods knew I didn't like sleeping alone in that room. But I had just met Jack, and I needed more time to assess his worthiness for my bed.

"Not the fool," I agreed. "But not tonight," I said, keeping my hand firm on his chest.

"One more?" he asked. "For the road?"

I had to laugh. "Just one."

It was a long, lingering kiss. I almost gave in. Perhaps next time I would.

7

I woke before Demetra could rouse me. It was another fitful night, my mind full of Jack's kiss and the weird events of the previous day. I opened the curtains to a gorgeous dawn. The garden below was blissfully silent.

After dressing and hiding the journal in the bottom drawer, deep underneath my clothes, I slipped into the hallway. Not hearing anyone bustling about, I forged ahead, making my way down to what I thought might be the servants' stairwell at the end of the corridor and descending the narrow staircase.

I was intensely curious about the secret passage to the *boschetto* that Giulia had mentioned in her journal. If I followed it, it may lead me toward something that could explain more about Giulia, but also more about me.

It seemed logical that a passage must originate in the cellars. Ignazio had mentioned that the floor below the *terzo piano*, the ground floor, was for service, so I passed it and kept going. When I reached the bottom of the stairs, I opened the door into blackness. A pervasive dank smell emanated from the dark. I felt around the edge of the door for a switch, but there wasn't any. There wasn't a single sliver of light to lead my way. I'd have to return when I could find a lantern or flashlight. Maybe I'd even bring Jack with me. Perhaps with all the weird things I'd already experienced since arriving in Bomarzo, I shouldn't take any chances. His brawn would protect me. And if he had to hold me tight, I wouldn't complain.

I went back up the stairs to the service floor, intending to ask someone for a flashlight, although I didn't know what excuse I might have for wanting one. Following the scent of something cooking, I entered the kitchen and was stunned to see that Ignazio was already looking toward the door, as though he were waiting for my arrival. Had I made any noise on my approach? The cook and his assistant turned in my direction, but they remained expressionless, as though they were looking through me instead of at me. It was the same blankness that Demetra and the servants at the dinners exhibited.

It wasn't the bustling kitchen I would have expected from a large palazzo. Instead, it was very old and, to my surprise, harbored no modern appliances. There were several tables, a heavy sink on one side, and a fire that roared in the grate, complete with a spit and platforms where pots could be set to cook the food. How had they managed to create such wondrous meals with such simple implements?

Ignazio crossed the room when he saw me, his enigmatic smile lighting up his face. "Julia! Are you ready for breakfast? Is there anything amiss?"

I hadn't thought I would find him there so early, nor was I prepared for the rush of butterflies that lit in my stomach when I saw him. Jack had fired up those same feelings the night before, with our kiss, but it was a small spark compared to the fire I felt when I looked at Ignazio.

"I..." My words failed me.

"Anything you need, Julia, just say."

"I woke early and decided to explore, that's all." Perhaps it wouldn't hurt to just ask about the lower level. "I found my way to the cellar, but I couldn't find the light switch."

"There isn't one. Would you like me to show you the lower levels? I'd be happy to give you a tour."

I hesitated. But our host was already in motion. He crossed the kitchen, pulled two lanterns down off a shelf and lit them. Then, as he led me down the hallway toward the stairs, he launched into a story about how the current owners, the Borghese family, had looked into wiring the lower levels but decided the expense wasn't worth it.

As we descended into the pitch-black cellar, I couldn't help but wonder why I hadn't said no. While I was curious about finding the passage, I wasn't sure I was so curious I wanted to scramble around in the dark looking for it. And yet, despite my trepidation about following Ignazio into the dark, I was enthralled by the sound of his voice, by his very nearness. Perhaps Ignazio and I were two lodestones tumbling against one another. We attracted, repelled, attracted, repelled. Lillian was always teasing me about my predilection to be attracted to men who were the most dangerous for me. Surely with Ignazio that was true. There was no safety here, just a heady deluge of desire—and a sense that he could flip my world in a direction I might not want it to go.

Then we were descending the stairs and my moment to say *no, I don't want to go down there with you* was slipping further and further away, until it was gone and we were walking through the darkness, our lanterns cutting into the black. I reasoned with myself that I wanted to see the space, to discover if there was, in fact, a hidden passageway of some sort that led down to the garden.

"This room used to be the kitchen," Ignazio said when we reached the bottom of the stairs, which led into a massive space large enough that the lantern light couldn't reach the walls.

"When they wired the *castello* for electricity, they moved the kitchen upstairs."

I couldn't see enough of the room to know if there was a fireplace or any of the furnishings you might find in a kitchen, though looking at the *peperino* stone floor, I could tell the basement had been carved from the rock upon which the *castello* was built. Ignazio strode from room to room with purpose, and with every step, I knew there was no way I could have come down there by myself. The never-ending darkness beyond our lamplight, the cobwebs, the sounds of mice or, more likely, rats skittering in the shadows—all that was only part of it. What shook me most was that I could sense a human presence surrounding us, centuries of history layered upon itself thick enough that it felt engraved upon the very air we walked through.

The darkness compelled me to keep close to Ignazio, closer than I wanted. But he knew this place and I did not. While I knew it ridiculous, I had a pervasive feeling that something might jump out, snatch me away, and drag me off...though perhaps I was already being dragged off by Ignazio himself.

A profound sense of relief flooded through me when we reached the opposite side of the room and entered a hallway. Seeing the two walls on either side of me was a great comfort.

"Where are the dungeons?" I asked. He had mentioned them when he first showed us around the palazzo.

"They aren't terribly impressive," he admitted as he opened a door to reveal a massive pantry lined with jars of food. "We use many of the cells for cold storage now."

"Are there any secret passages in the palazzo?" I was kicking myself for not asking him that before traipsing around in the darkness with him. I realized, with growing horror, that my companions had no idea where I was. Would the cook tell them if I disappeared? I had the strong sense that he wouldn't.

"Every old castle has secret passages, Julia," Ignazio said. "Some are merely for the servants to move about, unseen. But the old barons had many enemies. One never knew when there might be a need to escape from infiltrators. Or perhaps just get away from other family members."

"Where are they?"

"If I told you, they wouldn't be a secret anymore, now, would they?" He looked at me, his eyes glinting like sparks in the lantern light. "But, worry not, none go to your bedroom."

This did not bring me comfort. I also hated that he knew I was wondering just that.

"At the other end of the basement is a stairwell down to the road leading out of the city. Even our medieval counterparts found a reason to have an extra egress. That's the closest this floor has to a secret passage, though I'm afraid there's nothing mysterious about it."

I stayed close to Ignazio. He was quite animated and gave me a detailed history of the castle as we walked. Thankfully, his voice kept me distracted from the rodents I could hear scratching somewhere in the empty blackness.

We passed more storage spaces full of old furniture, building materials, and assorted boxes. A couple of the rooms were filled top to bottom with wine racks, some of which held bottles Ignazio told me went back over a hundred years. I would hate to be the servant sent down to the darkness to retrieve one of them.

Finally, we came to the end of the hallway. Ignazio waved a hand toward what he said was the door to a small area where there were still two or three dungeon cells and the aforementioned staircase, but then he doubled back, leading me to the massive room he had said was the kitchen. But instead of going up the steps, he went to the right a few paces, then homed in on a doorless entrance to a room about eight feet wide and perhaps twice as long. He held the lantern up so I could look in. On the far side, a small arched hole had been carved into the wall. A little metal grate had been bolted over the bottom half, perhaps to prevent one from falling in. In the center of the room there was a rounded impression in the stone as though some sort of mechanism may have been there centuries ago and was now long gone. The odor of moss and mold was unpleasant.

Julia...

The whisper, which seemed to emanate from the hole itself, made me jump. The hair on my arms and neck stood on end, though Ignazio didn't seem to register the whisper or my discomfort. He stepped into the room and thrust his lantern closer to the space in the wall.

"The well," he said.

"That's a well?" It looked utterly unlike any well I had ever seen.

"It is. It was the first thing they dug before building the castle. That they were able to bore deep into the rock is a feat in itself."

"How old is it?"

"Nearly a thousand years old."

I tried to imagine a medieval peasant woman hauling water up through that hole. That impression in the floor probably once held a winch. As I turned to ask Ignazio, a loud hiss sounded and a huge snake slithered across my foot.

I screamed and dropped my lantern, the oil spilling out and catching fire. It flamed up and suddenly Ignazio's arms were around me, pulling me back. Heat warmed my body. We were trapped in a corner near the well, the fire licking up the oil in the doorway.

"It will burn itself out," Ignazio reassured me. "It's a good thing it's all rock down here."

The smoke was thick and dark, and I began to choke. Ignazio held me close, smoothing my hair and whispering words I couldn't hear over my coughing. The heat from his body was nearly more than I could bear, but the fire just feet away was even hotter. I shook against him, burying my face into his chest, the smoke coating and searing my lungs. It wasn't long before it felt like a fire had been lit inside my chest and there was less and less air to breathe.

I looked back at the fire, hoping it would burn itself out soon. To my utter horror, a woman stood in the center of the blaze. She wore a blue dress fit for a baroque ballroom, her long blond hair piled high upon her head, and she held three fingers toward us. There was a frantic look in her eyes. Despite my growing inability to breathe, I let loose an expletive, realizing that this woman looked exactly like me. The world around me started to gray, like a movie fading out when the end came, and Ignazio's mouth was against mine, his lips sealed to my lips, his heat flooding into me.

Smoke. Cinnamon. Then nothing.

I woke in my room, the pillows amassed like a soft fortress around my head and shoulders, a lamp on the nightstand emitting dim light. Somehow, I was wearing my pajamas, not the dress from that morning.

How oddly hale I felt... I took a deep breath to be sure, but the smoke seemed to have had no consequence to my lungs. I didn't need to cough and wasn't burnt. But for the smell of smoke and oil in my hair, I would have thought it all a hallucination.

Rising, I went to the window and pulled open the heavy curtain to find it was dark. The entire day must have passed me by. And that cursed glow, verdant and eerie, was back in the garden. I kept the curtain open, trying to understand where it was coming from as it grew greener and brighter—angrier, it seemed to me—until it illuminated the garden. Then, with no warning, it winked out.

A knock at the door made me jump. I hoped it might be Jack. I needed a comforting face. But there stood Demetra, a tray of tea in her hands.

"If you are rested enough, the others are gathering for dinner soon," she said as she swept past me and deposited the silver tray on the table near the window.

"Do you know who took care of me?" I asked, thinking it must have been Ignazio. "Did you put me in my pajamas?" I didn't think I had been taken advantage of, but then again, the memory of his lips upon mine was still strong.

"It should have been me," she said, turning to me, her eyes full of anger.

"Who was it?" I asked, alarmed at the intensity in her voice.

She turned on a heel and left, not bothering to shut the door behind her.

I poked my head into the hallway to call her back, except she wasn't there. I shut the door in a rush, my heart hammering inside my rib cage. She couldn't have disappeared so quickly. What was happening to me? Sitting on the edge of the bed, my mind raced. I had expected Dalí to be the most surreal thing about this trip, but he was practically normal compared to the garden, the empty-eyed servants, the fantastical meals I had eaten, the fire, and the terrifying magnetism of Ignazio.

"Julia?" Gala's voice sounded at the other side of the door.

I never thought I would feel relieved to see Gala, with her snarky words and prickly countenance. She was no friend, but when I let her enter, I was infused with a wash of comfort that she was there, real, standing before me.

"You look a lot better than you did this morning," she noted, looking me up and down.

"You saw me this morning?"

"I did." She went to the window and shut the curtains. "You are a load of dead weight when you are out cold, you know."

"Were you the one to dress me?"

"Yes, you stupid girl. And not only that but you wasted a whole day of work! When they called me to your room, you were passed out. You reeked like smoke. Ignazio said he had already had the village doctor check you out, and you just needed to sleep it off. You wasted a whole day that Salvador could have been painting you."

The brief respite her presence provided quickly gave way to tension once again. "Gala, I was incapacitated," I said, exasperated. "I didn't intend to miss the sitting." I was incensed at her attempt to lay a burden of guilt upon me.

She folded her arms and stared at me. "What happened? Ignazio would not tell me."

I told her the story but left out the part about the woman in the fire. And I certainly did not tell her about Ignazio pressing his lips to mine.

"So, you went down into the dark with him, swooned, and he saved you."

"It wasn't like that," I said.

"Why wasn't he affected by the smoke?" It wasn't so much of a question of me as it was general pondering.

"I...I don't know. He should have been," I said, thinking of how he easily held me and stroked my hair to soothe me.

The thoughtful look on Gala's face was replaced by impatience as she went to my dresser and began to rummage through the drawers.

"You won't have time to bathe, so you'll just have to go stinking like a chimney." She tossed a pair of panties and a brassiere onto the bed.

"Stop. I can manage. I'm feeling all right now." I didn't want her to find Giulia Farnese's diary in the bottom drawer. She might tell Ignazio I had removed it from the library, or worse, be interested in it herself.

In a fit of exasperation, Gala picked up a hairbrush from the dresser. "You think you can manage? Without ruining another day's work?"

"Yes, I said I can manage," I snapped back, frustration mounting.

Gala hurled the hairbrush at me. It missed me by an inch and clattered against the wall. "Get yourself together. Time is money, and you're wasting both." She scowled. "Dress warm. We'll be dining in the Sacro Bosco tonight. You need to eat so you have strength for tomorrow. I'm not letting you wreck another day."

My breath caught. I thought of the green glow I had now seen twice. Demetra said no one ever went into the sacred wood at night. Why were we?

"And don't expect to be paid for today." She sneered at me when she reached the door. "We only pay models when they work."

She slipped out, leaving me standing there, stunned. That was seventy-five thousand lire out of my pocket, the equivalent of nearly a month's salary. And while I understood that if I couldn't complete the work I wouldn't be paid, what was even more galling was her violence, her complete lack of empathy, and the insinuation I had purposely intended to skip out on my duties.

I turned back to the dresser and looked for Giulia's diary. It was still there, hidden under a pair of slacks I had brought. Had Giulia said anything about the well in her diary? I had thumbed through the pages, but I didn't even know the Italian word for *well*. Besides, Gala had made it abundantly clear that I was not to miss dinner. Fuming, I put the book away and picked up the brassiere. As I dressed, my thoughts twisted and turned. Something was happening, something beyond my understanding. But I knew one thing for sure: the secrets buried in Giulia's diary were calling to me, and I had the distinct sense that the answers lay hidden in the shadows of the sacred wood.

8

"You're all right," Jack exclaimed, taking me up in a bear hug as I made my way to the front door, where the Dalís and their entourage were milling about. I fell into him, glad for the comfort after my ordeal. "Gala told us about the fire," he said when he had pulled away.

"She's perfectly fine," Gala hissed, glaring at me as she slipped a possessive arm around Jack. "Come along, *amore*."

Jack gave me an apologetic smile and then left with Gala.

"Where's Ignazio?" I asked, though I didn't want to see him. I was bracing myself for the moment when we'd meet again. The night was unusually warm, and I probably could have done without my cape, but I wrapped it tightly around me nonetheless.

"He is already down in the wood," Dalí said. He was dressed in a gray tweed suit with a pink tie, an unusual choice that worked for the eccentric artist. "Come, Paolo, bring the equipment." He pointed toward a camera bag with the silver-tipped end of his walking cane, capped by a detailed ram's head, also made of silver, then extended his left hand to me.

Paolo picked up the bag and dutifully followed us as we walked toward a dark car waiting at the bottom of the hill.

"No truck this time," I observed.

Dalí was horrified. "No. Not for dinner."

"I'm sorry I missed the sitting today," I told him as we walked toward the driveway. I was glad Gala and Jack were out of earshot. I didn't want her derailing my apology or deriding me again for fainting.

He gave me a broad smile. "You are lovely, my Proserpina, but you are not the only thing in my painting. You are recovered, no? We will resume tomorrow. There will be sun, I predict."

The car took us the very short distance to the entrance of the Sacro Bosco, which was lit by several tall torches. The closer we got, the tighter the knots in my stomach became. I still didn't understand what had happened at the well. I felt healthy and hale, not as if I had just inhaled a ton of oily smoke from the lantern fire. But it was puzzling that a doctor had checked me out and for something as debilitating as smoke inhalation, suggested I could merely sleep it off. And why would I have slept for an entire day as though I was recovering from some drunken bender? I had so many questions, and each one made me more and more anxious at the thought of seeing Ignazio once more.

This anxiety came to a peak when our host greeted us by the entrance to the garden. He wore a black tuxedo, and his hair had been slicked back, giving him a mysterious and somewhat sinister air. I couldn't meet his eyes. To my surprise, he didn't ask me if I was well, or even mention the incident in the basement. In fact, he acted like nothing had happened. While I found this baffling, I was also grateful that I could follow along and say little as he led us into the *boschetto*.

The trail's lanterns cast a dim glow on our path, and as we moved into the garden, like before, a strange familiarity enveloped me. A sense of déjà vu; I couldn't help but feel I had walked this path in some distant, forgotten life. Ignazio kept up a lively narration as we went, giving us the details of the stories and myths each statue evoked. I had worn my chunkiest heels, but I clung to Dalí's arm for balance as we navigated the overgrown path that led us past the looming statue of the giants.

We approached a massive turtle, steadfast with the winged goddess of Victory upon its back, an embodiment of triumph frozen in time. Next to the turtle was what must have been an ancient fountain, with Pegasus standing in silent guardianship at its center. Alongside them both, hidden within a shadow-filled ravine, an open-mouthed whale jutted upward, surrounded by the murmur of a bubbling brook, its low gurgle a haunting serenade to the night.

A sharp sense of being watched prickled at my skin, a gaze unseen but palpable, as if the statues themselves held a life force within their weathered contours. The feeling intensified as we moved past the statues toward the heart of the garden.

The trail wound through what Ignazio explained was known as a nymphaeum—a sanctuary dedicated to water nymphs— a small area of the *boschetto*, full of beautiful, curved benches and alcoves with worn images of the Three Graces and nymphs carved into the wall. According to Ignazio, a vaulted ceiling once covered the area.

As I peered at the worn carvings, a faint green luminescence flickered in the hollows of their eyes—a glow that vanished as quickly as it appeared, leaving me to question whether it had been there at all. The statues seemed to watch us with a silent intensity, their gazes following our every step. The nymphaeum held a dark undertone, a sense that we were intruders in a realm where the past was not quite asleep.

Beyond the nymphaeum, the footpath led us to the remains of an amphitheater, now covered in moss.

"Paolo, you were telling me that you like poetry," Jack said loudly enough for all of us to hear. "What would you recite?"

"*Sì*, recite something." Dalí waved the cameraman to the center of the amphitheater.

Paolo's face reddened but he acquiesced. "It's a bit of Ovid, from the *Metamorphoses*. I must speak Italian for this," he said, his voice shaking a bit. But as he began to speak, he seemed to gather courage, and his voice steadied, ringing out through the sacred wood.

Ignazio translated Paolo's words for us. "'I am dragged along by a strange new force. Desire and reason are pulling in different directions. I see the right way and approve it but follow the wrong.'" He eyed me intently as he spoke, as if to suggest that I was the one following the wrong way. I turned my head, unable to breathe beneath the heat of his gaze.

"*Brilliante*," I told Paolo as he made his way down the mossy stairs.

"Some serious razzmatazz," Jack said, clapping Paolo on the back. The Italian looked puzzled.

"*Fantastico*," I translated in the best way I could.

Paolo grinned, clearly pleased that his recitation was well received.

"Come now, dinner awaits." Ignazio pointed at a structure a little farther down the trail. It was a small, two-story building that looked more like a guard tower than a house, but it was leaning into a hill at a forty-five-degree angle. A stone bridge led from the crown of the hill to the top floor. There was a little clearing below the building.

"The tower was once the first thing you would see when coming through the garden entrance," Ignazio explained. "Remember the sphinxes I told you about?" He pointed to an overgrown path that was, indeed, guarded by two stone sphinxes.

"The warning that the visitor must decide if what they are seeing is trickery or art?" Jack asked.

"Exactly. And there—" he lifted his hand toward the tower "—you will have another opportunity to decide."

On top of the flat roof, a musician sat with his legs dangling over the edge. He began playing a mournful little tune on his trumpet.

"Something to remember," Dalí whispered. "Beauty in the dark."

He rocked slowly in time with the exquisite strain. The mournful melody of the trumpet floated down from the tower, wrapping around me in a soft, invisible veil of sound. In that shared moment of silent reverence with Dalí, a small kinship formed. For the first time, I thought that I understood a little about him—he became less of an enigma, less of an anomalous intrusion upon the world. I realized that this was a Dalí few might ever see. After a long moment, Ignazio laid a hand on Dalí's shoulder. "Come, we don't want our food to chill." He motioned for us to keep walking.

"This is the Casa Pendente," Ignazio said.

The leaning house.

"There are two ways in. From above and from below."

"Like heaven and earth," Dalí said.

"Our dinner will begin below," Ignazio announced, leading us up the little set of stairs to the lower entry. There was no door and the windows had no glass or shutters but were open to the elements.

The room was barely big enough to hold us, and the slant was disorienting. I knew we were all standing up straight, but we looked like we were impossibly angled, leaning forward, toward the far window, even though the house leaned the opposite way. The Casa Pendente didn't just lean, it also twisted up our equilibriums.

"Now, this is *surreal*," Jack joked, giving Dalí a little sock in the arm.

"As it should be," Dalí said, nodding in agreement.

To my dismay, I was seated with my back to the door, facing the glassless window that was tilted toward the stars. I didn't like not knowing who—or what—might come through the open door behind me. It also didn't escape my notice that Gala was careful to place herself between Jack and me. Fortunately, the table and chair legs had been altered so that we would not be subject to the slant of the building as we ate. Even so, I felt like I might fall backward at any moment. Once we were all seated, the room's snug dimensions left no space for the servers to navigate behind our chairs, forcing them to awkwardly reach around me from either side to serve each dish.

A meow at my feet caught my attention, and I was delighted to see Orpheus there, looking up at me. I reached down to pet him and he rubbed his head against my hand for a minute, then lay down beside my chair, staring at me. It was as though his blue eyes were pleading with me, but for what, I did not know. Perhaps he was as unenthused by the tiny gray dishes we were served as I was. The mushroom soup, oysters, sardines, mackerel, and gray cheeses with weird gray crackers were a far cry from the previous colorful dinners we'd been fed at the *castello*.

Paolo, who sat to my right, looked as uncomfortable as I felt, and neither of us ate much, which prompted Gala to admonish us for wasting food.

"I don't like sardines," I told her. She gave me a look of icy disapproval.

"Anch'io non mi piace," Paolo agreed, turning up his nose.

As if on cue, a servant appeared and whisked away our plates, replacing them with flat gray rocks smeared with an unappetizing gray paste dotted with little black seeds. Gala asked one of the servants what it was, but he only gave her a glassy look and departed without a word. Jack, having encountered the unusual dragon fruit on a prewar trip to Mexico, informed us of its identity. Contrasting its unremarkable gray insides, the fruit's skin was a vibrant yellow. I didn't even know cacti bore fruit at all, much less something so delicious.

"This is some spectacle," I observed. But, then again, everything in Bomarzo had been a spectacle. Even Ignazio and my companions were spectacular, like something out of a movie, except with brilliant color. I stared out at the sky beyond Dalí's head, the W shape of Cassiopeia's stars blinking in the darkness.

"All is as it should be!" Dalí responded, launching into a dramatic soliloquy, his hands waving wildly. "This is what other surrealists do not understand. We are on the edge of real and unreal. On the edge of life and death. Of black and white. Of the world and the Underworld! We are in a place where few will ever be. This! This is where the heart is. This is the point where the knife is touching the skin. The second before blood meets air!"

"Did you plan all of this?" I asked in disbelief.

Dalí looked at me as though I were daft. "Of course, my little Proserpina, of course."

Gala shook her head at me, contradicting her husband's words.

Ignazio's voice rang out from somewhere above us. "It is time to leave the emptiness of the Asphodel Meadows and join me in the Fields of Mourning."

"What meadow?" Jack asked. But I reeled with the names of these places, a chill coursing through me as some distant memory stirred, obscured by fog and shadows. An inexplicable sense of dread weighed down on me, as if I were on the precipice of recalling something awful, something that lurked just beyond the reach of understanding, hidden in the dark corners of my mind.

"Asphodel!" Dalí cried, addressing the room. "Now I understand. That's where we are. In the gray place in the Underworld where all the ordinary souls go. But not you, nor I!"

"Sounds like Limbo," Paolo remarked.

"No! Asphodel Meadows!" Dalí reprimanded him. But then he winked. "Sì, Limbo."

Two servants at the door indicated we were to rise from the table and follow them. But before I could do so, Orpheus jumped into my lap, lifted himself up to rub his face against my chin, then settled in as though he planned to take a long nap. His purring was loud and sonorous.

"Would you look at that," Jack said. I petted the little white beast, which, strangely, had the soft feel of an indoor cat, not one that lived outdoors in the elements. He pushed his face against mine again, and I sighed. Holding him gave me a sense of calm that I desperately needed. He was familiar, comfortable, almost like he had been a friend for much of my life. Somewhere in the dark void of my past I must have loved cats, even if I didn't recall ever having one.

"Orpheus should sing his song elsewhere," Gala said, waving an impatient hand at the cat. *"Amscray!"*

I looked at her, trying to puzzle out the word.

"I've been teaching her pig latin." Jack laughed.

I didn't want to upend Orpheus, but my companions were standing and waiting for me to move so they could join Ignazio upstairs. "Come on, Orpheus, let's go upstairs." I made to pick him up, but he squirmed, then pressed himself up against me in adoration.

"Orpheus worships you, O Queen of the Night," Dalí said. He looked serious.

"I wish he would worship me just a little less." I tried to pick him up once more, but he burrowed in. "He doesn't want me to leave."

Paolo reached over and deftly plucked the cat from my lap, and the beast gave a little cry of protest as the cameraman set him on the ground. Then he put his little body in front of me as if to impede me from making my way to the door.

"Amscray!" Dalí said to the cat, pushing his walking stick toward the feline. Orpheus dodged the stick, hiding behind my legs.

Paolo reached down and picked up the cat once more, holding it until I could exit the building. Once outside in the night air, Orpheus calmed down a bit, but he was still clingy, staying by my side as we followed the wordless servants up the path to the top entrance of the Casa Pendente, which sat at the end of a vast grassy area lined with monstrous vases on pedestals. Ignazio greeted us at the door, his hands folded in front of him. He had changed into a wild suit of red with black accents. I would not have been surprised if there had been a devil's tail when he turned around.

"Did you enjoy your meal in the Meadow?" he asked me with that damned, disarming smile.

"It was, um...unusual," I said.

"Next time, there should be more oysters," Gala griped.

"There are two courses to go, Signora Dalí." He may have been reassuring her, but he extended a hand to me. I ignored it and walked past him.

The tilt of the floor made me slightly dizzy, but I made my way to the open window, my eyes fixed upon the heavens beyond. The air was cool against the back of my neck, and I pulled my cape tighter about me. When I reached the window, I turned, and my world swayed as I watched Dalí and Gala walk around the small room, their bodies slanted.

"This defies all logic," Jack said, laughing.

"Imagine all of life on this tilt!" Dalí took hold of his wife and spun her around, nearly toppling them both. Paolo had entered the room last, and he helped stabilize the couple as five servants swept past us into an adjacent, equally small room where a high, narrow table ran the length of the longer wall, a candelabra in the center. They placed each dish, all red, on the table, then departed. We appeared to be expected to eat standing up—there wasn't enough room for chairs.

A servant deposited a salad of red before me, a plate full of radicchio, amaranth, currants, and strawberries.

"What did Ignazio say the name of this room is?" Jack asked.

"The Fields of Mourning," Gala said as she lifted the ruby-colored, spinachlike greens to her lips.

"The place where love has died! Where Dido resides!" Dalí

exclaimed, his voice ringing through the small structure. My heart clenched.

"Maestro Dalí is correct," Ignazio chimed in from the doorway, the flames lighting up his features. "The Fields of Mourning is where unrequited lovers are doomed to eternity. If you've read the *Aeneid*, you might recall that Queen Dido entered the Fields after she killed herself because her love for Aeneas was unrequited. It is a mournful locale, full of longing, desperation, loneliness, bleeding hearts." He looked at me as though he thought it was something I knew. And he was right—I knew the story of Dido, and while I had all too much familiarity with longing and desperation, there was something else in his look, an expectation that I knew more than just what the legends suggested.

"Why are the lovers doomed there for eternity?" Jack asked, unnerved.

"It is as the gods have willed it." Now it was Ignazio who looked mournful. "And no god may undo what another god has done."

"He quips Ovid again," Dalí chuckled, waving a fork toward Ignazio and, as if on cue, Ignazio faded back into the darkness. I wasn't sure what was more bizarre—Ignazio looking so stricken or Dalí seemingly having committed the *Metamorphoses* to memory.

I concentrated on my plate, thinking about the dead queen lost to the Fields of Mourning, and said little for the rest of that course, letting Jack hijack the conversation to explain American sports to Dalí. Instead, I focused on the wild array of red dishes that continued to appear on the table: tomato-and-red-pepper tarts, steak tartare, beet pasta with goat cheese and pistachios, little dishes of roasted red potatoes, blood orange pies, red cakes, and tiny bowls of grapes and cherries.

"We're moving toward the Underworld," Dalí announced as the servants escorted us from the dinner table to our next location.

As I moved to walk through the door into the slightly larger main room, I felt two tiny paws upon my leg. Orpheus again. He rubbed against me, purring loudly.

"That beast won't leave you alone," Gala growled.

"I feel like he's trying to tell me something," I admitted.

"It really is as though he's trying to stop you from going," Paolo said.

Somehow, I knew Paolo was right, but I couldn't avoid going along with the rest of the group. I moved around the cat and made my way to the door. But Orpheus raced out in front of me and stood in the threshold, his little cat voice lifting in the most mournful way.

"How strange," Jack said. He'd already crossed through the door and was watching the cat from the other side. "Perhaps he believes you truly are Proserpina?"

"I can't stay here forever, Orpheus," I said, leaning down to scoop him up. He continued to cry in my ear as we exited the Casa Pendente, and we weren't more than a few paces down the torch-lit footpath when he grew stiff in my arms. He dug his claws into my cloak and the hairs on his back began to bristle beneath my fingers.

"What is wrong with you?" Gala griped when I suddenly halted, causing her to run into me. She swiped at my shoulder with the back of her hand, a nudge to keep me moving.

I didn't bother answering as I pulled Orpheus from my shoulder and set him on the ground. He stood in front of me, hissing at something in the darkness.

"What is wrong with *him*?" Jack asked.

"Maybe there is a wild beast of some sort out there," Gala said, her voice lower, with a touch of nervousness that I hadn't heard before.

"Do not worry, Signora Dalí," Paolo said. "There are only boars and bears around here, and they wouldn't come so close with our voices and all the torches."

Jack walked a few paces in the direction of Orpheus's ire, past the torchlight. "There's a statue here, a big one, of a woman with a planter of flowers on her head," he called back. "Look, the *orco* is just up there." He pointed in the direction away from the woman, then looked back up at the reclining statue. "This is the statue Julia and I were looking at when we felt the earthquake the other day."

"Ceres," I said, an unexplained warmth spreading through me and the hairs on the back of my neck standing on end. I hadn't realized the monstrous goddess was so close. Was that what Orpheus was trying to warn me about?

"The mother!" Dalí's voice was loud in the dark silence.

I looked toward the statue, suddenly dizzy.

"No," I said.

"But she is. Ceres is Proserpina's mother. It is for her the earth weeps every winter as she seeks divine retribution for Pluto stealing her daughter."

"Ceres isn't her mother," I said, the memories slipping away like sand through my fingers but leaving a conviction behind.

"But she is," Gala broke in, parroting her husband. "Don't you know the myth of Demeter and Persephone—Ceres and Proserpina? It's the story of a mother protecting her daughter."

"Yes, I know what is written, but the myth is wrong," I said, adamant, my voice filled with an emotion I couldn't quite place. "That's not what happened. I'm telling you, Ceres is not her mother."

Dalí raised an eyebrow at me.

"You disagree with centuries of this known myth? And with the great Dalí?" Gala's glare was sharp, and I remembered how she was wont to slap people, and how quickly she had snatched away a chunk of the sum that had been promised me. I shook my head and turned away, even though I knew in my heart Dalí was wrong. That the mythology was false.

"*Andiamo,*" I said to Paolo, who was standing next to me. He

nodded and walked with me in pursuit of Orpheus, who had
trotted off down the trail.

"Who is Ceres, if not the mother of Proserpina?" he asked
me once we were out of earshot.

I answered instinctively, this truth welling up from someplace
hidden inside me. "Ceres and Proserpina were lovers."

Paolo chuckled. "Now, that, *amica mia*, was not what I expected you to say."

I could tell from his voice that he didn't believe me. I hadn't
expected him to. Many centuries of mythology stood against
me, and I had no proof beyond a deep internal certainty, nothing
that would ever give anyone pause to rethink the ancient stories.

The *orco* was a short distance away, its eyes and mouth lit
by fire. Servants came and went from its mouth, dark shadows
against the wild brightness. We started to head in that direction,
but Dalí redirected us.

"Come, I want to see where this trail leads!"

I groaned but dutifully followed him to a dark clearing, where
we found a massive rock embedded in the ground. A rectangle
carved out of the rock's center looked awfully like a hole for a
grave. The light from the torches on the path made the scene
look even more sinister, but Dalí stepped up and lay down in it,
unfazed. Paolo snapped photo after photo, his flash blindingly
bright.

"Now you." Dalí waved his walking stick at me.

I hesitated, but Jack gave me a little push at the small of my
back. I stepped forward a pace.

Julia... I stopped in my tracks. *Julia...do not. Julia...* I thought
of the woman I saw in the flames that morning, the woman who
wore my face, and suddenly felt short of breath yet again.

"No, no," I managed, my voice sounding more strangled than
I would have liked. "I don't want to dirty my dress."

Dalí couldn't disagree; he was brushing dirt and leaves off the
back of his suit. Besides, the servant leading us along the path,

devoid of any emotion or spoken word, simply extended a rigid, unyielding arm toward the path ahead, a clear, mechanical indication that we mustn't dally. Not wanting to argue with Dalí about lying in that creepy tomb, I immediately turned and followed our guide.

"We will return here to paint," Dalí said behind me.

I cursed under my breath but didn't pause. I was ready to be out of the dark woods.

9

We came upon the massive vase I had seen with Jack that first day, the one that signified Bacchus's entry into hell, and there was Orpheus again, rubbing up against its base. He looked at me and cocked his head.

Julia…

My heart sped up and I hurried past the vase, frustrated by the voice. I didn't understand what it wanted from me. Orpheus howled as I passed him, a horrible, sad, haunting noise. I picked him up and he calmed.

"Orpheus clearly doesn't want you to return to the Underworld," Dalí said, as he pointed with his walking stick at the stairs to the *orco* ahead. We had, it seemed, walked in a little circle.

The glow emanating from the Mouth of Hell was bright but sinister, highlighting the *orco*'s teeth. A red cloth covered the stone table, and from my vantage point, it truly did look like a tongue. The torches on the path highlighted the statues of Hannibal and his elephant and the dragon fighting off the lions beyond.

As I glanced between the statues, and back toward Ceres, I

could swear that the figures *shifted*. There is no better word for it—the movements were so subtle, and caught out of the corner of my eye. If I stared at them straight on, the movement seemed to be just a figment of my imagination, yet the pomegranate bushes near them stirred in a way that the foliage beyond did not. It was a scene from a nightmare, one that made me agree with Orpheus—I didn't want to return to the *orco* either. My previous experience in the Mouth of Hell wasn't a pleasant one, and its visage at night was rather terrifying.

Jack moved to my side. "Don't worry, baby doll. I'll be there to catch you if you faint again," he said in a voice too low for Gala to hear.

I smiled at him, glad for his attention and his reassurance. He held out an arm, and I took it. Gala immediately came and took his other arm. Her possessiveness was annoying, particularly in the presence of her husband, though he did not seem perturbed. No, he forged ahead to the *orco*, paused briefly to look inside, then turned to cut a compelling silhouette in the darkness as Paolo took photo after photo. To my surprise, Gala left Jack's side to go to Dalí.

"She loves the limelight as much as he does," Jack explained. He shifted so that his body was against mine. "Your nearness is beyond distracting," he whispered. "Let me come to you tonight. I'll keep the monsters away."

I looked up at him. My word, he was dreamy. To have him in my bed would not be a hardship. And I was sure there were monsters in the *castello*. The idea of having this huge man to keep me safe in the dark was suddenly very appealing. Throwing caution to the wind, I said, "I'll leave the door unlocked."

Not a moment later, the touch of a hot hand on my shoulder made me jump. A strangled noise escaped my throat as I realized it was Ignazio. I unhooked my arm from Jack's. Had Ignazio heard that I was going to leave my door unlocked? For a fleeting moment, memories of his perplexing kiss in the heat of the cellar fire had me imagining him being the one to climb into my bed and bring me immense pleasure.

I quickly banished that thought from my mind—he was dangerous. He was like a panther, waiting in the dark to strike. I was reminded of a movie I once saw, *The Lodger*, in which a woman rents out one of her rooms to a handsome man, and later he turns out to be Jack the Ripper.

"Are you ready for the next course?" Ignazio asked us.

I opened my mouth to respond, but my words died when I caught sight of two glowing green orbs in the darkness behind him, where the statue of Ceres rested.

"Why do you look like you've seen a ghost again?" Jack asked. His eyes followed the line of my sight, but the green glow winked out abruptly. Jack said nothing, so I suspected he hadn't seen it.

"Tomorrow may I use the telephone?" I asked Ignazio in a rush. I had to talk to Lillian. No longer certain of my sanity, I needed her voice of reason in my ear.

Ignazio raised an eyebrow. "I suppose that can be arranged. But there isn't one at the palazzo. There are very few telephones in Bomarzo—the war destroyed most of the lines and equipment, and they have been slow to replace them. But there is an old widow in town who I believe has one. I'll see if she will allow you to use it."

I let out a long sigh. "Thank you. I'd appreciate that."

"Come, the last course is waiting for you." He put his hand on my lower back and heat radiated through me, sending an electric rush of desire to my nether region. It seemed a possessive gesture, given my proximity to Jack in that moment, a subtle signal—to me or to Jack, I wasn't sure.

Gala, however, had no intention of letting me be the center of such attention. She stepped down from the *orco* and, unable to choose between Ignazio and Jack, took me by the arm and pulled me away from both men. I knew it wasn't an act of kindness, but I felt such great relief for her rescue. To be caught between two men who expressed desire for me may sound thrilling, but truly, it wasn't. It left me disconcerted and confused, two things I wasn't keen on feeling.

As Gala led me into the Mouth of Hell, I glanced back and saw Orpheus beyond Jack and Ignazio. He looked defeated. I paused in the doorway, hesitant to enter this sinister place. It was too dark for me to read the words carved into the monster's upper lip, but I remembered them. *"Ogni pensiero vola,"* I whispered to myself as I stepped into the giant screaming mouth. Thankfully, this time I felt nothing but a little extra warmth from all the tiny fires illuminating the space.

Gala indicated that I should take the seat at the head of the table, which was surprising—shouldn't the seat of honor be reserved for Dalí? But I quickly realized it was to set me apart, away from Jack. I sat in the luxurious chair that had been brought from the *castello* and looked down the length of the tiny table to the darkness beyond. Another bout of déjà vu hit me, an image of me sitting at the head of a different table, equally laden with delicacies, the queen of my domain. Was it a memory plucked from the emptiness of my past? I shook that thought off; the idea of me lording over a table full of expensive and exquisite food seemed a little too ludicrous to entertain.

Given the two courses we'd been served in the Casa Pendente, I expected the dishes in the *orco* to be one color, and I wasn't disappointed. Each morsel brought to the table was a shade of black. Salads of black lettuce topped by black beets, squid-ink risotto, charred aubergine, inky black pasta dotted with black mushrooms. Even the wine was so dark it looked black in the candlelight. I didn't know there were so many possibilities for black food! Every bite was even more delectable than the previous, leading to a surprising juxtaposition of the senses—being in heaven while dining in the Mouth of Hell.

When little plates of black garlic arrived to spread upon small slices of black bread, Dalí could barely contain himself. "This!

This is the food of death, of darkness. It drags me into my dreams. It reminds me of my supreme game."

"Your supreme game?" I asked.

"Yes! To imagine myself dead! On a slab of stone." He patted the table before us. "In my game, I am being slowly yet ravenously consumed by worms. They dangle from my vacant eye sockets, having gnawed away my sight. Beneath my ribs, their voracious jaws grind and mash, destroying the gossamer tissues of my disintegrating lungs. My heart holds out just a bit, for the sake of appearances, for it has always served me well. But the maggots are relentless, swarming over every inch of my divine corpse, their massive bodies undulating as they gorge themselves upon my flesh. At last, my heart can endure no more and ruptures in a great burst of putrid gore, unleashing a fresh torrent of wriggling spawn. I conjure every little detail with absolute scatological precision, imagining my complete consumption by these hellish creatures!"

Paolo pushed his plate away.

Dalí wasn't just eccentric; he was quite possibly deranged. What type of person imagined such awfulness?

"How is that fun?" Jack asked.

"Have you ever tried it?" Dalí countered in all seriousness.

"You suffer from a lack of imagination, darling." Gala gave Jack's shoulder a playful pat. He wrinkled his brow but didn't retort. Instead, he reached for his spoon to dig into the dessert, little cups of chocolate so dark it was almost black. Each one was dotted with a single pomegranate seed.

When the servant began to set the plate before me, I held up my hand. "No, thank you, I'm quite full," I said, though I knew Gala might scold me for insulting our host again.

But the man ignored me and set the plate down in front of me without a word.

"I guess you'll have to eat it." Jack laughed.

"I can't. There isn't another place in my stomach for it." I put it in front of Dalí. "Here, you have it."

"No!" he yelled, his eyes wide and bulging, his mustache twitching. "YOU WILL EAT THIS." His voice boomed in the small space, echoing off the *peperino* as he thrust the cup back in front of me. Alarmed by his furor, I picked up my spoon, and he instantly calmed down.

Gala raised an eyebrow at his erratic behavior but didn't say anything.

"Per què ha de ser tan difícil? Per què no et menges la maleïda llavor?" he muttered to himself.

While I didn't know any Catalan, it was close enough to Italian for me to understand it was something about me being difficult. Dutifully dipping my spoon into the black chocolate, I closed my eyes to savor the richness, the luxurious way the chocolate melted against my tongue. For a second, I felt grateful that Dalí had wanted me to eat it; I had never had a dessert so divine.

"No!" Dalí yelled again.

My eyes flew open with a start, and I almost fell backward.

"What did I do?" I cried, shocked. "I had the chocolate."

He pointed at the cup. The lone pomegranate seed had fallen into the depression made by my spoon.

"This is about a damn seed?" I asked. Up until that moment, I had thought he called me by the goddess's name in jest or out of some stubborn, deviant affection. But his fury made it clear he truly saw me as Proserpina's reincarnation.

He said nothing, only pointed dramatically at the cup as my tablemates looked on. Jack seemed amused, Paolo concerned, but it was Gala's frown that held the most weight. The thought of losing another day's salary pressed upon me like a physical burden. Resigned, I scooped up the seed with my next spoonful of chocolate, feeling its weight disproportionate to its size. As I slipped it into my mouth, Dalí exhaled as if he'd been holding his breath, a sigh of unmistakable relief permeating the air.

A warmth surged through me, a languid, mesmerizing heat that seeped into my very bones. My head swam, and a sensation of deep, unnamable loss overwhelmed me. It was a yearning for something elusive, a fleeting image of darkness and beauty so closely entangled it was impossible to distinguish one from the other. For a moment, I felt like I was teetering on the edge of a revelation, grasping for the substance of the vision. I closed my eyes to delve deeper into this enigmatic feeling.

When I opened them, Ignazio was standing before me, his eyes locked on to mine with an intensity, a hunger that unnerved me. The connection was so electric, so charged, that I had to look away.

"Much better," Dalí declared, a note of deep satisfaction coloring his words as he turned back to his own cup of chocolate.

I didn't finish mine and the maestro did not command me to. When the meal was complete, rather than having another glass of wine, I told Ignazio I would prefer to return to the palazzo. Dalí and Gala wanted to stay, and of course, they bade Jack to remain. Paolo graciously offered to escort me back.

"Find me in the morning," Ignazio told me after he had instructed a servant to lead us back to the car. "I will arrange for you to use the telephone."

The thought of talking with Lillian filled me with hope. She had always been a voice of reason for me. She would tell me what I should do—leave this world of freaks or stick it out for the money.

"Grazie infinita."

"Anything for you, Julia."

I backed away, unsure what to do with such adoration. Taking Paolo's arm, I waved to the others, and we followed dutifully behind the servant.

We said little, primarily because of the presence of the spindly servant leading us to the car and driving us back to the *castello*. The man's eyes were empty, devoid of sentiment. When he let us out at the base of the hill leading up to the palazzo, I released a huge sigh.

"He was a…how do you say?…*uomo insolito*," Paolo agreed, smiling at me.

"Yes, a very unusual man. Thank you for accompanying me back."

"It's nothing," he said.

On the way to our rooms, Paolo told me that he had been hired by Dalí just a day or two before coming to Bomarzo. He had known nothing of the artist before taking the job.

"He is also an unusual man," he said.

"Oh my, he is. And to be here in this place… Everything here is strange."

"But the pay is very good, no?"

I laughed. "*Sì*, it is."

The palazzo was eerily quiet, with not a soul in sight, but we were both jumpy, looking toward the dark corners with suspicion.

"I want to know more about this place," he told me.

There was so much I, too, wanted to understand. "Have you seen any…ghosts?" I asked hesitantly. Italians were terribly superstitious.

"No, but I believe there may be many here. Have you seen any?"

His openness to the idea compelled me to be honest.

"I think, perhaps, I might have. They keep calling my name."

He looked at me, his mouth in a round O of surprise. "Your name? Or the name of Giulia Orsini?"

"I'm not sure. But it's happened several times."

"It would not be surprising if there are ghosts here. That is why I would like to know more about the palazzo."

"I think I might know how we can learn a bit of its history." As I told him about Giulia's journal, he grew quite animated. "I haven't told the others about it. I think there's something important in it, and I didn't want them to become so interested that they'd take it from me."

Paolo nodded his understanding. "This secret is safe with me."

He walked me to my room, and I retrieved the journal from its place in the bottom drawer. I watched him thumb through it, a broad smile on his lips.

"This discovery, it is marvelous, Julia. I will read it and help you understand."

He hurried off to his room, clearly excited. Once he disappeared, I shut the door and almost locked it, but hesitated, remembering my words to Jack, that I would leave it open.

But there was a part of me that worried about Ignazio. Someone had, after all, left the tarot card under my pillow, and it was rather clear he was taken with me. I had no doubt he would be more than happy to take me to bed. Of course, another part of me wondered if that would be so bad. Then I thought of the ghost of myself in the fire, pointing at Ignazio. If there was any sort of warning I should heed, it was the one from my other self.

I leaned against the door. There wasn't a sound to be heard save for a bit of wind outside rattling a loose window shutter. I suddenly felt horribly alone, and I didn't want to be. Deciding to take a chance on Jack, I left the door unlocked. I closed my eyes, letting the darkness envelop me, my heart a soft drumbeat in the quiet room.

Finally, long after midnight, I felt the subtle shift of the mattress as someone climbed into bed with me. In my half-asleep state, I assumed it was Jack. Without opening my eyes, I pushed my body against the warmth next to me. The earthy scent around me seemed familiar, yet there was something different, something I couldn't quite place in my drowsy mind. Soft hands caressed me with the barest of movements, and although it would seem impossible to fall asleep in such an amorous moment, I must have been very tired, for I began to dream that Jack was a woman, large and powerful, cradling my body, wrapping herself around me from behind, her breasts against my back, her breath hot in my ear. Her flesh was soft, like the downiest pillows, and I let myself luxuriate in the sensation of her cool skin against mine. Then she kissed the tip of my ear, her tongue traveling across the tight skin, her hands roaming over my body, teasing my nipples with her fingers.

I moaned and rolled myself into her so that her mouth was upon mine, one of her hands between my legs, her other at my ear, whispering something I couldn't understand. Everything about this woman felt familiar, made me cleave to her. My hand found her hair and I held her as she devoured me with her mouth. We writhed against each other, and I felt truly alive, lost in multiple waves of satisfaction.

Then I was awake, Jack thrusting deep into me, my eyes flying open with the sensation of my cry, something I could not contain. I had wanted this, yet this communion wasn't what I thought it would be. Still lost in the sensation of my dream, it was hard to reconcile the real-life feeling of this big man above me. He filled me, pushing into me in a way that was quite pleasurable, but Jack was a bit of a disappointment compared to the ecstasy I had felt in my dream.

I didn't reach the same culmination he did, and when we lay next to each other afterward, I was relieved he either didn't notice or at least didn't comment. It seemed irrelevant; I had taken my pleasure with the woman I envisioned—but how could I possibly explain that to him? I could barely explain it to myself. And while he certainly had been partaking of me while I was lost in that vision, I also knew, instinctively, that the being who had given me such pleasure wasn't Jack. The woman in my vision was more than him, bigger than life, her spirit unable to be tamed.

"That was..." Jack began.

"Nice," I finished, not wanting to hear him gush sentiments I couldn't share.

He rolled over toward me, and his hand found my face. He stroked my cheek softly. "You are...unexpected, Julia."

"And so are you," I said, although I was sure we did not mean the same thing.

"I can't stay with you," he said. "Gala..."

"I understand."

He kissed me, a slow, tender kiss that was indeed nice. It was a skill at which he excelled. I found I wanted more, but he slid out of bed, put on his clothes, and was soon gone.

A heaviness filled me after he departed, my mind turning over all the sensations I had just experienced. Sleep came fast and easy.

I dreamed again of the woman caressing my skin lightly with her fingers, her voice in my ear. Leaning back into her, I tried to understand her words. Then my dream shifted—it was no longer her voice but Ignazio's. "You are mine," he said, his heat radiating through me. "Only mine." Smoke. Leather. Cinnamon. His scent was so heady that I could almost taste it.

He ran his hands along my arms, down across my belly, his fingers stopping above my sex, at the edge of my folds. A tease. I pushed myself into him, my body begging for more, but his hand did not shift. His lips caressed the back of my neck and my shoulder, every contact sending a deeper rush through me.

"She cannot give you all that I can," he whispered.

Somehow, I knew this was true, but I wanted him to prove it to me. One finger moved a little lower. I desperately pushed my hips upward, hoping for more. Then he abruptly turned to smoke, dissipating, the pressure against my back dissolving into nothingness.

I awoke with a start. Dawn light pooled at the edges of the drapes. I was alone, but my body was hot in the places where Ignazio's hands had lain against my skin. And I could have sworn the scent of cinnamon still lingered in the room.

10

I lay in bed, waiting until the sun was up enough that I could join the others for breakfast, turning over every aspect of the previous evening in my mind, trying to understand what I had experienced. Jack had surely come to my bed, and when I was readying for the day, I was relieved to find a used condom in the trash, proof that I had not imagined him there. But my fantasies of the woman and of Ignazio had to have been fabrications of my oversexed mind, though I couldn't shake the feeling that they, too, had been real.

"My beauteous Proserpina, come, sit," Dalí said, patting the chair next to him when I arrived in the small salon where breakfast had been arranged.

I followed his instructions, and a servant placed a demitasse cup of espresso before me, which I gratefully downed, then asked for another.

"Not much sleep last night?" Jack asked innocently, nudging me with his foot.

I nudged back. "No, not much."

Paolo also looked tired. *"Stai bene?"* I asked him.

"Sì, Signorina Lombardi. I am well. But I stayed up too late reading." He gave me a sheepish smile. I wished I could have asked him what he had found in the diary, but that would have to wait.

Gala appeared then, went straight to the window and threw the curtains wide open along with the glass and the shutter. Bright sunlight accompanied by a crisp breeze immediately wafted in. I pulled my sweater closed. "No clothes today, Julia," she said, stopping behind my chair and running her hands through my hair, arranging it on my shoulders. "It will warm up."

"I will capture the goddess within you," Dalí declared. "Proserpina is as beautiful as death. On the canvas, I will show this to the world, your deliciousness offered up from the grave, teasing the rest of the gods."

Ignazio and Jack would both be gazing on my naked body. I often felt naked enough under Ignazio's stare. And Jack had yet to see my body in the light. I groaned inwardly, but I had known this would happen, so I plastered on a smile.

Ignazio entered the room and all eyes turned toward him. *Like a magnet*, I thought. Gala went to him and linked her arm to his. "How is our handsome host today?" she purred.

But he smoothly untangled himself from her, not bothering to acknowledge her question. Instead, he turned to me. "Julia, Signora Rosati has graciously agreed to let you use the telephone. A servant will accompany you now to her house."

"Who do you have to call?" Gala spit at me, obviously furious. "You have a job to do today."

"Galachuka, darling, let her go," Dalí said. I was glad he was feeling charitable. For all his faults, he was kinder than his wife.

"It won't take me long," I said, praying silently to whatever god might be listening that she wouldn't dock my pay again. I grabbed a pastry off the plate in front of me and followed Ignazio out of the salon before Gala could say anything else.

"Did you have a restful night?" he asked as he led me out of the palazzo.

I took a deep breath, reassuring myself that he couldn't know of my dream. "I did, *grazie*."

He didn't follow up on that line of questioning, and I was relieved. Instead, he told me a little about the widow Rosati. She was highly revered in the town and very wealthy but a little doddering and often forgetful. Then he handed me off to a tall and gangly servant, Minos, who didn't spare a smile or a word for me. He led me through the warren of Bomarzo's narrow streets. Stopping at the door to a large medieval house covered in vines, he motioned for me to be the one to knock, then sat down on a nearby bench and stared off into the distance.

I knocked on the door. For a long moment, I was sure no one would answer but was finally rewarded with the sound of a person shuffling through the hallway, then the lock unlatching on the other side of the door.

A man who could have been Minos's twin stood there, in a shabby suit that looked like it must have been expensive long ago. "Signora Lombardi?" he asked. His voice was flat and empty.

"*Sì*, I have come to use the telephone," I said in Italian.

He guided me down a dark hallway adorned with stately paintings of the family's patriarchs, clouded with a varnish that hadn't aged well. The house smelled old, a mixture of dust, mothballs, and heavy, flowery perfume, and the small salon where the telephone sat seemed to have been cut right out of the eighteenth century. Rich tapestries covered three of the walls and the fourth boasted an enormous fireplace that had just been stoked. The chairs and tables looked expensive, though worn, with scuffed legs and frayed cushions.

"Signora Lombardi, you wish to make a call?" came a voice from the red velvet couch by the largest shuttered window. Moving closer, I spotted a tiny woman dressed in black, with black lace edging her sleeves, hem, and high neckline. Even her hair was black as night, not a single gray to be seen, though her wrinkled hands and face gave away her very advanced age. She was at least ninety, or maybe even a hundred. Rising, she took up the jeweled cane at her side, hobbling over to me with surprising speed for someone so old. The scent of rain clung to her.

"*Sì*, Signora Rosati. Thank you for letting me into your home. I appreciate your kindness." Her English was unusually clear, which surprised me, and I took it is a cue that I need not speak Italian with her.

But she just looked at me, squinting, a look of alarm spreading across her face. Then she began to shake her head, as though something were agitating her. "Who are you?" she asked in Italian, her voice suddenly becoming higher pitched. The servant who had brought me to the room laid a hand on her shoulder, and her confusion seemed to dissipate instantly.

"Signora Lombardi, pray tell, who are you calling?" she asked, returning to English, all signs of her previous agitation gone.

How odd, I thought, unsure what to make of her. "My roommate in Roma. I need her advice on a complicated matter."

"If you need advice, I would be happy to provide that to you." She smiled, but her eyes were cold.

I couldn't fathom how this strange woman's counsel would be helpful to me or why she would even offer such advice. "Thank you, but I am confident that Lillian can help me."

She raised a thin eyebrow but said nothing, letting the servant lead her out of the room. When she was gone, I went to the black Bakelite phone and hastily dialed the number to our apartment, holding my breath, hoping Lillian hadn't decided to go anywhere before she was due to work.

"*Pronto?*"

I breathed a huge sigh of relief. "Lily, I'm so glad you are home."

"Julia? Are you all right?"

"*Sì*, but I really needed to hear your voice." I rushed into the story of the last few days, leaving out some parts because I knew

I couldn't stay on the phone long. But when Lillian heard of the fire, she was resolute.

"You could have died, Julia. You can't stay there. You need to come home," she said.

I had been prepared to tell her I wanted to do just that, but now the words would not come.

"I...I can't," I said, still thinking of the flames and the woman who had appeared in their midst. The woman who looked just like me.

Somehow, I knew the ghost was me, but also wasn't. Her clothing was of a style I had never worn, and yet I could picture myself in those same garments.

I gasped with understanding. How had I not realized it before? The ghost didn't just look like me. The ghost was a *former* me. I was sure of it.

"Jules? Are you there?"

"*Sì*. I can't come home. You know how much I need the money. I'll be okay. I just needed to hear your voice."

I expected her to try to convince me to return, but she surprised me. "I have a few days off. I'll be there by nightfall."

"What? You don't even have a car."

"There must be a train. It's not like you are in Siberia, Jules."

Though I insisted I would be all right, she refused to listen. "I'll see you soon."

Signora Rosati appeared at the doorway as soon as I set the phone down upon the cradle. "You shouldn't let her come here," the old widow said, shaking her head. "No good will come of it. She is not of this place."

"Neither am I," I said slowly, a shiver creeping across the back of my neck.

"She wasn't invited."

"I just invited her."

She cocked her head and stared at me as though pondering my statement, then abruptly turned around and left the room.

I almost called Lillian back to tell her not to come. There was something in the widow's words that made me wonder if I would regret not heeding them. But I already felt bad that I had intruded upon the old lady and didn't want to further wear out my welcome.

When I departed the room and turned the corner, I ran right into the widow. She let out a horrible scream, raising her cane as though she intended to beat me with it.

"Who are you?" she cried, sliding back into Italian. "Why are you in my house? Giorgio! Giorgio! Help! Someone has broken into my house!" She began swinging the cane wildly, and I barely managed to back away to avoid being hit. She no longer smelled like rain but instead had that peculiar old-person odor that reminded me of the *nonna* who served me spaghetti at the *trattoria* around the corner from my apartment in Rome.

The spindly servant appeared. He said a few words that I couldn't hear, and mercifully, she lowered the cane. At the door I looked back. Signora Rosati had sat down upon the couch where I had found her, as though I had never interrupted whatever thoughts she might be having.

Minos stood when he saw me and, wordlessly, led me back through the streets of Bomarzo to the waiting car. As we sped down the hill toward the garden, I felt sure that Signora Rosati wouldn't even remember I had been there at all.

The sun was bright as I made my way up the trail toward Proserpina's bench, and while the light filtering through the trees should have lent the *boschetto* a less gloomy countenance, I did not like being alone in such a place. I rushed past the stone giants and beyond the fallen mausoleum where I'd first heard the whispers of my name. At the *tempietto*, I saw Orpheus waiting. I picked him up and cuddled him close, suddenly feeling desperate for comfort. The widow's words had left me with a terrible foreboding and worry about Lillian's arrival. The cat rubbed his face against mine, obviously glad to be held. He climbed to my shoulder and together we went toward the hippodrome, where the others awaited my arrival.

Ignazio saw me first and came to meet me on the stairs near the statue of Cerberus. My heart pounded when he stepped closer. *Damn it.* I hated the pull he had on me.

"You were able to reach Lillian?"

I nodded. "She is going to catch a train to join me here."

Ignazio's brow wrinkled with concern, but the look was gone as quickly as it had appeared. "It will take her to Attigliano, about seven kilometers away."

Seven kilometers. It would take her an hour and a half to walk to Bomarzo. She couldn't possibly be here before nightfall if that was the case.

"Would it be possible to arrange for a car to pick her up late this afternoon?"

Ignazio shook his head. "Not today. The train only comes once a week—few have need to stop here."

"Once a week?" My hope of seeing Lillian today suddenly fell.

"*Sì.* Then one must take a ferry across the swamp, and that only runs twice a day as well. It is not an easy thing to arrive in Bomarzo without a car, especially since the War. Now, don't look so defeated."

He put a hand on my shoulder but immediately removed it when I recoiled from his heat. I was trying hard not to cry.

"Worry not. The train arrives tomorrow. I will have Minos retrieve her," he said.

I took a deep breath, willing my tears to retreat. I wouldn't see her for another whole day. My trip would be half over when she arrived. But knowing she was coming to Bomarzo at all gave me courage.

Yet just as I was trying to muster that goodwill, I realized how forward I had been. I was sure there was a room for Lillian in the palazzo, but I didn't know how much Dalí had paid for this wild trip. She was another bed to make up and another mouth to feed.

Ignazio noticed my consternation. "What's wrong, Julia?"

"I…I might have been hasty in inviting her. I never talked to Dalí about it. I'll have them take the money from my pay…" I trailed off, wondering if Gala would even agree to such a thing.

"Don't worry, Julia. I will take care of everything for Lillian's stay. She will be my guest as much as yours."

I looked at him, shocked. "That's…that's very generous," I said, unsure why he would do such a thing but grateful all the same.

"It's nothing."

"I must return to Signora Rosati to call and let her know."

"No, no, give me her number. I will arrange everything," he said.

Although I was hesitant, I gave him our number.

It was only after he'd disappeared into the garden that I realized I had never told Ignazio Lillian's name.

11

"My beautiful goddess," Dalí exclaimed when he saw me. "Today I will paint you in all your natural glory." He held a pomegranate in one hand and waved it around as he talked.

"Off with the dress," Gala said, turning me around and unzipping my dress before I could say anything or change my mind.

At least Ignazio was not there, but Jack was, and I tried not to think of him standing off to the side. He knew my body but had not seen it. I suddenly felt shy, a feeling I couldn't have if I were to make it through the day. Reminding myself that I had done this dozens of times, I allowed Gala to pull the baby blue dress off over my head, then my slip, and pretended not to notice Dalí's stare, or Jack's, focusing instead on the cool autumn air that pimpled my skin. I removed my brassiere and panties and handed them to Gala, who folded my clothes and set them neatly on a nearby camp chair. Lowering myself to Proserpina's bench, I lay back and let Dalí arrange me. The stone wasn't cold against my bare skin as I would have anticipated, but warm, as warm as I was, and familiar, as though I had sat on the bench hundreds of times before.

Dalí positioned me on my side, then whipped out a pocketknife and began to cut into the pomegranate. The juice dripped over his fingers as he pulled out a handful of the arils. After separating them from the pith, he laid the seeds across my body, one by one, up one leg, across my thigh and along my side and my arm.

"So beautiful," he gushed. "You are a vision, a dream. If there were no Gala, no gorgeous Gravida of mine, I would have to penetrate you."

I gasped at this proclamation.

Gala flicked the edge of her husband's ear with her finger. "Don't tease the model, *estimat meu.*" Though I didn't understand her Catalan, I could tell from her tone that it was said with endearment. I honestly did not understand these two people, nor did I want to.

Just then, Dalí placed two arils upon my left breast, pinpricks of warmth against my areola. I closed my eyes, wishing the day was over, not just beginning, and tried to ignore the weirdness of everything around me. I thought of Lillian and how these people might receive her. Dalí needed to know I had invited her, but I'd wait until Gala left, for I feared she would be quite angry with me.

"Maestro Dalí," I ventured once we were alone, "that phone call I made was to my roommate, Lillian. She is going to join me here tomorrow."

Dalí looked at me as though I had just sprouted another head. "But, little goddess, why? Why would you do that? Why would she come here?" He put down his brush and waited for my answer.

I gaped at him, unsure of what to say. That I was afraid of Ignazio? That I was hearing voices whisper in my ear when I walked through this place? By hell, I decided, logic be damned, perhaps a little truth wouldn't hurt.

"I'm afraid of ghosts. I think this place is haunted."

He said nothing for a moment, then nodded. "Yes, yes. It is. I am haunting it! I walk with the gods and ghosts of the *boschetto*. I hear their music and I make it mine. This haunting is delicious, delirious!"

Unsure what to make of his raving, I listened and tried to keep my expression passive. When he quieted, he stared at me for a few moments, then finally said, "You do need a friend, my muse, my Proserpina. For I am not that." And, with that, he went back to painting as though I had never had the conversation with him.

Finally, Gala returned and broke the silence by instructing Paolo to take pictures of Dalí painting me. She was certain that *Art News* would want to publish them.

"They will, but such magnificence will be better represented in *Time*," Dalí pronounced with confidence. "*Time Magazine* will want them. Or *Life*."

My first thought was that I didn't want the entire world to see my breasts—a photo in a magazine wasn't like a painting, a work of true art—and I was about to protest when it dawned on me that neither my nudity nor my name would be of any import whatsoever. The editors of whichever magazines ran the photos would not only black out my parts, but they would never even bother to find out who I was. Dalí would be the star of the piece, would receive all the accolades, and I would merely be "the model."

Of course, this realization made me feel even worse, so I tried to divert my anxious mind by taking an imaginary walk through Rome's Borghese Gallery, my favorite museum, a place where I often went when I needed solace. I wandered through the gilded halls, admiring the statues and paintings, flitted through the rooms, wanting to see Bernini's masterpieces. My mind led me directly to my favorite statue, and as I stood in front of it, I had a startling insight. While I had always admired the piece for Bernini's skill—how he could make marble hands gripping flesh seem so real—I hadn't, until that moment, realized the statue I so deeply loved was that of Pluto dragging Proserpina off to the Underworld.

I was jolted out of my daze when Dalí declared it was time for lunch. Without a thought for me, he led Jack and Gala up the stairs before I knew what was happening. Paolo came toward me, his head turned, a blanket in his outstretched hand. I chuckled at his modesty, considering he had just spent considerable time photographing me in the nude.

"Signorina Julia, they have gone to the *orco* to eat," he said once I'd put my dress back on. "I will bring you there."

I shivered at the thought of eating inside that damn monster again.

"But first, I wanted to talk to you about Giulia Farnese's journal."

I sat back down on Proserpina's bench and patted the seat. Paolo joined me and extracted the journal from his camera bag. "She was an unusual woman. Not only did she keep the *castello* running while her husband served as a *condottiero*, but…"

"*Condottiero?*" I asked, unfamiliar with the term.

He thought for a moment. "A soldier for hire."

I nodded. "A mercenary. That's interesting."

"*Sì*, but more interesting is that Vicino Orsini didn't come up with the idea for the *boschetto*. It was Giulia who inspired her husband, though the ideas for the statues did not come from her. They came from her chef, Aidoneus." He paused to gauge my reaction. "Have you heard of Aidoneus?"

"The name seems familiar, but…" I couldn't quite place where I had heard it.

He looked up at the worn face of the goddess in whose lap we sat. "Some stories say that Aidoneus is another name for the Roman god, Pluto."

"Or for the Greek Hades," I breathed, trying to understand what such a thing meant.

"*Esatto.* But this Aidoneus is different. There is some thought he might have been real, not a myth, and that he was married to a woman named Proserpina many centuries ago."

I gaped at him, trying to grasp what this could mean.

A crackle of branches on the path behind Proserpina's bench caused both of us to jump to our feet. Paolo quickly shoved the journal into his bag.

"What's taking you so long?" Jack asked, coming into view. "We're getting hungry."

"I was telling her about the little town where I grew up," Paolo lied.

"Well, hop to it and tell her on the way."

I squeezed Paolo's arm, a small gesture to thank him for keeping the journal our little secret. He gave me a nod and a smile, but he looked worried. Hopefully we'd find more time to continue this conversation sooner rather than later. "Why do we have to go to the Hell mouth to eat?" I wondered aloud as we traversed the overgrown route. "Why can't they just set up a table near the bench?"

Jack shrugged. "There's already a table there. Why drag another one into the garden?"

My mind focused on steeling myself to take on whatever new thing might happen in the mouth of the *orco*, I tripped on an overgrown root and went flying. Jack caught me without effort, lifting me up and cradling me in his arms. "Be careful, Julia," he warned, holding me tight. "I would hate to see that pretty face marred by the rocks of Bomarzo."

Dreading lunch, I didn't want to leave the safety and comfort of his embrace. But he righted me, then relinquished me, though he did extend his arm for me to hold as he led me into the Mouth of Hell, where Dalí and Gala waited impatiently. No sooner had Ignazio told us about the various *tramezzini*— little triangular sandwiches on crustless white bread that he said were popular in Venice—than Dalí laid in, loading up his plate with two or three of each kind. I felt dizzied by the choices: prosciutto and cantaloupe; cucumber, mayo, and herb; asparagus and egg; artichoke; *bresaola* and arugula; mortadella and roasted red peppers; eggplant and mozzarella; cherry tomatoes and asiago cheese; tuna, egg, and olive.

"*Squisito!*" Dalí raved.

"These are far superior to those sandwiches they serve at tea in London," Gala agreed, though she had only taken one.

They were right about the sandwiches being delicious. But the white bread was sticky in my mouth, and I asked Ignazio for something to drink. He gave me a little bow before pulling a thermos from a bag at his feet. He uncapped it and poured an enticing ruby-colored liquid into the goblets before him, then handed me a glass, his fingers brushing against mine. My breath caught with his heat.

"What is it?" I managed, although the seed floating in my glass gave me the answer before Ignazio confirmed that it was indeed pomegranate juice.

"With a little gin," he added, nodding at Dalí, who tipped up his drink in a toast.

Just as I lifted my cocktail to drink, Paolo's elbow crashed into mine, sending the glass flying. It burst into pieces as it hit the *peperino* wall at the back of the monster's mouth, the juice leaving a dark stain against the rock.

"*Mi dispiace!*" he cried. Scrambling past me, he began picking up the broken glass shards, but Ignazio waved him off.

"Worry not. My people will clean it up," Ignazio assured him as he poured me a fresh goblet.

Paolo put his hand on my arm and squeezed an unmistakable warning. He did not want me to drink the juice.

"I've changed my mind," I said to Ignazio.

"You must have a glass," he insisted.

"Drink! Drink!" Dalí said, his eyes bulging. "You need the

ruby strength, the power of the sacred pomegranate. Proserpina would never say no to such ambrosia."

"This one would," I said. I dared not look at Gala. But there was something in Paolo's warning that made me willing to take the chance.

"I'd prefer water," I told Ignazio.

"I have none here."

I shook my head. "Then I will be fine without anything."

Finally, Ignazio set the goblet upon the table and left. I swore I felt the ground tremble as he walked down the trail away from the *orco*.

"Why did you do that, you stupid girl?" Gala sniped at me. "He is our host."

"I'm not going to eat and drink everything forced upon me," I said, refusing to give in to her.

"If you do not drink it, you will wear it instead," Dalí said. "We will pour it over you, letting it flow across your limbs."

Gala stared at me, daring me to say no.

I shivered, thinking of how cold and sticky that would be.

"Just drink it," Jack said, his eyes imploring me. "It would be better than wearing it."

Paolo's knee pressed against mine, his foot pushing along my shoe, warning me without words. I felt trapped, a mouse between two cats with no graceful way out.

My desire to remain clean and dry won out. I picked up the goblet and was about to lift it to my mouth when I heard a horrible yowl. Orpheus jumped onto the table, scattering the remnants of the *tramezzini*, and leaped at me, knocking the new glass out of my hand so it too shattered on the smooth stone beneath our feet. A drop of liquid hit my cheek and I wiped it off with my hand.

We stared at the cat in disbelief as he sat down on the table, his tail flicking back and forth, then calmly began to clean the few spots of pomegranate juice off his paws.

"It seems I wasn't meant to drink the juice after all." Checking the thermos, I noted with satisfaction that there was also no more left to drizzle upon me.

Jack picked up the cat and tossed him out the mouth of the *orco*, ignoring my cry of protest. He cursed as he let the cat go.

"The little beast scratched me." He held up his arm, upon which there was a long gash with a few beads of blood.

Down the path, Orpheus sat and stared at me. I swear he gave me a little nod of his head before he took off into the bushes beyond the statue of the dragon fighting off the lions.

12

Outside the Mouth of Hell, a wild storm had begun to brew, darkening the sky and whipping the wind up around us as we walked. It soon became apparent that we wouldn't be able to work that afternoon. Jack and Paolo gathered up Dalí's equipment and we headed back to where the truck usually waited for us. We looked up the long dirt road that led to the village and the palazzo on the top of the hill. There was no sign of transport in sight.

"It's only a fifteen-minute walk," I said, trying to be cheery. "The exercise will be good for us."

"Fifteen minutes up the side of a mountain," Gala barked at me. "This is *your* fault. If you hadn't angered Ignazio, he would have been here, waiting." She said something else in Russian and then stomped off, leading Dalí by the hand.

"Don't let her bust your chops," Jack said after they were out of earshot. "I've not known her long, but she's always been fussy. And she's not one for liking other dames."

"Do you think Ignazio didn't come because he's angry with

me?" I asked as we trudged up the road. The first few raindrops were beginning to fall.

"Maybe," Jack said.

I looked at Paolo, the only Italian among us.

"It is rude to say no when offered food, but it's also rude to force someone to eat something. I cannot say, Signorina Julia."

We walked the rest of the way in silence, the wind growing stronger and stronger. I wished I had a ribbon to tie back my hair and keep it from flying into my mouth. Dalí and Gala had run ahead, but I stayed back with Jack and Paolo, who were burdened by the equipment. The rain was coming down harder, and by the time we reached the town, we were drenched and Dalí's painting was ruined.

"I'm sure they will be furious with me," I said, looking at the smeared paint.

"It's not your fault," Paolo said.

"Tell that to Gala."

"Don't worry, I'll get her off your back," Jack assured me. "She turns into a kitten with the right words."

Not wanting to know what words those might be, I was relieved that Gala, Dalí, and Ignazio were nowhere to be found when we returned to the palazzo.

"I think I'm going to spend time in the library this afternoon," I said, mostly for Paolo's benefit. I hoped he would tell me more about the diary.

"I wouldn't mind falling asleep on the couch as you read to me." Jack winked, and I blushed. "But I don't want to rile Gala up any further."

I left them to finish putting away the equipment and headed up the stairs. At the top landing, Demetra materialized from the shadows. A bolt of lightning flashed, illuminating her hollow eyes. A waft of petrichor hit my nostrils, and while it seemed to emanate from the maid, I knew that mustn't be true. It had to be from the rain on the stones of the *castello*.

"Madonna Julia," she said, bowing her head in deference, "I have drawn you a bath."

I had never been called Madonna before and was grateful for all the art history classes I had taken or I wouldn't have known it was an archaic way of addressing noblewomen who had gone by the wayside centuries past.

Her action surprised me. "But how did you know I even needed one? Or when I would be coming back?"

Demetra only looked out the tall arched window toward the dark skies. A massive crack of thunder made me jump. "I can assist you with your bath if you desire. Let me help you out of those wet clothes, shampoo your hair." She sounded eager, which made me uncomfortable.

"No, no. I will be fine on my own," I insisted as another flash of lightning brightened the corridor.

I made my way to the bathroom, locked the door, removed my dripping garments, and slipped into the tub. The maid had put a silky oil that smelled of oranges and almonds into the bathwater. Closing my eyes, I luxuriated in the warmth.

Julia...

My eyes flew open. The room was empty.

Julia...

I couldn't tell where the voice was coming from. "Who are you?" I whispered back.

I am Julia.

I did not like this game. "No, I am Julia. Please, leave me alone."

Thunder broke above the house. The lights flickered wildly before dying completely, and I was immersed in absolute darkness.

I couldn't breathe. I sat there, listening for movement, terrified that I would hear someone—or something—in the room with me.

BOOM! A massive crack of thunder shook the house.

I huddled in the bath, my heart pumping so furiously I

thought for sure I would die of heart failure and they would find my lifeless body naked in the tub in the morning.

She loves you, the voice said, so faint I wasn't sure I heard what it had said.

He loves you, it said again. *Love you, love you, love you...* The whispers swirled around me.

"Go away," I hissed.

Silence.

Lightning flashed again, and mercifully, I could see no one in the room with me. I was getting out of the tub when the power returned. Quickly, I stood and grabbed my robe, wrapping it tightly around myself.

Don't... The whisper was loud in my ear.

I put my hand on the door handle.

Don't let them...destroy you.

I pushed the door open, only to find Ignazio walking down the hall toward me. My heart began to pound hard. I held my clothes tightly against me, making sure the bathrobe didn't reveal too much.

"How was your bath?" he asked. I hated that his husky voice was so delicious to my ears.

Lightning flashed again at the window on the stairway landing. "I don't like bathing with such a storm raging." My voice shook.

"I won't let anything hurt you, Julia," Ignazio said, stopping a few paces from me. It seemed he had forgiven me for refusing him earlier. "Worry not." He gazed past me, out the window, and his eyes took on a briefly vacant look. "The thunder will pass soon."

"You sound so sure of that."

"I am." He nodded as though I had just passed some sort of evaluation. "We still have time."

"Time for what?"

"Time until dinner," he said, flashing me his heart-melting smile.

"Ah, that," I said, though I had the distinct feeling that he was referring to something else.

He reached out a hand and cupped my cheek. I froze, unsure of what to do. Instinct told me to rip my body away, but everything about his touch seduced me into ignoring any warning bells. I thought he might lean forward and press his lips to mine, but then he was gone, down the stairs, leaving me shivering in my robe in the dim hallway.

He loves you...

I ran from the voice, slamming the door to my room behind me. As I lay down on my bed, struggling to catch my breath, I tried to make sense of the messages I was hearing. If the ghosts were from my past lives, what could that mean? Who was sending them here? They were incomplete and often faint. I was the only one who seemed to be hearing them. What were they warning me about?

Unable to make heads or tails of this eeriness, I found the courage to dress and go down the hall to the library. As I'd hoped, Paolo stood by the window, staring into the valley beyond.

"Sometimes, when I look at the garden at night, I see a green glow," I said as I approached him.

He turned to me, then looked back at the garden and pointed. *"Come quello?"*

I looked out the window. It wasn't night, but the storm clouds had cloaked the *boschetto* in darkness, and emanating from the Sacro Bosco was a sickly green light. It played at the edges of the *tempietto* and seeped up through the trees.

"You see it, too?"

"Sì. This is the first time."

"Then I'm not imagining things." Relief filled me.

We stared at the glow for a few moments before it abruptly winked out.

"What do you think it is?" I asked in a low voice.

He looked at me for some time before responding. "I think there is something down there—something not from our world."

Three days earlier, I would have laughed at such a thought, but after everything I had experienced since arriving in Bomarzo, it seemed as plausible an explanation as any. I sat on the couch, and he joined me, taking Giulia's journal and another slim volume out of his bag. He put the journal back and thumbed through the book. *La storia di Bomarzo* was etched into the spine. *The History of Bomarzo.*

He thumbed through it. "I found this book in the library. There's not much in it, but I read something interesting. You remember the big vase in the middle of the garden?"

"Yes, it seemed important to me."

"There are ashes of a woman inside."

"I knew it," I gasped.

He raised an eyebrow at me. "You did?"

"I told Jack I thought someone was buried there. I don't know how I knew it."

"Her name was…"

I knew what he was going to say.

"Julia," we said in unison.

"*Sì.* She died on that spot one hundred years after Giulia Farnese married Vicino Orsini and came to Bomarzo. The Della Rovere family owned the property after the Orsini, and they buried one of their nieces there. She had loved the garden."

I put a hand on his arm. "Remember when I told you I could hear someone calling my name?"

He nodded.

"I've seen ghosts too."

Paolo gaped. *"Fantasmi?"*

I nodded. "They look like me."

Paolo stared at a point on the floor as if trying to comprehend what I was saying. He drew a deep breath. *"Reincarnazioni?"* He began talking to himself in Italian and I only caught a few of the words, all a little incredulous, with a few Hail Marys thrown in for good measure. Finally, he turned back to me. "How can that be?"

"I don't know if they are reincarnations." The possibility unsettled me more than I cared to admit. I pointed at the journal. "Does the book say how the woman died?"

"Legend has it that she died from eating six cakes over the course of a week or so, each topped with a rotten pomegranate seed."

I thought of all the ruby seeds that had dotted every dish I'd been served since my arrival in Bomarzo. They'd even dotted my body.

"Couldn't anyone tell that they were rotten?" My question was more to myself, voicing the doubt that gnawed at me.

Paolo didn't have an answer, nor had I expected him to. It seemed too implausible that pomegranate seeds would kill the poor woman. The idea of them being rotten was too convenient of an explanation for her death. Then it hit me.

"Wait, six seeds?"

Paolo nodded.

"Like Proserpina."

He traded the history book for the journal and opened it. "Giulia also writes of another story the local peasants told of the *boschetto*—about it being haunted by the spirit of a woman who died in a cave surrounded by pomegranate bushes. I think this must be the story Ignazio was referring to when we first came to the wood."

I wondered if her name was also Julia. "How did she know all this?"

Paolo shrugged. "Stories of this nature are often passed down from generation to generation. If I were to tell you all the legends of my village, you would be just as amazed."

"What else does Giulia write about?" I looked at the journal in Paolo's lap.

"She was in love with Aidoneus."

"Does she say that in the journal?"

He shook his head. "Not so directly. But it is clear in her descriptions of him, and of their lovemaking, and of the longing she has for him between the times she sees him."

"Did Vicino ever find out?"

"I don't know. Beyond discussing care for the home or their conversations about the Sacro Bosco, it seems he didn't pay much attention to her in life."

He picked up the worn volume and thumbed through it. "She used to wander through the wood with Aidoneus and they would dream up fantastical stories about the rocks scattered about. Later, she'd recount these stories as dreams to Vicino, never mentioning where they'd originated. The history book—" he jerked his thumb toward the volume in his pack "—tells us that Vicino had her sketch the monsters that supposedly visited her in her sleep. He then used those sketches to help inspire the creation of the *boschetto*.

"Signorina Julia, there is something else you should know."

I had a feeling I wasn't going to like what he was about to say.

He drew his lips into a fine line, as though measuring his words before he spoke. "Her descriptions of Aidoneus... Well, he sounds just like...Ignazio. Pale green eyes. Heavy brow. Dark hair. And she often wrote that he smells of smoke and...*canella*."

Cinnamon.

"That's not...possible." I couldn't believe what I was hearing. "Wait, does she mention his hot hands?"

He nodded, his eyes growing wide. "Ignazio... His hands are like this?"

"They are. He radiates heat." I felt lightheaded.

"There is one more thing." He flipped to the back of the journal. "In her last entry, Giulia seems very worried about something, maybe an unwanted pregnancy. To help her, Aidoneus had been preparing a special, um, *pozione*...for her every day.

He was going to bring her a sixth dose after her evening meal. He told her she would be cured within the week."

My heart sank. "Let me guess. The potion was made of pomegranates."

"*Sì*. There is a little portrait of her in one of the salons, which has her date of death as the same date as the last journal entry."

"Dear god." I shuddered.

"That is why I didn't want you to drink the pomegranate juice today, Signorina Julia." He paused as if not wanting to speak his next words. "How many seeds have you eaten?" His voice was nearly a whisper.

I thought back. There was the one in the parsnip soup the night we arrived, the apple-and-pomegranate fritter that first time in the *orco*, the date-and-pistachio candy from Poliphilio's dinner, and atop the cup of chocolate from the meal in the garden.

"Four. It would have been more if you and Orpheus hadn't intervened earlier."

Paolo closed the book and handed it back to me. "You must be very careful."

"This is madness," I said, straightening. "A bad dream."

Paolo reached over and pinched my arm.

"Ow!"

"Not a dream, Signorina Julia."

I ran my hand over the journal cover, wondering what happened to Giulia. "There's something I don't understand."

"How much of this are we supposed to understand?" Paolo joked. "*È tutto ridicolo.*"

"I agree, it is ridiculous—all of it. But what I find most confusing is that all these women named Julia eat the seeds and die. They can't all have been Proserpina reincarnate, or it wouldn't keep happening, right? They would end up in the Underworld and stay there. But their ghosts linger."

Paolo knitted his brow in thought. "Are they really ghosts? Could they be something like memories, or echoes of you, like...

impressioni you left behind in the world. Do they respond to you when you see them?"

I thought for a moment. "They do, but in a restrained way. It's as if they're bound within certain confines, compelled to re-play crucial moments, and offering small glimpses of insight or warnings."

"*Ecco qua.*"

There you have it. I had to admit that Paolo's idea of the ghosts being impressions of me made sense. I had never heard of such a thing, but perhaps that was what ghosts often were? Memories?

"I don't know," I said. "Maybe our minds are just drawing strange parallels because this is such a creepy place."

"Maybe. But they are compelling parallels."

As I put the journal back on the shelf, thinking it would be safest there, I remembered the secret passage and asked Paolo if Giulia had mentioned it again.

"Ah, *sì.* I think it is somewhere in this room. *Perchè?*"

"Maybe it leads to something that would give us a hint about all this."

He shrugged, then gave me a big smile. "And because it is a secret passage. Everyone wants to find the secret passage."

I chuckled. He was certainly right about that.

Soon we were examining every little nook and cranny of the library, pressing the edges of the wallpaper, feeling under drawers in the desk, tipping back books on shelves. We hadn't been at it long when I heard Dalí bellowing for Paolo.

"He must have seen the painting," he said with a sigh. He gave me an apologetic look, then headed toward the sound of the maestro's voice.

As I watched him walk out the door, my gaze landed on a tiny bronze detail on a corner of the lintel—an arrow pointing toward the bookcase on its left.

Julia...

I ignored the voice and followed the arrow, which led to another at the edge of the bookcase. This one pointed down. The arrows were so tiny that if you didn't know what you were looking for, they would be easy to miss among the decorated bookcases.

Julia...

The truth was, I was losing my fear of the whispers, hearing them now for what I thought they surely must be—a warning. About what, I could hardly imagine, much less say aloud. About Ignazio? About the seeds? About my potential death?

I felt along the edge of the bookcase until I found another bronze arrow, this one an arrowhead without a shaft, pointing toward the wall. I pressed it, and suddenly, there was a whoosh and a slight sucking sound as the corner of the library seemed to pull backward in upon itself, revealing a door. It opened to an extremely dark set of stairs. The air was stale, and I was pretty sure no one had used the passage in centuries. I marveled that Vicino Orsini had found someone with the technology to create a staircase like this.

Beyond the library, I could still hear Dalí's voice, and occasionally, I caught my name. Much as I wanted to find a light source and descend into the passageway, I was sure they would miss me soon. I did not see any way to pull the door closed, but when I pressed the arrow again, the bookcase and the corner swung back toward me and clicked shut.

Just as I turned away from the secret door, Dalí appeared in the library. "My little goddess, you must come now. Those fools! They destroyed you, and they melted your visage. I must make it anew. Now!"

Reluctantly, I let Dalí lead me to the salon, where he had me lie upon a table, one leg and arm dangling, my head barely propped up by a pillow. I was naked, but a fire raging on the grate not far away kept me warm. Dalí had blissfully forgone the notion of the pomegranate seeds and seemed focused primarily on capturing my image with the intention of adding any adornment later. He banished everyone with the instruction that no one was to enter, not even Gala. When Dalí first began to paint, I tried to spark conversation about his technique, but he commanded my silence with a grunt and a sharp wave of his hand.

So I lay there for hours, with only a few short breaks. I had not yet seen Dalí in such a fervor, so deeply invested in his art on the canvas rather than the art of his personality.

My mind ran wild, thinking over every meal I had eaten, every interaction with Ignazio, and every whisper of the ghosts. I didn't understand how Orpheus fit into this puzzling mix, but his actions were so deliberate that I was sure he did. Nor did I understand the connection of these ghostly women to this place and why all their names were Julia. But, above all, I couldn't get my head around this person named Aidoneus.

"Maestro Dalí, do you sometimes find that life is more surreal than your paintings?"

He frowned. I thought I had annoyed him, and he might not answer, but then he fixed his wide eyes in my direction. "No. My paintings are more surreal, but they are also safer."

"I wish I could live in one of your paintings," I said wistfully.

"But you do, little Proserpina," he said, turning the canvas toward me so that I could see my body rendered in paint, stretched across a vast ocean, floating, my hair falling to touch the water, my eyes open, staring at the viewer.

"My name is Julia," I said, suddenly angry at his insistence on calling me Proserpina. Perhaps Dalí was entangled in the murderous scheme that was unfolding around me. He was practically possessed with the idea of me eating the pomegranate seeds, demanding my compliance.

"You are who I say you are! You bear the name that I give you, the name that will live on for centuries after you, that will be forever emblazoned upon this canvas. You are Proserpina, a woman stolen from her life, stolen from her loves, doomed to darkness. Now HUSH." He slashed an arm across the air toward me, like a sword sweeping off a champagne cork. "HUSH!"

When we finally finished, it was late. Ignazio had left me and Dalí a warm platter of bread, roasted chicken, an assortment of savory pastries, and some more Elysium wine. Despite my desire to taste the heavens again, I decided I would not have any wine that night. I wanted my wits about me, even though, to my relief, there wasn't a single pomegranate seed in sight.

While we ate, the others played Machiavelli, a card game Paolo had taught them. "It's a little like rummy," Jack explained when I joined them. The goal of the game was to be the first person to play all their cards. After my first hand, Gala and Dalí, who'd been downing the wine incessantly, had become so intoxicated that they started undressing each other right there, in front of us. Embarrassed, Paolo quickly excused himself, and I, not wanting to be an unwilling part of the Dalís' orgy, followed suit.

"*Dio mio,*" Paolo cursed after we had escaped the salon. "They are wicked."

I wasn't sure I thought of them as wicked, just oversexed, but I didn't say as much. While I had been privy to a number of sexually deviant situations in the art world, the Dalís took it to another, much more uncomfortable, level.

"No *melograni* tonight, at least," he said.

I had always loved the Italian word for *pomegranate*, not only because of the way it rolled off the tongue but also because of the imagery it evoked, an apple (*mela*) with many grains (*grani*). But now it had taken on a darker meaning for me, and if I never heard it again, I would not mind. "*Sì,* I am glad for that."

"Be careful, Signorina Julia." He gave me a little nod, then left me at the door to my room.

13

I awoke to a commotion in the hallway. It was still dark and I flipped the switch on the lamp at my bedside. Gala and Dalí were bantering loudly outside my door, and Jack was shushing them.

"Your room is that way, the last one down the hall," he told them.

"Ish this your room, Jack?" Gala slurred. "Come to ours."

"I was already there," he said to her, like he might a child. "You wore me out, Gala, darling. Now I need to sleep. So do both of you. And, yes, this is my room." He rattled the door-knob, and I wondered if he knew it was my room or if he was also too drunk to remember who slept where.

"Galachuka! Come! Let me undress you. Let me worship you." I could barely understand Dalí between the liquor and his heavy accent, but the sound of his voice fading out seemed to indicate that he was leading Gala away.

Jack rattled the knob again and softly knocked two times. "What a schnook," he whispered when I opened the door. "She'll believe anything when she's deep in the sauce." He stepped into my room and locked the door behind him.

"Including the gobbledygook that this is your room?" I asked.

He gave me a broad grin. "Exactly."

I rolled my eyes at him.

"Oh, come on, doll, you'll let me stay for a little bit, won't you?" He picked me up with sudden swiftness and brought me to the bed. "It's a big bed and a dark, scary house. Let me hold you in my arms and keep you safe." He laid me down and then leaned in to kiss me.

I had not planned on letting anyone into my room tonight, yet despite my best intentions, here was Jack—warm, strong Jack. And I *did* feel safe in his arms. In fact, the low level of fear I'd been harboring dissolved with his touch. Then I let him kiss me—slow, deliberate, and careful—and the world around us both seemed far away. His earthy smell was comforting, and he tasted faintly like apples. I wondered if Gala had stolen his Elysium wine and left him drinking calvados.

I watched him undress, his hard, chiseled body beautiful in the light from the small lamp at the bedside. He was ready for me, but he wasn't in a hurry. He climbed into bed and roamed his hands all over my body, caressing every inch of my skin, teasing me with his fingertips, his tongue, and his lips. The longer he touched me, the more he felt familiar, deeply familiar, as though I had known him for thousands of years and his hands had explored my body countless times. We were melting into each other, rivers flowing between us, our pleasure lapping up against our very banks. At some point, I lost myself, and he must have, too, but I don't remember it. When I woke later, it was still dark, the bed was cold, and Jack was gone.

I pulled my robe around me and went to the door to lock it again, but for some reason, I felt compelled to open it and look down the hall first. And there was Ignazio at the end of the hall, by the stairs, striding toward me with purpose. I was so stunned to see him I couldn't respond. I watched him, transfixed, danger and desire coming closer with every step.

When he reached me, he said nothing, only stepped inside my room and pulled me close. I let him. He buried his face in my hair and wrapped his hands around my back. Dark autumn enveloped me, smoky, heavy, and hot. So hot, I thought I might burn with fever, with desperation. I had never imagined wanting someone as much as I wanted this man before me. Everything about Jack paled in comparison. I tried to speak, but he shushed me and pulled off my robe. Then he dropped to his knees and worshipped me. I almost lost myself in a cry of pleasure, but he rose again, placing his hand over my mouth before I could make a sound.

"Mine," he whispered, his breath warm in my ear. Closing my eyes, I let his husky voice seduce me. "Only mine."

Then he was gone. There was no embrace, no hand upon my mouth, no one touching my skin, only the cold air of the room and the lingering, faint scent of smoke. I opened my eyes and found that I was alone, leaning against the bed, naked. Shocked and terrified, I picked my robe up off the floor, wrapped it around me, and checked the door. It was locked.

As I climbed back into bed, I heard the voice again.

Julia...

I turned my head toward the sound, and there, near the door, was that same image of me that I had seen in the fire, though, this time, it wasn't nearly so concrete, but faint, almost transparent. The apparition pointed at the door and held up three fingers. Then she winked out.

For the next few hours, I sat in bed with all the lights on, playing over the events of the morning in my mind. I could come up with only two plausible explanations. Either I was going completely mad, or there truly were supernatural forces warring over me. I leaned toward the latter, if only because the others around me had been on the edges of the same experiences.

At some point, I must have succumbed to sleep, too weary
to drift into the nightmares I anticipated, for it was a knock on
the door that stirred me awake. Bright sunlight crept around the
edges of the curtains, and, in the light of day, the night before felt
like a strange dream—a vivid one—but there was no evidence
that either Jack or Ignazio had ever been in my room.

I opened the door, and there stood Gala, hands on her hips.
"What are you doing, lolling about in bed?" She pushed past
me and went right to the wardrobe. I was surprised to see her
so hale. She was twice my age, and I knew older women didn't
bounce back from the booze the way someone my age could.
She threw a dress at me, a red, flowing gown with black trim,
muttering about the hard work that went into Dalí's paintings,
how useless I was, and how it should have been her image on
the canvas, not mine. I narrowly managed to dodge the pair of
shoes she threw at me. "This job is gravy for you and you want to
muck it up by sleeping all day." She began to mutter something
about it being one of the few times she let Dalí have his way.

"That's not true, Gala. This job is important to me."

She pulled up the shade to my window and blinding light
flooded into the room.

The light was green.

"Get a load of that," I said. She only nodded, her mouth open
in shock.

By the time I reached the sill, the light had shifted, muted a
little, and it was just sunlight again.

"Did you see where it was coming from?"

She shook her head, and the two of us stood there, staring
down the valley, our eyes searching for whatever could have
made such an alien glow.

"I've seen it before," I confessed. "At night, in the *boschetto*."

She turned to face me. "I told you this place was wrong,"
she said, taking my hands in hers and squeezing them tight, too
tight. "I knew it from the moment I met you that there was

something off, something wrong with you. We should never have brought you here."

I tried to pull away. "There's nothing wrong with me."

"There is. That's why Salvador wants you for this painting, not me. He says you are more surreal than anything he has ever seen." And with that, she let my hands go and the conversation was over.

There was another knock on the door. I went to it, grateful for the interruption. It was Jack.

"Good morning, you beautiful birds! Dalí says it's time to get this show on the road."

Gala went to Jack and linked her arm in his. He waved at me to follow. *"Andiamo."*

I had missed breakfast, but Paolo had been thoughtful enough to save me a napkin with a cream-filled *cornetto*. Ignazio was absent, which I was both relieved and frustrated by—I wanted to confirm that he would be retrieving Lillian from the train station in Attigliano.

Dalí seemed particularly delighted to see me that morning. "My beautiful Proserpina, how the sun shines on your hair! Today we will fashion you a crown of laurel leaves. This dress, it becomes you. We will leave it on. You'll hold a pomegranate in your hand. YOU! You are the goddess of the Underworld today. You are the embodiment of Pluto's love and desire." He continued on, raving about Cerberus and Mercury and Ceres, and I quickly lost track of all the gods and monsters he named.

It was chilly in the *boschetto*, and I was grateful Dalí let me keep my clothes on, but my thoughts were fixed on the pomegranate he had with him. A whole fruit in my hands was fine with me; I just hoped there were no plans to cut it open. In the end, Dalí decided that I would sit upright, my feet on the ground, my back against the bench. The stone goddess would surround me while I sat in her arms, the fruit in my hands, a laurel crown that Gala had fashioned on my head. This position wasn't nearly as comfortable as lying down, but at least I wouldn't be at risk of falling asleep and would be more aware of my surroundings.

Dalí was in a good mood, and Gala, too, was in fine spirits that morning. The two regaled us with stories of their travels to London, Paris, and New York.

"Tell them about when you nearly died at the International Surrealist Exhibition in London," Gala instructed her husband.

Dalí set aside his paints and told us that in 1936, as part of the surrealist demonstrations, the opening talk was given by the poet Dylan Thomas, who was dressed entirely in green, and he offered teacups full of boiled string to everyone present. "Do you like it weak or strong?" he asked. While the crowd was tittering about this bizarre event, Dalí entered the hall with two wolfhounds on leashes in one hand and a pool cue in the other. But apparently, he was also wearing a deep-sea diving suit. "It was hot, but I did not care. It was a quest into the depths of the human subconscious!"

"And it was hermetically sealed," Gala explained.

Dalí rose from his seat and began to demonstrate. "Not long into my lecture on the sublime nature of diving into the subconscious mind, I began to feel faint, so I waved my arms for help. But the audience did not believe me! I was pounding on my helmet, staggering, but everyone thought this was part of the show. No one came to my aid until I finally fell upon the ground, and Gala, my Gravida, saved me."

Gala laughed. "I did save him. When he began flailing about on the floor, I knew something was very wrong. But imagine, it was a crowd of artists, none of whom had ever been within five meters of a diving suit. We tried to get the helmet off but couldn't figure out how to unbolt it. Finally, I pried it off with his pool cue."

"So, what happened?" Jack asked, amused.

"I finished my lecture. It was not my time to die." Dalí stared at me, his eyes bulging as though there was something in those words I should understand. I held his gaze until he finally picked up his brushes and began to paint again.

Eventually Jack, Gala, and Paolo became bored and went on a walk around the *boschetto*. Dalí painted me in silence. He didn't even open his mouth to complain when Orpheus jumped up on the bench and settled himself into my lap. I cradled him in my arms, holding the pomegranate out in front of him, and he reached out a paw and patted my hand three times. I took one hand off the pomegranate to pet him, and he seemed to settle down. But as soon as I took up the fruit once more, he again patted my arm three times.

"What are you trying to tell me, little kitty?" I whispered. He looked at me and blinked, quite deliberately, three times. I was so surprised I almost dropped the pomegranate.

But Orpheus wasn't the only one trying to warn me about three things. The ghost in the fire and the ghost in my room had both raised three fingers in the air. "Three what? Why is that number significant?" I whispered to him, as if the cat could respond.

Just then, a turtledove came to rest on one of Proserpina's outstretched arms. I expected Orpheus to attack the bird, but to my surprise, he ran off into the bushes instead. The dove watched the beast disappear into the garden before taking flight and disappearing among the statues.

"Did you see that?" I asked Dalí.

"A cat and a dove?" he asked. "*Sì. Madre natura* works in mysterious ways."

I sighed. To him, nothing was as strange as what he saw with his mind's eye.

A little past noon, Gala came down the stairs into the hippodrome and bade us come for lunch. Dalí obliged her with a kiss and set his brushes aside. When he took the pomegranate from my hand, I was glad.

"Julia, that dress becomes you," Ignazio commented, flashing me a smile when he saw me coming up the path.

Crimson heat rose to my cheeks. "Thank you," I managed, still unnerved from my dream encounter with him the night before. I drew upon what courage I could. "Signor, you are picking up my friend Lillian today, right?"

Ignazio nodded. "My driver will leave for Attigliano this afternoon. She will be here in time for dinner."

I breathed a sigh of relief. "Thank you."

"Anything for you, signorina."

I didn't dare look at him, unable to stop thinking about his hands upon me. Surely it had been a dream, but it didn't feel like a dream. I hardly dared to admit to myself how much I wanted his touch again.

Turning away from him, I went into the *orco*'s mouth. I sat next to Paolo and tried to cleanse my mind by focusing on Lillian's arrival. My friend would be here soon, and if I knew Lillian, she wouldn't put up with any shenanigans, ghosts, or whatever Ignazio was. Gala, I was pretty sure, would hate her. For the first time in days, I was filled with hope.

But that feeling didn't last long. The *peperino* table had been laid with simple fare, salads, meatballs, and *bruschetta*. Dalí took the liberty of making a plate for me, but my heart sank when I saw that pomegranate seeds dotted every dish he'd served me. Rejecting his offering, I took a hunk of bread, slathered it with butter, topped it with some sliced figs, and decided that would be my lunch. I wasn't going to ingest another seed of my own volition.

"You need to eat more, my goddess." Dalí deposited a *bruschetta* with ricotta, olive oil, and a pomegranate seed on my plate. "We have a long afternoon ahead of us, and you must keep up your strength."

"I'm not that hungry," I said, feeling Ignazio's eyes boring into me. He stared at me so intensely that I thought he might burn a hole through me. It was as though he was trying to will me to eat the food Dalí had proffered. I smiled awkwardly at him, then turned back to my piece of bread, heat rising to my cheeks.

"I'll have it," Paolo said, plucking the *bruschetta* off my plate.

It was an impolite gesture, one that caused Ignazio to turn on his heel and leave the *orco*, but it made me want to hug the cameraman.

"Why did you do that again? You should have eaten it," Gala scolded me once Ignazio was out of sight. "You are always insulting our host."

I didn't even bother to answer her, and Dalí happily filled the silence gabbing away about how, as an adolescent, he would regularly throw himself from the top of the stairs at school for attention. When I'd had my fill of both bread and Dalí's narcissism, I excused myself by saying I was going for a walk. Jack rose to join me, but Gala's hand on his arm stopped him in his tracks. When Paolo also moved to follow, I waved him back to his seat as well. I wanted to be alone, away from them all, to try to make sense of my thoughts.

I headed toward Proserpina's bench, but instead of taking the fork back to the hippodrome, I went right, past a few lesser statues, until I reached the well-worn ram of Aries. Patting its snout, I wondered about the artist who had fashioned all these creatures, when a flock of turtledoves swarmed above me, their wings making a deafening sound. They came to rest on the path, their sonorous coos filling the *boschetto*. Then the flock began to walk away from me, their gray heads bobbing, the orange on their wings bright in the sunlight. They moved together, like one living organism, with purpose. I couldn't help but follow them.

They approached the statue of Ceres. Most pooled around her enormous legs, a few perched themselves on her arms and moss-covered shoulders, and the rest on the edges of the flower basket atop her head. Unease gnawed at my insides as we drew near, a silent warning whispering in the back of my mind. Yet the enchantment of the birds, with their soothing coos and the hypnotic flutter of wings, lured me closer, overshadowing my intuition. When I reached Ceres's feet, buried in the earth, I looked up at her face. She seemed so serene, so sweet, so relaxed.

While I gazed upon her visage, it seemed to come to life, her lips curling into a slight smile, her head turning slowly to look at me. Then her left hand, which rested on her knee, turned upward before my eyes. I was too entranced to be afraid. The forest around me was filled with the sound of the turtledoves. Their wings brushed against my legs and my arms, their feathers soft and warm. A strange force compelled me. I wanted to take her hand, to hold my body against hers, to feel the stone turn to flesh and wrap me in her comfort.

I reached my hand toward her massive hand, and as I brushed against her index finger, the bushes around the statue burst into flames, causing the turtledoves to fly upward in a cacophonous swirl. With a scream, I spun around, relieved to see the way behind me was clear. Orpheus stood just beyond the fire, mewing at me. I ran toward him, and he led me away from the flames to the clearing beyond the *orco*. And when I looked back at the statue of Ceres, it was stoic. There was nothing—no smoke, no fire, no turtledoves, no evidence to suggest that anything I'd just witnessed had actually occurred.

My heart in my throat, I hurried back to the Mouth of Hell but found that my companions were no longer there. I was baffled by their absence—how did they not see all the doves? The statue of Ceres was visible from the opening of the *orco*. They were probably waiting for me at Proserpina's bench, Dalí impatient for my return, and Gala ready to dock my pay. The weight of the last few days crushed down upon me. I entered the *orco*, sat down at the stone table that was its tongue, and cried.

When I finally pulled myself together and returned to

Proserpina's bench, only Dalí and Paolo were there, and while I was sure they could see I had been crying, neither of them dared to ask why. Dalí arranged me for the sitting, but I barely registered him moving my arms and hands. I was numb and empty inside. Only when he placed the pomegranate in my hands did I feel a spark of emotion rise within me. I repressed the urge to hurl it to the other end of the hippodrome. If I managed to finish out the week, I vowed I would never touch another pomegranate so long as I lived.

Dalí let me look at the canvas when we were done for the day. It was different from the piece he'd painted the night before. In this scene, I sat on a bench at the edge of a vast field, staring off into the distance, my golden locks framing my face, the blue sky beyond, with dark clouds impinging on whiter ones. The pomegranate in my hand had uneven jade and ruby stones embedded in its side, and its crown had been made into jeweled points. It was hardly complete, but it was already breathtaking. I thought of Gala's words—how Dalí wanted me because I was so surreal—yet I was the least surreal thing in the painting. I looked as I should, I thought. It was everything else around me that was wrong.

14

I was overjoyed to find Lillian waiting for me at the *palazzo*. Seeing her gave me the jolt of determination I had lost earlier when I cried in the Hell mouth. With my friend by my side, I would be able to see the week through, I was sure of it.

"Lily!" I threw myself into her arms and buried my face into her shoulder. She hugged me tight.

Gala cleared her throat behind me. My heart sank. Dalí must not have told her Lillian was coming. I let my friend go and turned to face Gala.

"This is Lillian?" Dalí asked, striding forward before I could make the introduction. He took Lillian in his arms as though she were his dancing partner and twirled her around.

Gala looked like she might whip a knife out and stab one of us.

Lillian gave Gala a broad grin and went to her. She grasped both of Gala's hands in hers and gripped them tightly. "I am honored to meet you, Signora Dalí. I have heard so much about you."

Gala did not look pleased by Lillian's bold behavior. "I've heard nothing about you," she barked, withdrawing her hands.

Lillian wasn't deterred. "I'm Julia's roommate. She tells me you are an inspiration to her, a woman who knows what she wants in life and isn't afraid to take it."

I had said no such thing, of course. But I had seen Lillian do this before. She was a marvel when it came to smoothing things over, assuaging doubts, and bolstering her friends. I had told her how difficult Gala was, and this was her way of mollifying the Russian. It worked. I glanced at Gala and saw the slightest twitch of pleasure at the edge of her lips.

Ignazio cleared his throat, drawing all our attention in his direction. "Miss Parker, I am pleased that my driver has delivered you to Bomarzo without issue. I have arranged a room for you next to Julia's." He turned to Gala. "Ms. Dalí, I am taking care of Miss Parker's expenses, so please do not concern yourself about that."

Gala huffed but didn't say anything.

Lillian stared at Ignazio, and I knew she recognized him from the brief description I had given her over the phone. "You must be Ignazio. Thank you for putting me up. Julia has told me much about you."

He raised an eyebrow. "Is that so?"

"It is," she said matter-of-factly, linking her arm in mine, a protective gesture.

I thought I saw the hint of a smirk on his face, but it was gone as quickly as it came.

In any case, Dalí had already managed to shift the conversation, rattling on about our impending dinner, and for that, I was grateful. He waved his hand at our host. "I require snails tonight, Ignazio. Snails and armadillos, under the stars, with bats in the sky and monsters in the valley below. Fig-stuffed armadillos. And jasmine for my Gravida."

"Surely, you realize there are no armadillos in Italy," Lillian exclaimed, squeezing my arm. It was the first "Dalínian" thing she'd witnessed.

Dalí guffawed. "There are, but you must know where to look."

"You'll get used to him soon enough," Jack said.

I didn't think it was possible for anyone, save perhaps Gala, to get used to Salvador Dalí, but I laughed as if Jack had just cracked a joke, and as if there was nothing unusual or off-putting about our ringleader. Then I took my friend by the arm and led her away from my strange companions. By the time we reached the top of the staircase my emotions burst forth.

Lillian pulled me into a hug. "Oh, dear heart, stop your tears. It can't be as bad as all that, can it? They don't seem completely terrible."

"Seem! That is the deception here," I cried. "Nothing is as it seems."

As if on cue, Demetra emerged from the library and strode toward us, her eyes fixed upon Lillian. "You." She spit the word as though it were poison.

Lillian tilted her head. "Me? I'm a friend of Julia's."

"You should not be here. You weren't invited."

I stepped forward a pace, placing myself partly in front of my friend. I had an overwhelming desire to protect Lillian. "I invited her."

The old woman shook her head. "That will only end in regret." She pointed down the stairs. "Go. Now. While you still can," she said to Lillian.

I took Lillian's hand and led her past Demetra to my room. When I looked back, the maid had vanished. I pulled Lillian inside and locked the door.

"What an oddball," she said, plopping down on my bed. "She reminds me of the driver that brought me from Attigliano. Maybe they are related. They both have the same strange coldness."

I shrugged. "The servants here are all like that. But that's not even the weirdest thing about this place."

"This place *is* weird. Why would she tell me that I should not be here?"

"She's said other weird things to me too."

I gave Lillian the lowdown. "And Gala is also always telling me that I'm somehow 'not right,' that I'm 'out of place,' that something is wrong with me, and that they shouldn't have brought me here."

Lillian's eyes grew wide. "That makes no sense."

"I know. But that's not even that strange. Not compared to everything else that's been happening since I got here."

"Dimmi," she said. "Tell me everything."

I drew her to the love seat in the corner of the room, a rush of relief washing over me. As we sat, I began to unravel the intricacies of the past few days: the ghosts, the eerie green glow emanating from the garden, the moving statues, and the peculiar dinners. I told her a little bit about Dalí's odd fixation on feeding me pomegranate seeds and briefly mentioned the mysterious diary I'd unearthed. I also armed her with information about the artist's generally bizarre mannerisms and Gala's bitchiness so she wouldn't be caught too off guard.

Then, with a hesitant breath, I broached the topic I'd long avoided—my lack of a past. "I've always let you believe I was a New Yorker, through and through," I confessed. "I wish I'd been brave enough to tell you the truth."

Lillian's expression softened. "You know I am always here for you. So tell me, what is the truth?"

I sighed, gathering the fragments of my earliest memories. "The first thing I remember is walking out of the Pantheon, a couple of years past, just after the war ended. I had nothing but the clothes on my back, a purse filled with lire—an amount equivalent to $2,000—and a letter of acceptance for a full-ride scholarship to the *accademia*." The words came out in a rush. I had never told anyone the truth before. "The first person I spoke to was an American woman. She noticed my confusion and asked if I was lost. It was her kindness that led me to the school, where an administrator welcomed me and helped me get settled, and arranged for a doctor to treat my amnesia."

Lillian listened intently. "Damn. It's almost like you just

popped into existence. I know, that's out-there, but wow, what a story."

A chill ran down my spine. I had always felt exactly like that, as though I had literally appeared in the world. But she was right—that was too out-there.

"Wait, how did you get the scholarship?" she asked.

"An anonymous benefactor. The school couldn't tell me anything. I don't think they even knew." A strange sense of relief surged through me at sharing this with her. "None of it has ever made sense. It's like I'm a character from a story, stepping into a world that was somehow prepared for me, yet completely foreign."

Lillian's expression softened, a mix of surprise and understanding. "I have always admired your confidence, Jules. You seemed so...self-assured, so worldly. But there have been moments when little things didn't quite add up."

"Like what?"

"Well, your knowledge of art and history for one. It's as if you have memorized hundreds of books. And you often have a faraway look in your eyes, as if you were searching for something lost."

"I've always felt out of place, Lillian. Like a puzzle piece trying to fit into the wrong picture."

She smiled then, a big happy grin that brightened her eyes. "Do you remember how we met? I mean, the very first time?"

"We met at a gallery opening sponsored by the *accademia*. But tell me what you remember." I didn't want to admit that I wasn't sure if I should trust my memory; everything had become so convoluted and I wasn't sure what to believe.

"I saw that tree and I knew I had to meet you. I asked around and a curator at the show pointed you out to me. You were staring at someone else's painting, some weird, surreal thing I couldn't get into. You seemed so captivated, yet so lost. I remember thinking you were like a character from one of those paintings—enigmatic, mysterious. I told you how much I loved your painting, and after we talked for a few minutes, you said you wanted me to have it. I tried to refuse but you were adamant."

"And that's when I asked if you knew anyone who was looking for a roommate?"

Lillian bobbed her head in affirmation. "That's right. It's so strange you don't remember that. But that's okay. We'll figure this all out." She patted me on the shoulder. "So now you are caught up with our history at least. But really, Jules, you should have told me about your memory."

"I was too embarrassed." While I was glad she knew the truth, the one thing I couldn't bring myself to mention was that I'd slept with Jack. If I told her about that, I'd inevitably tell her about the dreams, about the woman who came to me, and the deep underlying desire I had for Ignazio. I could barely articulate those feelings to myself, much less to someone else, even someone as dear to me as Lillian. "It sounds *pazzo*."

"Well, it's definitely some bad business," Lillian said, shaking her head. "Tell me, you don't really think that you are somehow connected to Persephone—I mean, Proserpina?"

"I don't want to believe it, but with the warnings from the ghosts, and from Orpheus...I don't want to eat another pomegranate seed and find out. Why chance it? I don't want to be the next Julia buried in the garden."

"Well, even if the whole thing seems rather far-fetched, don't you worry. I've got your back, Jules. I'll eat all the pomegranates so you can't."

I hugged her, grateful again beyond measure. "So, you believe me?"

She chuckled. "Let's put it this way. I don't disbelieve you. But there is a lot to get to the bottom of in all this weirdness. Besides, this is better than a Nancy Drew mystery!"

I probably should have expected such a reaction from my friend. She was always up for a challenge.

"There's more," I said, feeling energized by her excitement. "Come, let me show you."

When we reached the library, I was pleased to find Paolo lounging on one of the couches. Lillian blushed when he stood to greet her with kisses upon both cheeks. It hadn't hit me before that moment, but he was exactly Lillian's type.

But we didn't have time for flirting. Anyone could appear at the library door at any moment, and I was determined to show them my find before that happened.

"*Ooo,*" Lillian said as I led them around the library and pointed out the thin golden arrows. She reached out a hand to touch the final arrow in the corner, and again, the hidden door slid back with a whoosh. "Holy moly," she exclaimed as Paolo simultaneously let loose a *"Madonna."*

I shushed them, and we looked down the stairs into the blackness.

"We need a flashlight before we can go down there," Lillian said.

"I have a couple of torches in my camera bags," Paolo offered. I smiled, amused by his use of the British word for *flashlight.*

"Let's check it out tonight after everyone has gone to sleep." Lillian was giddy, like a child excited about going to a birthday party. "Maybe there are secret chambers down there full of fascinating things."

After the episode in the cellar, I was more than a little anxious about exploring this place, but the idea that perhaps I may learn more about the green glow in the *boschetto* bolstered me. I touched the arrow, and we watched the door close before joining the others for dinner.

It was cool on the terrace, but several little fiery lamps around the periphery helped to warm us up. I was surprised to see such a rustic table, given that the rest of the furniture in the *castello* was so opulent. There was no tablecloth. The plates were simple Tuscan majolica, the stemware of thick red glass. The servers looked as if they had just stepped out of a restaurant in Rome. Though I appreciated this bit of normalcy, I was disappointed for Lillian, who had not yet witnessed the wonders of Ignazio's hospitality. But my friend had also not had many extravagant experiences, and she found everything about the meal enchanting, especially the food, which was also more rustic than our previous feasts, featuring deeply traditional Italian foods: potato croquettes, *passatelli* noodles made from breadcrumbs; *zampa burrata*, calf's foot in butter; pappardelle in a rabbit sauce; veal scaloppine; lentils with prosciutto; and plates of roasted white truffles.

"Have you been eating like this all week?" Lillian asked me.

"Better, in fact."

"Impossible. This is literally the best meal I've ever had."

"I see you haven't had many fine meals." Gala sniffed.

Lillian didn't let the woman rile her. "You're right. I've not been part of the glitterati, which is why I appreciate it so much."

"Wait! Where are my snails? My armadillos?" Dalí cried as the waiters brought out the sweet dishes, a bevy of little tastes: cake with pine nuts; *mostaccioli* and *amaretti* cookies; and *zuppa inglese*, a cake from the northern region of Emilia-Romagna made from a unique red liquor called *alkermes*. "Ignazio!"

Our host merely lifted a hand toward the door leading back into the palazzo, and two servers brought forth platters of beautiful marzipans in the shape of snails and armadillos.

Dalí was incensed.

"Forgive me," Ignazio begged, laying a hand on the maestro's shoulder.

The spell that fell upon Dalí was immediate. He relaxed his shoulders and let out a small sigh of satisfaction, lifting one of the miniature armadillos to his mouth.

"Forgiven," he said, closing his eyes in savory bliss.

Lillian pressed her knee against mine, a distinct what-on-earth reaction to the way Dalí had so easily fallen under Ignazio's influence. I was feeling the same. The gesture confirmed what I had already begun to suspect, that Ignazio held a very particular sway here. It wasn't just the magical touches that he brought to every meal. No, the sway he had was over the very people of this place, over my companions. Or at least over Dalí. And certainly, over me.

I downed a glass of wine, hoping to calm my nerves. Did this mean Ignazio could also control me?

The servers set a platter of little, rustic, fava bean–shaped cookies before me. I plucked one from the plate, pleased it didn't look to have anything to do with pomegranates. The exterior was hard, the interior slightly soft, with a slightly sweet orange flavor.

"What are these called?" I asked, intrigued.

"Fave alla Romana o dei morti," Paolo explained. "Roman beans of the dead. They are usually served on All Saints' Day. I don't know why."

Ignazio cast his gaze at me. "The ancient Romans believed that fava beans represented the souls of the dead. They were used as offerings to Proserpina and Pluto to pacify any restless ancestors or spirits in the Underworld."

I averted my eyes and put the cookie down, unnerved.

"How do you know Julia?" Jack asked Lillian.

"I was struck by one of her paintings, a rendering of a tree standing in a pool of bright, cherry-red–colored water, on exhibit at the *accademia* art show. I sought her out at the gallery party to tell her how much I loved it and was shocked when she gave it to me. We got to talking, and she told me she was looking for a roommate. Two weeks later, I moved in."

"I knew right away we would be fast friends," I added for color, despite not recalling any of the moment.

"You are an artist?" Jack asked me. "You haven't mentioned that."

"Yes," I said sheepishly, feeling Dalí's eyes on me and knowing full well how he felt about female artists. "I graduated from the *accademia* last year. I have a small studio in Rome. Still a bit of a starving artist, which is why I model." I tried to sound nonchalant, but Dalí's dismissive words about women painters still stung.

"Modeling will take you farther," Gala sniped.

"What is your medium?" Jack asked.

"Oil, mostly," I said, grateful for his interest. "But I have been working lately with some of the new Magna acrylics, which dry much faster."

"Are you a surrealist?" he asked.

Dalí threw back his head and laughed. "She is a muse, nothing more."

Flames of embarrassment washed over me. I wanted to crawl under the table and hide.

"Julia is a dynamite abstract expressionist." Lillian put her hand on my arm, cool and calming, as she spoke to Jack. "Her paintings are wild and full of color. Viewing them leaves you feeling positively sublime."

Lillian was only standing up for me, but I wished she had kept her mouth shut. I could feel Dalí's irritation rising.

"Isn't it amusing?" Gala interjected, a cold smile playing on her lips as she glanced at Lillian. "How often those who cannot create, promote. Julia, dear, you really ought to surround yourself with people who truly understand art." Her eyes lingered on Lillian, the implication clear.

Gala's words hung in the air like a thick fog, suffocating the conversation. Lillian, however, seemed undeterred, her eyes narrowing as she met Gala's challenge.

"Well, Mrs. Dalí," Lillian began, her voice sweet but with a hint of steel, "I believe that true appreciation of art doesn't require one to create it. Understanding and passion can be found in those who merely witness the beauty, don't you think?"

Gala's smile was fixed, a mask that failed to conceal her irritation. "Darling, you mistake simple admiration for genuine understanding. It's quaint, really, how people like you believe they can comprehend the profound depths of artistic genius."

Lillian's cheeks flushed, but her voice remained steady. "Perhaps, Mrs. Dalí, you mistake pretension for wisdom. Art is a language spoken by many, not just the so-called geniuses."

Dalí glanced between the two women, his eyes dancing with amusement. But Gala's expression had turned frosty, and her reply was clipped. "And yet it's the geniuses who shape the world, while the admirers merely gawk."

"Or exploit," Lillian shot back, her eyes locking on to Gala's. "After all, without those who truly value art for its essence, the geniuses might starve."

The room fell into an uncomfortable silence, the tension palpable. Gala's eyes narrowed further, a challenge in her gaze. But before either woman could continue, Ignazio appeared in the doorway, a glass carafe of golden liquid in his hand.

I interrupted the conversation. "Lillian, our host has the most wonderful concoction you must try." I waved at Ignazio, who came to our table with a dazzling smile. "He says it's from Elysium, and I think he might be right."

Ignazio filled our goblets with the shimmering elixir, then raised his glass. "I propose a toast."

"Yes, a toast!" Dalí cried, jumping to his feet and raising his glass.

"To the power of art to bring people together," Ignazio said, lifting his glass a little higher.

"To art," Jack said enthusiastically, clinking his glass with Dalí's. Gala snarled but brought her glass to meet Jack's.

Ignazio winked at me as we touched glasses, and again, conflict rose within me. Could this man indeed be Pluto...or Hades...or the Devil? Sipping at the wine, I savored the heady scent and each delicious drop on my tongue. I should have warned Lillian to indulge carefully, but I was lost in thought about Ignazio. I couldn't stop thinking of him kneeling at my feet in my bedroom, and I hated myself for turning over the moments of pleasure more than the confusion and terror I felt when he vanished.

Dalí was obviously delighted to have another person to regale with his tales, and he made a grand show of doing whatever he could to shock Lillian. He told us stories of how he pushed a childhood friend off a bridge just to do it and how when he first met Gala he so wanted to impress her that he dyed his armpits blue, then cut them up to be bloody and scabby, before making a paste that smelled like ram manure to smear all over his body.

"Fortunately, he had second thoughts and showered it all off before he came outside." Gala chuckled, the wine clearly having dissipated her anger. "But he wore a pearl necklace and had a red geranium behind his ear."

Lillian nodded politely, smiling and laughing at all the right spots. But I knew my friend, and she was mortified. More than once, she nudged my leg with her hand or her knee. Yet as the evening progressed—and as Dalí poured more of the golden Elysium wine into her goblet—she seemed to relax into the weirdness, even egging Dalí on, teasing Gala, flirting with Paolo.

Dalí had just poured another round when the first crack of thunder sounded, a massive crash of the heavens right above our heads, causing us all to jump in fright. A moment later, the skies lit up bright as a blue-white sun then plunged us back into darkness, releasing a deluge of rain upon our heads. The wind kicked up and blew out the candles and torches that had lit up the terrace. We only had a few feet to run, but by the time we shut the doors behind us, we were drenched. Ignazio arrived a moment later with a servant bearing a pile of towels.

"The night is young," Dalí proclaimed as he toweled off his hair. "It is time for SNAPDRAGON." He said this last word with a grand flourish, elongating the sounds.

Gala clapped her hands together like a little girl. "Yes. How perfect!"

"What is Snapdragon?" I asked.

"Go and change into something dry, then return to the small salon and you'll find out." Gala had never sounded so gleeful.

She took Ignazio by the arm and led him out of the room, giving him some sort of instructions in a low voice.

We trudged upstairs to change. Lillian was disappointed.

"I'm guessing it's probably not the best night to go to the garden," she said to Paolo and me as we headed back downstairs a while later.

Unlike my friend, I was relieved to spend the evening playing Snapdragon, which, it turned out, was a game, usually played on Christmas or, sometimes, on Halloween, that had been popular as far back as the Renaissance. Shakespeare even mentioned it in *The Winter's Tale*—though it had fallen out of favor sometime before the Great War because it was rather dangerous.

"We're going to do what?" Lillian asked, incredulous as Ignazio poured sweet brandy into a shallow dish, just barely covering the fruit therein.

"You will reach into the flames and pluck, with your beautiful hands, a fruit or a nut," Dalí explained.

A growing horror rose within me as I noticed that, in addition to raisins, currants, and figs, the bottom of the dish was laden with pomegranate seeds. How would I avoid snatching one up through a hot flame that could burn me as I tried?

A servant turned off the lights, and we were suddenly doused in a flickering dimness, lit only by a pair of candelabras in different corners of the room.

Ignazio capped the brandy and set it aside. He handed Gala a matchbox, and she gleefully struck a match against its side, then lit the bowl on fire. It glowed blue as the alcohol burned.

"Now we snatch away. The person who eats the most wins," Gala declared. "Ignazio, will you keep track for us?"

He nodded. "Of course, Signora Dalí. I would be happy to track all your fiery snacks." His eyes caught mine, and he winked, then retrieved a pad and pen from the credenza.

"What will we win?" Lillian asked.

"A hundred and fifteen thousand lire," Dalí declared.

"*Dio mio,*" Paolo breathed.

I sucked in a breath and glanced at Lillian. She nodded at me, her eyes wide.

"But," Dalí added with great dramatic flair, "if Gala or I win, you get nothing."

I had the sneaking suspicion that this game had nothing to do with the money—it was merely a convenient way to get me to eat a pomegranate seed.

"And we commence." Dalí clapped his hands together very fast.

Having played the game before, he and Gala did not hesitate to stick their hands in the flaming dish, pluck out fiery fruits and pop them into their mouths. Dalí's morsel was still lit with blue flames, and I couldn't understand how he wasn't worried about his mustache catching fire. Jack and Lillian quickly mastered the game, too, but Paolo and I were more tentative—he because of the fire, me because of the damn seeds.

The first morsel I took was a fig. It was boozy and warm but didn't burn my fingers or my tongue. But, as I was about to grab a second piece, Ignazio tossed something into the flames and the fire flared up gold and bright, causing us all to jump back.

"Just a little salt." He grinned. In the firelight, he looked almost demonic, his mouth in a sly smile, one eyebrow arched, his pale eyes boring into me, making my heart race.

Over and over, our hands danced in and out of the flames. If it weren't for my fear of consuming another pomegranate seed, I think I would have had a wonderful time. The game was dangerous, adventurous, and a tad ridiculous.

Soon I was moving fast, my hand flying into the blue flames. I didn't drop any, trusting that this wouldn't have been a game that families and their children played over the centuries if it was that hazardous. Each time I stuck my hand into the flickering blue, I became more confident that I could avoid the pomegranate seeds.

Until I didn't.

As soon as it hit my tongue, my stomach flipped. I looked up to find Ignazio staring at me, his eyes anticipating what I already knew, and I decided I wasn't going to swallow it. The room was dark, and the atmosphere chaotic. Sure I could get away with hiding the seed, I tucked it under my tongue and went for the next piece. It was an almond. I chewed the nut with my tongue sealed to the bottom of my mouth, the pomegranate seed safely nestled beneath. But Ignazio never took his eyes off me. I had no clue when I would be able to throw away the seed, and I hoped the awkwardness of it being under my tongue when I spoke wouldn't make anyone ask if I was feeling all right.

The fire eventually died down, and the remaining pomegranate seeds and currants sat at the bottom, the almonds, figs, and raisins snapped up by virtue of their size. All eyes turned to Ignazio for the final tally. He gave me yet another long look, and I was positive he knew I'd never swallowed the seed. My cheeks burned with crimson heat. He was going to say something, I was sure of it. He would tell them I cheated. But instead, he turned the notepad around so we could see the scores.

"Julia has won, by one piece over Signora Dalí," he announced. Gala scowled.

Lillian let out a little shout of excitement and gave me a big hug.

"Dang nabbit. I really thought I had that one." Jack snapped his fingers in disappointment.

"Wow," I said, careful to keep my tongue in place. "I can't believe it." It was only a few words, and everyone was talking simultaneously, so they missed the slight shift in my speech.

"What a gas," Lillian exclaimed. "And no one got burned." She sat down next to me and reached for her glass of wine. "A toast to our winner."

"Yes." Ignazio took up the carafe of wine and began refilling our glasses. "It will help wash down what is left of the flames." He was joking, of course, but the look he gave me when he refilled my wine made it clear that he expected me to wash down something more.

I took a sip and spit the pomegranate seed into my glass. Then I set the goblet down in front of Lillian. I nudged her with my knee, then tapped the glass with my finger, hoping she would get the hint before anyone noticed the seed floating in my wine. She did, and she immediately drained my goblet, seed and all.

Just as she set it back down on the table, a massive crack of thunder sounded overhead. It was so loud none of us even realized at first that it was thunder. Instead, we all dropped to the floor to put the table above us, the survival training of the War still so instinctively drilled into us.

From my vantage point on the tiles, I saw Ignazio storming out of the salon. At the door, he turned and gazed down at where we huddled, his eyes catching mine. The anger there set my heart to even more furious pounding. He'd done this, I was suddenly sure. He knew I hadn't eaten the seed, and he'd brought on this storm with his rage.

My ghost—for that was how I had begun to think of her— appeared a few feet away from where Ignazio's stare burned into me. This me wore a gown from the previous century, with an Empire-style waistline and her blond hair piled high upon her head. Like the other ghosts, she held up three fingers. Lightning flashed, briefly illuminating the darkest corners of the room. Then the ghost was gone, winking out at the moment the heavy wooden doors slammed shut behind Ignazio, a simultaneous crack of thunder rattling the windows.

Lillian crawled out from under the table first. She reached a hand down and pulled me out.

"Maybe I'll just stay down here," Gala joked.

Another flash of lightning and the main lights went out, leaving the room once more bathed in the pale flames from the candelabras.

"Then again, maybe I won't," she said, scrambling out from under the table and into Jack's arms.

"Where is Ignazio?" Dalí asked. "IGNAZIO," he bellowed.

I knew our host wasn't going to return. He was absolutely furious with me for thwarting him.

Dalí and Gala exchanged exasperated glances, their irritation palpable as they discussed Ignazio's sudden absence and the premature end of the night's revelries. Gala's voice was tinged with disdain. "This is simply intolerable," she muttered. "Such a lack of decorum, and now the party ends so abruptly."

Jack glanced nervously at Lillian's unsteady form. "Perhaps it's for the best," he suggested. "The storm outside is getting worse, and Lillian seems...quite affected by the wine."

"We should get Lillian back to her room." Paolo gestured toward the candelabras. "Let's take the candles."

I took one, the flame casting a dim, flickering light that barely penetrated the darkness of the palazzo. With the candle in my left hand, I reached out with my right to support Lillian, who leaned heavily against me, the effects of the alcohol increasingly evident. "We need to put you to bed," I told her, motioning to Paolo for help.

We made our way down the hall and up the stairs. The palazzo was creepy enough during the day, but at night, without any interior lighting and a storm raging, it was downright terrifying.

"The thunder and lightning... It's not moving away," Jack said as we reached the top of the landing. "It's just hovering over us."

"This storm is a humdinger!" Lillian yelled, her voice echoing through the palazzo between the claps of thunder. She was very drunk, and Paolo had his hands full keeping her upright.

Gala swept past us, her voice sharp. "Enough of this. Salvador, Jack, come with me. This night has lost its charm."

"Lemmee just sit on down here," Lillian slurred as their figures made their way along the hall, toward the safety of Dalí's room. She started to slide down the wall.

"No, no, Lillian, my room is just up ahead. You can sit there." I struggled to keep the candle steady, its light flickering as I helped Paolo lift Lillian back to her feet.

"This Paolo guy," she said, poking her finger at his chest.

"He's a dreamboat." She gave him a sloppy kiss on the cheek. "You could... You...you could stay with me tonight."

"No, signorina. Not tonight," he said. "You are adorable, but *troppo alticcia*."

He was being kind. She was downright drunk, not tipsy. "I'm sorry, Paolo." I sighed as he helped me get Lillian into my room and onto the bed. While I wasn't thrilled about my friend's drunken state, I was glad for her company, though she passed out as soon as I took off her shoes and tucked her in, clothes and all.

"This is my fault," I said as we watched her sleep.

Paolo shook his head. "No. I saw how she drank down the wine. She didn't know how powerful it is."

"She only drank it down like that because it was my glass, and I had spit a pomegranate seed into the goblet."

"So, you did have a seed. I wondered how you managed to play the game and not get one," he marveled.

"I think Ignazio knew I didn't eat it. You didn't see the way he looked at me, right before he left in a huff. This might sound ridiculous, but I think he caused this storm. It started at the exact moment that Lillian drank down that seed."

"*Merda,*" Paolo cursed. "I thought this *tempesta* seemed un-natural. But controlling the weather?"

"I know what it sounds like. But I think that's why he didn't come to help us when the lights went out."

"We have seen some strange things, but I feel like that is... how do you say?...a stretch?"

"I hope you are right. I also don't think I won the game, either... I wasn't moving as fast as the rest of you, so how can I have eaten the most? He must have rigged it, but why? But I'm going to share my winnings with you and Lillian. It's only fair."

His laugh was rueful. "Signorina, if you are the one that is right, and Ignazio can control the weather, we have bigger problems. If you make it out of here alive, you deserve all that money."

15

Lillian woke me by opening the curtains and letting the bright sunlight wash over me.

"Let's get the day started, lazybones."

My friend seemed utterly unaffected by the amount of wine she had consumed the night before. What miracle beverage had Ignazio been serving us that no one ever woke with a hangover? I pulled myself out of bed with the realization that it was the only night I had really slept since I had arrived at Palazzo Orsini.

"You sure are chipper this morning," I observed.

"Why wouldn't I be? We are in a beautiful castle, and we have an adventure ahead of us. Plus you are sitting for one of the most important artists in the world. And you just won a handsome sum last night."

I rolled my eyes. "Right. A castle full of ghosts, with a host trying to kill me with pomegranate seeds, and an artist whose stingy bitch of a wife is running the show."

She sobered and pulled me up by the hand. "Jules, we'll figure this all out. I promise. Maybe Ignazio isn't as terrible as you think. He seems like a nice enough guy."

I stared at her, incredulous. "You don't believe me?"

She hugged me. "I do! I promise I do. I just feel like there is so much we don't know yet. Though you are right about one thing—Gala's pretty awful."

That got me to crack a smile. "She really is."

"Let's get going. I want to see this weird garden. And tonight, we're definitely going down into that passage." Her eyes were bright with anticipation.

"Now I see where this is going," I teased. "You just want to spend some time with Paolo in the dark."

"Ha! So what if I do?" She threw a pillow at me, and we made our way down to breakfast, laughing.

The day was beautiful, and despite the cool air, it was by far the best weather we had experienced since our arrival. Ignazio was absent for breakfast, so it was Minos who drove us to the *boschetto.*

"Where is Ignazio?" Gala inquired, a note of irritation in her voice. Minos merely shrugged and retreated to the cab of the truck.

"He's clearly mute," Gala scoffed, rolling her eyes as we started on our way. "No man is that silent."

"None of the servants talk," Paolo pointed out.

That wasn't entirely true. Demetra had spoken to Lillian and me, but neither of us saw fit to challenge his assertion.

"They are well trained," Dalí announced with a self-satisfied air, a hint of pleasure in his eyes. "Just as they should be. Seen and not heard."

Lillian's expression tightened, and I could almost feel her biting back a retort. She glanced at Gala, then looked away, her face betraying her distaste. Though outspoken, thankfully, she seemed to understand that challenging Dalí in that moment would be futile.

Jack carried a duffel bag I had never seen before over his shoulder, and he smirked when I asked him what was in it.

"This bag here is full of wonderful things. Something I suspect you might greatly appreciate today." He snorted with laughter.

"What sort of things?"

"Towels."

"Towels?" I parroted, not understanding.

He winked at me. "You'll see."

"I'm not sure I like the sound of this."

Jack only gave me a knowing smile and helped me into the back of the truck.

After entering the *boschetto*, Dalí forced us to make a quick detour to show off Proteus Glaucus and his wide toothy mouth to Lillian, who the artist seemed to have taken a liking to. Gala, visibly irritated, stomped off with Jack and Paolo to set up for the sitting.

Lillian immediately went up to the sea god and sat in his wide mouth on one of his bottom teeth. "So, who is this funny monster?"

"Proteus Glaucus—a tale of transformation, of becoming something other than what one was born to be." Dalí waved his cane in the air as he talked.

Lillian looked intrigued. "What do you mean?"

I explained about Glaucus and the story of the Scylla.

"That doesn't sound like any sort of transformation that I would want," Lillian said.

Dalí's eyes twinkled. "Transformation is the essence of art, my dear. The artist transforms the mundane into the sublime. Even the muse undergoes a transformation, from mere mortal to eternal inspiration." He gestured at me with his cane. "Now, my little muse, it is time for you to inspire."

He abruptly turned away from us and strode down the path. I

had curled my fists into angry balls, and with a big sigh, I forced myself to relax them.

Lillian knew me well. "Don't listen to him, Jules. He lives in a world of his own imagination, not reality. Come on, let's go. This will all be over before you know it."

We followed after Dalí, and with each step I willed myself to be calm.

When we caught up, he was with the others near the whale in the bubbling brook, the turtle, and the empty Pegasus fountain.

"When you said it was a forest of monsters, I wasn't sure what to expect," Lillian said as we neared. "But jeepers, this is wild."

"I'll show you around, Signorina Parker," Paolo offered, sounding eager. "Maestro Dalí will be painting for a long while and there will be time."

"I'd like that," Lillian said with a wide smile.

Jack and Gala were helping Dalí set up his easel so it was facing the Pegasus fountain. It was a strange structure, with a raised, hollow dais, upon which a rearing Pegasus was striking a hoof against a pile of rocks. The Pegasus wasn't that big, certainly not the size of a regular horse.

Gala was standing in the shallow, moss-covered basin of the fountain. "Over here," she instructed. *"Le temps, c'est de l'argent."*

Time is money. I hated her obsession with the latter. But I now understood why it had long been said that she was the reason Dalí was famous. His head was in the clouds; her feet were down on earth. At least she extended a hand to help me up.

Once I was standing inside the basin, Gala immediately started to unbutton my shirt. I shooed her away. "I can do it."

She stood back. "Then do it. We haven't got all day."

"My Gravida, don't pester the *modelo*."

Gala gave her husband a withering look. "If I didn't pester these people, nothing would get done. We'd waste half the day."

"She will model, I will paint. If it takes a little time for that to happen, what does it matter?"

Gala stood on the edge of the basin and waved Jack over to help her down. "The longer you take to paint, the fewer paintings you have finished and the less money we have," she said as he placed her on the ground.

Dalí waved a dismissive hand. "What is money compared to enjoying the moment and readying ourselves for the eternal glory of art?"

"Money is what keeps you in paints and me in furs," Gala retorted.

Jack, sensing the tension, tried to defuse the situation. "Why don't we all take a deep breath? The setting is perfect, the light is just right. And Julia isn't dawdling..." he said, pointing to me. I had just taken off my skirt and tossed it to Lillian. "Don't worry about them. Come with me. I found a certain spot in the garden I want to show you."

Before leaving with Jack, Gala went to her husband and said something I couldn't hear but that seemed like a reprimand. He only harrumphed and began mixing his paints.

I was to stand for this session, which did not delight me in the slightest. It would be much colder with the air flowing around me, and I was bound to be tired standing in one position for so long. Dalí instructed me to raise my hands high toward the mountain of rocks upon which Pegasus was striking its hoof, releasing the waters of the Hippocrene—the inspiration for the Muses. The idea was that I would act as though I were catching flowing water, but when I protested that it would be hard to keep my arms above my head for long, he acquiesced. I could rest my hands on the rocks, but from time to time Dalí would instruct me to hold the pose.

I suspected it would be a long, cold morning.

When Dalí began painting, Lillian took Paolo up on his offer to show her the garden.

"Why am I posed this way?" I asked, once we were alone. "Your work is so visionary. How does your model help you when what you paint is so surreal?" My hope was to engage his artistic pride and have him teach me something...anything.

Dalí paused. "What a perfect question for this perfect painting. You are standing in the font of the Muses. As Pegasus rears his mighty hooves to strike against the rocks of Mount Helicon, releasing the waters of the Hippocrene, you become more than a model. You transform from a beautiful woman into a Muse. Today you are standing beneath the flowing font of inspiration. You are the one to light the divine spark of my art on this glorious day. Bask in the sunlight, in the water flowing over you, in the gift you give to the world!"

This did nothing to help me understand how he painted. I tried a different tack. "How do you transform my image onto the canvas? What aspects of what you see are most important to you?"

Dalí paused, his brush hovering in the air as he considered my question. "Ah, Proserpina, it is not merely the physical form that I capture. It is the essence, the soul, that I seek to render. Your presence, your energy—they are as crucial as the lines and colors. It's an alchemy of reality and imagination. The key is to look beyond what is visible to the naked eye and capture the intangible aura of the subject."

His words, hinting at a deeper artistic philosophy, intrigued me. "So, it's about capturing more than just the physical appearance? It's about portraying the unseen aspects?"

"Yes, precisely," Dalí responded, his eyes alight with passion. "Each subject, each muse, has an aura, a unique spirit. An artist must learn to see and translate this onto canvas. It is what elevates a painting from a mere portrait to a masterpiece."

I shifted slightly, trying to find a more comfortable position for my hands on the cold rocks. "But how do you capture this aura?"

"It is an intimate duet between artist and the muse, where emotions pirouette and leap into a realm that transcends the physical. The canvas becomes a portal to a world where the tangible and intangible embrace in a passionate tango of colors and forms."

While this still told me nothing, I was encouraged by his response, and decided to ask about the creative process from a more personal angle. "But what if the muse wants to be the one holding the brush? What if she wants to create, not just inspire creation?"

Dalí had turned back to his canvas. "That is not the role of the muse. The muse is the mirror that reflects the artist's genius." He sounded irritated.

A knot tightened in my stomach. "A mirror only shows you what's already there. It doesn't add anything new. But what happens if the muse decides to look into the mirror?"

Dalí paused, lifting his eyes to meet mine. "She sees only illusion, because the muse is eternal, unchanging. She is the constant in a world of variables, the North Star guiding the artist's hand."

I sighed, feeling the weight of centuries of muses who'd been relegated to the background. "Maybe it's time for the North Star to turn comet, charting her own bright, burning course across the heavens." My own aspirations felt like that comet, yearning to blaze a trail of creativity and recognition.

Dalí frowned, considering my words. "My dear Proserpina, your spirit glows with the intensity of a thousand suns. Yet you must understand—the muse is the egg from whence the great artist is hatched. She is the womb-like cocoon where his nascent genius gestates until bursting forth in a rapturous explosion of creative splendor. Without his muse, the poor artist is but a shriveled larva, helpless, mute, and destined to perish in obscurity."

I shook my head, unmoved by his dramatic metaphors. "But the muse contains multitudes, just as the artist does. She, too, deserves the chance to shape her own visions, to give birth to creations made of her essence. Why must she always remain your silent incubator?" My thoughts drifted to my own pieces, hidden away, waiting for some gallery to give them the light of day.

Dalí waved his hands wildly, nearly upsetting his palette. "Because, my dear, the muse must be the gardener patiently tending the seeds! Yours is the soul of the *Mona Lisa*'s smile, eternally serene and endlessly enigmatic. To demand more would rupture the delicate cosmic order that produces true art."

Though he attempted to elevate my role to pacify me, I was still confined to being his muse, not granted any agency as an artist myself. It also dismissed all the women artists who came before me.

I tried a different angle. "You say Gala is your eternal muse. That together you form the divine couple. Yet you deny other women that creative power. Why must Gala be the exception?"

Dalí bristled at my questioning. "It is simple—Gala possesses the ferocious, tenacious spirit of a warrior muse! Other women are content as placid lakes reflecting my brilliance. But Gala's psyche is a snarling whirlpool, threatening to pull me into unknown depths. She commands by refusing to submit—thus she compels me to ever greater heights."

"So no woman can be your equal unless she dominates you? We either idolize you or torment you?" I challenged, feeling a surge of frustration at the narrow path laid out for women in art.

Dalí threw up his hands dramatically. "You fail to grasp the mystical symbiosis between artist and muse. It is a dangerous dance—one wrong step could destroy us both."

I held his gaze firmly. "I think you enjoy standing safely on the pedestal while women remain below. But I dare you to think differently. I believe true inspiration comes when the muse is unbound." My words were bold, but inside, I harbored doubts about my own ability to break free from these constraints.

Dalí's eyes flashed with irritation—he was not accustomed to being challenged so bluntly. He avoided my eyes and went back to painting. I sighed. But after a few minutes, he said, without looking up, "The muse nurtures the artist's spirit. This, too, is art. Do not underestimate your part in all this, Proserpina. Few will ever have so much divine inspiration as you."

He wouldn't say more unless it was to instruct me to lift my hands or turn my face a certain way. My further attempts at conversation were met with stony silence.

After an interminably long, chilly morning standing in the mossy basin, Dalí finally declared that I could lower my arms and put my clothes back on. Our companions had not returned at all during our session and I wondered if I was the only one who had lost their clothes in the course of the morning.

Dalí was quiet as we walked back up the path toward the orco, but when I ventured to ask if it was because he was angry with me, he shook his head and waved me off, indicating he was merely lost in thought.

A meow at my side drew my attention to Orpheus. He looked up at me with his blue eyes and meowed again until I picked him up. He immediately climbed onto my shoulder. Dalí seemed to soften in his presence and he reached up to pet the beast.

The orco was empty, but we heard voices on the hippodrome behind the monster, so we made our way toward Proserpina's bench. A table had been set on the patchy grass that sprawled out between the goddess and the three statues of the siren, mermaid, and Fury.

Three mute servants poured us wine and set dishes before us. I scanned the food but didn't see any pomegranate seeds. Orpheus took up a spot under my chair and his tail swished against my leg as we ate.

Ignazio was nowhere to be seen, probably still fuming over my refusal to down another pomegranate seed. When Gala asked about our host, the waiters ignored her, as though she had not spoken to them at all. Irate, she grasped one of the men by the arm.

"I'm speaking to you," she hissed.

The man, who was about sixty with a head of perfectly coiffed, peppered hair, only stared at her blankly, as if he couldn't quite comprehend what he was looking at. Finally, exasperated, she let his arm go. He turned from her as though nothing had happened.

"What's wrong with these people?" she said, waving her hands at the servants who were making their way up the path toward the entrance, pushing a food cart in front of them.

Dalí seemed unperturbed. He pulled his wife down onto the chair next to him. "They are only doing their jobs, my Gala. Come. Come, eat."

"It is very strange how they act," Lillian agreed. "That was one of the first things I noticed when I arrived."

I knew Lillian was trying to butter up Gala by siding with her, but tacking on the part about her arrival only set Gala further on edge.

"You shouldn't even be here," she screamed at her. "We never invited you." She jumped out of her chair and stepped away from the table. "All of this, it's all wrong. Every last bit of it. You need to go. I want you to leave on the first train tomorrow. Out of our sight."

Lillian's eyes grew wide and her mouth dropped open in shock. None of us could believe what we were hearing.

"If she goes, I'm going with her," I said, putting my napkin down.

Dalí gave a great cry and stood up from the table, his chair knocking over behind him. "No, no, no, my Galarina. You cannot do this. No, no, no, no!"

While the others watched him stagger away from us toward Proserpina's bench at the end of the hippodrome, I was distracted by a grinding sound that emanated from somewhere behind me. I turned to look. The Fury's stony webbed wings were not at her side, but raised, as if in alarm. Her eyes briefly flashed green. Orpheus dashed out from under my table and ran toward the statue, hissing at it. Horrified, I tried to get Lillian's attention, but Dalí's cries had reached a crescendo, filling the garden, and all eyes were upon him. I turned back to the Fury and she was as she always had been, wings lowered, immovable, her stone face passive. Orpheus was walking toward me, tail high in the air.

When Dalí reached the bench, he had collapsed beside Proserpina's stone base. While we could no longer see his face, he continued his demonstrative sobs and moans.

"Go to him, Gala," Jack said softly. "He needs you."

Gala looked stricken, as if torn on what she should do—stand her ground or go to him. Finally, after several more gulping sobs from the artist, she caved and went to comfort her husband, kneeling on the ground beside him, her arm over his shoulder.

I turned back to the Fury. She was as before, cold stone. Orpheus was back under my chair, his tail thumping against my ankle. I wanted to believe I had imagined the whole thing, but I was sure I had not.

"What just happened?" Lillian asked, her voice soft so it wouldn't carry to the couple.

"You mean the Fury?" I ventured, hoping she might have seen it too.

She gave me a quizzical look. "No, with Gala. Why did she say all that?"

"She has wild mood swings," Jack said. "She can be angry and irrational some days."

I was about to say something about Dalí's more demonstrative mood swing when it hit me. "She's going to be even madder when she finds out that there is no train tomorrow."

"I was thinking that," Lillian said. "It only comes once a week."

"Does he do this often?" I asked, looking toward the Dalís.

"Sometimes," Jack said. He reached across the table for a roll and began to butter it. "He has strange, crippling anxiety attacks. I've only seen it a few times. Once a grasshopper landed on his easel and I thought he might literally die of fright. Only Gala can calm him when he gets this way."

Paolo and Jack tucked into their food, but I didn't feel much like eating, and Lillian didn't either. We watched Gala dry Dalí's tears with a handkerchief. Then she pulled him up off the ground.

When they returned, neither of them acknowledged what had just happened. Dalí sat down next to me and raised his glass of wine. "My little goddess, I will paint you in the mouth of the whale this afternoon!"

I wanted to groan, but given all that had happened, I plastered on a smile. Now I knew why Jack had a duffel bag full of towels. At least I'd be nowhere near the Fury.

Ignazio never showed for lunch, and while I didn't end up eating, it seemed as though the meal was blissfully pomegranate seed free. I had a flutter of hope that perhaps it all had been some weird set of circumstances that really amounted to nothing. A hope that I might just end the week as a simple artist's model and then go home, back to our flat in Rome, and to my life, which I mostly liked, as a struggling artist.

The whale was barely a stone's throw from the Pegasus statue, separated only by a thin bubbling brook. I stared at the giant, open-mouthed whale head that jutted up out of the earth next to the stream, as though it was emerging from the sea. The mouth was open stone, hollowed out and lined with thick heavy moss and full of fallen leaves. Jagged teeth framed the top jaw, and a circular eye gazed ever upward. The little stream flowed around the stone head. It wasn't a large body of water, and I could probably reach over it and scramble into the mouth of the whale on my own, but with the moss, it was very possible I could slip and fall into the stream.

Jack noticed my consternation. "Don't worry, I'll help you."

"I'm supposed to sit there?" I asked, pointing at the gaping maw.

Gala made a sound of exasperation. "What were you hired for, Julia?"

"It was merely a question, Gala," I said, trying to keep my tone measured. While she had seemingly acquiesced to her husband's demand that I remain in Bomarzo, I was wary that she might once again change her mind.

Jack stepped forward, offering his hand. "I can carry you over."

"Oh please, Jack. She can manage. It's just a bit of water and stone. She's not crossing the River Styx."

Jack, to his credit, ignored her. He took off his shoes, rolled up his pants, then stepped out into the water. Once he was sure he had solid footing, he reached out to me. I let him take me up into his arms.

Gala called out, "Careful. You wouldn't want to drop her. Though I'm sure she'd make a lovely water nymph—drenched and desperate."

"Very lovely," Jack whispered in a voice only I would hear. "But it would be you making everyone else desperate," he said as he turned to place me in the mouth of the whale.

"Now get out of there," Gala said, not giving Jack another second with me. He let Paolo help pull him back onto land. "Off with the clothes," she called to me. *"Tout de suite."* She clapped her hands at me and stood at the brook's edge, expecting to relieve me of my garments.

I felt like I was on a stage, one where I was completely trapped, surrounded by stone and water. Reluctantly, I removed my clothes, wrapped them in a ball, and relinquished them to Gala's waiting arms. I let her bark posing instructions at me until she was satisfied, my limp body arranged as though I was a prize that had just been snatched up by the whale. I found myself wishing that Orpheus hadn't wandered off after lunch. Having his little warm body against mine would have been a comfort, one I think Dalí might have tolerated.

Everyone stood on the other side of the brook, watching, and I was relieved when Dalí began painting and they grew bored and wandered off once again. I attempted conversation with him, but he was all business and only grunted out short replies. He didn't need to say so, but that afternoon, I was clearly only the muse.

Dalí was so engrossed in his painting that he didn't notice—or care—that my eyelids were growing heavy. The sun was warm on my skin, and the sound of the bubbling brook had a lulling effect. Before I knew it, I had drifted off to sleep, perched precariously in the whale's gaping maw.

In my slumber, I found myself wandering the Sacro Bosco in a different time, the garden vibrant and teeming with life, a tableau from the Renaissance unfurling around me. The air was filled with the sound of lutes and flutes, their melodies intertwining with peals of laughter. Men and women in elaborate Renaissance attire mingled around me, their clothes rich with brocades and velvets, the women's gowns flowing and the men's doublets ornately embroidered.

I was drawn toward a grand feast set under a canopy of lush vines. Tables were laden with sumptuous dishes, reflective of the era's lavish banquets, and around them, people were engaged in spirited conversations, their gestures animated and lively. There, in the midst of it all, was Ignazio. He stood out even in this opulent setting, clad in a finely tailored doublet, his presence commanding yet enigmatic. Our eyes met across the crowd, a moment transcending time. His gaze was intense and familiar. I began to walk toward him when I was jolted awake by a gentle, hot touch on my shoulder.

Blinking against the sunlight, I looked up to see Ignazio standing in the brook. His eyes met mine, and it set my heart to racing. I sat up and wrapped my arms around my knees, both for warmth and to cover up some part of my nakedness. How long had Ignazio been standing there? I looked beyond him and saw Dalí's easel had been packed up and my companions were nowhere to be seen.

"Sleeping on the job, are we?"

A flush of embarrassment surged through me. "I didn't mean to fall asleep. Where is everyone?"

"Lillian and Paolo returned to the palazzo earlier this afternoon. I imagine they intended to come fetch you, but, well…" His mischievous smile said what his words did not. While I loved Lillian and thought it sweet that they had probably shacked up, I was frustrated that they'd left me in this predicament.

"Jack helped Dalí pack up, and Gala asked me to bring you back to the truck. They're waiting for us there." Ignazio leaned over to the other bank, picked up my bundle of clothes, and handed them to me.

After putting them on, I reluctantly sat on the edge of the mossy whale mouth and let him pick me up. I couldn't help but gasp when his heat enveloped me. I was warmed, instantly. As he set me on the opposite bank, I thought I saw steam rising from the water around his legs, but before I could say anything, he had stepped up beside me, taking up a towel Jack had left behind.

I was grateful for his help, but also a bit wary. "Thank you, Ignazio. But where have you been? You missed lunch."

"I had some matters to attend to. I hope my absence didn't cause too much distress."

I couldn't help but think of the pomegranate seeds and the tension that had been building since my arrival. "Your absence was…noticed," I said cautiously.

"Obligations," he said simply, turning to lead the way back to the truck.

We walked in silence for a few moments, the tension palpable but unspoken. I was still unnerved by the Fury lifting her wings. Finally, I ventured, "It's been an unusual day."

"Unusual is a matter of perspective," he said. "Especially in Bomarzo."

He got that right. I didn't know what to respond to that, so said nothing.

After walking for a few moments, he spoke. "I have been impatient with you, Julia. And for that I'm sorry."

I drew in a breath. "Impatient?"

He gave me that enigmatic smile that made him even more alluring.

"Yes, impatient. It was unfair. You deserve better."

I wanted to ask him what he meant but he continued, "I heard Dalí telling Gala about your conversation on art. It seems you have a passion for painting."

I couldn't help but let loose a heavy sigh. "I imagine he was disparaging."

He gave me a sympathetic smile. "Dalí thinks of himself as a supreme being, but I assure you, he's often wrong about many things."

"Yes, he is very dismissive about women being painters," I explained.

"A perfect example. Some of the best painters in the world are women. Do you know of the Venetian painter Giulia Lama?"

I gaped. "You are familiar with Lama? She is one of my favorite painters." Few knew of Lama outside art scholars who studied the late baroque era.

"Yes, very familiar. Her mastery of chiaroscuro was remarkable, and yet she remains largely unrecognized."

I was surprised to find this sort of connection with Ignazio. "It's a challenge, being a woman in the art world, even today."

"I can only imagine. And what of your own work, Julia? I'd be very interested to see how you express yourself on canvas. Is your style similar to Lama's, or do you have a different approach?"

I was taken aback by his interest. "My work is quite different. It's contemporary, exploring themes of identity and transformation. I use a lot of abstract forms and colors."

"A modern approach, then," he said thoughtfully. "I would very much like to see your art. Perhaps it might be displayed in the palazzo. This is a place of myth and transformation after all."

This was the last thing that I expected. "I...I'd be honored," I said, realizing it was true.

We had reached the truck where Gala, Dalí, and Jack were waiting, and I found I was disappointed that the conversation had ended. Ignazio helped me into the truck bed, his hand briefly touching mine as I climbed in. Again that jolt of heat surged through me. "Until later," he said, his voice neutral but his eyes holding a glint of something unreadable.

On the return, as we bumped along, my mind turned over Ignazio's words. Then it hit me. He had said he was *very famil-iar* with Lama.

"Are you all right?" Jack asked, startling me out of my thoughts.

"Yes, I am, thank you."

But I wasn't. I was too busy thinking about the painter, whose name was *Giulia*.

16

I found Lillian alone in her room. She opened the door to let me in, then returned to the vanity to continue reapplying her makeup. Her hair was slightly disheveled, and she had a dreamy look on her face.

"I was beginning to think you'd been swallowed by one of Bomarzo's monsters," I said, adopting a playful tone to mask my underlying frustration.

Lillian looked at me in the mirror. "Oh, Jules, you won't believe the afternoon I've had. Paolo is just…incredible."

"That's wonderful. I'm happy for you."

My friend knew me too well. "But? What's wrong?"

I sighed. "You do realize you left me alone in the garden, right?"

Her eyes widened. "Oh god, I didn't even think… I'm so sorry, Jules. We lost track of time."

"It's fine, really. I fell asleep. But guess who woke me up?"

"Oh no. Ignazio?" She set down her box of mascara and turned to me. "What happened?"

"Fortunately, nothing. But it was…odd. He's been absent all

day, and then he suddenly appeared when everyone else was gone."

I explained about his weird apology and his familiarity with Giulia Lama.

"But he didn't hurt you?"

"No, he helped me out of the whale's mouth. Then we walked back to the truck."

Lillian came to me and enveloped me in a hug. "Thank god. I'm really sorry, Jules. It wasn't intentional, I promise. Paolo and I just got carried away."

"I get it, Lil. New love is intoxicating. Just…maybe next time, set an alarm?"

Lillian laughed. "Deal. So, what's on the agenda for tonight?"

"I'm not sure. But we're supposed to be ready in an hour."

When Ignazio had dropped us off, he had exchanged a cryptic glance with Dalí before the two of them headed toward the kitchen. "Dinner will be at six," Ignazio had said in a loud voice without looking back at us. I could only imagine what kind of Dalínian spectacle awaited us—and dread how many pomegranate seeds I would see on each plate.

My expectations about dinner were not only met but exceeded when Lillian and I stepped into the grand hall. Dalí stood with Ignazio near the crackling fireplace, the former resplendent in a tailored black suit and flamboyant brooch in the shape of a distorted eye. His cravat was a swirl of colors that only Salvador Dalí could pull off. Ignazio contrasted in a deep burgundy velvet blazer and charcoal trousers, a striking silver-and-ruby ring glinting on his finger.

Four circular tables graced the corners of the room, each draped in a sumptuous tablecloth that seemed to embody an element: deep oceanic blue for water, a rich, loamy brown for earth, a pristine white, evoking the lightness of air, and a blazing red that practically smoldered for fire. Our companions had already been seated at the blue table and were making small talk.

But what truly captured my attention was the centerpiece in the middle of the room—a butter sculpture, intricately carved. It was a breathtaking rendition of the Pegasus statue, complete with cascading buttery water flowing over rocks. And there, at the base of the sculpture, was a figure unmistakably modeled after me, hands outstretched as if to catch the stream of inspiration flowing from above.

I gaped. A sculpture like that had to have taken the better part of a day to create and I had only left those rocks behind a few hours past. "How did you...?"

Dalí shushed me with a theatrical flourish. "The muse quickens the hand, little goddess. All is possible with such divine inspiration. Shall we begin?" He gestured toward the first table where everyone was seated. "Tonight we dine through the elements, and we start with Water—the realm of emotion."

He sat next to me, and Lillian took a seat on my other side, next to Paolo. Gala was engaged in some deep conversation with Jack about Americans and their love of ice in every drink, and how strange the idea of cold, sweetened tea was. I, too, had no love for iced tea, and normally, I would have defended Gala's position, but her anger that afternoon had me on edge, so I kept my thoughts to myself. Ignazio stood near the kitchen entrance, his eyes meeting mine briefly as he oversaw the blue-suited servants carrying trays of lobster bisque with saffron. He gave me a knowing smile, which set my heart to pounding.

As I expected, a single pomegranate seed floated atop the bisque, a vibrant red against the orange hue of the soup. Dalí caught my eye and gestured toward the seed with a subtle nod, but I chose to leave it untouched, swirling it around with my spoon instead.

"The pomegranate seed—a symbol of binding, of commitment," Dalí mused, watching my hesitation. "I forgive you, darling Proserpina, for now. Tonight you may put your worries and your fears aside. Let us commit only to the experience. To the emotions that water stirs within us."

Put my worries and fears aside? I wasn't sure what he meant by that, but I had no intention of letting my guard down.

The oysters Rockefeller were next, each one a tiny universe of flavor, nestled in its shell. The cured sardines offered a salty contrast, perfectly complemented by the rye bread. The watercress-and-orange salad was a refreshing palate cleanser, preparing us for the courses yet to come. Each dish was a work of art, presented with the same meticulous attention to detail that Dalí applied to his paintings.

As we finished the water course, I couldn't help but feel a sense of anxiety building, like the rising tide. Despite Dalí's advice, I wasn't fond of the emotions that this course, or any of the upcoming courses, might bring.

Ignazio appeared with a decanter of Elysium wine. A few sips of the *digestivo*, and the heaviness of the first course seemed to lift, making room for what was to come.

The plates were removed, and we were ushered to the next table. Jack made an attempt to sit next to me, but Gala wouldn't hear of it. She swatted him on the shoulder, and he gave me a sheepish smile as he stood to switch chairs.

Ignazio's resonant voice rang out across the room. "From the depths of emotion, we rise to Earth, the grounding reality that holds us." He clapped his hands and the servers in earthy brown-and-green attire returned. Much like at the magnificent dinner inspired by the *Hypnerotomachia*, the servers seemed to be changing their dress for every course. A hearty venison stew was the centerpiece, its rich aroma filling the room. It was accompanied by roasted chestnuts, petite glasses of potato-and-leek soup, and a platter of roasted beets, turnips, and carrots. My stomach turned when I saw the root vegetables were dressed in a rich pomegranate sauce.

"Just say no," Lillian whispered to me. "They can't make you eat it."

"I know, but I make everyone so angry."

She squeezed my hand. "Let them be angry. I'll stand with you if they are."

Gala threw a piece of bread at us. "What are you gossiping about? Don't be rude!"

I expected Lillian to retort something about the rudeness of throwing food, but she wisely refrained. "Girl problems," she said instead, giving Gala a knowing eye. "You understand."

Gala pursed her lips but only nodded her head. I pressed my leg against Lillian's, a silent laugh between us.

A server moved to spoon the sauced vegetables onto my plate, but remembering how they ignored my refusals in the past, this time I blocked the attempt with my hand. He hesitated, spoon hovering uncertainly. A sharp clap from Ignazio broke the tension, and the server returned the spoon to the platter. Ignazio offered me a knowing smile, as if granting an unspoken favor. Relief washed over me, but it was tinged with a sense of distrust. His smile, while seemingly generous, left me wondering what he truly had in store for the evening.

At the end of the Earth course, Dalí instructed us to stand and make our way to the table that represented Air.

"At the conclusion of Earth's grounding embrace, we take wing," Dalí said. "Let us ascend to the realm of Air, where the zephyrs of freedom dance with the breath of life itself! A place where the imagination soars and the soul is unshackled. Air, where the molecules of inspiration collide with the atoms of audacity. Where the very air we breathe is laced with the intoxicating perfume of anarchy and the ozone of original thought. Prepare yourselves, for tonight we dine on the very essence of liberation. It may leave you breathless."

"So, tell me again, what does this table represent?" Jack laughed.

"FREEDOM! FREEDOM!" The artist lifted his hands to the sky.

Dalí's words hung in the air, filling the room with a sense of exhilaration. But as I took my seat, I couldn't help but feel a dissonance between his poetic description of freedom and my own reality. Here I was, surrounded by people who seemed to live life on their own terms, unshackled by societal norms or expectations. And yet I was anything but free. The weight of the pomegranate seeds, the lingering gaze of Ignazio, the unspoken tensions—they all felt like invisible threads, pulling me in directions I wasn't sure I wanted to go. Freedom? I could hardly imagine it.

The servers, now dressed in flowing white, brought in the next course, highlighted by a goat-cheese-and-spinach soufflé that seemed to defy gravity. It was accompanied by puff pastry twists with herbs, mini quiches with asparagus and Gruyère, and miniature angel food cakes, each one dotted with three damned ruby seeds.

As soon as the cake landed on my plate, Lillian's hand snatched it and popped it into her mouth. *"Delizioso,"* she declared. "So good I needed two."

Next to me, Dalí grunted but stuck his fork into a quiche without further comment. I didn't dare look at Ignazio. I was glad when the server didn't attempt to replace it with another cake.

After another dose of Elysium wine, Ignazio brought us to the final table. His voice was like a smoldering ember, heating the room with its intensity. "Fire is the catalyst, the transformative force that turns potential into reality. Tonight we feast on the very essence of desire, the heat that fuels our most primal instincts."

As we took our seats, I couldn't help but feel the tension in the room rise like the temperature of a flame. The table was set ablaze with reds and oranges, and the centerpiece was a bowl of actual fire, flickering and dancing in a mesmerizing pattern.

The servers, now dressed in fiery hues, brought out the Baked Alaska, setting it in the middle of the table. With a flourish, Ignazio produced a match and set the dessert afire. The room gasped as the fire danced atop the dish, casting flickering shadows on everyone's faces.

"At last! A dish as contradictory as love itself—cold and hot, sweet and fiery," Dalí exclaimed.

Gala leaned over to Jack and whispered something in his ear, loud enough for me to hear. "Darling, I expect a performance as fiery as this dessert later tonight."

Jack chuckled, his eyes meeting mine for a brief moment. "Oh, don't you worry. I know how to fan the flames of passion."

Ignazio caught my eye as he served the Baked Alaska, his gaze lingering just a moment too long. "I trust you'll find this course…enlightening."

I felt a shiver run down my spine, despite the heat of the room. Ignazio's presence was like a flame I was both drawn to and afraid of getting burned by.

As we moved on to mini churros with cayenne-pepper sugar and the flambéed, spiced poached pears, Dalí steered the conversation toward themes increasingly risqué. He licked the sugar off a churro, then leaned back in his chair, a devilish grin spreading across his face. "Imagine, if you will, as I have witnessed, a night in Paris, where the air is thick with the scent of absinthe and the promise of forbidden pleasures. There, in a dimly lit room adorned with velvet and lace, the boundaries of the flesh are tested. The male organ, that phallic totem of virility, becomes a paintbrush, and the female form, a canvas of voluptuous landscapes, each curve a hill, each crevice a valley. And I, the voyeuristic maestro, orchestrating this symphony of skin and sin, where every moan is a note and every climax a crescendo!"

Lillian's mouth fell open in shock. No one spoke for a moment. Then Gala giggled. "I remember that night." Her hand moved under the table, conspicuously, in Jack's lap. Jack closed his eyes for a moment, reveling in Gala's touch, then abruptly opened them again, fixing them on me. "So, Julia, which element do you find most stirs your passions? Water, Earth, Air, or Fire?"

Caught off guard, I hesitated. "I think I'm still figuring that out."

Ignazio, who had been directing the servers, paused. "Don't be shy, Julia. You are drawn to Fire, are you not?"

The room seemed to hold its breath, waiting for my response. My heart leaped into my throat as Lillian's leg pressed deep into mine.

I thought of Dalí's description of Air. "No, I'm drawn to freedom."

Ignazio nodded. "Then it seems we both want the same thing." He held my gaze. Heat rose to my cheeks.

Lillian came to my rescue. "And what sort of freedom do you want?"

Ignazio's eyes remained locked on to mine as he responded, "The freedom to pursue what sets our souls aflame, without the constraints others may place upon us."

The atmosphere in the room became charged, as if his words had added fuel to an already smoldering fire. I felt both seen and exposed, a paradox that only Ignazio seemed capable of evoking in me.

She pushed harder. "And what, pray tell, are the constraints that have been placed upon you?"

Ignazio's gaze finally broke from mine to meet Lillian's challenging stare. "Constraints are often self-imposed, are they not? Fear, doubt, the weight of expectations—these are the chains we forge for ourselves." His eyes flicked back to me, as if inviting me to break free. "But sometimes, the key to those chains is held by another."

"I wish I had the key to those chains," Gala said, reaching out a hand to run it across Ignazio's arm.

Dalí suddenly stood, knocking over the chair behind him. "Gala, the supreme, divine Gala holds ALL THE KEYS."

Gala laughed and let her husband lean down to kiss her. Ignazio gave me a knowing wink, then returned to directing the servers. What did he mean by someone else holding the key? It certainly wasn't me.

The course ended with a demitasse cup full of spicy hot chocolate, sensuous and smooth. I never wanted the flavors to dissipate, but all too soon the last drop was gone.

"Bravo, Signor Dalí. What a meal," Lillian declared as the last plate was removed.

Jack patted his belly. "I feel so perfectly full. Not too full, just perfectly full. What's next, Dalí?"

The artist raised his walking stick into the air. "My friends, we ascend upon the realm of Quintessence." He charged forward toward the small salon, leaving us to wonder what he meant.

"No seeds," Lillian said to me as we followed Dalí across the immense hall, our footsteps echoing on the stone floor. "They hardly even tried."

I was worried about that. But before I could express my fears to her, we had reached the salon's ornate double doors. With a flourish, Dalí pushed them open.

The salon had been rearranged, and rather than the couches and plush chairs that had been there before, individual chairs were positioned in a circle facing each other. Ignazio stood in the center.

"Welcome to the Quintessence Salon," Ignazio announced, holding out his hands. His eyes met mine for a fleeting moment, and a shiver ran down my spine. "Quintessence, or Aether, is considered the fifth element," he continued. "It's the essence that fills the universe and the celestial sphere. It's the divine breath that gives life to all things. Tonight we gather here to explore our own quintessence, to delve into the mysteries that bind us, both earthly and divine."

Dalí clapped his hands together, drawing our attention back to him. "To celebrate this celestial gathering, we shall engage in a game—one that will reveal our deepest mysteries and dare us to confront our most hidden desires."

He paused, looking at each of us in turn before his gaze settled on Ignazio. "I've asked Ignazio to participate in this game. His role is crucial, for he will be the arbiter of our choices. Are you up for the challenge?"

Ignazio gave the maestro a single nod. "I accept, Dalí. Come, sit. Let the game begin."

My breath caught in my throat.

The chairs bore name tags, clearly designed to prevent us from sitting next to familiar comforts. I found myself between Gala and Paolo, while Ignazio occupied the seat directly across from me—a placement that unsettled me more than if he had been right beside me.

Minos appeared and handed Ignazio a black top hat with a red band. I expected our host to put it upon his head, but instead he drew out a slip of paper. "Jack, this question is for you. A truth you must answer."

Jack grinned. "Fire away."

Ignazio read from the slip. "If you could replace the moon with any object, what would it be?"

Jack answered immediately. "That's an easy one. If I could replace the moon, I'd put up a giant baseball. That way, every night would be a ball game, and we'd all be swinging for the fences."

Gala rolled her eyes. "How very droll, Jack."

"Quintessentially American," Dalí exclaimed, not letting his wife bring down the mood. "Next!" He looked at Ignazio.

Ignazio fixed his gaze on Paolo. "Ready?"

The cameraman laughed. "No. But go ahead."

"You are to compose a poem about the last person you kissed." Ignazio snapped his fingers and Minos presented Paolo with a notepad and a pencil.

Lillian burst out laughing. "This will be good."

Paolo took the implements with a sigh. "I fear I am a terrible poet."

"Even better," Jack said.

While Paolo composed his poem, six servers appeared with glasses of wine. I noticed Ignazio did not partake.

Finally, Paolo looked up. "It's in Italian. *Mi dispiace.*"

"I'll translate," I said. I felt bad for him. His face was red with embarrassment.

He handed me the slip, and I read it aloud:

"*Labbra si incontrano*
In un attimo di magia
Il cuore trepida."

"A little haiku. And now, the translation." I couldn't help but grin when I looked at Lillian. She knew enough Italian to understand the poem and I could see the adoration in her eyes. I would mostly be reading the poem for Jack.

"'Lips meet
In a moment of magic
The heart trembles.'"

Gala's laughter broke the silence. "How utterly sentimental, Paolo. Now, Ignazio, would you be so kind as to draw a question for me?"

Ignazio reached into the hat. "If you could be any mythical creature for one day, which would you choose?"

Gala swirled her wineglass before taking a sip. "An intriguing question. A siren. Imagine the power of captivating anyone with just the sound of your voice."

My mind immediately wandered to the siren statue in the garden, situated at the far end of the hippodrome, opposite Proserpina's bench, next to the Fury whose wings had moved.

The stone figure was a paradox—both hideous and sensual. Her bifurcated, scaly tails were spread wide in place of legs, while her thick, stone-like hair veiled her intimate areas. She was a creature of contradictions, embodying both allure and repulsion. Fitting, I thought.

"Dalí, your turn." Ignazio handed the artist a slip of paper.

Dalí leaned back in his chair and read the slip out loud. "'Pick someone in the room and describe how they would be as a lover, using only metaphors.'"

His eyes twinkled mischievously as they landed on me. "Proserpina! A lover like her would be a surrealist dreamscape, a labyrinth of sensuality where each turn reveals a new wonder. She would be the brush and the canvas, both the muse and the art, a swirling vortex of passion where the boundaries between reality and fantasy blur. She would be the moon pulling the tides of desire, a symphony of ecstasy where each note is a shiver down the spine, each crescendo a climax of soul-shattering intensity. A dalliance with her would be like plunging into a sea of liquid gold, where every touch is alchemy, transforming the mundane into the extraordinary."

I wanted to crawl under my chair and hide. Jack caught my eye and winked at me.

"Damn, Julia. Now even I want to make love to you." Lillian laughed, breaking the tension.

Ignazio had been staring at me throughout Dalí's monologue, and his gaze remained unbroken, even as the room erupted in laughter and playful banter. The intensity of his stare was almost palpable, like a physical touch, and my cheeks heated under the scrutiny. He said nothing, however, and only pulled another slip of paper from the hat and handed it to Lillian.

Lillian's eyes widened as she read it. "'Choose someone to dance with, but the dance must be entirely improvised and as surreal as possible.'"

A mischievous smile spread across her face. "Well, this should be interesting. Paolo, would you do me the honor?"

Paolo grinned and stood, offering his hand. "With pleasure."

The two moved to the center of the room, and for a moment, they simply stood there, staring into each other's eyes as if searching for some unspoken cue. Then, as if struck by the same bolt of inspiration, they began to move.

It was unlike any dance I'd ever seen. Lillian started by mimicking the movements of a marionette, her limbs jerking in exaggerated motions as Paolo pretended to hold invisible strings. He then transformed into a matador, and Lillian became the bull, charging at him only to spin away at the last moment.

The dance evolved, becoming more abstract with each passing second. Lillian suddenly dropped to the floor, curling into a ball and rolling around Paolo, who responded by leaping over her as if jumping over a rolling log. They moved in a series of bizarre, yet oddly harmonious, movements—sometimes mirroring each other, sometimes in stark contrast. All of it was simultaneously mesmerizing and hilarious.

At one point, Lillian stood perfectly still, as if frozen in time, while Paolo circled her, making sweeping gestures as if painting her into existence. Then, in a sudden burst of energy, Lillian sprang to life, pulling Paolo into a series of quick spins before pushing him away, only to pull him back in a magnetic-like force.

As they took their final pose, Lillian bending backward in a dramatic arch with Paolo's hand supporting her, the room erupted into laughter and applause.

Dalí was the first to speak, his eyes shining with delight. "*Bravo! Bravo!* A dance worthy of the surreal. A living canvas."

Lillian and Paolo, still catching their breath, bowed deeply, their eyes meeting for a lingering moment before they returned to their seats. The atmosphere in the room was electric, charged with the energy of their performance. But I only felt dread.

The hat of fate was now down to two choices: mine or Ignazio's.

Ignazio extended the hat toward Dalí, who theatrically plucked a slip of paper from it. He twirled it around in the air, as if casting a spell, before handing it back to Ignazio.

"You must choose one who has not chosen!" Dalí declared, his voice booming in the small room.

A groan escaped my lips. What mortifying task would that slip assign me to perform with Ignazio?

"Don't fret, Julia," Lillian reassured me. "If he decides to toss you into the stratosphere, we'll be here to catch you." Her words were playful, but the underlying message was clear: I wasn't alone, and she would be there to protect me, come what may.

Ignazio read the slip. "'Engage in a staring contest with your chosen partner. The first to blink or look away loses. The winner gets to ask the loser any question they desire, which must be answered truthfully.'"

Oh, dear god, no. Not a staring contest. There was no way I would win this. I caught Lillian's eye, and while she tried to plaster on a smile for me, I could see that she thought the same. But at least he wouldn't be touching me.

Dalí instructed us to position our chairs facing each other, a few feet apart. The group rearranged themselves around us to watch and egg us on.

"*Udachi,*" Gala muttered to me in Russian as she pulled her chair away from mine. "You'll need it."

I didn't need a translator to tell me that she also thought I was about to lose.

I closed my eyes and waited for Dalí to give us the signal. The room fell silent, the tension palpable.

"Begin!"

His shout made me jump and my eyes flew open. Like a moth drawn to a flame, I locked eyes with Ignazio. The iridescent quality of his pale green eyes seemed to shift with the flickering candlelight, casting an almost ethereal glow that was both captivating and unsettling. It was like staring into the soul of a creature not entirely of this world, and the intensity of his gaze made it difficult to look away. His stare pulled me, silently challenging me, daring me to delve deeper, to discover what lay behind those enigmatic eyes. And in that moment, I felt both vulnerable and strangely exhilarated, as if I were standing on the edge of a precipice, teetering between fear and fascination.

Then, suddenly, I plunged into the abyss. My world shifted and went gray, then brightened. I was no longer sitting in that circle in Bomarzo, but instead standing in a chamber unlike any I'd ever seen. It was as if I'd stepped into a realm where the very fabric of reality had been woven with threads of beauty and enigma. The walls were alive with murals that appeared to breathe, their colors vivid yet ethereal, like the hues of a twilight sky. They depicted scenes both celestial and earthly, as if capturing the essence of two realms in one sweeping panorama.

The room was bathed in a soft, otherworldly light emanating from orbs suspended from the ceiling. They glowed with a captured sunlight that felt both distant and intimate, like a cherished memory. The bed before me was a masterpiece, its frame carved from obsidian but adorned with an intricate filigree of silver and gold. The sheets whispered secrets of unimaginable softness, their colors a blend of pomegranate red and the deepest shades of midnight.

Ignazio stood before me, his jacket and tie missing, and his shirt undone. "All of this is up to you," he said.

He stretched out a hand and I could not help but take it. Pulling me forward, he lifted his hands to my face, his eyes never once leaving mine.

"I will ask my question of you now."

The question? My mind was hazy, but it came to me, yes, the question I must answer when I lost the staring contest.

"What is it?" I breathed. I didn't want to talk. I wanted... Dear god, I wanted him. No, no, I didn't. This made no sense. My mind whirled with the contradiction.

"Do you like this?"

His mouth found mine and I closed my eyes.

The room erupted in squeals and groans. Jack's whoop reached me first. "Julia, you barely even tried."

I swallowed hard, trying to make sense of what had just happened—and what was happening around me.

"Absolutely weak," Gala sniped.

"The question," Dalí shouted. "The divine question must be asked."

All eyes turned toward Ignazio.

"I don't need to ask my question," Ignazio said, his voice low but carrying easily in the hushed room. "I already know the answer."

The room seemed to hold its collective breath, as if waiting for a revelation. Ignazio's gaze never wavered, daring me to challenge him, to question what he claimed to know. But I couldn't. Because deep down, a part of me feared he was right—that he did know, and that knowing gave him a power over me I didn't fully understand.

Lillian broke the silence, her voice tinged with a mix of awe and concern. "Well, that was...intense. What's the next dare?"

Ignazio handed the hat to Dalí. "Please, continue on without me. I have duties to attend to."

He left and did not look back.

As the hat of dares and questions began to circulate again, I sank back into my chair, my heart still pounding, my lips still tingling from the dream of his kiss. I was caught in a whirlpool of emotions—desire, confusion, a hint of fear.

The game resumed, the room buzzing with laughter, dares, and the clinking of glasses. But it all felt like background noise, a distant echo that couldn't reach the place where my thoughts were spiraling. I participated, laughed at the right moments, even completed a dare, but my attention was elsewhere. How could Ignazio have evoked such a vivid vision? Was it a trick of the mind, or something more? And if it was more, what did that mean for me? What kind of power did he hold, not just over my thoughts but over my very senses?

As the evening wore on, I felt increasingly disconnected, as if I were floating above the scene, watching but not truly engaged. Finally, Lillian, sensing my detachment, leaned in and whispered, "I think it's time we call it a night."

I nodded, grateful for the escape. Lillian and Paolo accompanied me back to my room, where I explained what had happened during the staring contest. I implored Lillian to stay with me.

"Please. I don't think I should be alone."

Lillian hesitated. I sighed. She had obviously hoped to be with Paolo that night.

"Never mind," I said. "Just go. I'll be okay." Although I wasn't sure I would be.

Lillian gave Paolo a quick but passionate kiss. *"A presto."* See you soon.

"I came here for you, Jules," she said when the door closed. "Of course I'll stay."

She hugged me, and I fell into her, sobbing.

"Only one more day. You can do this," she said, wiping away my tears. "We'll get through this together."

Over her shoulder, the curtains were slightly open, and between them there was a little sliver of light. A green glow. I blinked, and it was gone.

17

In the middle of the night, I woke to find the room shrouded in darkness except for the soft glow of light from the hallway under the door. I reached out instinctively to the other side of the bed, only to find it empty. Lillian was gone. A pang of sadness hit me. Her passions had won out over our friendship, at least for the night. But could I really begrudge her that? Besides, Ignazio seemed perfectly capable of exerting control over me despite me being in the company of others. What use would it have been if Lillian stayed?

I tossed and turned, the sheets tangling around my legs as my mind replayed the evening's events. Ignazio's kiss, the vision he'd conjured, the unsettling mix of desire and apprehension he stirred in me—it all swirled in my thoughts like a tempestuous sea. Sleep remained elusive. But I had to admit, Dalí had ultimately been right. Nothing had harmed me last night. I had not eaten a seed. Though I'd lost myself in a fit of tears on my friend's shoulder, perhaps I had not needed to be so afraid after all.

Finally, as the first rays of dawn began to paint the sky in hues of pink and gold, I heard the door creak open. Lillian tiptoed into the room, her face flushed and her eyes shining with a mix of exhaustion and exhilaration. She caught my eye and gave me a sheepish grin.

"Please don't be mad," she said as she crawled into bed next to me.

"I can never stay mad at you," I replied.

"We have one more hour to sleep," she said, her eyes already closing.

I chuckled. "You mean *you* only have one hour to sleep." But she was already lost in the arms of dreams.

I had thought we might return to Proserpina's bench to paint that day, but Dalí had other plans. Instead, he led us to the strange, exposed tomb we had seen a few days before.

"It's Etruscan," he declared when we arrived, drawing out the word for effect. He said he had asked Ignazio about the tomb. "Nearly three thousand years ago, a body was buried here. Worms devoured the flesh. Eviscerated the organs."

"Thieves probably stole the lid and animals must have taken away the bones," Gala informed us far less dramatically than Dalí had. "Now strip down, Julia, and climb in."

I stared down at the mysterious space. The rock where the grave was carved wasn't big, perhaps eight or nine feet long and four feet wide, mostly buried in the earth. It was so nondescript that it would be easy for any man or beast stumbling across the rock to fall into the little grave. It looked horribly uncomfortable. The burial spot itself was a simple square rectangle carved down about three feet into the rock, with a ridge around the top where a lid must have rested. I wasn't entirely sure my body would fit within it. Jack bent down and began clearing out the dirt and leaves that had collected in the depression.

"Here," Lillian said, recognizing my discomfort. She took off

her long black wool coat, folded it, then leaned into the grave
and arranged it so my backside would have some cushioning.

After removing my clothes and handing Lillian my thin cape,
I sat on the edge of the grave. Despite the intense sun, the stone
was ice-cold, and I did not remain there for long. I lowered myself
into the shallow hole, grateful for the soft warmth of Lillian's coat.

"Excelente," Dalí exclaimed, looking down at me. "Now, to
make you a delight for the worms." And with that, he and Gala
squatted on the edges of the grave and began arranging my body
so I looked as corpse-like as possible, my legs straight, my hands
folded below my breasts. Gala arranged my hair so it curled
slightly against my shoulders.

Dalí reached down and closed my eyes. "Imagine the worms
crawling across your skin, the beetles slicing up your organs
with their pincers."

I opened my eyes. "That is not what I want to imagine while
lying in a grave."

"Shush!" He closed my eyes again, and I tried to lie still, as
still as possible. The coat filled the recessed space beneath me
but did not afford me any pillow, and I wondered how long I
could manage to rest upon the *peperino* before a headache or
neck ache set in. I opened my eyes again when I heard Dalí instructing Jack to set up the easel.

"I told you that you'd have to take off your clothes," Lillian
teased. "I just had no idea it would be so creepy."

"It's definitely creepy," I said. "And cold."

"I'll make sure you get to warm up," she said.

"No, you won't." I laughed. "You'll be too busy warming up
Paolo."

She looked off in his direction and grinned. "Guilty as charged."

Annoyed by the distraction, Dalí shooed her away, but I
reached up to stop her. She took my hand. "Ask Paolo about
Julia's diary," I instructed her. "There must be more to it. The
ghosts pointed me to it for a reason."

She squeezed my hand. "I will. And don't worry, we won't leave the garden," she said as Dalí shouted at me to put my hand down. And then she was gone, and the maestro appeared at the side of the grave to reposition me and close my eyes again. Once he was satisfied with my pose, he placed something in my hands, and I didn't need to open my eyes to know it was a pomegranate.

After quite some time, I was startled by a rustle and a soft coo at the edge of the grave. I opened my eyes and saw a turtle-dove looking down at me, its head cocked in curiosity. A moment later, five more joined, the orange of their wings shining bright in the sunlight.

"Magnificent. How very Dalínian," Dalí whispered so as not to scare them away.

I lifted my head slightly to look at him. A glare and a fast motion of his hand made clear that I was to remain in position. Then his brush began flying across the canvas again.

I laid my head back down, but I didn't want to close my eyes for fear one of the birds might land on me. I tried to soothe myself by listening to the sound of Dalí's brush flying across the canvas again. Still, all I could think about were the birds at the *tempietto* on the day we first came, and the turtledoves that flew into the window the night of the *Hypnerotomachia* dinner. Their presence at the grave wasn't coincidental, of that I was sure. My mind went to Ceres and the immense flock that had surrounded her the day before. Each of the deities had birds they called their own. And while I didn't have my *Bullfinch's Mythology* or a copy of Ovid's *Metamorphoses* to verify this idea, I was confident turtledoves were beloved of the goddess.

I watched the birds through half-closed eyes. They did not leave but continued to stare down into the grave, occasionally pecking at the moss on the edge of the opening. What would happen if they decided to descend upon me? These dark imaginings were worse than what Dalí had suggested. Instead of worms, I pictured the doves ripping out my hair, pecking at my skin, and poking out my eyeballs. Finally, I could take it no more. Sitting up, I waved my arms at the birds, and thankfully, they flew off without incident.

"I need a break," I told Dalí.

"Yes, yes, fine."

"Ignazio is setting up lunch," Jack said from his camp chair nearby. His eyes alighted upon my bare chest.

I pulled Lillian's coat around me and scrambled out of the grave. After I'd dressed, I went to look at Dalí's work. He grunted but sat back to let me see the canvas. It was a sketch in oil and not nearly finished, with half of my body missing, but the heart of it was already there. It was a stark painting, with a dark background and the open grave in its center, my body aglow in the recess of the Etruscan tomb. The pomegranate in my hands had split and the jeweled seeds were ruby bright. I had never imagined myself looking quite so beautiful. But it was me—Dalí hadn't embellished my features with his wild imagination. He had omitted the turtledoves.

"We'll bring the final back to Paris," Gala said to Dalí as she looked over my shoulder. "Rouchard will buy it for a small fortune." I had no idea who Rouchard was, nor did I care, but I couldn't help but wonder if he'd keep it in his private collection or loan it to a museum. Letting my imagination run wild for just a moment, I imagined myself standing before it in a gallery, people milling around, wholly unaware it was me glowing in that grave.

Gala took both her husband and Jack by their arms and led them the short distance to the *orco*, leaving me to follow. But the path they took went past the statue of Ceres, and I wasn't keen on being anywhere near it if I could avoid it. Glancing around, I spotted Paolo and Lillian descending the stairs near Proserpina's bench.

I headed in their direction, though it meant passing the vase where I'd first heard the ghostly whispers. I'd happily subject myself to those over the imposing statue of Ceres, though I was relieved the only audible sound that caught my ear was of Paolo and Lillian chattering away. Lillian's parents had died in an accident when she was a teen in Seattle, and she had come to live in Rome with an aunt. Her Italian was far superior to mine.

"Oh, Jules, Paolo told me all about the diary," she explained when they reached me.

I motioned to her to lower her voice. We could see the *orco* from where we stood, and who knew how the sound might travel. "The acoustics in the *boschetto* are weird," I explained.

But she waved me off and wrapped her arms around me in a bear hug. "The cook that Giulia Orsini mentions... Aid...o..." She looked at Paolo.

"Aidoneus," he said.

"At first, I thought Ignazio might be a descendant of Aidoneus or maybe a reincarnation of him. But what if...?" She paused for dramatic effect.

"What if?" I nodded at her to get on with her thought.

"What if Aidoneus and Ignazio were the same person?"

I had already thought of this, of course, when Paolo had first told me about the mysterious cook. I'd never met anyone like Ignazio, with his mesmerizing eyes, electrifying heat, heady scent, and it gave me the distinct impression he was more than what he appeared to be.

But before I could admit that perhaps my friend was on to something, Dalí interrupted us. "Come! Eat!" He was standing in the Hell mouth, waving to us.

"We don't pay you to dawdle," Gala chimed in.

Lillian rolled her eyes at me but was the first to step in that direction. "This is truly the most incredible thing," she exclaimed as she went up the stairs and into the Mouth of Hell. "To dine inside such a creature—how many can say they have done such a thing?"

I wished I had the same sort of excitement my friend had. But I dreaded every step I took toward the monster. Every time I entered it, something terrible had happened. I hadn't seen Ignazio since the staring contest, and the memory of our encounter lingered in my mind, leaving me unsettled yet yearning, trapped in a whirlwind of emotions I couldn't fully understand and wasn't sure I wanted to. Yet he greeted me with a broad smile, as though nothing had transpired between us.

"Julia, welcome."

I hated myself for the way my body responded to his presence, every fiber gravitating toward him while my mind told me I was utterly foolish for harboring such desire.

"Thanks," I said nervously. The previous night's reprieve from the seeds was unlikely to continue. I wondered what he would do when I refused another pomegranate seed, and what might happen to me if I ate them all. I was damned no matter what I did.

"Mmm, heaven," Lillian murmured as Ignazio described the decadent meal before us: saffron risotto with white truffles, baked scallops in a rich béarnaise sauce, warm pheasant pâté, and fresh oysters, each dotted with a dreaded pomegranate seed. She bit into one of the gold-dusted arancini and, while raving on and on about the succulent flavors, positioned her half-eaten rice ball quite purposefully, so that I could see a single pomegranate seed embedded within.

I stared at my plate, fuming.

Julia...

I heard the ghost but didn't look up. Thinking back to the vision of me in the empire-waist dress from a couple of days past, three fingers outstretched, it dawned on me. Every time I had seen my ghost, it had held up three fingers. Suddenly, I understood what the visions were trying to tell me. I placed two arancini on a plate and turned to Ignazio, my heart pounding with desperation, desire, and no small amount of fear. "You'll join us for lunch, will you not?" I asked.

He visibly brightened but shook his head. "Thank you, Julia, but I must not."

"You must," I insisted. "We enjoyed the game with you last night, so why not today? And it is only fitting that you enjoy a meal with us after you have done so much to make this week so…special." I struggled with the last word—there were no words to describe our time in Bomarzo.

Gala took my bait, as I hoped she would. "Yes, you must stay." She took Ignazio by the arm and sat him down between us. A jolt of heat went through me as his knee brushed up against mine.

"Here," I said, handing him the plate before he could say no. "Take one."

He began to rise, but Gala pulled him back down. "Stay, please."

I took his other arm and echoed Gala. "Yes, please stay."

Lillian added her voice into the mix. "Please, as the others said, we'd love for you to stay."

"The ladies rule the room." Jack laughed.

Ignazio turned his head and looked at me.

"For me," I said, barely loud enough for anyone to hear. Boldly, I pressed my knee against his.

I felt him soften. "Very well, Julia. But I'm not hungry."

Gala glared at me, recognizing that he had decided to stay because of me.

Jack and Gala raised their arancini, and we all followed suit. I glanced at Ignazio. Our eyes connected, and for a moment, I was lost, wishing the rest of our companions were no longer there, that it was just us, alone to dine upon each other.

I examined the golden rice ball in my hand. If I ate it, I would be consuming my fifth pomegranate seed. Paolo and I had already determined that if there really was some curse upon the Julias of this place, it would manifest after I'd eaten the sixth seed. But if my theory was right and I could get Ignazio to eat a seed as well, it might be worth it. I took a bite and swallowed.

As the taste of the *arancino* filled my mouth, a strange sensation overcame me, a mysterious pull into the shadows of my

own mind. I saw myself strolling through grand, torch-lit corridors, the walls lined with black marble and hung with dark
tapestries depicting scenes of an unworldly splendor. I wandered
through shadowy gardens filled with twisted, thorny vines and
blossoms that exuded a heady perfume. The air was cool and
tinged with the scent of damp earth, echoing faintly with the
murmurs of unseen rivers. An inexplicable joy surged through
me, a contentment in the darkness that was profound and enveloping, yet bewildering. The place was both beautiful and
foreboding, a palace that was at once my sanctuary and a maze
hiding secrets.

A chill tingled my skin as the vision receded, leaving me at
the table with a lingering sense of having touched something
ancient and profound. I looked around, slightly disoriented, my
heart filled with an odd yearning for the dark splendor I had
glimpsed.

"Your turn, Ignazio," I egged him on. Leaning toward him, I
brought another *arancino*, a pomegranate seed embedded within,
to his mouth. He didn't turn away. The rice ball touched his
lips, and he bit it and swallowed, closing his eyes.

This time, the earthquake's grip was immediate and violent.
But as the world shook around us, something peculiar happened.
Ignazio seized my hand, and it was as if we were not simply
fleeing the chaos, but directing it. The ground quaked beneath
our feet, yet it moved with us, not against us. We rushed out
from the *orco*, and the earth roared around us, a symphony of
destruction nearly deafening in its intensity.

I was terrified, but I couldn't shake the sensation that Ignazio
and I were somehow at the center of the tempest, like puppet
masters pulling at unseen strings. A long crack opened in front
of us, an unsettling dance of destruction, its edges grinding and
shifting as if beckoning us closer. It was as if the chasm was a
mouth, and we were both its voice and audience. Trees shivered,
chestnuts pelted the ground, and yet, amid the pandemonium,

a pomegranate rolled to a gentle stop at my feet, a symbol of something I couldn't quite grasp.

Down the path, it seemed Ceres's eyes flashed bright green for the barest second, but I could not be sure. I stared at the statue, but there was no movement, only cold stone.

"Are you all right?" Ignazio's voice was tender in my ear, yet laden with something I couldn't identify.

I nodded and reluctantly pulled away from the comforting heat of his arms and our inexplicable connection, the magnetic pull that had briefly united us with the chaos.

"Now do you believe us about the earthquake we felt the other day?" Jack asked Gala, his eyes wide with the remnants of terror and confusion.

Paolo slowly went toward the place where the crack had been, Lillian in tow. "It's gone," he said. "As though it was never there."

"All of this is very Dalínian," Dalí cried out. "Even the ants declare it so." He pointed at the earth. Instead of a crack, there was a growing line of dark ants.

"Death marches forward," Gala breathed.

Dalí waved his cane in the air. "Our mortality is evident. Impermanence is all around us."

"So, ants mean death?" Jack asked.

"*Sì! Sì!* Or sometimes they mean overwhelming sexual desire." The artist winked at me.

I took Lillian and Paolo by their arms. "Will you walk me back to the tomb? I'm not hungry anymore."

"*Certo.*" The cameraman grabbed his bag and slung it over his shoulder. "We can take some more photos while we wait for the others."

"Excellent idea," Dalí declared. He waved us off toward the path to the Etruscan hole in the stone, then stepped gingerly over the line of ants and headed back into the Mouth of Hell, Gala and Jack following behind.

"Hot damn. What happened back there?" Lillian exclaimed when we were far enough down the trail to be out of earshot.

"You ate another seed, Signorina Julia," Paolo said, incredulous. "If you eat one more, you might—"

"—die," I said, finishing the thought for him. "I know. But I wanted to make sure Ignazio had one too."

"Wait, you want *him* to eat the seeds?" Lillian asked me.

I told them about the ghosts' signs and Orpheus's warnings. "I don't know what else they could mean other than I should try to get him to eat three seeds. And when he has eaten them, wild things have happened." I cited the birds hitting the window as evidence. "But I don't know. I'm just guessing." I was starting to question if finding out about my past was worth endangering my future. I looked to Lillian for guidance. "Maybe we should go back to Rome."

Just then, Jack came crashing down the overgrown path, interrupting us. "Dalí wants you ready to go when he returns," he said, throwing an arm around my shoulder as though we had been best friends forever. "Time to lose the coat." He gave me a squeeze.

I chuckled awkwardly and pulled away. "I don't know if I can model this afternoon," I said. "I'm too on edge." I raised a hand so they could see that I was still shaking.

"You'll have the wrath of Gala on you if you don't," Jack cautioned. "She's in one of her foulest moods." He pointed toward the *orco*, where Dalí and Gala were in a heated conversation.

"Why is she so angry?" Lillian asked.

Jack shrugged. "She is the most mercurial creature I have ever met. When she's in a good mood, she's glorious. But when she's in a bad one, stay out of her way."

"She's always in a bad mood when it comes to me," I groused.

Lillian tried to bolster my spirits. "Only one more day. You can do this." She smiled, then helped me undress and settle back into the grave, arranging my arms and legs, although I suspected

Gala would do it again when she arrived. She was a woman who always had to put her mark on things.

"You do look beautiful," Lillian said as she laid some of my hair across my shoulder.

"You're just jealous. You wish it was you lying here, cold and naked for the whole world to view."

"How did you guess?" She swatted my shoulder playfully, then made way for the Dalís, who both repositioned me several times before finally agreeing on a pose. Gala was most definitely in a mood, and she was particularly rough, pulling my hair so hard that I swatted her hand at one point. I expected her to retaliate, but instead, she backed off, spoke a few harsh words to Dalí, and departed, dragging Jack along with her. The tension flowed out of us like someone had released the air from a balloon.

"We have to come back here when everyone is asleep," Lillian whispered, nudging me awake hours later. "I want to see this place at night."

I no longer had any interest in traipsing around the *boschetto* in the dark but didn't have the opportunity to say so.

Lillian sat next to Dalí on the drive back to the palazzo as he animatedly described one of his surreal visions, his hands gesturing wildly, moving closer and closer to Lillian's face as he spoke.

"A rhinoceros horn curving into the infinite horizon, the perfect symmetry of an ant's antennae in juxtaposition with the chaos of a crumbling world," Dalí raved, his eyes alight with creative fervor. "Imagine a garden of flamingos, each bearing the face of a different philosopher, or a sea so tranquil that it reflects not the sky but the dreams of those who gaze upon it. That's where art transcends reality, you see?"

Lillian, eyes widening as his hand came too close for comfort, instinctively reached out and took hold of his wrist, pulling his palm toward her to avoid being accidentally struck.

"You have a high Mount of Mars," she said quickly, improvising a distraction. "This signals great ambition, and..."

"Genius," Dalí exclaimed, momentarily forgetting his vision as he looked at his own palm, both fascinated and slightly confused by Lillian's unexpected move.

"Yes, great genius," Lillian agreed, smiling as she guided his hand back to his lap, seizing the opportunity to steer him away from his wild gesturing.

"You are a *modelo*, too," he said, but it didn't sound like a question.

"No, I sell coats and hats and shoes."

"Ah, that is where women can truly excel, in fashion. My shoe hat? My collaboration with Elsa Schiaparelli?" He started to gesture again but seemed more mindful of Lillian's space.

"I have seen it. Truly brilliant," Lillian said, her eyes dancing with amusement.

Dalí settled back, seemingly still intrigued by the palm reading, and the drive continued without further incident. Lillian winked at me, a triumphant grin on her face.

"Does anyone know what dinner is tonight?" Jack asked, changing the subject. "I can't believe it's our last night. I can tell you now, I'll miss the food."

"Dinner will be Dalínian!" Gala declared.

"Perfectly so," Dalí agreed. "Gastronomy is the one subject of which I will never tire, and tonight, you will be delighted by *my* delights. You will be exalted by all that is placed before you. Tonight there WILL be snails." He waved his cane around, whipping it dangerously close to Paolo's head. "There will be frogs. Baby turkeys! Crayfish! Peacocks! Quail! Siren shoulder! Pierced hearts! Toffee with pine cones and old-champagne sherbet!"

"You're making my head spin," Lillian said. "I didn't even know you could eat some of those things."

"This will be a *Dîner de Gala*," the artist cried out. "You will see, my little shoe seller. You will see."

18

After returning to the palazzo, we retired to our rooms for rest and refreshment. On the way upstairs, Jack regaled us with tales of other *Dîners de Gala* he had attended—luxurious dinner parties over which Gala always presided as the guest of honor, despite important people in attendance such as Laurence Olivier, Vivien Leigh, Humphrey Bogart, Bob Hope, and Gary Cooper. All of the dinners featured strange food, costumes, and wild staging, as though you were walking into a surrealist movie to dine.

So when Lillian and I returned to our rooms to find costumes we were supposed to wear to dinner, we weren't completely shocked. I was trying to understand my new getup when Lillian burst into my room, her arms full of shimmery blue-and-gold fabric.

"I'm to be a sea goddess of some sort, I think," she said, arranging the beautiful dress on the chair so I could view it. It was light and airy blue silk, covered in thousands of little scales that glinted in the light. "It has a train, a crown of netting and shells, and a little trident."

"Salacia," I said, the word coming unbidden to my lips.

"It is definitely salacious." She laughed. "It's practically see-through."

I shook my head. "Salacia," I corrected her. "She was a nymph and the consort of Neptune."

"Ah," she said. "Well, she came by her name honestly, I suppose."

She pointed at the black silk-tulle dress splayed across my bed. It was adorned with a long front panel of intricate black-and-gray beadwork flowers, which fell from the waist to the floor. Three tiny bloodred hearts were embroidered into the lower third of the panel, and a long, elegant black braided rope was attached to the waist.

"Who are you?" she asked.

"Take a guess." I sighed, examining the drawing that illustrated how the rope should be employed to hold the tulle in place. I was annoyed that the tulle would barely cover my breasts, leaving a wide empty space of flesh between them. Modeling nude made me feel less vulnerable than this dress did.

"The Queen of the Underworld."

"Righto!" I rolled my eyes. "It's a gorgeous dress, but I'm so tired of being Proserpina." I fingered the crown of black flowers with ruby centers meant to accessorize it.

"Don't worry, Jules. This is just a costume. The rest of it? We'll find an explanation, I'm sure of it."

I raised my eyebrow at her. "So far all signs point to one explanation, and it is there in that damned dress."

"Oh, come on. It's not *that* dire. Do you think if you put on the dress you'll turn into Proserpina?"

"I suppose not." I sighed again. "But after today's earthquake, I'm starting to think the money isn't worth it. I feel like my life is in danger, Lillian."

She tried to reason with me. "You've been scared, sure, but you haven't been hurt, have you? You need that money. And more importantly, you need answers. I'm here now, and Paolo is on our side. We're not going to let you out of our sight." She paused, then gave me a mischievous grin. "Well, we might slip off for a bit..." She giggled. "We are planning on seeing each other in Rome. Oh, Jules, doesn't he look a bit like Sinatra?"

"Does he kiss like Sinatra?"

Lillian rolled her eyes at me, but then she gave me a vigorous nod. "He's so dreamy. But that's beside the point. We only have one more day. We'll be looking out for you."

I knew my friend didn't want to leave. She was keen to see where things would go with Paolo. And Lillian could be stubborn once she had her mind set. Unless clearer danger presented itself, it would be pointless to try to convince her that we should leave early.

"Hey," she said, sitting up. "What if I go as Persephone and you go as Salacious Sally?"

"Salacia," I corrected her. It felt wrong to hear the name twisted into something else. "There is no way Dalí would stand for it. And Gala would have a fit."

"I don't like her. She's been nothing but snotty to me since I arrived. Dalí is an oddball, but you were right about Gala. She really is a bitch."

"A bitch that holds the ends of Dalí's purse strings," I said, lifting up the dress I was meant to wear. The tulle flowed across the bed.

Once we'd dressed and done our hair and makeup, Lillian picked up her trident and pointed it at me. "I command you to have a good time tonight." She could always make me laugh and forget my worries, and despite the gravity of my situation, I found myself reveling in the levity she brought to Bomarzo.

"Can a goddess command another goddess?" I asked, playing along.

"I suppose if one cursed another, right? I mean, that must have happened."

"Yes! After Aurora slept with Venus's lover, Mars, Venus placed a curse on her so that she'd only fall in love with mortal men."

Lillian waved her trident at me again. "Then tonight, beautiful Proserpina, I curse you to have a good time."

I was about to retort when a loud knock on the door caused us to jump.

"By the gods," Jack said, looking us up and down when Lillian opened the door. "You are both...breathtaking."

"Well, aren't you also rather easy on the eyes," Lillian said with a grin.

I had to agree with her. Jack's toga left most of his chest exposed, his muscles rippling beneath the single swath of fabric draped over one shoulder. He held a scepter in one hand, a large bronze key in the other, and a golden diadem lay nestled in his gilded curls.

Lillian looked puzzled when Jack turned around to reveal a papier-mâché face with a beard on the back of his head. "Who are you supposed to be? A two-faced god?"

"He's Janus," I told her.

Jack puffed up his chest. "That's right. I am your god of beginnings, gates, passages, doorways, and endings, or at least, that's what the note with the mask said. I must say, it is my pleasure to escort you to our dinner destination, a place bound to be equally surreal."

"It seems at least one face of god Janus is chivalrous, too," Lillian teased. A second later she gave a little squeal of delight as Paolo trotted by in a toga decorated with the same luminous scale design as her dress, with a diadem made of seashells on his head. It was immediately clear that he was Neptune.

"It seems Dalí has a bit of matchmaking in him," I mused to Jack.

"Then I should have been made Hades," he whispered in my ear, his voice hungry.

"I wish you were," I said, knowing without a shadow of a

IN THE GARDEN OF MONSTERS

doubt that if Ignazio played any role tonight, it would be as the god of the Underworld.

But Ignazio was nowhere to be found when we arrived in the *sala grande*, which had been transformed to feel like Mount Olympus itself with tufts of cotton clustered around the base of beautifully painted papier-mâché mountains formed to resemble rocky peaks poking through the clouds. A servant sporting a short white toga and gleaming gold cuffs on his wrists accompanied us to our seats at the table, which had been laid with a gilt-edged linen tablecloth adorned with dozens of white candles of varying lengths.

No one would be playing footsie under the table tonight, for not only had the silver chairs been set nearly five feet apart, but they'd also been staggered so no two diners faced one another. Worse, Lillian had been seated at the opposite end of the table from me, across from Jack, and for me to have a conversation with her, I might have to shout. This was especially true if I was to be heard over the quartet of clarinetists, who began to play something akin to a march as the Dalís entered the room, the artist gallantly holding Gala's hand in the air. They, too, were in full costume, he in a white toga with armlets of burnished metal, a crown of laurel leaves on his head, and a lightning bolt fashioned from papier-mâché in his free hand. Gala glowed in a diaphanous dress of pale amber with a cloak of bright peacock feathers, a radiant diadem on her head, and a scepter in her free hand.

"This! This is a *Dîner de Gala*. A tribute to the goddess that she is," Dalí exclaimed, bowing before his wife. Then he raised his lightning bolt over his head. "Tonight you will experience the bounty of Olympus!"

And with that, he led Gala to her seat, one of two elaborate gold chairs at either end of the table. Once he'd taken his place opposite her, he gave each of us the once-over and, seemingly satisfied, struck his scepter on the ground with a loud thump.

Immediately, six dead-eyed servants appeared at our sides to pour the wine, a golden liquid heady with an aroma of elder-flower and strawberries.

"Let us toast to Gala." Dalí lifted his glass in the air. "To the beauty of Gala, to the glory of her visage, the bounty of her words."

Gala basked in the praise, her smile belying the venom I knew ran in her veins. I picked up my glass reluctantly. She was the last person I desired to toast. But I took a drink and, despite the deliciousness of the wine in my glass, forced myself to restrain. I half hoped Lillian wouldn't restrain herself, and we wouldn't have to hike down the secret passage after all.

Then Dalí clapped his hands together three times and Ignazio entered the room.

I held my breath and took him in. He was the true embodi-ment of Pluto in a red toga that exposed a well-chiseled chest, an iron crown resting on his head, and, in his hand, a dark bi-dent. He moved with grace and his eyes shone with purpose. And his purpose was me. He came to stand before my place at the table and bowed.

"Beautiful Proserpina, you are, as ever, radiant," he said qui-etly enough so that only I heard his compliment.

It was the first time he had ever called me by that name. My stomach filled with butterflies—though perhaps it was more apt to think of locusts, as there was nothing delicate about the feelings that Ignazio inspired within me. He was dark, dangerous, and determined. I held his gaze, equally determined. I had no idea how I would do it, but I vowed to hold my own against this man.

He turned to Gala and gave her a sweeping bow, more elegant than the one he had given to me. "My queen, we are ready to delight your senses."

"By all means," she replied, raising her hand in a gesture of permission.

Ignazio stole one more hungry glance at me, then looked at

Dalí, nodded, and snapped his fingers. Again, the servants swept in, this time setting before us the first course—a dish containing what seemed to be an egg that had been breaded and fried and some sort of greenish-brown paste spread on a small slice of rye toast, surrounded by gold-gilt almonds arranged attractively around the edge of the plate.

Dalí's voice rang through the room. "I, the divine Salvador Domingo Felipe Jacinto Dalí, declare this meal dedicated to my queen, the magnificent Gala, to begin."

Paolo managed to catch my eye and mouthed something to me, which I thought might have been *"Stai attento."* *Be careful.* This time, he would not be close enough to knock anything containing a pomegranate seed out of my hand, nor would Lillian be able to swallow another seed for me.

"Mangia," Dalí shouted in Italian, then in Catalan, *"Menja."*

I examined the toast on my plate and, not seeing any seeds, took a bite. It turned out to be rich and pleasurable, and I detected a hint of alcohol but couldn't identify the other ingredients. "What's in this?" I asked.

Dalí was delighted that I wanted to know. "This is avocado toast. Never have you tasted anything so marvelous. You will experience a delirious concoction of avocados, almonds, lamb brain, and tequila. And a delightful fried egg stuffed with goose rillettes. I thought it quite Dalínian to begin this dinner with breakfast."

"A divine beginning for this gathering of gods," Gala said, licking avocado off her fingers.

What followed was a parade of food born from Dalí's imagination—prawn parfaits made from egg and sausage and decorated with prawns waving their pincers in the air; snail stew; a soufflé of cauliflower and garlic topped by a skewer of fried frogs; ramekins of frogs' legs; and a dish Dalí called "snail saltimbocca," which was nothing like the saltimbocca *alla Romana* of chicken and veal in white wine that I had grown accustomed to. His dish, made of fried snails with garlic sauce, was far more complex.

I carefully dissected every morsel of food before eating it, to ensure I wouldn't ingest another pomegranate seed. So far, I'd found only two, stuffed into the egg, but I'd managed to tuck them under the empty prawn shells, glad that no one sat close enough to me to notice, though I was sure I'd been caught red-handed when Dalí suddenly screamed out, *"Absolutament no!"*

As it turned out, he hadn't seen me squirrel away the seeds at all. Instead, he was yelling at Paolo, who tried to photograph the obscure but exquisite dishes before us. They were not ready to be seen by the world, Dalí insisted, and Paolo obliged him, putting his camera back in his pack.

Between courses, Ignazio brought us an herbal *digestivo* that made me feel as though I hadn't eaten a thing, which was fortunate because next came a tower of crayfish, which the servants shelled before us, then served in a broth, eel pâté and eels with beer, sardines in little bread boats, and an entire turbot with skewers of sausages rising out of its back. It was hard to imagine eating some of these things, but aware of Gala's eye on me, I sampled a little of each dish, and, to my surprise, every one delighted me. If you had told me that same afternoon that one of my favorite bites of the night would be jellied codfish, I would have grimaced, then laughed in your face. But now I was wishing for seconds.

"This is magical stuff," Lillian remarked to Ignazio as he poured us another *digestivo*.

"Your Maestro Dalí would not want you to miss any of the magic of the food at hand." He gave a nod toward the artist.

"We have not yet seen our friends of the land," Dalí explained, and as if on cue, the servants brought out plates of pheasant in port sauce, steamed and stuffed larks, roast duckling, pigs' feet in piecrusts, pork chops on a bed of flaky pastry, boar shank with black radishes, and a "siren shoulder," which turned out to be a lamb shoulder with anchovies and caviar.

"There's more," I told Lillian. We still had dessert to come, and I knew how much the Dalís loved their sweets.

The "toffee with pine cones" turned out to be candies with pine nuts. The old-champagne sherbet, Dalí informed us, was made from a ten-year-old bottle of Veuve Clicquot. It was accompanied by a banana pie made with rum-soaked biscuits and a tiny plate with a chunk of chocolate, chock-full of what I guessed to be about fifteen pomegranate seeds.

I had a few bites of the pie and a little of the sherbet, both of which were divine, but I dared not eat much or my feigning at fullness might not be believed. The liquor we had been drinking made me feel like I still had room to eat a horse. Of course Gala gave me a stern look when I pushed away my plate of chocolate untouched, and I wondered if she would reprimand me later.

Finally, Dalí brought the meal to an end. Ignazio indicated that we should stand, and within moments, the tables and everything on them had been cleared from the room. They took the golden chairs and lined them up along the wall.

"You have dined upon the delights offered to the glorious Gala, the one true goddess who graces us tonight with her presence. Now," Dalí exclaimed, "it is time to dance!"

I silently groaned. I didn't think of myself as a great dancer. Besides, how could anyone be expected to dance after such a feast? But the music began, a slow waltz I recognized as a traditional Italian song called the *"Serenata Napoletana."*

Jack came forward and took Gala by the hand. Lillian already had a hand on Paolo's arm. And I stood there awkwardly as the couples danced. Just as I began to walk toward Dalí, thinking I would stand next to him and watch, Ignazio appeared in the doorway. I wanted to curse.

"Dance, my darling Proserpina. Your Pluto awaits," Dalí commanded me. *"Danse!"* he instructed again in French. He spanked me with his lightning bolt, forcing me to move toward Ignazio, who had crossed the room with surprising speed.

Ignazio wrapped an arm around me, finding the small of my back with one hand, holding my hand with the other. Heat, smoke, and cinnamon circled around me as we began to move across the tiles of the *sala grande*. I tried to catch Lillian's eye as we swept by her, but my friend was lost in Paolo's embrace.

I had never danced the waltz without counting my steps, but in Ignazio's arms, I could hardly think, much less count. Nor did I need to. We moved together as though we were one, as though we had been dancing together for centuries. *Together for centuries.* That thought came to me as we spun, as my feet moved effortlessly, in time with the clarinets. It was an alarming thought, but one I could not shake and one Ignazio seemed to validate with his whisper in my ear.

"This is something you have missed," he said.

I had no response for him. While I rarely danced and had never danced with him before, his words rang true within me. How could I feel as though I genuinely had missed waltzing with him?

Over his shoulder, I caught a glimpse of the windows along the western wall, through which a green glow was evident. The *boschetto* was alive again.

Julia...

The whisper was soft, and I wondered if I had imagined it. Ignazio and I moved together like fire, like heat rising. We spun, our bodies moving with a rhythm the music could barely reach.

Julia...beware...

The whisper grew louder, and it shook something loose inside me, a sliver of anger. Who were the ghosts warning me about?

I wanted to find out. "Do you know the name Aidoneus?" I asked Ignazio. It was the question I'd wanted to ask if I had won the staring contest.

He pulled me closer. "It means *husband*," he said, his voice like silk.

That was not the answer I had expected. His skin burned against mine, and I wondered if I might burst into flame or melt into the earth.

"You made a choice." His breath was hot summer in my ear. "You can make it again."

"What choice?" I asked, alarmed.

Beware...

The windows overlooking the *boschetto* glowed with a new intensity. I wondered why none of my companions noticed.

"You chose me. And you can choose me again."

Before I knew what was happening, his lips were against mine, crushing against me until I softened, fell into him, and nearly lost myself. The night before had barely been a kiss at all, a brush of the lips, enough to whet my appetite. This was something more, a promise...dare I even think it?...a commitment.

Julia, beware...

The whisper gave me the courage to break away once more. It didn't matter how much I wanted him... I couldn't give in. "No. I can't do this. I *won't* do this."

I looked around. No one had noticed us—they were all lost in the dance, Dalí sublime in his golden chair, tapping his thunderbolt against the arm in time with the music.

Ignazio suddenly fell into a kneeling bow at my feet. "My ardor for you got the better of me. Forgive me."

The windows glowed bright green, a wild light that pulsed. Like it did that first day I arrived, it was keeping time with every fluttering beat of my heart. I backed away from the windows, away from Ignazio. The world spun around me again, and I closed my eyes, willing everything to disappear. When I opened them, Ignazio was nowhere to be found, the windows were black with the night, and I was standing next to Dalí, Gala was waltzing with Jack, and Paolo with Lillian. She grinned when she saw me looking in their direction.

"Pull up a chair, dear Proserpina," Dalí suggested, indicating with his lightning bolt that I should retrieve a chair from the other side of the room. The golden one next to him was unoccupied, but, clearly, it was reserved for Gala.

"You are troubled," he said as soon as I had sat down.

I was surprised. Dalí wasn't one who seemed to care about or even notice the people around him.

"This place, it is...unsettling," I said. I wasn't sure how I could possibly tell him any of my real concerns.

"As it should be."

"Why?" I asked.

He regarded me with new interest. "Why?" he parroted.

I nodded. "*Sì*. Why should it be so unsettling?"

He looked down, as though he were ashamed of the answer. "We are caught here, in between everything."

I waited for him to explain but he only stared at the tiles. I touched him on the arm. His skin was cold, and he recoiled as though my hand was poison.

"I'm sorry," I said, flustered by his reaction. "You just looked lost."

"*Sì*. We are all lost." He spoke as though he were in a trance, a blank stare on his usually animated face.

"What does that mean, Maestro Dalí? What are we caught between?"

"All of this," he said, waving the lightning bolt around at the room in front of us, "could be different, Julia. All of it. If you weren't merely a muse and you were an artist."

I gritted my teeth. "I am an artist."

"Then prove it. Paint this away. Change it. Paint your way forward. You are the only one in the room with the power to do so. My paintings are only a door. I cannot make you step inside."

This time it was he who reached out to touch me on the arm. His fingers were like ice. "One more, Julia. You know what you have to do." He put a hand into the folds of his toga and pulled out a little pomegranate, held it toward me.

I stood, furious, and tried to keep my words measured. "No. I won't. *Buona notte, Maestro.*"

I departed as calmly as I could. When I reached the hallway beyond the ballroom, I leaned against the wall, willing my heart to slow and my wits to return.

19

Lillian burst through the door, sliding to a halt and sighing when she saw me leaning against the wall. "Julia, what happened?"

I was so relieved to see her, to know I wasn't alone in the *castello*. She had said that she and Paolo wouldn't let me out of their sight, and she hadn't lied. "I'm fine. I just... I just couldn't stay in there any longer."

"You...you...didn't eat a seed, did you?"

I gave a rueful chuckle. "If I had, I don't think you'd be talking to me."

Paolo appeared, shutting the door behind him. *"Grazie a Dio,"* he said, the slight worry lines on his forehead relaxing when he saw us.

"Come, let's go before the others find us here." Lillian took me by the elbow and propelled me down the hall.

"But the dancing just started," I said, confused. "Gala will be furious if we leave now." I was aware of how ironic that sounded coming from my mouth, considering I had been the one to leave first.

Lillian paused and put a hand on my forehead. "Are you all right?"

"What do you mean?"

"Non ti ricordi?" The worry lines had returned to Paolo's brow.

"What are you talking about—what don't I remember?"

"Julia, we've been dancing for the last two hours. You danced with Jack, with Paolo, and even with Dalí."

That couldn't possibly be true. Dalí would never have danced with any of us, nor would Gala have let Jack so much as lay a finger on me.

"That doesn't make sense. I only had one dance with Ignazio, and a conversation with Dalí while I watched Gala and Jack and the two of you dance."

Paolo and Lillian looked at each other, then back at me. "Ignazio left right after dinner," Paolo said, furrowing his brow. "He wasn't here for any of the dancing."

"Come, let's talk about this somewhere else." Lillian led us up the stairs to our rooms.

Paolo's room was the closest to the top of the stairs, so we ducked into it and Lillian locked the door behind us. The clock at his bedside showed that two hours had passed. My head spun with the thought of it. How could that be? I explained to my friends what had happened to me in the *sala grande*.

"Che pazzo," Lillian said.

"Very crazy," I agreed. "If these…beings…can manipulate what we are seeing and thinking, what chance do I have of avoiding all the seeds? Both Ceres and Ignazio seem to have it out for me."

"You have managed so far," Lillian pointed out. "You only ate that last seed because you wanted Ignazio to eat one. And sure, what you tell me about your encounters with Ceres sounds pretty scary. But I think if Ignazio or Ceres wanted to harm any of us directly, they would have by now."

I reminded them about the fire.

"It could have been an accident," Paolo said.

I shook my head. "No, now that we're talking, I'm sure it was Ceres. I don't know how I didn't realize it before, but I'm sure of that now. The snake slithered right over my foot."

"Why couldn't that have been an accident?" Lillian asked.

The words came to my lips unbidden, yanked out of the recesses of my memory. "Serpents are sacred to Ceres. The myths tell of her yoking two huge snakes to her chariot. They even printed coins with this image on them in ancient times."

Lillian raised an eyebrow. "I forgot you are a mythology geek. How oddly convenient."

"I have thought about that," I admitted. Why had I gravitated so much toward the myths? "It is alarmingly coincidental."

Lillian furrowed her brow. "According to mythology, Ceres didn't want Proserpina to go to the Underworld, right? So, if you somehow are Proserpina, why would she want to hurt you? You're already in the Overworld. I think we should explore the *boschetto* and find her statue. She may be the key to figuring all this out. Paolo, what did that journal say about the secret passage?"

"*Non tanto,*" he said. *Not much.* "Giulia Orsini was the one who convinced her husband to put it in. She suggested it as an escape route in case bandits ever stormed the castle."

Lillian put her hand on the doorknob. "I want to find out what that green glow is and why it beats in tune with your heart, Julia. This is our last chance to get to the bottom of this. Paolo, meet us in the library in a little bit? Make sure no one sees you."

He gave her a brilliant smile. "*Certo, signorina.*"

We left Paolo to return to my room. As I touched the doorknob, the ghostly whisper was suddenly strong in my mind. *Julia, beware...*

Aside from the whisper, my conversation with Dalí weighed on me. It was a warning, a serious one.

"I don't know if this is a good idea, Lily," I said once we shut the door behind us.

"Don't worry. You'll be with Paolo and me. And it's just as I was saying. You've had some bizarre encounters, but you haven't been hurt yet, right?"

"I suppose you're right."

"We'll tread carefully, watch each other's back. If anyone wants to get to you, they'll have to go through me first." She tossed me a pair of her trousers to wear, which were much more suitable than the dresses I had brought with me.

"All right, tough guy. I'll hold you to that." As I pulled on the trousers, the fabric cold against my skin, a sense of resolve began to build within me. Perhaps Lillian was right—I hadn't been hurt yet. Maybe I just needed to confront these fears.

Paolo waited for us in the library. The lights were off, but the full moon illuminated the room. He handed Lillian a flashlight.

My earlier resolve wavered. "Do we really need to do this?" I asked as Lillian pushed the golden arrow to open the hidden door.

She rolled her eyes at me. "Jules, this is a secret passage in a castle. Of course we do! This is a childhood dream come true."

"I'm not sure if it's a dream or a nightmare," I muttered.

"We'll get to the bottom of this, I promise," she said, giving me a little hug. Then she turned her flashlight on and began to descend into the tunnel.

The stairs were dry and solid, carved directly out of the mountain's rock. At one point, I started to count them, but after I hit five hundred, I stopped because of the growing dread of having to climb them after we ended our folly. Sound in the long, dark hallway was strange and muted, and it was easy to hear the person behind you, but not so easy to hear the person in front of you. It was quite dark, even with the flashlights. I would have given anything to light up the torches in the holders we passed, but we had nothing to light them with.

Eventually, we reached a heavy bronze door, green with age. Paolo lifted the thick wooden beam securing the door and set it aside. With considerable effort, he pulled the door inward, its terrible screech echoing as it scraped against the stone floor.

"I'm sure it was quieter long ago," Paolo said. "After four hundred years we should be grateful it opens at all."

The sound of rushing water indicated we were near the stream along the wood's south side. Somewhere in the distance, a wolf howled.

The door was behind some thick overgrowth, and it took us a good ten minutes to clear a route through the bushes. The wood beyond was bathed in pale moonlight. The path took us along the bank of the stream, and then we were at the location where we crossed over on the wobbly boards to enter and leave the wood. Lillian lit the way across. The familiar feeling that I had stepped from one world into another hit me, hard, an invisible curtain that brushed across my body as I crossed the stream into the *boschetto*.

"We shouldn't be here," I said when I reached Lillian on the other side.

"Oh, come on, Jules. We came all this way."

"'All this way' is only about a quarter of a mile, you realize," I pointed out. "This place is creepy enough during the day. I'd rather wander around in a cemetery than be here at night."

"We're already here. We can't go back now." She was down the trail before I could argue further.

We traipsed along the path toward the monstrous statues. The terrain was rough enough during the day, but at night, it was far more treacherous with less light. I kept my head down to better traverse the occasional jutting rock and the tree roots snaking across the path. As we neared, I lifted my head toward the giant. Its face was bright in the moonlight, stone eyes determined.

I took a step forward but stopped in my tracks when I thought I saw the giant's eyes blink. I gasped. It blinked at me again.

"What is it?" Lillian asked.

"I...I..." I froze, pointing at the statue, unable to find the words to explain what I had seen. How could I tell them that I thought the figure was alive? At that moment, it appeared to be just a cold rock, its eyes lifeless.

"There's nothing there," Paolo said.

Lillian disappeared behind one of the giant's legs. "He's not so impressive in the dark," she said, shining her light up to where his manhood should be.

I couldn't take my eyes off the giant's face. Would it blink again?

A plaintive meow sounded behind us. I tore my gaze away and found Orpheus sauntering up to us, his white fur aglow in the moonlight. He began winding around my legs. I reached down and picked up the little beast. His very presence made me feel better.

"Keep watch for me," I whispered in his ear.

He immediately pushed his forehead into my chin and rubbed his cheek on mine before giving me a little lick with his rough tongue. Giving him a soft squeeze, I set him down to keep up with my companions, who had already started down the path again. I had no intention of being left behind in the dark. I was glad to see the little cat follow.

We passed the moss-covered tortoise, the Pegasus fountain, and the nymphaeum, heading toward the amphitheater where Paolo had recited lines from Ovid. If dimly, the moon gave enough light to our surroundings to leave eerie shadows as it filtered through the trees. It was cold, quite cold, and I was glad I had brought my heavy cloak and wore my thickest socks. The air was still, with not even a whisper of a breeze caressing my cheeks. Aside from the sound of the stream, the garden itself was silent. Not a bird stirring, just us crashing through the dark space, avoiding fallen branches and rocks.

The path was edged with a tangle of bushes and trees in the space between the nymphaeum and the theater. Lillian swept the beam of her flashlight across the bushes and woods. There were dozens upon dozens of pomegranates. None of the bushes had been there earlier in the day. How had they sprung up so fast?

One of the fruits had fallen to the ground at Lillian's feet. She grabbed it and chucked it into the darkness. The wind immediately kicked up, rocking the trees around us, whipping my hair into my eyes and mouth. Orpheus yowled at my feet. I picked him up and hugged him close.

As we passed through the amphitheater toward the Casa Pendente, a growing sense of dread began to rise within me. We were moving ever closer to the statue of Ceres. My last encounter with the turtle-doves and the fire was still too fresh in my mind.

"Do you see that?" Lillian had stopped abruptly, and I almost ran into her. We had reached the edge of the little clearing where the tilted house stood. Orpheus leaped from my arms and ran into the bushes.

I peered past her and saw a faint green glow emanating from the ground-floor window of the leaning house.

"*Dio mio,*" Paolo blurted, extinguishing his flashlight. Lillian did the same.

"We should go back," I whispered.

"We'll never know what is going on if we don't investigate," Lillian insisted. She sounded as excited as I was afraid.

"It's too dangerous. Whatever forces are at work here are much stronger than us," I cautioned.

"*Andrò.*" *I'll go.* Before Lillian or I could protest, Paolo was already heading toward the house.

"We can't let him go alone," Lillian said, grabbing me by the arm.

As we neared the leaning house, I began to feel short of breath.

My heart drummed inside my rib cage. Paolo had already reached the top when we approached the bottom of the Casa Pendente's short staircase. As his feet found the landing, the green glow winked out, leaving us in darkness. I almost screamed, but Paolo switched on his flashlight and trained the beam into the tiny, slanted room. He took a step forward. Lillian and I hurried up the stairs and followed him.

The room was empty, save for the moss streaked across the concrete below the front-facing open window, moss I hadn't noticed when we dined in the tiny room.

Paolo walked across the slanted floor to the little adjacent room on the left. He shone the flashlight inside, then turned back to Lillian and me.

"Niente."

"Nothing? How could that be?" Lillian asked. She crossed the room in a few wobbly steps to see for herself. The space was empty, with no sign that we had dined there a few days before.

A thud above our heads froze us in place. Our gazes swiveled toward the concrete ceiling. We waited, not daring to move, for another sound to come. Goose bumps rose across my neck and arms, and my heart felt like it was clawing to get out of my body. After many excruciating moments, I motioned Lillian and Paolo toward the door. As terrifying as it might be that someone—or something—was above us, it would be far worse if we ended up trapped inside the tiny room. They turned off their flashlights, and we made our way as quietly as we could down the stairs and back to the clearing, where we turned toward the leaning house.

The green glow had returned, shining through the second-floor windows, growing brighter, brighter, brighter, until I had to shield my eyes with my hands to block out the blinding light. Then it vanished, and we were again plunged into utter blackness. I pulled Lillian close, and she held me, soothing me like a child. "Shh, you'll be okay, Jules," she whispered.

It took a few minutes for my eyes to adjust once more to the dim light of the moon. The house's windows were black rectangles against the whiteness of the carved stone exterior. We watched the house in silence for a good five minutes, until Lillian's restlessness got the better of her.

"We can't just stand here all night. We came here for a reason—let's find out what that green light is. *Andiamo.*" She patted me on the shoulder, flipped on her flashlight, and headed toward the stairs on the other side of the house that led up to the top of the hill and the second floor.

And Ceres. And the Mouth of Hell.

No! I wanted to scream at her. *Don't go!* But she was already turning the corner, her flashlight bobbing as she walked. Paolo was on her heels. I sprinted to catch up with them.

At the top of the stairs, my heart racing, I looked for Ceres ahead of us, a mere sixty or seventy feet away, but it was too dark, and bushes obscured the statue of the goddess despite her closeness. To the left of the house, the moon lit up the weedy vase-lined promenade with Neptune at the far end.

Paolo and I crept after Lillian, who was moving slowly through the brush to the little bridge that led into the top floor of the leaning house. After a pause to listen for movement, she turned onto the bridge and shone her flashlight into the house. Glancing back at us, she shook her head. Nothing there. She pointed in and to the left, to the second room of the house, then began to move toward the door, but Paolo stopped her, stretching his arm out in front of her to indicate he would check out the house, not her.

I held my breath. Paolo's dark figure moved inside, his flashlight barely lighting the way, then cautiously peered around the corner into the adjacent room. He disappeared for a second, before returning to us, shaking his head.

He held a pomegranate in his hand.

"It was on the floor in the center of the room," he explained.

Lillian took it from him, weighing it in one hand. "I'm tired of these games. Isn't the statue of Ceres near us somewhere?"

Julia...go back... The whisper of the ghost was loud in my ear. *Hurry. Go back...*

I thought my knees might give beneath me. "We should go, Lillian. This is madness. We shouldn't be here."

But she had already turned around, her light moving toward the darkness, where I knew the goddess rested in the bushes. Paolo motioned with his hand to come along, then trotted after her.

I almost left them and turned down the path back toward Orlando and the woodsman and the secret passage beyond. But they had the flashlights, and there was no way I could traverse the quarter-mile tunnel in total blackness. I swallowed hard and followed. When I reached them, Lillian and Paolo were shining their flashlights on Ceres's face, illuminating her serene features and the bowl on her head. I gasped. The flowers that had been so bright and alive earlier that day were dead, the stalks brown and shriveled, falling over the edges of the bowl.

"Some goddess of nature she is," Lillian joked, her voice loud in the silence of the *boschetto*. "Can't even manage to keep her flowers alive."

As soon as they were uttered, I wished I could shove those words back into my friend's mouth. *Don't make her mad*, I wanted to scream at her.

Yet Lillian thrived on impulse. She lifted her arm and threw the pomegranate as hard as possible at the goddess. The fruit burst across her chest, the bloodred juice spraying across her bared breasts.

"*I suoi occhi.*" Paolo pointed at the goddess's eyes, which had slowly begun to light up green.

It was as though I was rooted to the spot, unable to move. I watched her eyes brighten, and then there was movement on her shoulder, the stone cherub that rested there coming to life, extending its hand, one finger outstretched, pointing at us.

A massive rumble began beneath our feet.

A few paces away, I heard Orpheus's little voice rise in a yowl.

I finally found my voice. *"Run!"*

My friends did not hesitate. We bolted from the goddess. Orpheus ran ahead of us, his white fur glowing in the moonlight, a beacon in the darkness. We followed the cat past Hannibal's elephant, past the maw of the *orco*, and the vase where one of the Julias was buried, then up the stairs toward Proserpina's bench. The rumble grew louder, the trees swayed dangerously, and the ground shook beneath us as we ran.

We passed the little statue of Cerberus and raced up the stairs toward the *tempietto*. When we reached the top, there was a roar behind us. Orpheus yowled in response, a terrible, unnatural sound I had never heard from a cat. I ventured a look back, and in the darkness at the bottom of the stairs, a three-headed dog at least twice the size of a horse reared back. Cerberus made a noise that was deeper than a bark and louder than the roar of a lion. It was facing away from us, toward the inner part of the garden. After a wild howl, the beast suddenly went silent, and that was even more terrifying.

The ground shook, nearly drowning out my scream with its rumbling. We were nowhere near the secret passage, but the road back to the *castello* was right before us, beyond the arch in the wall and its broken gate across the field. None of us needed words to convey to each other that we should head toward it.

Lillian tripped just before we reached the gate. Her flashlight flew out of her hand and went dark somewhere in the field. Paolo and I stopped to help her up, but as she rose from the ground, she yelled at us to keep running. Behind us, across the field at the top of the stairs near the *tempietto*, a massive figure loomed, its green eyes bright. It was the giant statue of Orlando Furioso. Something was slung over its shoulder. My blood went cold.

"Go," I screamed.

Orpheus jumped through the gate. Paolo and I followed, Lillian on our heels. We had to climb over a few crumbled stones from the arch over our heads. But then we were past it and on the road leading to the village and Palazzo Orsini.

We were out of the garden but not out of danger. The ground continued to shake.

Then, to my horror, it began to snow.

It had been a warm day and evening, and there hadn't been a cloud in the sky. Besides, it rarely snowed in the Lazio region of Central Italy. And yet the wind whipped up around us and the flakes began to fall, fat and wet, sticking in clumps on my coat and catching in my eyelashes. Soon it was falling hard enough that we could barely see in front of us. I was terrified we might slip in the accumulating snow, but none of us dared slow down.

The only indication we were heading in the right direction was the low rock wall that edged the road to the village. Somewhere along the way, Orpheus disappeared in the blinding whiteness. I hoped he would find his way to someplace warm and safe.

My legs burned and I was sure my companions also felt the strain of our pace, but we continued on. Paolo raced along beside me, and from time to time, I caught flashes of Lillian's red cape out of the corner of my eye. The ground still shook, but the strength of the tremors had diminished, and the rumbling was no longer constant. Instead, behind us, there was a cadence, a thud, thud, thud, like footsteps of stone.

It seemed like forever before we neared the open arch of the Bomarzo gate. When I saw it looming above us and the little lights of the village beyond, I began to cry, tears freezing on my face as we found new energy to reach the palazzo at the top of the slope.

An explosion of snow and rocks erupted in a loud boom before us, stopping us in our tracks, the flying debris forcing us to double over to protect ourselves. Lillian huddled against me. When the powder had cleared, we cried aloud at the sight of the stone creature before us—it was the figure the giant statue in the *boschetto* had been tearing apart.

A flash of memory ripped through me, of Ignazio's description of Orlando Furioso raging through the woods, filled with jealous rage that his lover did not return his affections. The broken statue was the woodsman that Orlando threw across the field. The stone man's head had rolled to a spot in front of Paolo, its face staring up at us, its mouth a rictus of horror. Its body was broken, and its legs and arms had detached and skidded across the ground, making tracks in the snow.

Thud. Thud. I looked back but could not see the stone giant through the snow, only its glowing green eyes, the same as the statue of Ceres. *"Andiamo,"* Paolo screamed, and we flew into action, scrambling to move around the broken statue before us.

I ran as fast as possible, my lungs aflame with the searing cold. I didn't look back for fear I would find Orlando right behind us, readying to toss us aside with a heavy fist.

When we reached the door, Paolo and I began to pound upon it, hard, and when Minos opened it, I fell inward, stumbling into the palazzo, grateful for the hard tiles beneath me. The door shut behind us, and I lay there with my eyes closed, desperate to get my breath back.

"Dov'è Lillian?" Paolo's voice was frantic. He scrambled to his feet and pushed the servant aside. Opening the door, he ran back out. But Minos just stood at the door, his head cocked, looking at us like nothing unusual was happening.

"Lillian," Paolo screamed into the snow as he ran back down the street toward the village entrance.

I jumped up and ran after Paolo into the blizzard, finding him at the Bomarzo gate in a heap on the ground. One leg was twisted unnaturally. He wasn't moving. Digging my hand under his scarf to feel a pulse at his neck, I was relieved to find one. I couldn't tell what had happened. Did he slip and hit his head? Did something knock him out? I knew I wouldn't be able to lift him.

And where was Lillian? She had been behind me at the village arch, and next to me when the statue fell in front of us. *"Aiuto!"* I screamed for help down the long brick corridor toward the palazzo. I hoped the snow didn't deaden my cries as I alternated my shouts for help and for Lillian.

Just as I was beginning to wonder if I would have to drag Paolo back to the palazzo myself, Ignazio and Jack appeared at my side. Ignazio cursed as he drew close, something that sounded like "damn her." Then he was kneeling next to Paolo. The snowflakes didn't seem to touch him at all—I thought of his heat when he touched me and understood.

He looked Paolo over. "We can't set that bone here. Help me." Ignazio and Jack gingerly picked up Paolo, doing their best to avoid jostling his broken leg. As we moved through the snow, the storm intensified around us, snowflakes lashing at us like shards of ice, driven by a wind that seemed to cut through every layer of clothing. Visibility was reduced to almost nothing; the palazzo that was usually just a short distance away appeared as a vague shadow amid a blinding white landscape.

With each step, my ruined shoes sank deeper into the snow, now accumulating at an alarming rate. I trudged behind them, my heart heavy and eyes squinting against the harsh wind. Every few paces, I glanced back, my eyes straining through the increasingly impenetrable wall of swirling snow, hoping against hope that Lillian would somehow emerge. The severity of the storm made it clear: venturing out farther, even for help, was becoming perilous, if not impossible.

"Was Lillian with you?" Jack asked me after he and Ignazio had laid Paolo down on one of the long couches in the small salon where we'd earlier danced for minutes—or hours.

I couldn't answer Jack. I could only nod and cry.

Jack brought me to a nearby settee and sat down next to me. I curled into him, glad for his warmth, for his strength. As he comforted me, a woman I had never seen before entered the room and went to Paolo's side. Tall and spindly, she, too, looked remarkably like Minos. She examined Paolo and said a few words to Ignazio before leaving the room.

"Paolo will be fine," Ignazio reported, pulling up a chair to join us. "He must have passed out from the pain when he broke his leg. We won't be able to get to the doctor in this weather, but Furia is fetching materials to stabilize it until we can get someone here to set it in plaster."

Furia. Fury. Even in my distressed state, I thought it an odd name for a woman. I half expected her to sprout wings.

Our host leaned toward me, his voice gentle, concerned. "Julia, we won't be able to go after Lillian until the storm breaks. Mother Nature is angry, and I fear this blizzard of hers is too much for even the strongest in this house to brave."

I buried my face into Jack's shoulder. Deep in my heart of hearts, I was sure Lillian was dead, and it was because of me. I should have just gone home. I should never have agreed to go to the *boschetto.* I should have stopped her from going near Ceres. I should have known she would throw that pomegranate.

"What is going on?" Dalí stood in the doorway in a plush bathrobe and red silk pajamas. Gala pushed past him into the room. She, too, was in a bathrobe and wore a kerchief over the curlers in her hair.

"What happened to him?" she asked when she saw Paolo stretched out on the couch. Furia had just finished setting the broken bone in a splint.

Ignazio beckoned to the pair to sit with us. Dalí folded himself into a chair, but Gala refused. She stood beside her husband, arms crossed, waiting for an explanation.

"He took a fall in the snow," Ignazio explained. "He will recover, but his leg is broken."

Gala stared at him, hands on her hips. She cursed in Russian, and I didn't need to know the language to realize that she was upset that their cameraman was now out of action. She didn't care one whit about Paolo himself.

"Snow? In the Lazio?" Gala said. "I'm sure it is nothing. It never snows here."

I was about to charge over to the window and rip open the curtains to show her, but she whirled on me before I could.

"You need to get to sleep. We have one day left to paint, and you better be ready. Jack, you come with me."

I gaped at her.

"Gala, darling, sit down," Jack said. "Something bad has happened."

She opened her mouth to retort, but she must have seen something in his eyes to know that perhaps she should listen, so she sat down on a chair next to her husband.

"Julia, Paolo, and Lillian were out in the storm," Ignazio said.

"Lillian disappeared," I blurted out, my tears beginning anew.

"This is ridiculous. You said there was snow?" Gala asked with a frown. "If that is true, why would you go out in a storm?"

I ignored her. "We need to tell the police," I implored Ignazio, anger rising through my sorrow.

He shook his head, his face sullen. "There isn't much of a police force in the village, but the moment it is safe to go outside, I'll fetch the *commissario*."

Jack patted my back to soothe me as I sobbed uncontrollably.

"Do not worry, little Proserpina," Dalí chimed in. "We will find your friend." He sounded genuinely concerned, and he looked resolute, but I had been around him enough to know that he was likely more interested in the thrill of discovering someone dead than anything else.

Gala wasn't nearly as magnanimous. "You shouldn't have gone out in the middle of the night. What on earth were you thinking? This is not a vacation, Julia Lombardi."

She spoke my name with more than her usual venom. I expected her to continue berating me, but she only tugged at the shoulder of Dalí's robe to make him rise and follow her back to their quarters.

"Come, Julia, you need sleep," Jack said softly, rising.

I couldn't move. "Someone should stay with Paolo, and wait for Lillian, in case she finds her way back."

Ignazio put a hot hand on my arm. "He'll be taken care of, and I'll be here, Julia. You should rest." There was something different in his voice—something akin to resignation.

Jack brought me to my room. I expected him to stay and comfort me, but he unceremoniously left me at the door and bade me good-night. As he turned from me, I thought I saw him smirk, but that didn't make sense.

Telling myself that grief was working my mind overtime, I locked the door behind me, but I didn't undress, in case I needed to go to Lillian if she returned. I didn't expect sleep, yet it engulfed me in an emptiness of black as soon as my head hit the pillow.

20

I awoke at dawn. The first rays of the morning sun had barely begun to filter through the trees. To my astonishment, there was no snow on the ground at all. The road from the *boschetto* to the village was clear.

A knock at the door jolted me from the view. It was Jack.

"You saw all the snow, didn't you?" I pointed to the window.

He nodded. "Snow squalls can be terrifying," he said, his voice holding a hint of condescension.

I wanted to scream at him. *It wasn't just a squall.* We had been trudging through several inches of snow by the time we reached the village gate. Ceres had sent the giants and the snow. She had purposefully tried to kill us. I couldn't even begin to explain it to him. Irritated, I pushed past him and made my way to the small salon.

Gala frowned when she saw Jack trailing behind me. "Did your friend turn up?" she asked, her tone making it clear that she was still annoyed. The look on my face must have said enough because she didn't wait for me to respond. "You should never have invited her here. It wasn't your place. You've ruined our last two days. We're not paying you for them."

I could only stare at her, mouth agape. Lillian was *missing*. I could hardly fathom how she could be so cruel.

"Now, now, Gala, darling, I think she's earned her pay," Jack said, sidling up to her.

She shrugged him off. "*You* certainly haven't."

Dalí gave me a sympathetic smile. "Worry not, my Proserpina. We will find your friend. And I will pay you." This last part was said in a conspiratorial whisper as Gala stepped aside to give Jack a dressing-down.

Ignazio appeared, a tray of pastries in his hand. "Take one, and we'll go search for Lillian. The truck is waiting."

I had no appetite. "Did you send for the *commissario*?"

"Yes. He's gathering up his men—they're volunteers, mind you. I'll remain here to await them."

I was relieved but also concerned about such a small police force. After thanking Ignazio, I asked if we could go to the *boschetto* immediately. Though I didn't want to return to the garden, I was sure my friend was there, and I was anxious to begin the search for her. I didn't have high hopes of finding Lillian alive. Yet looking for her gave me purpose, something I could do. I had to at least find her, and for that I would brave Ceres's twisted wrath.

There wasn't any snow outside the garden, but once we left the truck and crossed over the makeshift bridge into the *boschetto*, I was surprised to see a dusting still remained. I shivered, not so much with the cold, but because the unnatural feeling of Sacro Bosco and its stone statues filled the air around me even more than usual as I stepped foot on the trail beyond the planks that crossed the stream.

I stopped the group at the fork in the path. "We should stick together," I said. I could see the giant head of Orlando Furioso on the lower path, the feet of the intact woodsman in his hands. With the woodsman disappearing from the road, I wasn't surprised to see the statues had returned to the proper places. But Lillian was missing, Paolo had a broken leg, and I did not doubt what I had seen in the snow the night before. Now the sight of the giant men made my heart pound faster.

"We would cover more ground if we split up," Jack reasoned. My jaw dropped.

"You can't be serious?" I said. But I hadn't told my companions about the horrible events of the night before and I knew they wouldn't understand my fear. They thought that Lillian had merely gotten lost in the snow.

"Excellent. *Aniré per aquí.*" I didn't understand Dalí's Catalan, but he immediately headed down the upper path toward the top of the Casa Pendente—and the statue of Ceres.

"No. You shouldn't go alone!" I yelled after him. He waved at me and kept going like he hadn't heard me.

Gala pointed up the trail past the toppled Etruscan mausoleum toward the *tempietto*. "It's daylight," she said, as though that negated any danger. "You go find Salvador. We'll check the Pegasus fountain." She nudged Jack in the direction of Orlando and the woodsman, past which were the fountains and the nymphaeum. Jack gave me a casual wave and went with her, ignoring my worry about being alone.

I flipped them the bird behind their backs, which gave me only the slightest modicum of satisfaction. But I was glad I would be traversing the opposite side of the *boschetto* from Ceres. I hoped Dalí would be all right when he reached her statue, but I had no intention of taking direction from Gala.

After she and Jack were out of sight, I backtracked and made my way through the brush to check the entrance to the secret passage. I called for Lillian, hoping that if she ended up there she might hear me. Silence. It was too dark for me to go far into the tunnel, so I was forced to abandon the passage and return to the garden.

As I passed the overturned mausoleum where I had first heard

the whispers, I laid my hand upon the rock, wondering if I
would hear them again, but everything was silent.

I spent the next fifteen minutes going over all the places where
I thought Lillian might have hidden from the storm, starting
with the most obvious—the *tempietto*, which was empty. Dreading the thought of finding her body, I tried not to imagine what
wild animals might have gotten to her before we did. I looked
in and around the little temple, around Cerberus and around
the statues of the sirens. There was a little bit of patchy snow in
this part of the *boschetto*, including on the bench of Proserpina,
and enough to make the stairs slippery as I made my way down
into the heart of the garden toward the area around the *orco*.

As I reached the bottom of the stairs, I spotted Dalí in the
distance through the trees, across the bramble of weeds and
bushes, standing over the open Etruscan tomb where he had
last sketched me. He held a little sketchbook and a pen and was
drawing furiously. The world seemed to shrink around me, tun-
neling my vision into a point, the point where his pen hit the
paper. I knew what he was drawing.

I ran toward Dalí, past the worn statue of Aries's ram, until I
came to the edge of the tomb. And there was Lillian, her coat
gone, her shirt ripped open, exposing her left breast. Snow covered her stomach and legs. One arm was slung over her head,
resting on the edge of the tomb, her fingers reaching upward.
Her eyes and mouth were open, caught in a moment of pure
terror. As I stared at her body in shock, an astonishing, iridescent green beetle climbed out of her mouth.

Screaming, I fell to my knees at the side of the tomb. I was
vaguely aware of Dalí backing away and stuffing his notebook
in his coat, but the only thing I understood in that moment was
that my friend was dead.

My words from the day before ripped through me. *You're just
jealous. You wish it was you lying here, cold and naked for the whole
world to view.*

I did this to her. I should never have brought Lillian to Bomarzo.

At some point, I became aware of others gathered around us, then Ignazio helping me up, his hands hot, his smoke enveloping me with an odd comfort. "Oh, Julia," he whispered. "Julia, I'm so sorry. This should never have happened." In his embrace, I felt his deep sorrow—not for Lillian, but the sorrow he had for me.

A tall man with curly dark hair, a mustache, and gray suit stood at the edge of the tomb, barking orders in some unintelligible Italian dialect. The *commissario*. Ignazio led me away, telling me that the inspector would take care of everything. I didn't have the energy to tell him he was wrong. There was nothing for the *commissario* to take care of. Lillian was dead. She was dead because of me—because I dragged her there.

I barely registered Ignazio whisking me away to the palazzo and providing me with some sort of liquor I willingly drank to dull the pain in my heart. Heading outside, I sat on the terrace, staring down at the *boschetto*, at the little figures I could see moving among the trees, combing the garden for clues, the *commissario* peppering Gala, Jack, and Dalí with questions.

He would later ask the same questions of me. But for a long while, I just stared down at the *boschetto*, my heart a dull, empty thing. Ignazio sat there with me, but he did not do or say anything. I don't know what I would have done if he had tried to talk with me, or touch me, even in sympathy. He hadn't been the one to harm Lillian—somehow, I was sure of it—but he was wrapped up in all this, and I didn't have a single iota of trust in him. But he only sat there with me, and for that, I was glad.

The *commissario* was gentle with me and my less-than-stellar Italian, and I was relieved I didn't seem to be under any suspicion. But I didn't tell him what really had happened—how could I? We got caught in the storm and one moment Lillian was behind me and the next she wasn't. We went down to the *boschetto* to see what it was like at night. No, we didn't see any other people in the garden. No, I didn't know her family, but she had an aunt in Rome whom I had never met. Yes, I knew where she worked. Yes, I loved her. Yes, she was my best friend.

"Will you help me return to Roma?" I asked the *commissario* as the interview was ending.

He pursed his lips. "You will all need to remain here until we have concluded our investigation."

"Even Dalí?" I asked.

The *commissario* chuckled. "No man is above the law, signorina. Not even him."

My guess was that Gala had not yet had a chance to grease this man's palm. I could easily see them departing quickly if she gave him enough cash.

Besides, neither Dalí nor Gala knew what had happened out in the storm. And when they questioned Paolo on the morrow he wouldn't give up the truth either. The mental hospitals in Italy were known to be torturous places, and neither of us wanted to end up in one.

I went to Paolo that afternoon and sat in the chair at the edge of his bed until he awoke. I wanted to be the one to tell him about Lillian. The doctor had come while we were in the *boschetto* and had set his leg with plaster. A pair of crutches leaned against the wall.

After I told him about Lillian, he asked me to help him sit up. Once he was upright, his head and back against the backboard, he patted the spot next to him. "Come here." I climbed onto the bed next to him and he held me while I cried.

I sobbed long and hard, and he let me.

"What happened when you went back for her?" I asked.

"I don't know. I must have slipped."

"I wish you could have known her better," I told him. "I am sorry for that."

"Do not be sorry. I am glad she was in my life, even if for just a couple of days. She loved you, Julia. Cherish her memory. Remember all you learned from her, all you loved about her. Let those memories be your solace when darkness looms."

We sat in silence for a few minutes. My tears had dried, and a little shell was starting to form around my heart, hard and protective.

"I think I will eat the last seed," I finally said.

He pulled back to look me in the eye.

"No, Julia, no, you must not."

"Lillian died because I wouldn't give in to the forces of the *boschetto*," I said. "I don't know why they want me to, but it seems like I should, regardless of what will happen to me. I don't want anyone else to suffer the same fate because of me."

"Julia, you'll die."

I nodded. "I think that's true."

"You can't give in to them, Julia. Think of all the ghosts. You'll become one of them. You don't want that terrible fate, roaming around Bomarzo till the end of time."

"If I don't, you might die. Dalí or Jack or Gala might die. Lillian's death was a terrible one. She died in fear. In total, abject terror. Whatever killed her will come for all of you."

Paolo shook his head. "You don't know that. Anything could have happened to Lillian. Don't do this, Julia, please. Lillian wouldn't want you to."

I had been sure of my decision until he said these last words. He was right. Lillian would not want me to. She would want me to fight these forces, to defy them.

But look what defying them had gotten her.

When I left Paolo, I searched for Dalí and found him on the terrace, thankfully alone, painting the valley before him. I was surprised to see trees cropping up on his canvas—he was fonder

of the desert, of clean lines that served as a backdrop to his surreal visions.

"I'd like to see the sketchbook I saw you with earlier," I said
to him, no longer caring if I got paid or if I sat for him again.

He set down his brush. "I don't think you need to..."

"I do."

He stared at me, but I refused to budge. I held out my hand
expectantly.

He seemed unsure what his course of action should be. I don't
think many women had been stern with him except for Gala, and
perhaps his mother, long ago. He reached into his coat pocket
and handed me the worn Moleskine. In his eyes, I saw something that I don't know if many had ever seen or might ever see
from him again—shame.

I flipped through the notebook, past images of me, Gala, slippery clocks, fuzzy bees, partially imagined humans, spindly elephants, and strange landscapes. Finally, I came upon the sketch
he had been making at the edge of the Etruscan grave. Lillian's
terror stared up at me, her breast bared, her leg and arm askew.
I hated how talented he was. I hated that he had captured the
image so perfectly. And in that moment, I hated him.

The thought of slapping him, as I had seen women do in
movies, crossed my mind. But I knew that for Dalí, that would
mean little. His face was just skin and bone; his art was his soul.

Instead I ripped the drawing out of the book, holding the
delicate paper up to his eyes so he could see the destruction.
Dalí's face paled; he looked as though I had struck him physi-
cally. His lips quivered, but he said nothing.

When I handed the Moleskine back to him, his eyes would
not meet mine. I went to the edge of the terrace and ripped up
the sketch, letting the pieces float in the wind, dropping to the
boschetto below like fallen snow. I watched them fly away, my
heart broken into as many pieces.

He came and stood next to me, and we looked out toward

the garden. He didn't apologize for his drawing. Even if the thought had occurred to him, I don't think he had the slightest idea how to do so. I had destroyed something irreplaceable, something that had sprung from his twisted, brilliant mind. And I felt no remorse.

"Salvador." Gala's call sounded like a command and the artist took it as such, turning at once and going to her. "We can't leave for at least a few days," she said stoically.

So, the *commissario* hadn't taken her bribe after all.

"You need to get back to work on the sets for the Opera, but now we're stuck here." She sneered at me, her tone accusatory.

This time, I didn't resist the urge to slap her. But as my hand connected with her face, I realized that real life was not like the movies. There was no orchestral swell, no gasping audience. There was only the sound of flesh against flesh, the sharp sting in my palm, and the look of pure shock in Gala's eyes.

Her mouth dropped into an O of surprise, but if she said anything to me, I didn't hear her. I had already stepped back inside.

21

There was no funeral parlor to take Lillian's body to in Bomarzo, so until the *commissario* had enough information for the investigation and they could return her to Rome, they had to keep her in the palazzo. The coroner in neighboring Viterbo had been sent for but would not arrive until the next day. Gala didn't want Lillian laid out where she'd be a constant reminder of her inconvenient death, so the salons were nixed. Ignazio had the *commissario* bring Lillian to the library, where she lay on a long walnut table.

Paolo's words about Lillian gave me the courage I needed to go to her, late in the afternoon. Although the sun still filtered through the big windows, the room was lit with four or five candelabra, and a fire crackled in the grate.

Someone had closed Lillian's eyes and mouth, dressed her in a white shirt, smoothed down her hair, and laid her hands at her sides. The bottom half of her body was covered by a sheet. She looked like she was sleeping. I was grateful she no longer looked afraid.

I wanted to tell her I was sorry, but I couldn't make the words come. I couldn't speak at all. I knew I would fall apart, and there was so little holding me together. Instead, like Ignazio had done with me, I sat with her in silence, staring at the fire. I didn't hear any whispers during my vigil, but I had the distinct feeling I wasn't alone, that my ghosts were there with me, mourning at my side.

Eventually, my body's needs broke through the numbness of my grief. With a lingering kiss to Lillian's cold forehead, I excused myself to use the bathroom down the hall. Inside, I caught my reflection in the mirror, a stark reminder of the day's toll. My appearance was a wreck, hair askew and tear-streaked cheeks. I could almost hear Lillian's teasing voice, chiding me about my disheveled state. The thought brought a fresh wave of tears, blurring the reflection that so vividly echoed my inner turmoil.

I allowed myself a few moments of unchecked sorrow, the bathroom echoing with the sound of my crying. Gradually, the sobs subsided, and I set about repairing the damage. Splashing water on my face, tidying my hair, I worked to regain some semblance of composure.

On my way back, I was nearly at the library door when I heard Jack calling my name. He and Dalí approached, a study in contrasts. They were a funny sight, even in the midst of my grief—one dark and one light, one taller than the other, one solid and strong, and the other thin and slight. Everything about them was opposing, yet here they were together.

"We wanted to pay our respects," Jack said, his voice somber.

"Properly," Dalí added, bowing his head a little.

Given our recent confrontation, I was taken aback by his lack of animosity. The thought of Dalí hovering over Lillian's lifeless body again gnawed at me, but it seemed ungracious to turn them away now. With a reluctant nod, I led them into the library.

When I saw the empty table, I froze, my heart sinking into my stomach. "She was here…right here, a moment ago." Panic clawed at my chest. "Who could do this? Why would someone take her?"

"What's that?" Dalí pointed, his eyes narrowed, his voice tinged with a nervousness that was uncharacteristic of him.

I followed his gaze to the corner of the library. The door to the secret passage was ajar, a dim light glowing from the darkness beyond.

"Whoever did this must have taken her to the garden. This passage leads there," I said.

I rushed to the corner and peered down the stairs. The torches had all been lit. I knew it was foolish, but I didn't hesitate. I started down the stairs, not caring if Dalí or Jack followed, which of course they did. Their footsteps and ragged breathing sounded behind me. I don't know what I expected to do when I found Lillian—if I did—I only knew I had to find her. Or I would die trying. The footsteps that were following us in the snow the night before were from some creature far bigger than me.

As I navigated the secret passage, its contours seemed to change under the torchlight. Chisel marks told a story of laborious excavation, and soot-blackened spots above each torch marred the ceiling. While I could see easily and didn't have to rely on the cautious bob of a flashlight, the passage felt just as interminable as it had when we first discovered it. Finally, I had to stop to catch my breath, allowing Jack and Dalí to catch up.

Dalí looked unnerved. "This might be a bad idea," he muttered, glancing around the stone walls as if they could close in at any moment.

It was such a ridiculous statement I almost laughed.

Jack looked pensive, his eyes squinting as if trying to pierce the darkness ahead. "You have to wonder, with Lillian gone so suddenly... Could be we're not alone in this place. Could be some deranged killer lurking in the shadows," he said, his voice low and ominous.

A shiver crawled down my spine. "You really think a murderer would be hiding here?"

Jack shrugged, his eyes shifting, evasive. "Who knows? People do all kinds of horrible things for reasons we can't always understand."

Dalí looked from me to Jack, as if sensing an unspoken tension. His eyes darted nervously. "Indeed, madness and genius often walk hand in hand, but a killer—that's something else altogether."

Jack smirked at Dalí. "You should be excited about this. An excursion into the heart of one of the most surreal places on Earth."

Dalí narrowed his eyes at Jack. "This is not a game."

"Isn't it?"

I don't know what compelled Jack to say such a thing, but I think he saw the horror written on my face. He quickly put his arm around my shoulders and hugged me tight. "Don't worry, Jules, we'll find her."

"Let's keep going." I pulled away, unsure what to think about what had just happened, and doubly irritated that he'd called me by the nickname that Lillian always used for me.

We resumed our journey down the dark passage, but Jack's words hung in the air, each step forward accompanied by a growing sense of dread.

"If there is a killer," Dalí said as we continued on, "we have nothing with which to defend ourselves."

I didn't slow my pace. "Then maybe you should go back."

"Don't be silly, Julia. We're not leaving you," Jack said. "Right, Dalí? I know that I'm seeing this through with you to the end."

Something about his declaration of loyalty fell flat. But if physical danger did lurk at the end of the tunnel, perhaps I would be grateful to have his brawn at my side.

Finally, we reached the bronze door. It was wide open, and the last dim rays of the setting sun glowed against the green metal. We raced down the path, across the boards at the stream, and through the veil that separated the *boschetto* from the rest of the world.

Orpheus waited for me on the other side. He jumped into

my arms, meowing. "I don't have time for you right now, little one," I said as I put him back down on the ground. Jack was the last one to cross the stream, and as he neared, Orpheus suddenly gave a hiss and a yowl before running back into the bushes. We looked around for the disturbance but saw none. Had he been hissing at Jack?

We took the path toward the heart of the garden, the one that Dalí had taken when we were looking for Lillian. As we turned the corner and came upon the dried-up fountain of Neptune and his dolphin, like the night before, a tangle of bushes and trees had grown up. But the bushes were different, only leaving room for a path that snaked between them in the direction of Ceres, who loomed between the trees about a hundred feet away. While that made me nervous, I was more immediately concerned with the type of foliage that had appeared. The pomegranate trees were bursting with fruit.

And that fruit was bursting.

"Mon Dieu," Dalí cried. I couldn't tell if he was horrified or amazed. Perhaps a bit of both. There were dozens upon dozens of the ruby fruits, each split open horizontally, revealing rows of seeds, some still unripe and white, others bloodred. They hung on the vine, arils bared like vicious fangs, their downward crowns reaching out like little tentacles, turning the pomegranates into horrifying little monsters.

"These," he said, examining the opening in the skin that looked like a mouth, "are the most Dalínian fruits I have ever seen. If only Paolo were here with his camera."

"They're all split," Jack marveled. He looked at me. "What could it mean?"

"How should I know?"

"I just thought you might," he said, raising an eyebrow.

He sauntered over to a bush, plucked one of the fruits, and held it out to me. I recoiled, horrified.

"She's not fond of those," Dalí said, coming to my rescue and snatching it out of Jack's hand. I was shocked. It was the first time that Dalí didn't try to make me eat a pomegranate. I wondered why. I only had one more seed to eat, and if he was some sort of mechanism for my destruction, wouldn't he want me to eat it?

"What a terrible Proserpina you make." Jack chuckled, but I sensed he was being serious. And mean. Something was not right about him, and I didn't like it.

"Truly terrible," I agreed, bristling. "Come, we don't have time for this."

Dalí chucked the pomegranate into bushes beyond the statue of Neptune. The wind immediately kicked up, rocking the trees around us, whipping my hair into my eyes and mouth.

"Maybe you should have eaten it," Jack said. He yanked another pomegranate off the bush, one with a jagged line of unripe white seeds.

Orpheus ran up between us and began a horrible caterwaul, a mournful, terrible sound. Jack snarled and gave the beast a swift kick, knocking him into the bushes.

"What is wrong with you? Why did you do that?" I screamed, pushing past him to part the bushes in search of Orpheus, but Jack spun me around to face him. His mouth was twisted into a snarl and his eyes were suddenly green, not that beautiful blue that I had once admired.

"I'm tired of this game," he said, but his voice wasn't his voice. It was the same one I heard every time I had encountered Demetra in the hallways of Palazzo Orsini. And then I understood. Demetra, named after Demeter, the Greek name for Ceres. I cursed myself for not making the obvious connection sooner.

His eyes flashed green, just as the giant's had last night.

This wasn't Jack. It was Ceres. Or at least, he was being controlled by her.

He yanked me toward him, pulling me into a one-armed embrace that pinned my arms to my sides like a vise. With his other hand, he pushed the pomegranate toward me, pressing the fruit against my lips.

I clenched my mouth tight, my screams muffled. I tried to struggle, but he held me fast. The pomegranate was hard against my face, smashing my lips against my teeth. I was sure he was going to break them when suddenly he crumpled, his hands loosening and falling away. The pomegranate rolled toward the bushes where Jack had sent Orpheus flying.

"No one defiles my *modelo*," Dalí said, dropping the rock in his hands. There was a splotch of blood on one side.

On impulse, I threw my arms around him. "Thank you." I didn't know the reason he saw fit to stop Jack, but I was grateful for it.

He stiffened in my embrace, and I pulled away. He lifted a hand, calloused from holding his brushes for hours at a time, to wipe the tears from my cheeks.

I turned from him to look for Orpheus, digging through the leaves, but he wasn't there.

"Come, it's getting dark," Dalí said, putting a hand on my shoulder and looking down at Jack's body. "Let's find Lillian before he wakes up."

"What happened to him?" I sighed as I stared down at the prone figure. He looked like the sweet brawny boy I had liked the moment we met, not the twisted creature that Ceres had turned him into.

"It's this place," Dalí said. "It gets into your head. Even I, the great Dalí, have felt its sinister pull. Come. We need to find your friend." He guided me down the pomegranate-lined path.

As we made our way farther into the heart of the garden, an even stronger sense of dread began to rise within me. It wasn't just Jack's terrifying actions, but the fact that I already knew what we would find. I was anxious to get away from Jack and the pomegranates, but we were being herded in a specific direction—and I knew it was a trap, set with Lillian's body as the bait. We would find her inside the Mouth of Hell.

The promenade before the statue of Neptune had a wall with dozens of large vases around its perimeter. One had to walk down toward the Casa Pendente, then past the statue of Ceres, before turning back toward the ominous *orco* in the hillside, passing Hannibal's elephant and the fighting dragon on the way. If we wanted to avoid Ceres, we would have to climb the wall, which wasn't convenient—or possible, with the newly grown wall of pomegranate bushes.

As we came close to the statue of the goddess, I saw a ghost of myself standing near the path in front of her. It was growing dark, and her blue glow was faint as she flickered in and out of my vision. She—or I—wore a dress right out of the Renaissance, with a long, full brocade skirt, belted under the bust, the billowing sleeves slashed elegantly to show through the *camicia* underneath. Her hair was intricately braided with ropes of pearl.

Suddenly, a memory surged through me, so vivid it was as if I'd been plunged into another lifetime. I found myself in my bedroom in Bomarzo, but everything was new, the walls adorned with tapestries and fine art, and the soft glow of candlelight filling the room. The door opened, and he walked in—his face a composite of lifetimes and love, the lines of Aidoneus, Ignazio, and Pluto woven into one countenance.

He approached me cautiously, holding a small vial filled with a dark liquid. "This is the last pomegranate potion," he said softly, his eyes brimming with a cocktail of love, regret, and something I couldn't quite place.

I nodded, knowing that in the society of that lifetime, an illicit child would spell doom for both of us. I trusted him, loved him, across all lifetimes. With trembling hands, I opened the vial and drank its foul contents. As I swallowed, I felt the familiar texture of a pomegranate seed slide down my throat.

Almost instantly, pain enveloped me, racking my body in torturous waves. His face, so full of contradictions, was the last thing my eyes grasped before darkness overwhelmed me. In that terrible moment, I realized it wasn't just an unwanted pregnancy I was erasing—it was my very life, my existence in that cycle, sending me spiraling back to the Fields of Mourning under the weight of an eternal curse.

Back in the garden, the Renaissance ghost of me suddenly raised a single finger, a haunting warning echoing across the fabric of time itself.

Dalí obviously didn't see her since he walked by without acknowledgment. I could almost hear the rustling of her gown as she disappeared into the fading light. Thankfully, the stone goddess behind her did not move.

Another version of me waited near Hannibal's elephant. This ghost was clad in medieval dress, with flowing skirts, a corseted bodice, and long, belled sleeves. As I approached, I felt a strange pull, a kind of magnetic force that beckoned me into the depths of a forgotten memory. There I was, in a castle's stone-walled chamber, standing near an expansive wooden table laden with rustic dishes—bread, meat, cheeses, and fruit.

This time, it was a goblet of wine that was handed to me by the same man, whose soul stretched over lifetimes. His eyes met mine with an inexplicable mix of love, sorrow, and inevitability. "For your health, my lady," he said softly, urging me to drink. "Pomegranate wine."

Hesitant but not wanting to offend, I lifted the goblet to my lips and took a sip, the single pomegranate seed sliding over my tongue. I was surprised by the taste for an instant, followed by a feeling of dread as I swallowed. A crushing weight settled over my chest, heavier and colder with each passing second. I looked at him, desperation flooding my eyes. "What have you done?" I wanted to scream, but no words escaped.

The room spun around me, and just like before, my last sight was his face, stricken with unbearable grief as he watched me collapse, my life extinguishing like a candle snuffed out by an unforgiving wind.

As we passed the medieval ghost in the garden, she, too, raised a single finger. The fabric of my reality began to unravel as I started to understand the threads of my past.

Again, Dalí passed without as much as a glance. She winked out as I passed her.

At the dragon fending off the wolves and lions, another ghost waited, arm outstretched, one finger pointed toward the sky. This version of me was dressed like all the women I had ever seen in ancient Roman statues, with drapes of fabric about her body and over her head like a hood, with sandals and bracelets ringing her thin wrists. I was reminded of something Dalí called me on one of the first days—Julia of the Julii. I didn't understand why then, but upon seeing this ghost, I did, as some odd memory lit up in my mind. The Julii were an ancient Roman family of great nobility—the clan that Julius Caesar himself came from. This was a Julia from centuries past.

As we grew close to this Julia, a vision overtook me so powerfully that I nearly stumbled. I was in an elegant atrium, adorned with frescoes and opulent decorations, the kind that would be found in the house of a Roman patrician. The same man—this time dressed in a toga and wearing a laurel crown—offered me a plate of stuffed dates. His eyes were a deep well of mixed emotions: love, regret, and sorrow.

"Try one, Proserpina," he said, the name as strange and familiar to me as the earlier incarnations had been. "They're made just for you. I know you don't like pomegranates, but try one more… You may just like this one."

Reluctantly I took a date and bit into it. The sweetness enveloped my senses, but then my tongue touched something different—a pomegranate seed hidden within the treat.

My vision began to blur; my limbs felt weak. "What's happening?" I gasped.

His smile faded into a look of terror, the joy in his eyes giving way to realization and then unbearable grief. "No, no, no," he cried, rushing to catch me as I fell to the ground.

"Stay with me," he pleaded, holding my limp body. "Please, stay with me. This wasn't supposed to happen. Damn you, Ceres."

I wanted nothing more than to stay with him, but a force stronger than both of us was pulling me away. The last thing I saw was his anguished face, immortalized in that moment, forever to be repeated over a string of lifetimes. My vision tunneled, the edges darkening. My spirit was being pulled away, traveling at an unimaginable speed through the fabric of existence, into the place where love had been thwarted—the Fields of Mourning.

When the memory cleared, I was back in the garden. The Roman ghost before me raised her single finger, a signal that reverberated through time, wrapping my newfound understanding in layers of tragic, eternal truth. It was a curse, a hundred-year cycle, and unless broken, it would carry on infinitely. My resolve hardened; something had to change. I would not endure this again.

We reached the base of the stairs leading into the open maw of the *orco*. If Lillian was in the Mouth of Hell, she wasn't lying on the table that also served as the monster's tongue.

Dalí led the way into the *orco*. We had only climbed a couple of stairs when Orpheus ran up beside me. He gave me an agonized cry. I stopped, my heart full of relief that he was alive.

Bending down to pick him up, I hugged him close. He licked my cheek and a burst of understanding washed over me. I saw myself in a black and beautiful palazzo in the Underworld, and Orpheus, the man, rushed into the room, his lute bouncing against his back. "Ceres is coming for you." His voice was urgent, explaining that Ceres stood on the banks of the Lethe, ready to cross, raging about a curse.

"I brought this for you," he said, holding out his hand.

Oh, Orpheus. He had brought me a pearl from Mnemosyne's pond.

I gathered my courage and went to Ceres, carrying the pearl

from the goddess of memory under my tongue to help me hold a shred of remembrance, a glimmer of truth through countless lifetimes. It was this pearl that helped me remember just enough to leave the ghosts, providing cryptic warnings and guidance across the veil separating life and death.

Orpheus the cat meowed softly, jolting me out of the memory. He rubbed his face against mine, as if acknowledging the immense tapestry of events and emotions that had led to this moment. I knew that there was an essence of the real Orpheus within the beast, helping me, like I had once tried to help him.

Dalí's shout rang out from the interior of the *orco*.

"She's here."

I ran up the stairs. Dalí was at the back of the mouth. Past the central table, in the last light of the dusk, I could make out Lillian's bare feet. She was lying on the carved bench that lined the interior.

I was about to go around the table toward them when suddenly a rough hand spun me around. Jack. Pushing me into the table, my lower back connecting with the stone, he pinned me there with an elbow—because his hand held something.

A pomegranate, burst on the side, a tiny mouth of ruby seeds gaping at me. Jack shoved his fingers into the fruit, ripping out a chunk of arils and pith.

He shoved the seeds into my face, pressing them against my closed mouth. His fingers parted my lips, and before I could understand what was happening, he forced apart my teeth. I bit at his fingers, and he pulled his hand back, but he had done what he set out to do. The seeds were in my mouth. I held them under my tongue, refusing to swallow. I could taste blood, and my lip hurt where it had cut against my teeth as he pressed the seeds into me.

"Swallow!" the voice that wasn't Jack's said.

Then Jack was yanked backward.

A shout rang through the *orco*. "No one touches her with violence."

Jack howled when he hit the stairs outside the Mouth of Hell. Then there was no sound. I sat up in time to see his body roll to a stop on the path.

Ignazio stood there, a dark shadow against the lighter shadows of the dusky garden behind him. "Are you all right?" he asked. He was only a few feet from me, and I could feel his heat radiating, a sharp contrast to the cold stone of the table.

Outside the *orco*, Orpheus cried. His little blue eyes implored me. The Julia of the Julii ghost stood next to him. She balled her hand, held up one finger, and then pressed it against her lip. *One more.*

I knew what to do.

I pulled Ignazio to me, one hand on the lapel of his jacket, the other around his waist. He didn't resist. I lifted my face to his and his lips met mine and parted, his tongue searching.

I blew an aril into his mouth. Then I pulled back and took a fist to his chest, hitting hard, forcing him to gasp and swallow the seed.

Ignazio's eyes grew wide, then found mine. They flared, bright fire in his pupils. Everything about him transformed, hot, white, yellow fire. His arms wrapped around me, and he kissed me. His heat became my heat.

The ground beneath us shook. I heard Dalí yell something in Catalan, felt Orpheus rubbing against my leg, and the brush of ghostly fingers across my cheek, and somewhere beyond us, I heard a woman crying, a woman I knew was Ceres.

The kiss tasted like home—a home I had forgotten and yearned for in every fiber of my being, through every incarnation. It tasted like the sweetest pomegranate, which I now knew that I loved, its juice both tart and sugary, complex yet straightforward. In that instant, the weight of our shared histories lifted, as if the air around us had become less dense, more forgiving. I felt the redemption of our love in its purest form, a love that had battled against the trials of immortality and the spite of a jilted lover. Pluto's breath caught, a moment of vulnerability as our lips parted, and I knew then that he felt it too. It was as if we had ventured into some sacred space, a sanctuary that could only be unlocked by our union. We had returned to each other, and there was no curse, no vengeance, no mortality that could ever pull us apart again.

Then the whole world fell away. There was no Julia or Ignazio, no Dalí, no Jack.

Only Pluto and Proserpina.

22

We stood on a massive precipice of shining ebony at the very edge of the Underworld. Our gazes stretched over a grove of golden oaks with glittering acorns toward the star path that ran along the banks of the mystical River Lethe, born from the tears of its namesake goddess. There was no sun, but the sky was full of brilliant and vivid hues of every shade of red and pink and purple. I could see Kharon, the ferryman, up in the distance where the River Styx met up with the Lethe, his hand outstretched, waiting for a coin of passage from the souls who had come down the star path and were ready to board. The star path was the last place a living being might walk before reaching the dock that would take them into their final resting place.

In my past, Ceres had been my lover, but she turned against me when she discovered my infidelity and my deep affection for Pluto. She cast a formidable curse on us. The true path to breaking this curse was obscure yet simple: it required me to persuade Pluto to willingly consume three pomegranate seeds.

However, Ceres, in her deceit, had convinced Pluto of a dif-

ferent, false remedy. She made him believe that every hundred
years, my reincarnation had to consciously consume six pomegranate seeds to free us both from her spell. These seeds, which
she convinced me that I patently didn't like, were presented to
me in various methods by Pluto's earthly form. They were never
hidden; I always had the choice to see and consume them.

Tragically, this was a ruse. He had convinced me to eat the six
seeds twenty-six times over countless years, and each consumption led to my death. The cruel cycle was perpetuated by the effects of the River Lethe: upon returning to the Underworld, its
waters wiped our memories clean. Ceres had ensured this selec-
tive amnesia.

Pluto remembered only the necessity of my consuming the
seeds, not the repeated tragedies that followed. He was oblivious to the reality of my recurring deaths, forever locked in the
belief that the next cycle would be our salvation. Every century,
he was convinced it was our chance to finally break the curse,
oblivious to the sorrowful loop we were trapped in.

A soft, tinkling bell echoed in the distance, and Pluto's expression changed, as if pulled back to reality by its call. With a reluctant wave of his hand, he summoned Ceres. "You may come."

She materialized before us, wearing a gauzy gown of white,
cinched at the waist with a metallic belt, and her auburn hair
was piled high upon her head, entwined with a thin golden rope.
She was breathtaking, and I remembered all the reasons why
I had once spent eons as her lover. Around her neck dangled a
pendant shaped like a wheat stalk, a symbol of a love that once
was—a love that had instigated this never-ending cycle of joy
and sorrow. I had given it to her in the early days of our romance.

Pluto tightened his hot grip on me. "Say your piece, and say
it fast," he urged Ceres, the undercurrent of his voice carrying a
challenge, a boundary. "I would be all too happy to banish you
from this place, and with no small amount of pain."

"I wanted to acknowledge that you won." She gazed intently

at us, her eyes searching our faces. "In my bitterness and pain, I thought my love for Proserpina was unparalleled, all-consuming. But seeing the love that you two share, a love that has survived countless lifetimes of separation and heartache... I was wrong."

A complex mix of emotions crossed her features—regret that to me seemed tinged with relief. "And so, my curse is undone. I relinquish its hold over you."

I found I had no anger toward my former lover, only something akin to pity. But one thing galled me. "You didn't have to kill Lillian, you know."

"I suppose it was rather cruel," she responded. "But you were starting to figure it all out, and I was loath for my game to be over. I never thought you'd solve the riddle in just three millennia."

Her eyes flickered to Pluto. "I have to admit, it was brilliant to take on the guise of Aidoneus, to convince Giulia to inspire her husband to create the Sacro Bosco. And all those monuments to help with your familiarity—Orcus, Cerberus, your bench. As soon as I got wind of that—" she broke off and looked at me, as I was the one who needed the explanation, not my husband "—I planted the seeds within Vicino Orsini to create my own statue. And, of course, found a local goodwife to call my own."

"The servant, Demetra. What did you do with her?" I asked.

"She's home and no worse for the wear. And you didn't even know she was right under your nose." She snickered at Pluto.

Heat rose around us. Pluto's patience was low, and he was ready to cast her out. But I stayed him with a hand on his arm. There was one thing I had to understand.

"The curse wasn't enough for you, though. You changed our story. Why?" I understood why Ceres cursed Pluto and me, but she had planted the seeds of rumor that I was her daughter and had been forcibly ripped from the world. Her subversion of the myth that humans ended up passing along through the centuries was baffling to me.

"Would you want to be remembered through eternity as the

jilted lover?" Her nostrils flared with anger. "No! You wouldn't have. And I still don't. It was Jupiter who introduced his brother to you, and for his role in tearing us apart, I demanded he change the memory of our love in the minds of gods and men. Mine would be the plight of a mother in distress."

"Jupiter can do that?" I marveled.

"He had some help from Gaia herself, who called upon her daughter."

Gaia, one of the primordial deities. And while she had many sons and daughters, Ceres was speaking of Lethe.

"I'm not sure I like the idea of people thinking I'm your daughter," I said.

"Too bad," she sniffed.

"I tire of this," Pluto said, his ire at a peak. "You have your answers. Begone, and never come back."

"I should have listened to Venus," she said, her voice softer, forgiving. "When she heard what I had done, she told me that true love would win. I doubted her. But neither of you gave up."

Then she was gone.

"Come, I want to show you something." I took Lillian by the hand.

"Oh! It's the garden! But everything seems so pale, so dull," she said as we left the dark stars of my sacred grove and the Sacro Bosco materialized around us.

"You are spoiled by Elysium," I told her. "There is more color there." It was her first time out of the Underworld, and I had forgotten how strange that might feel for a mortal who had passed.

We stood on the path between the statue of Ceres and the *orco*. The garden was different—rejuvenated, restored.

"Is this the past?" Lillian asked.

"This is the future," I said with a smile. "See?" I pointed at a young couple standing near the base of the *orco*. "That's Giovanni and Tina Severi Bettini. Remember I told you that we filmed at the *tempietto*? They saw Dalí's film and were inspired by the garden, and upon visiting, they fell in love with its magic. The Bettinis will dedicate decades to Bomarzo's renewal. Each sculpture will be meticulously restored. Gravel paths raked smooth, hedges pruned, the chaos tamed. They'll open the gates so people can experience this sublime place for themselves." I waved my hand and the garden transformed again, statues repaired and cleaned of their moss, vines neatly trimmed back from weathered inscriptions. Visitors strolled in awe along paths once overgrown.

"It's not so creepy now. It's mystical, magical even," Lillian said in wonder. "Thank you for showing me this."

Next, I took her to one of Dalí's exhibits in New York, at the Museum of Non-Objective Painting on the Upper East Side. There was one painting I wanted to see, and I thought she might too.

I propelled her to a gallery in the back of the museum, where a crowd had formed. Salvador Dalí stood in the center of it, gesticulating wildly with a white staff topped with a golden dove. He wore a flower behind his ear and his mustache was exceptionally long and curled upward. Gala stood to the side, flanked by three young men vying for her attention.

Lillian's eyes widened. "Dalí!" she exclaimed. A flicker of something complex crossed her face—nostalgia mixed with an uncomfortable familiarity. "He is such a living paradox."

"What do you mean?" I asked.

"He's so deeply selfish, yet completely vulnerable and insecure. Before my spirit found its way to the Underworld, I watched him sketch my lifeless body. It was as if he was trying to capture something he himself was afraid of losing—his essence, his mortality. Yet the act itself showed how disconnected he was from the human experience, how consumed by his own mind." She sighed, her gaze still fixed on Dalí. "It's a strange mix of emotions, watching him now. I feel pity for him, for his eter-

nal struggle to seize something he could never fully grasp…"
She trailed off.

"But?" I prompted.

"But—" she smiled, her eyes meeting mine "—I also feel
warmth. It's strange, isn't it? To feel warmth for someone who
violated such a private moment? But he has a special sort of cha-
risma, the kind that makes it very hard to dislike him for long.
You cannot help but to be drawn toward him."

I knew exactly how she felt.

Putting an arm over my friend's shoulders, I hugged her tight.
"Genius often comes with its own set of damning flaws, and
Dalí is clearly no exception. But here's the thing, Lillian. We're
all flawed beings, even gods. Perhaps that's what makes us eternally fascinating to each other."

Dalí struck the bottom of his staff against the floor, its sound
turning every head toward him. He was talking with a young
reporter who held a notebook in his hand. "When someone
important dies, I can feel it, sometimes very intensely. It is a
monstrous and reassuring feeling. Because that dead person has
become one hundred percent Dalínian. From now on, they will
watch over me, over the great fulfillment of my work."

He sauntered over to one painting. "This is a poem about
death."

Lillian gasped. "I thought you destroyed them all."

I chuckled. "All except that one. It isn't a painting of me, but
it's about me."

She jabbed me in the ribs with her elbow. "A muse, not an
artist."

"This time Dalí was right. But remember what I said about
him being flawed."

The painting wasn't large, about three feet wide and two and
a half high. It had a typical stark, Dalínian landscape, where
sparse trees with tiny leaves decorated a desert scene. An abnor-
mally large, bizarre floating box broken into four corner quad-

rants comprised the focal point of the painting. Hovering in its center was a massive pomegranate, its crown forward. On the top of the box was a tiny figure of a man playing a trumpet, his legs dangling off the side, just like the musician that night in the *boschetto*.

A man next to us lectured his bejeweled wife about the musician. "The trumpeter challenges our notion of scale," he said.

"No, he challenges our perception of reality," Lillian said, leaning conspiratorially toward the man.

The couple was startled at Lillian's interjection. They gave her a funny look and backed off, making their way to another corner of the gallery.

"They don't know what to do with me, do they?" Lillian observed.

I nodded. "You are the one challenging their perception of reality. Seeing the dead is unsettling for them, even though when you are with me you appear real enough in the flesh. It's strangest for them when they hear you speak."

Dalí had painted a skeleton of some horned creature into the foreground of the image. "You see death, but this is not death. Look into the center, at this jewel of a fruit, the most perfect fruit ever devised by the gods. It floats, a key into a door, a door of death."

He paused for dramatic effect. The reporters and gallery visitors hung on his every word. "And you all want to snatch it out, to open it."

Dalí suddenly noticed me standing there. His mouth opened, and his eyes bulged. He broke through the crowd, moving toward me.

"Proserpina..." he said. "Oh, Proserpina!"

When he came close, I leaned toward him and brought his face to mine. I kissed him softly on the forehead and let him go. He turned around. He would not remember seeing me. "This painting. It is the heart of Proserpina herself!" The crowd began murmuring, not entirely sure if they knew who Proserpina was, but then someone shouted out "Persephone!" and the crowd murmured with approval.

"Paolo is here," Lillian said, her voice full of joy.

"I know. That's why I brought you. I thought you might want to say goodbye. He will only know you for a minute, so do not tarry."

Lillian threw her arms around me. She kissed my cheek and then went to where Paolo stood at the side of the room, camera in hand. His leg had healed, and he, like his employer, remembered nothing about the week in Bomarzo, save that they visited and filmed a short movie, complete with a white cat on Dalí's shoulder as he entered a simple, white *tempietto*.

I watched as Lillian put her hand on Paolo's cheek. His eyes brightened, and a smile bloomed on his lips. He reached into his pocket and handed her a piece of paper. She broke into a broad grin when she saw what was written on it. Then she tucked it back into his hand before kissing him deeply. "May the gods always find you in favor," she said when she broke away. He lost the moment, but a smile remained as he snapped photos of Dalí mesmerizing the crowd.

"What was on the piece of paper?" I asked when she was once more by my side.

She sighed. "It was the haiku he wrote for me."

We watched the scene in the gallery for a moment before she asked, "Whatever happened to Jack?"

"He boarded a plane to America a few days after Bomarzo. He remembers nothing."

Lillian nudged me. "Look."

Gala had pulled one of her young paramours toward her and slid her hand down toward his crotch.

"At one of his gallery showings, no less," Lillian said, astonished.

"I wish I was surprised," I said.

Lillian looked at me. "What do you mean?"

"I was curious, so I read Gala's thread of fate. In years to come, she will find herself—by her own actions—thrust into the background of the great Salvador Dalí, responsible for making the money and convincing him to work. But she never really sees him for who he is, only a means to wealth and security. His feeling for her is one of the great loves in all of history, and through her life, she feels so little for him. The world will blink, and she will find herself in Tartarus soon enough, where she will dine every night on her own bitterness."

Lillian glanced back at the gallery scene. "That's really tragic. She has no idea what she's throwing away."

"Nor does she care," I replied, my eyes meeting Lillian's. "Some people are so preoccupied with their own desires that they fail to recognize the profound emotions others hold for them. In her lifetime, Gala won't realize the depth of Dalí's feelings, nor will she confront her own emptiness. But in the Underworld, she will have an eternity to reflect on it."

"But what about Dalí?" Lillian asked.

"Dalí will continue to paint, to create, and to love, in his own eccentric way," I said softly. "His love for Gala will be both his curse and his muse. He will pass into the annals of art history as a genius, loved and misunderstood in equal measure."

Lillian took a moment to process this, staring at the earthly spectacle before us one last time. "It's a strange thing, to look at the living like this."

I pulled her away from the scene.

As we reentered the Underworld, my hauntingly beautiful realm of shadows and half-light, I couldn't help but think how life's richness often lay hidden beneath its surface, visible only to those willing to dig a little deeper.

"You know, I've been thinking. Snaring Salvador Dalí was a bit of a dramatic touch," I teased my husband when I returned.

He folded me into his arms, and I was filled with his scent of leather and smoke.

"It wasn't easy convincing every incarnation of you to return to Bomarzo. And you know how much I love drama. You were an artist in this life. Besides, Dalí is a lover of food. Better to have someone else trying to get you to eat the seeds, and if it seemed he was orchestrating the show, I thought perhaps there was a stronger chance."

I laughed. "All those wild dinners? They were a bit excessive."

"So is Dalí." He smoothed my hair back from my face. "You know, sometimes I think I should thank Ceres."

I raised an eyebrow. "Thank her?"

"We have been ripped from each other's arms so many times. Every time my love grew a hundred-fold. Every time she strengthened our bond." Pluto kissed my temple and ran his fingers across my cheek. "I won't let anyone take you away from me."

"No one will ever dare," I said, letting him kiss me again. And again.

★ ★ ★ ★ ★

AUTHOR'S NOTE

In the fall of 1948, the great Salvador Dalí visited one of the most unusual places in Italy, the Sacro Bosco, an abandoned Renaissance-era Mannerist garden full of stone statues of mythological beings and monsters. This little wood, or *boschetto*, is located an hour north of Rome. Dalí's visit sparked new interest in the strange place, which had fallen into significant disrepair after the death of its creator, Pier Francesco Orsini (4 July 1523–28 January 1583), who was also called Vicino. The garden is commonly said to be a memorial to his late wife, Giulia Farnese. Over the years, the *boschetto* had become a place of fascination for figures such as Johann Wolfgang von Goethe, Jean Cocteau, Mario Praz, and, of course, Dalí. Dalí filmed a one-and-a-half-minute film in the garden (viewable on YouTube), which sparked the world's interest in the unusual place.

I describe more about the history of the Sacro Bosco in the section after this Author's Note.

Palazzo Orsini is on the hill above the garden. Vicino Orsini's father, Giovanni Corrado Orsini, began constructing the palazzo in 1519 on the remains of a centuries-old castle. After his death, Vicino finished the construction of the palazzo. Today the building has been partially sold off to private owners, but much of it is now the administrative offices for the town of Bomarzo. While I have visited the garden several times, Palazzo Orsini was closed during the writing of the novel due to the COVID pandemic, so I relied on photos, historical accounts, and floor plans to create my story. The well in the basement does exist, although there is no evidence of any secret passage to the garden.

Vicino Orsini married Alessandro Farnese's great-niece, Giulia Farnese, in the 1540s. In his letters, Vicino describes Giulia as a "prudent and magnanimous" wife. She is often mentioned as one of the most faithful and dedicated great ladies of Italy, keeping his estate in order while Vicino was off waging wars for the Pope. She died in 1560 after Vicino began work on the garden but before it was fully finished. Unlike in this novel, Giulia did not leave a journal behind.

When considering writing a Gothic novel set in Bomarzo, I wasn't sure I wanted to include Salvador Dalí. He's a larger-than-life, often controversial figure. He was kicked out of the Surrealist group for overt racism and a fascination with fascism. But he is also one of the most recognizable and influential artists of the twentieth century, and his influence cannot be overstated. The more I studied the artist, the more I realized that the presence of Dalí and Gala made sense for this story. In their lives, they constantly flirted with power, immorality, and wickedness. Dalí had a love of the grotesque. And Bomarzo had undoubtedly influenced him, as is evidenced by the sets he designed for the Rome Opera that year, which featured a monstrous, open-mouthed *orco*.

Dalí was a narcissist, but like many narcissists, he also had a certain charm, and I enjoyed playing with the juxtaposition of his depravity and genius. His life is well-documented, and he wrote two autobiographies, *The Secret Life of Salvador Dalí* and *Maniac Eyeball: The Unspeakable Confessions of Salvador Dalí*, from which I pull a few wild stories. I also draw upon *Comment on deviant Dalí, les aveux inavouables de Salvador Dalí*, by André Parinaud, for Dalí's story about being devoured by maggots.

Dalí's wife, Gala (born Elena Ivanovna Diakonova), is a more mysterious and infamous figure. She was Dalí's manager and muse, but she was not a faithful wife. Her escapades with younger men, which lasted until she was in her eighties, were known to, and sanctioned by, Dalí. Later in life, he even bought her a castle to entertain her paramours in the summer, and the couple agreed that Dalí would only visit if he received Gala's written invitation. For three years before she met Dalí, Gala was the wife of poet Paul Éluard, with whom she had a *ménage à trois* with artist Max Ernst. She and Éluard had a daughter, Cécile, but upon meeting Dalí, she turned her back on the eleven-year-old and rarely spoke to her again. Gala was not well-liked by most people, and there are some accounts of her violent nature at parties. She took great advantage of Dalí during their relationship, but this seems only to have endeared her to him even more. She was the subject of countless paintings; he even signed many works with her name. Gala was also said to be clairvoyant and a great lover of the tarot. In 1984, five years before his death, Dalí released a special edition tarot deck in which he appears as *El Mago*, The Magician, and Gala as The Empress.

Readers of my other novels, *Feast of Sorrow* and *The Chef's Secret*, may know that I love writing about food in history. And while *In the Garden of Monsters* is a Gothic novel, it is also an ode to food. I feature many traditional Italian dishes, but you'll also find historical meals such as the dinner inspired by one of the fantastical meals within the *Hypnerotomachia*.

I also pay homage to Dalí's great love of food, highlighting many of the dishes featured in Dalí's 1973 cookbook, *Les Dîners de Gala*. Within the pages are incredible and fantastical depictions of food, including a tower of crayfish and a recipe for avocado toast (long before the dish became popular in the 1990s and 2000s). The cookbook's recipes are extremely elaborate and difficult for a home chef to pull off, but if you want to try your hand, the cookbook was recently reissued by Taschen, along with a companion book, *The Wines of Gala*.

Dalí had a special place in his heart for pomegranates, and they appear in a number of his paintings, including *Dream Caused by the Flight of a Bee around a Pomegranate a Second before Waking*, which I described in the first chapter. He transposed pomegranates with jewels in his painting *Grenade et l'ange* (Pomegranate and Angel) in his *Flordali* series. In 1949, he created a jeweled brooch with jeweler Henry Kaston—a gold heart filled with ruby red pomegranate seeds. According to auction house Bonhams Skinner, Dalí is said to have commented about the piece: "The many-celled reddish pomegranate berry pulses with life. The slightly acid flavor of the fruit is agreeable, as acidity stimulates human accomplishment." In the novel, all of Dalí's paintings in Bomarzo are lost except one, which he is sharing at the gallery in the final scene. This painting is a real one, quite obscure, untitled, and painted in 1948. I took the inspiration for the trumpeter on the tilted house in the garden from this artwork.

As for the retelling of Hades and Persephone, I have had a lifelong love of Greek and Roman mythology and the power of these stories to fascinate people for centuries. You may be asking why I chose to subvert the myth and make Ceres Proserpina's lover rather than her mother? The simple answer is: Why not?

And finally, if you want to try your hand at some of the recipes in this novel, head to my website, crystalking.com, for inspiration. If you blog or share your recipes on social media, please tag me or use the hashtag InTheGardenOfMonsters. I'd love to see the results!

Buon Appetito,
Crystal King

#InTheGardenOfMonsters

ACKNOWLEDGMENTS

In the spring of 2021, everyone was itching to rejoin the world. The first thing I did when I emerged from my pandemic cocoon was go on a writing retreat at the Highlights Foundation Retreat Center in rural Pennsylvania with four fellow authors, Kris Waldherr, Heather Webb, Jenny Brown, and Julie Carrick Dalton. It was there, in a little cabin of my own, that I began writing *In the Garden of Monsters*. The early support of these authors was invaluable in helping me find my way into this wild story.

I first visited the Sacro Bosco in January 2018. At the time, I had no intentions of writing anything related to the garden; it was a mere side trip after seeing the nearby town of Caprarola, where part of another book I was working on was set. But it took hold of my mind, and years after, when I contemplated writing a Gothic novel, I realized that it was the perfect location for such a book to take place. Once I began working on the story, I visited the garden again, this time with the invaluable help of Thomas Robinson and Stefano Guida.

There were several early readers, whose advice and insight assured me that it was a story worth telling. Thank you to my writing partners, The Salt & Radish Writers—Anjali Mitter Duva, Jennifer Dupee, and Henriette Lazaridis—and also to Melissa Ayres, Kirby Crum, and Jason Alvarez. Gracelyn Monaco helped me proofread the Italian components of the novel.

I am especially grateful for my agent, Amaryah Orenstein, who helped me hone this story and share it with the world. So much of this novel has her touch upon it, and because of that, it's a better tale.

My fantastic editor at MIRA, Dina Davis, who immediately dived in and got right to the heart of the book. I thank my lucky stars that this novel fell into her hands. I couldn't have imagined a better partnership.

To everyone at Harlequin and MIRA who helped bring this novel into the world, I owe you my deep gratitude. Thank you to the editorial team, including editorial director Nicole Brebner; editorial assistant Evan Yeong; proofreading manager Tamara Shifman; copy editing manager Gina Macdonald; copy editor Jerri Gallagher; and, in managing editorial, Katie-Lynn Golakovich. Marketing: Ana Luxton, Ashley MacDonald, Puja Lad. Channel Marketing: Randy Chan, Pamela Osti, Maahi Patel. Digital Marketing: Lindsey Reeder, Brianna Wodabek, Riffat Ali, Ciara Loader. Art (thank you for my amazing cover!): Erin Craig, Elita Sidiropoulou, Sarah Whittaker, Denise Thomson. Typesetter: Monica Czerepak. Subrights: Reka Rubin, Christine Tsai, Nora Rawn, Fiona Smallman. Audio: producer Carly Katz and narrator Carlotta Brentan. Publicity: Laura Gianino. And thanks to the leadership team, Loriana Sacilotto, Amy Jones, Margaret Marbury, and Heather Connor, who believed this book should find its way into the hands of readers. And finally, thanks to the MIRA sales team for helping this book land on so many bookstore shelves.

There are so many others who have supported me and my writing, including dear friends: Graziella Macchetta, Leanna Widgren, Gregory McCormick, Phil Ayres, Dan Daly, and

Patrizia and Beniamino Bellini. Megan Beatie has been a huge champion of my novels from the very beginning. I also have to give a huge shout-out to my fellow Grubbies, and especially to the Wonder Writers, the best community of supportive friends I could hope to be part of. There are too many of you to name, but I am indebted to you all.

Thank you to those who have always been there for me, Mom, Dad, Misty, and Chase.

I agreed to work with MIRA just two days before I learned that I had early-stage breast cancer. Working on edits for this novel was the absolute best way to keep my mind occupied before and after surgery and radiation (and, yes, I'm okay now!). Cancer is a lonely, terrifying, and awful thing to go through, but I am lucky to live in a place where there is some of the best cancer care in the world. I am forever grateful for my surgery and medical oncology teams at Mass General Brigham and to the radiation team at the Hoffman Breast Center.

And, of course, I have to thank my husband, my partner, my chef, my knight in shining armor, *amore mio*, Joe. He is as much a part of these books as I am.

THE HISTORY OF THE SACRO BOSCO

During the Renaissance period in Italy, the creation of fantastical gardens was a significant reflection of the era's artistic and intellectual awakening, particularly in the Lazio region, which encompasses Rome and the towns surrounding the city. These gardens, like the Villa d'Este in Tivoli, Villa Farnese in Caprarola, and Villa Lante in Bagnaia near Viterbo, were not just about aesthetic beauty but also served as manifestations of philosophical and mystical ideas. They featured elaborate sculptures, fountains, and grottoes, each symbolically intertwined with myths, allegories, and classical references. The emphasis in these gardens was on creating a harmonious blend of art and nature, inviting visitors into a world where the real and the surreal merge. The Villa d'Este, renowned for its innovative water features and artistic design, the geometrically precise and architecturally integrated Villa Farnese, and the Mannerist, surprise-laden layout of Villa Lante, each in their own way, embodied the Renaissance fascination with blending artistic imagination with the natural world.

Nestled among the wooded hills of Bomarzo, Italy, lies a garden unlike any other of its era or beyond. The Sacro Bosco ("Sacred Wood"), also known as the Park of the Monsters, forsakes manicured lawns and symmetrical flower beds for a realm of the bizarre. Giant sculpted monsters lurk within the foliage, a building leans at a precarious angle, and inscriptions offer cryptic riddles rather than guidance. The Sacro Bosco stands as a testament to Mannerism, a movement that defied both rational explanation and classical aesthetic norms.

The garden is the brainchild of Pier Francesco Orsini, who went by the name Vicino. Vicino was born in 1523 and, after a greatly disputed inheritance, eventually acquired the centuries-old palazzo in Bomarzo and the surrounding land after his friend Cardinal Alessandro Farnese ruled in his favor (Farnese is subsequently honored on plaques within the garden). Vicino followed in his father's footsteps and became a *condottiere*, a mercenary for hire. He spent over a decade in this profession, fighting as a soldier on behalf of Cardinal Farnese and his grandfather, Pope Paul III, and then later for Pope Julius III and Pope Paul IV. Many of Vicino's letters survive, and we know that he was a romantic, an intellectual, and a lover of food who also had a penchant for sexual pleasure.

While Vicino dedicated the garden to his wife, Giulia Farnese (not to be mistaken with her relative Giulia Farnese, who was the lover of Pope Alexander VI), he had a number of passionate lovers during his marriage to her and afterward, when he wrote to Alessandro that he was grateful to be able to have more than one girlfriend. The garden's dedication was likely designated out of respect for the Farnese family and in gratitude for Giulia's excellent handling of his estate when he was at war. But in truth, Vicino more likely built the garden to be admired by his peers and to serve as a testament to his intellectual loves and pursuits. The little wood, or *boschetto*, as he often called it, was as much a wonder in his time as it is today.

The garden is at the base of the hill where the medieval *borgo*—or village—of Bomarzo spills down one side. The distance from Palazzo Orsini to the garden is approximately a half mile. Rather than walk, Vicino rode his horse from the palazzo to the garden every day.

Vicino enlisted the help of Pirro Ligorio to design the garden. Ligorio was the renowned architect behind the gardens at Villa D'Este in Tivoli, and he worked on St. Peter's in Rome after the death of Michelangelo. The sculptures themselves were likely created by several workers led by sculptor Simone Moschino, the son of Francesco Moschino, who helped Vicino redesign parts of Palazzo Orsini upon the hill above the garden.

The Sacro Bosco once had an artificial lake that was created by damming up the stream that ran through the garden. This lake helped feed the numerous fountains that are scattered throughout the *boschetto*. This lake no longer exists, but archaeological evidence of its location has been discovered.

Scholars are still debating the hidden meanings behind the development of the specific statues and their placement in the garden. It is possible that at least portions of the garden were inspired by Ludovico Ariosto's epic poem *Orlando Furioso,* as well as the mysterious text *Hypnerotomachia Poliphili* (in English, *Poliphilo's Strife of Love in a Dream*), thought to have been written by Francesco Colonna. Vicino was enamored by the Stoics and the ancient Greek philosophers and was likely also influenced by the works of Dante and Petrarch. There is some thought that the garden is laid out according to particular alchemical theories, and that the sculptures pertain to the stages of transmutation, that of turning ordinary metals into gold, which was also a metaphor for human transcendence.

Amid the garden's wonders, key sculptures demand attention. The gaping maw of the ogre, also known as the *orco*, represents an entrance to the underworld and confronts visitors with the grotesque embodiment of death. There is a stone table inside the mouth of this monster, which, when viewed from the *orco*'s exterior, looks very much like a tongue. Inscribed above the monster's mouth are the words *Ogni Pensiero Vola*—All Thoughts Fly. This likely echoes Dante's words in *Inferno*, "Abandon all hope, ye who enter here." It also references the phenomenon that words spoken in the mouth of the monster may be heard from down the path.

The statue of Proserpina, or Persephone, is a massive stone bench that faces down a green hippodrome lined with stone pine cones. Her lower body becomes the bench, and her arms look posed to wrap around any who sits upon it. She is eroded and moss-covered today but must have been quite regal in the garden's original incarnation.

The twisted house, defying architectural logic, adds a sense of disorientation and symbolizes a world thrown off-balance. It is a two-story building that leans against a wall, and a short bridge leads from the upper level of the garden to the top floor. There are windows, but they have never held glass. It is extremely disorienting to stand and walk in the tiny rooms of the house.

The battle of giants is one of the most striking and memorable sculptures in the garden. This particular sculpture depicts a dramatic battle scene between two giants, creating a powerful visual narrative that captures the viewer's imagination. It shows one giant overpowering the other, with the victor seemingly emerging from the ground to grasp his opponent in a fierce embrace. The figures are rendered with exaggerated features and expressions, characteristic of the Mannerist style that pervades the garden. The muscles are tensed, and the faces are contorted in expressions of rage and agony, conveying the intensity of their struggle. The statue serves as an allegory for the internal battles that humans face, such as the struggle between good and evil, or the fight against one's own demons. The size and dynamism of the sculpture make it a focal point within the garden, drawing visitors into its dramatic story. The giants' statue, like many of the sculptures in the Sacro Bosco, is open to interpretation. It has been suggested that it could represent the mythological battle between Hercules and Cacus, a fire-breathing giant, or more likely, as the plaque nearby suggests, it could represent Ludovico Ariosto's character Orlando Furioso in his fight with the woodsman. However, research laid out by Horst Bredekamp suggests that the giants were not both men, but that it was possibly depicting the rape of an Amazon (who would lack breasts and therefore was misidentified previously as a man). Obviously, for the purposes of the story, the idea that it was Orlando Furioso wrestling with a woodsman made more sense.

Vicino Orsini died in 1583, and while his sons likely inherited the palazzo and garden, they seem to have been unable to fund its upkeep. The holdings were sold to the Lante Della Rovere family in 1645 and to the Borghese family in later years, but for the better part of five centuries, the Sacro Bosco was neglected and overgrown. Statues toppled over and eroded, and the lake dried up. There was once a wall around the garden, and it, too, has vanished, the stones likely ending up as part of the homes up on the hill.

In the early part of the twentieth century, news of the strange place reached the ears of many writers and artists of the time, and it was visited by the likes of Italian art critic Mario Praz, poet and novelist Jean Cocteau, and several others of the Surrealist movement, including, of course, Salvador Dalí. By this time, most Bomarzo villagers avoided the location due to rumors of a woman dying there centuries past. Still, the farmers whose land abutted the *boschetto* let their sheep graze among the statues. Dalí made a little film about the *boschetto*, and it took the world by storm. In the film, he walks into the *tempietto* with a white cat on his shoulders, an inspiration for the inclusion of Orpheus in the novel.

A few years after Dalí's visit, in 1954, Giovanni Bettini purchased the land from the Borghese family and, after an exorcism to banish any lingering evil spirits, restored it, enabling thousands of visitors to experience the garden every year. His wife, Tina Severi Bettini, died in an accident during the restoration process, and she and Giovanni are now memorialized in the *tempietto*. There is no evidence that Giulia Farnese was ever interred there.

In the Garden of Monsters attempts to stay true to the garden's layout as it would have been in 1948 when Dalí visited, before the Bettini family moved a few of the sculptures (such as the sphinxes at the entrance), and when it was still wild and overgrown. There were fewer trees at that time than there are today, and there is no proliferation of wild pomegranate bushes, but this is where poetic license came in to help shape the story.

Today, the Sacro Bosco draws visitors from around the world. Its monsters, its leaning house, and its enigmatic symbolism continue to fascinate and bewilder. While modern art historians analyze its place within the broader Mannerist movement and seek to unveil hidden meanings, casual visitors, too, are captured by the sheer power of the bizarre. Walking through the Sacro Bosco is a departure from the ordinary. It is a journey into a world of deliberate artifice, where the strange and grotesque confront us with unsettling questions about our own nature, fears, and place in an incomprehensible world. The garden remains a living riddle, offering no easy answers but inviting endless possibilities for exploration and introspective wonder.

In my studies of the garden, I found the following books especially helpful: *The Garden at Bomarzo* by Jessie Sheeler (in English); *Vicino Orsini il Sacro Bosco di Bomarzo* by Horst Bredekamp (in Italian); *Bomarzo il Sacro Bosco Fortuna Critica e Documenti* by Sabine Frommel; and *Hypnerotomachia Poliphili: The Strife of Love in a Dream* by Francesco Colonna and translated by Joscelyn Godwin.

I am also indebted to local Etruria expert Mary Jane Cryan for her insight into the area. Art historian Katherine Coty also graciously lent me her time to discuss the garden and her research paper *A Dream of Etruria: The Sacro Bosco of Bomarzo and the Alternate Antiquity of Alto Lazio.*

It's possible to visit the garden, often called the Parco dei Mostri (Monster Park), now maintained by the Società Giardino di Bomarzo. More information can be found at www.sacrobosco.eu.

IN THE GARDEN
OF MONSTERS

CRYSTAL KING

QUESTIONS FOR DISCUSSION

Caution: There may be spoilers in the discussion questions.

1. Julia has no memory of her past, and no clues about where she's really from except her American accent and her letter of acceptance to the *accademia*. How do you think this influenced her decision-making before going to Sacro Bosco and after she arrived? How do you think she would have done things differently if she had her memory? What would you do if you had no memory of your past?

2. Salvador Dalí is a famous eccentric artist who really did visit Sacro Bosco. Lillian calls him "a living paradox." What did you know about him before reading *In the Garden of Monsters*? If you know his work, which is your favorite? What did you learn about him in this story? Has your impression of him changed? Do you agree with Lillian's thoughts on him?

3. *In the Garden of Monsters* changes the relationships in the myth of Hades and Persephone. How does the novel's por-

trayal of these mythological figures differ from traditional interpretations? What new dimensions do these characters gain in this retelling? What do you think of the shift? Did you see the twist about Ceres coming? How do these changes impact your understanding or appreciation of the original myth?

4. Food plays a large role in this story as an instrument to get Julia to eat the pomegranate seeds. Which meal was your favorite? Would you try all of the food? Do you think any of the meals hold a particular symbolism?

5. Julia pushes back on the idea of being just a muse, but Persephone has been one of the biggest muses throughout history. Why do you think Julia continued to model rather than taking another job when she felt this way? When she regains her memories, do you think that changes her feelings on this matter? What kind of power do you think muses hold?

6. Dalí doesn't believe women can truly be artists, but there have been talented female artists throughout history. Who are your favorites? How do Dalí's thoughts on this tie into the other themes of the book?

7. Gala is based on Dalí's real wife. When Proserpina says Dalí's "love for Gala will be both his curse and his muse," what do you think she means? Did you know about Gala before reading this book? What is your impression of her? Do you agree with the other characters' opinions of her?

8. Sacro Bosco is a real garden full of monsters in Italy. Had you heard of it before this book? Did this story make you want to visit it? Which statue was your favorite?

9. The garden in the novel is a central element. What does it symbolize, and how does its meaning evolve throughout

the story? How does the garden reflect the internal states or journeys of the characters?

10. Julia is haunted by echoes of her past lives throughout the story, revealing that she and Pluto have gone through this journey for centuries. Why do you think this time was different? How do you think the monsters in the gardens changed the outcome? What set the couple free?

11. *In the Garden of Monsters* explores one take on ghosts and what they are in our world. Do you believe in ghosts? Have you ever seen one? Do you think they are just echoes of past lives, as they are here, or something more?

12. The novel blends historical elements with mythological ones. How does this combination affect the narrative? Does it enhance the realism of the story, or does it serve another purpose?

13. "We're all flawed beings, even gods. Perhaps that's what makes us eternally fascinating to each other." What do you think of this statement from the book? Do you agree? How has this theme shown up for each character? Do the changes to the original version of this myth highlight this message for you, and if so, in what ways?

AUTHOR Q&A—CRYSTAL KING

What was the inspiration for writing *In the Garden of Monsters*?

Around the time COVID hit, and publishing was in a strange place, I was thinking I might want to try something different in my novels. I was having a conversation with a friend of mine, the author Kris Waldherr, who had just written a really wonderful Gothic novel about the women of Frankenstein, *Unnatural Creatures*, and we were talking about how Gothic novels have recently grown in popularity. I began to wonder: If I were going to write a Gothic, what would I write? I immediately thought of the garden I had been to a couple years before, in Bomarzo, Italy, the Sacro Bosco. It's the perfect place for a Gothic story. There is a strange castle in a tiny remote town on the top of a hill, and below it is a garden literally full of statues of monsters and mythological gods. And that was it. I knew I wanted to write a book there.

What is so interesting about this garden?

In 1552, an Italian prince, Vicino Orsini, began developing
the garden, which he later dedicated as a memorial for his wife
upon her death in 1560. He hired sculptors to turn the tufa and
peperino stone in the valley below the castle into all manner of
mythical creatures. Not only do you have the *orco*, or the mouth
of hell, the demesne of Pluto/Hades, but across from it is Ceres
(the Roman name for Demeter). Farther along in the garden,
there is a bench depicting Proserpina (Persephone). There are
sirens, dragons, nymphs, and monsters carved from stone. It's
a place utterly unlike any other garden you have ever been to,
and even in its day, it was highly unusual.

The Sacro Bosco was a product of its time, reflecting the
Renaissance's fascination with alchemy, astrology, and the
supernatural. It was an era where art and science were not yet
distinct disciplines, and the park embodies this intersection of
knowledge and imagination. Traditional Italian gardens have
a specific geometric rationality, with well-laid paths, fountains with water games, and inspirational sculptures. Unlike
the manicured gardens of Renaissance Italy, the Sacro Bosco
was designed to blend with the natural environment, creating a sense of being lost in a mystical world, with sculptures
carved where stones already jutted from the earth, seats hewn
from rock to fit into the natural landscape, a tilted house that
will make you dizzy, and a myriad of fantastical stone creatures to discover.

There are many theories on why Orsini created the garden in
the way that he did. Some scholars think that it may have been
designed based on the idea of alchemical transmutation—the
idea of turning lead into gold or, more importantly, transforming the spirit into something purer. However, as I mentioned
in the Author's Note, there are also schools of thought that he
based the garden upon the early Renaissance epic poem *Orlando*

Furioso by Ludovico Ariosto, or that he was influenced by the medieval story *Hypnerotomachia Poliphili* (which is featured in Ian Caldwell's popular novel *The Rule of Four*). My sense is that he included elements of all these things in this garden.

When Salvador Dalí's little film clip ignited the imagination of the masses, it essentially helped put the garden on the map and led to the purchase and renovation of the garden, which now any visitor can go see. It's about an hour north of Rome and very much off the beaten path. It's surprising to me how many Romans I've met who aren't familiar with the garden. But it's definitely worth the trek.

What inspired you to include Salvador Dalí in this novel?

I was first intrigued by Dalí's involvement in the garden when I saw the video he made at the Sacro Bosco (you can find it on my website, www.crystalking.com/dali). It's a minute and a half long and features him among the statues in the garden. I have to admit, at first, I wasn't sure if I wanted to include Dalí. I hesitated because I knew he was controversial and had ideas about the world that would definitely have gotten him canceled today. He was a narcissist, and he had very unorthodox views about sexuality, politics, people, food, and certainly about painting and sculpture. And besides, I didn't even really like his art very much. But I figured I'd do a little research about him, and it wasn't long before I was really hooked. His life was pure drama, pure spectacle. He had a brilliant, curious mind. And the more I learned about his art, the more I realized how talented and highly influential he was.

He was a true Renaissance man, a master of multiple art forms, including painting, sculpture, and drama. Beyond his artistic endeavors, he penned autobiographies and even a novel, *Hidden Faces*. His passion for food was evident in his cookbook and in his art. His career was marked by extraordinary collaborations with figures like Italian fashion designer Elsa Schiaparelli, Walt Disney, and Alice Cooper. His diverse projects ranged from designing five hundred ashtrays for Air India to creating the iconic Chupa Chups lollipop logo. Posthumously, his unique and captivating tarot deck was published, adding to his legacy. His prolific output was significantly influenced by his wife, Gala, who played a crucial role in his creative process.

The more I learned about the couple, the more I realized I wanted to include them in my story. *In the Garden of Monsters* is very different than retellings of the Persephone myth, and I liked the idea of including some of Dalí's surreal ideas as part of the story. I knew I didn't want him to be the main character, but he was a perfect vehicle for delivering up so much of the plot. It helped that Dalí already saw pomegranates as a symbol, which he included in many of his paintings. And voilà! That was it. I would tell the story from the point of view of a model he hires and brings to Bomarzo for a week to paint. Of course, Gala had to come along. Dalí's relationship with his wife was just as surreal as everything else about him was, and her controlling, demanding nature was the perfect counter to his flamboyant, over-the-top antics.

I did my best to represent Dalí in a way that was true to the person that he was in life while recognizing his many shortcomings.

There is so much food in this book, which makes sense, given that your past novels were about culinary figures. How did you decide what food to include?

I honestly think that this book has more food in it than my previous novels. That's partly because the Persephone myth revolves around the six pomegranate seeds, so that gave me a lot of opportunity to incorporate food as part of the plot. The story takes place over the course of a week, and every night, there is a dinner, and every day, there is a lunch that the characters participate in. Julia lived many lives and would have tasted foods from all sorts of historical points in time, so I approached food as sort of a compendium of flavors through the centuries. There are dishes from Salvador Dalí's 1973 cookbook, *Les Dîners de Gala*; the early Renaissance text *Hypnerotomachia Poliphili*; Bartolomeo Scappi's *L'Opera*, published in 1570; Pellegrino Artusi's 1891 cookbook, *Science in the Kitchen and the Art of Eating Well*; as well as many Italian regional favorites that have been popular in modern times.

My husband and I love trying to re-create some of the historical recipes. He's the chef, and I'm the baker, so it works out well. Some of the dishes we make all the time at home are recipes we've collaborated on for my novels.

This novel is also a bit of a ghost story. Have you always been drawn to the supernatural? Do you believe in ghosts?

Regarding my attraction to the supernatural, I find myself in a curious position. While I can't claim to be a staunch believer, I'm also not among the 18 percent of Americans who, according to a 2009 Pew Research study, have experienced ghostly encounters. My stance is more agnostic when it comes to the paranormal. However, what truly captivates me is the historical and cultural significance of ghosts. The concept of ghosts has ancient roots, tracing back through thousands of years of human history. This enduring fascination reflects our collective desire to understand the mysteries of life and death. Questions like whether parts of us linger after we're gone, the existence of an afterlife, and the possibility of maintaining contact with those who have passed are not just intriguing but also deeply human. These questions and the myriad ways different cultures and individuals have tried to answer them provide a rich tapestry of inspiration. Ghosts, in this context, are more than just spectral figures; they are a gateway to exploring the profound mysteries of human existence. They offer an endless treasure trove of story fodder, allowing writers like me to delve into, understand, answer, or even playfully engage with these age-old questions.

Your first two books are more traditional historical fiction, but this one has a fantasy bent. Are you done with writing more true-to-life historical novels?

My writing is deeply influenced by my fascination with the past, particularly Italy's rich and varied history. The country's long and storied heritage serves as an inspiring backdrop and offers an endless wellspring of inspiration. While I am still dabbling in historical fiction, I am also interested in writing novels with more contemporary and fantastical settings, infusing them with historical elements. My passion for ancient myths stretches back to my childhood when I gravitated toward the stories of the gods and goddesses who, although they had so many human qualities and failings, also had magic and powers to bend the world to their will. Their stories are also history, even if they are mythological. (A fun fact: people in Greece still often believe their family lineage is descended from the gods and consider them their ancestors.) And today we still know and love the stories of these thousands-year-old myths, which makes infusing them into the present day in my novels great fun.

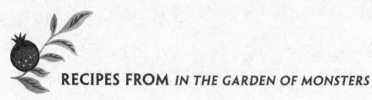

RECIPES FROM *IN THE GARDEN OF MONSTERS*

by Crystal King and Joseph Doucette

One of the joys of food writing is creating and eating the foods that I'm writing about. Sometimes this means re-creating historical recipes and making them more palatable for modern audiences, and other times it is merely developing the dishes that began in my imagination. I am fortunate to have a husband who is an excellent cook, and my own forte tends toward baking. Between us, we have a lot of fun in the kitchen and cooking for friends. These three recipes from In the Garden of Monsters *are our imagined creations.*

DATE, POMEGRANATE, AND PISTACHIO BITES

In the novel, these delicious treats don't have pomegranates incorporated within the recipe and are instead dotted with a single pomegranate seed on top. I find that incorporating the seeds gives these morsels a wonderful richness. If you don't want to break open a pomegranate yourself, you can sometimes find the seeds in the precut fruit area of your grocery store, or often frozen. You can find edible gold powder online or sometimes in the baking section of your local stores. You need quite a bit of it to coat all the bites, however, so using powdered sugar is an easier, sweeter, and more economical route to go. Because of the pomegranate seeds, these are best eaten cold. The flavor also deepens after a day or so in the fridge.

Makes approx. 24 bites

INGREDIENTS

1 ¼ cups (125 g) pistachios, shelled
¼ cup (35 g) almonds
2 cups (375 g) pitted Medjool dates
¾ teaspoon rosewater
½ teaspoon ground cinnamon
⅛ teaspoon ground cloves
2 teaspoons honey
¼ cup (37 g) pomegranate seeds
½ cup (60 g) powdered sugar
Optional: edible gold powder

INSTRUCTIONS

1. In a food processor, combine all ingredients except the pomegranate seeds and powdered sugar. Puree until the mixture is sticky.

2. Add the pomegranate seeds and pulse into the mixture. You want to incorporate the seeds, not chop them finely.

3. Take 1 tablespoon of the mixture and form a ball.

4. Roll the ball in the powdered sugar. You can also opt to roll them in edible gold powder instead, for a more luxurious display.

5. Refrigerate for at least 30 minutes before serving. You can also freeze them in an airtight container for a month.

GILDED CHICKEN

This recipe is a simple and delicious glimpse into our Renaissance past and makes for a delightful display at a dinner party. In the novel, during Poliphilo's dinner, the characters feast on gilded capons. A capon is an old chicken and will have a bit of a gamier flavor than a regular chicken. They are not always available (but you can ask your butcher), and chicken is a perfectly good substitute. This recipe would also work equally well with other types of fowl. You can adjust the recipe fairly easily depending on the size of the bird. Make sure you use fresh herbs, as you are stuffing the bird with them. Also, for the sauce, avoid pine nuts sourced from China, which tend to have an unpleasant aftertaste. Nuts from Turkey, Greece, Italy, or Spain are more expensive but worth the price. A tip: keep your pine nuts in the freezer to help preserve the flavor.

4 servings

INGREDIENTS

For the bird:

1 capon or chicken
1 shallot, quartered
1 large lemon, quartered
1 bunch (handful) of fresh thyme
1 bunch (handful) of fresh tarragon
Salt and pepper to taste
Olive oil to drizzle
Edible gold powder

For the sauce:

2 teaspoons sugar
2 ½ lemons, juiced (not from the lemon you stuff the bird with)
½ teaspoon cinnamon
4 tablespoons pine nuts, toasted and very finely chopped
4 tablespoons butter
12 oz (340 g) chicken stock
2 teaspoons chopped tarragon

INSTRUCTIONS

For the bird:

1. Sprinkle salt into the cavity of the bird.

2. Stuff the bird with shallot, lemon, thyme, and tarragon, and then tie up the bird.

3. Add the bird to a low-sided roasting pan or, ideally, a cast-iron skillet.

4. Salt and pepper the top of the bird, then drizzle olive oil over the skin.

5. Sprinkle with edible gold powder.

6. Roast at 375°F (190°C) for 90 minutes or until it reads 165°F (74°C) on a meat thermometer. For the first hour, tent the bird with foil. Remove the foil for the last 30 minutes to brown the skin.

7. Remove the bird from the oven and pan but leave the drippings. Let the bird rest for 10–15 minutes before carving.

For the sauce:

1. Add sugar, lemon juice, cinnamon, and pine nuts to a bowl and stir. Set aside to let the sugar dissolve.

2. Add pan with drippings to a stovetop burner.

3. Add butter and chicken stock. Cook down by half on medium heat.

4. Add sugar/lemon mixture to the ingredients in the pan. Cook on medium heat for a few minutes until it begins to thicken.

5. Add the chopped tarragon. Cook for another minute, then remove the pan from the heat.

6. Carve the chicken and serve with the sauce.

TORTA ALLA RICOTTA

During the first lunch in the mouth of the *orco*, one of the desserts is a ricotta tart. This delicious pie traces its origins back to the Renaissance and may even hearken back to medieval times. Bartolomeo Scappi, the protagonist in my second novel, *The Chef's Secret*, includes a recipe for a cheese tart in his 1570 cookbook, *L'Opera di Bartolomeo Scappi*. Scappi's version was much loved by Pope Julius III but was made with provatura cheese rather than ricotta. Today, ricotta pie is considered to be a particularly Sicilian treat, and every *nonna* has a different recipe for it, which may sometimes include chocolate, lemon, raisins, or even orange flavors. To keep with Scappi's tradition, this version includes rosewater in the crust, which gives the tart a delightful flavor to balance with the elderflower and ricotta. If you don't have elderflower extract but you have a bottle of St-Germain liqueur handy, that will work as well.

8 servings

INGREDIENTS

For the crust:

1 ¾ cups (250 g) all-purpose or 00 flour
⅓ cup (67 g) sugar
pinch of salt
½ teaspoon baking powder
½ cup (113 g) cold unsalted butter
2 eggs
3 teaspoons rosewater
extra flour for rolling

For the filling:

1 ½ cups (360 g) ricotta cheese, whole milk
¼ cup (34 g) pine nuts, ground into a paste in a mortar or food processor
2 large eggs
½ cup (100 g) sugar
1 tablespoon grated ginger
1 teaspoon elderflower extract
pinch of salt

INSTRUCTIONS

1. Combine the dry ingredients in a food processor and pulse to mix. Add the cut-up butter and pulse until the mixture is coarsely ground.

2. Add the beaten eggs and rosewater and pulse until the dough comes together.

3. Form the dough into a smooth disc and wrap the dough in plastic wrap. Let it rest in the refrigerator for at least an hour. Remove the dough from the refrigerator and roll it with a rolling pin (lightly flour the surface and pin if the dough sticks).

4. Butter a 9-inch tart mold or pie pan. On a lightly floured surface, roll the pastry into an 11-inch circle and place it inside the pan, pressing it against the edges. Pass the rolling pin over the edge to eliminate excess dough. Prick the bottom of the pastry several times with a fork to let steam escape and keep it from bubbling. Let it rest in the refrigerator for at least 10 minutes before filling it.

5. Add all filling ingredients to a mixer bowl and blend until combined.

6. Add the filling to the tart pan and bake in a 350°F (176°C) oven for about 55 minutes.

7. Remove from oven and let it cool completely on a wire rack. Cover and refrigerate until well chilled.